EVERYMAN, I will go with thee,

and be thy guide,

In thy most need to go by thy side

HENRY FIELDING

Born at Sharpham Park, Somerset, 22nd April **1707,**
seat of his maternal grandfather, Sir Henry Gould, judge
of the King's Bench; his own father served under
Marlborough, later becoming a general. 1719–24, at
Eton, along with the elder Pitt, the elder Fox, Charles
Hanbury (Williams), Thomas Arne and George
Lyttelton, later a leading statesman, and Fielding's
friend. 1728–9, studied literature at Leyden. 1729–37,
wrote plays in London; the main surviving results are
some songs (including 'The dusky night rides down the
sky'), the burlesque *Tom Thumb*, two adaptations of
Molière (*The Mock Doctor*; *The Miser*) and two political
satires (*Pasquin*; *The Historical Register for 1736*).
Walpole retaliated with the Licensing Act (1737).
1734, married Charlotte Cradock of Salisbury, commemorated in Sophia and Amelia. 1737, entered Middle
Temple, and tried journalism in *The Champion* (1739–
1741), which reveals the wide reading and generous
attitudes later displayed in the novels. Ridiculed
Richardson's *Pamela* (1740) with a shrewd travesty,
Shamela (1741), and with *Joseph Andrews* (1742). 1743,
Miscellanies (3 vols., including *A Journey from This
World to the Next* and *Jonathan Wild*). Severely harassed
by poverty and family troubles; his wife died 1744.
Anti-Stuart-and-Popery propaganda in *The True
Patriot* (1745–6) and *The Jacobite's Journal* (1747–8).
1748, appointed Justice of the Peace for Westminster,
later for Middlesex also; as Bow Street magistrate
struggled with poverty, crime and corruption. 1749,
Tom Jones. Despite failing health worked indefatigably,
with his blind half-brother Sir John Fielding, to clean
up legal malpractices and street violence. 1751, *Amelia*
and *An Enquiry into the Causes of the Late Increase of
Robbers*. 1752, *The Covent-Garden Journal*. 1753, *A Proposal for Making an Effectual Provision for the Poor*.
1754, fatally ill from his exertions and disease; sailed
for Portugal, but died soon after arrival. 1755, *Journal
of a Voyage to Lisbon* published.

HENRY FIELDING

Jonathan Wild
The Journal of a Voyage
to Lisbon

INTRODUCTION BY
A. R. HUMPHREYS
Professor of English in the University of Leicester

NOTES TO BOTH WORKS BY
DOUGLAS BROOKS
Department of English Language and Literature,
University of Manchester

DENT: LONDON
EVERYMAN'S LIBRARY
DUTTON: NEW YORK

© *Introduction, J. M. Dent & Sons Ltd, 1964*
and 1973 (additions)
© *Notes, J. M. Dent & Sons Ltd, 1973*

All rights reserved
Made in Great Britain
at the
Aldine Press · Letchworth · Herts
for
J. M. DENT & SONS LTD
Aldine House · Albemarle Street · London
This edition was first published in
Everyman's Library in 1932
Reprinted 1973

Published in the U.S.A. by arrangement
with J. M. Dent & Sons Ltd

No. 877   Hardback ISBN   0 460 00877 3
No. 1877   Paperback ISBN   0 460 01877 9

INTRODUCTION

EVEN good critics have responded very variously to *Jonathan Wild*. Scott could not make out 'what Fielding proposed to himself by a picture of complete vice, unrelieved by anything of human feeling'. Saintsbury, on the other hand, thought it second only in ironic force (and superior in unity of effect) to Swift's incomparable *Tale of a Tub*. 'Fielding', he observed magisterially, 'has written nothing greater.'

In the preface to the *Miscellanies* (of which *Jonathan Wild* formed the third and last volume) Fielding distinguishes three classes of men. There are the rare good and great ('the true sublime of human nature'), the good who are not great (a lesser species, but loved for their virtues), and the great who are not good ('the perfection of diabolism'). In the careers of Wild and the Heartfrees he makes, with unflagging vigour, his most decisive confrontation of the evil and good in human nature. Yet if Scott overlooked Thomas Heartfree and his lady his oversight is pardonable; the passivity with which they are rendered is all but overwhelmed · by the creative force invested in their fell incensed opposite. 'Hypocrisy, cruelty, avarice and lust', Sir Leslie Stephen remarks of Fielding's methods generally, 'have to be stamped by hard blows, not cured by delicate infusions of graceful sentimentalisms.' Though a real enthusiasm for virtue does in fact share the book with an assumed enthusiasm for villainy, the ironic grasp of evil imposes so potent a stress that to save the Heartfrees from obliteration one is almost driven to an inadmissible critical procedure— that of importing from other works the abundant evidence that Fielding loved goodness at least as passionately as he hated vice. The Heartfree story, meant touchingly to recommend virtue, slips into sentimentality: Heartfree himself lacks the energy which Fielding knows to be necessary and without which, as he admits in the preface to the *Miscellanies*, the good man, though not 'absolutely a fool or coward', yet 'partakes too little of parts or courage'. Wild is viciously 'great', Heartfree guilelessly good.

Human nature needs goodness and strength. Yet goodness is to be loved; guilelessness is virtue; Heartfree does not lack moral or physical courage; and the Heartfree scenes, read sympathetically, reveal a warm appreciation of love and honesty. It is in fact because the book favours goodness that it works so forcibly against wickedness—the 'human feeling' that Scott could not see in it is the very motive for its existence. Yet what it displays most prominently is not the beauty of goodness but the ugliness of evil, and the menace of the power which corrupts.

The *Miscellanies* appeared in April 1743, fourteen months after *Joseph Andrews*. When *Jonathan Wild* was written is not quite clear. Several allusions refer to events of 1742, yet Austin Dobson is surely right in thinking that, having achieved *Joseph Andrews*, Fielding would hardly turn so soon to write in a vein so different, so much fiercer. Publication had in any case been delayed. In June 1742 the *Daily Post* advertised proposals for the *Miscellanies*; the third volume, it announced, would contain

the history of that truly renowned Person, Jonathan Wyld, Esq: in which not only his character but that of divers other great personages of his time will be set in a just and true light.

Publication, the *Post* continued, had already been halted by 'melancholy accidents' in the winter of 1741–2. Further delay was to be caused by other misfortunes, including the grave illness of Fielding's beloved wife. Material in a late stage of preparation by the end of 1741, but not published until 1743, may well have been amplified in 1742 by references to current events, and anti-Walpole satire relevant to the Opposition campaign of the 1730's and early 1740's might appear in a work issued after the Prime Minister fell in February 1742.

A hypothesis to account for the discrepancies of dating is that the book shows three strata of composition.[1] The first is the biography of Wild, without the Heartfrees. This biography is the story of the real Jonathan, though with invented additions, a complete and unfailingly ironic analogue-satire on political greatness, part of the anti-Walpole campaign. Wickedness is consistently applauded, and no goodheartedness impairs the ironic pose. The second stratum relates the Heartfrees' persecution by Wild; here

[1] The hypothesis is well worked out in F. Homes Dudden, *Henry Fielding*, i. 470 ff, 1952.

goodness is a foil to greatness, and the reversal of good and evil is much less steadfast—indeed Fielding permits himself an evident sympathy with the victims. The third stratum is Mrs Heartfree's foreign adventure which, in the 1743 edition, includes a Lucianic fantasy (IV. ix; 1743) entitled 'A very wonderful chapter indeed: which, to those who have not read many Voyages, may seem incredible; and which the reader may believe or not as he pleases'. This is in fact one of Fielding's many satires on travellers' tales, the subject already of a satiric paper in *The Champion* of 20th March 1739–40, and to be resumed in the preface of *A Voyage to Lisbon*. When the whole work was revised in 1754 for separate publication the Lucianic chapter was excised, but even so the travel romance sits unconvincingly with the rest of the book. The Wild biography, then, is probably concurrent with Fielding's Opposition campaign in *The Champion* in 1740, and, when the *Miscellanies* were being compiled between 1741 and 1743, was amplified with later allusions and with the humaner element of the Heartfree story (which shows some influence from *Joseph Andrews*), Mrs Heartfree's wanderings being adapted from a travel-satire written earlier and for other purposes. Disparate elements not wholly assimilated probably account for the puzzles over the book's date. The 1754 revision reflects the different political circumstances. Walpole was now dead and Fielding was supporting Pelham's Government, not the Opposition. The satire on Sir Robert was therefore somewhat though not wholly broadened into general satire on Great Men, and one chapter of political attack was omitted (II. xii; 1743). Thus amended the book appeared in March in the text commonly accepted since then.[1]

The Wild of history was born in 1682 or 1683, of honest working folk in Wolverhampton. Making his way to London he fell into evil ways (like Hogarth's Idle Apprentice) and landed in jail. On release he acted as intermediary between criminals and their victims, restoring stolen goods for a reward and maintaining a gang by bribes and threats. For some years he flourished mightily. At last, however, as Fielding relates, a violent attack made upon him by a subordinate villain named Blueskin—the subject of Swift's *Blueskin's Ballad*—caused inquiries to be made. His trial

[1] The World's Classics edition reprints the 1743 version with an appendix listing the revisions.

and subsequent execution at Tyburn on 24th May 1725 caused immense excitement. Ballads, biographies factual and fictional, and potboiling pamphlets of all sorts burst forth in great numbers, many of which, including Defoe's *True and Genuine Account of . . . the late Jonathan Wild*, Fielding was to study for his own version. That racy collection, the *Lives of the Most Remarkable Criminals* (1735), begins its account thus:

> As no person in this collection ever made so much noise as the person we are now speaking of, so never any man, perhaps, in any condition of life whatever had so many romantic stories fathered upon him in his life, or so many legendary accounts published of him after his death.

What is more important is that satirists at once exploited the ambiguities of the villainous 'benefactor'. The anonymous *Life of Jonathan Wild, Thief-Taker General of Great Britain and Ireland*, published at Northampton in 1725, anticipates Fielding's line:

> We need make no apology for collecting these Materials and offering them to the publick; For here they will meet with a system of Politicks unknown to Machiavel; they will see deeper stratagems and plots form'd by a fellow without Learning or Education than are to be met with in the conduct of the greatest Statesman.

Wild, the pamphlet explains, 'show'd early signs of a forward genius', and 'laid the foundations of all his future greatness'. In *The Champion* of 4th March 1739–40, on 'Reputation', Fielding himself took '*Jonathan Wyld*' (the variant spellings provide a jest in the second chapter of the novel) as an instance of a man become unintentionally famous.

Yet through the features of Wild there peer also those of Walpole, so the fact that the statesman subscribed for ten sets of the *Miscellanies* has a pleasing piquancy. He had for years been the Opposition's imperturbable butt. In May 1725 *Mist's Weekly Journal* treated the executed Wild as a 'celebrated statesman and politician' and left no doubt that the real target was Walpole; among the newspaper accounts Fielding consulted this may well have been one. In *The Beggar's Opera* (1728) Gay satirized 'Robin of Bagshot, . . . alias Bluff Bob, . . . alias Bob Booty'; his Peachum (a version of Walpole) declares to Lockit (a version of Wild) that thief-takers, receivers of stolen goods, and statesmen

alike live by plundering, plotting and betraying their
friends. Swift remarked in *The Intelligencer* of 25th May
1729 that *The Beggar's Opera* likens criminals' 'betraying,
undermining, and hanging each other to the several arts of
politicians in times of corruption'. *The Craftsman* made
much of the supposed analogy between Wild and Walpole,
and on the latter's fall it concluded that two Great Men had
met their deserts, the one being hanged and the other dis-
graced. For the twenty preceding years the term 'Great
Man' had meant Walpole; it runs as a motif through
Jonathan Wild. Fielding himself attacked Walpole's
bribery in *Don Quixote in England* (1734), *Pasquin* (1736),
The Historical Register for 1736 (1737) and *The Champion*
(1739–41), Walpole had driven him from the stage with the
Licensing Act of 1737. The title of 'Prime Minister', a
recognized appellation of Walpole (though disowned by
him), gave Fielding another foothold for attack; *The
Champion* of 8th May 1740 ends with the prayer, 'FROM
THE PRIME MINISTER GOOD LORD DELIVER US. AMEN'. And the
ancestral tree Fielding draws up for Wild is a parody of
William Musgrave's *Brief and True History of Sir Robert
Walpole and his Family* (1736) in which, to forty pages on
Sir Robert, thirty-eight go to his ancestry.[1]

But *Jonathan Wild* transcends Walpole and the immediate political scene as much as it does Wild, and it rises
into that 'masterpiece and quintessential example of irony'
that Saintsbury calls it. *The Champion* of 3rd May 1740 had
made an impassioned attack on the falseness of the great
and the inhumanity of conquering heroes. In disavowing
personal application, as he does in the preface to the
Miscellanies, Fielding was not being merely ironical:

> A second caution I would give my reader, that as it is not a
> very faithful portrait of Jonathan Wild himself, so neither is it
> intended to represent the features of any other person. Roguery,
> and not a rogue, is my subject; and as I have been so far from
> endeavouring to particularize any individual, that I have with
> my utmost art avoided it, so will any such application be unfair
> in my reader.

Behind the ironic disclaimer lies a genuine point. The
book's aim would be limited if a single criminal, a single
politician, were its object. The murderous destructiveness of

---

[1] J. E. Wells, 'Fielding's Political Purpose in *Jonathan Wild*',
Publ. Mod. Lang. Assoc. America, vol. xxviii, 1913.

Great Men is an evil Fielding projects far past the Wilds and
Walpoles of contemporary England on to the Alexanders
and Caesars of world history, and condemns with all the
power at his command. There was nothing new in this; an
age-old hatred of military megalomania, paralleling an age-
old laudation, was suddenly reinforced in the eighteenth
century by the meteoric career of Charles XII of Sweden,
publicized through Voltaire's account of his 'glorious mischief', and later taken up in Johnson's *Vanity of Human
Wishes* as a supreme instance of that vanity.[1] Yet humbler
readers cannot congratulate themselves that the satiric gale
winnows only the great. They are themselves liable to be
blasted by that indignation against inhumanity which
blows against 'poor Heartfree''s callous neighbours—'this
detestable picture of ingratitude', as Fielding frankly calls
it (II. viii)—or the shockingly callous commander of the
jail (IV. v.).

Fielding's other novels are more attractive, but none conveys more force and pressure of mind and attention. The
satiric and narrative strokes are perpetually alive (save for
one or two over-laboured disquisitions). The many-sided
parody of grandiloquence is admirable. Wild's upbringing is
a skit on polite and genteel education; romantic courtships
and highflown sentiments on love and honour are equally
taken off. The intellectual poise is grandly diverting; Fielding
disciplines his material with a powerful formality, giving his
narrative a cogency and deliberation which imitate the
grand stances of serious history and learning. The balanced
and triple clauses with which the book opens, and the
incisive character of Wild (in IV. xv), have been thought
indebted to Clarendon's *History of the Rebellion* (a work
which Fielding had in his library), and certainly these
passages show a resemblance to Clarendon's early pages and
his 'short character' of Charles I (in Book XI of the *History*).
The similarities may be generic rather than specific, but in
any case, whether or not Fielding has a particular original
in mind, he catches admirably the lofty tone of the formal
historians with whom his library was stocked—Clarendon,
Rymer, Rushworth, Thursloe, Whitelocke, Burnet and

---

[1] F. Homes Dudden, *Henry Fielding*, i. 465 ff., gives a list of Fielding's
hostile references to military leaders. W. R. Irwin, *The Making of
Jonathan Wild*, pages 44–79, surveys the tradition of antipathy to
'heroes'.

others. In particular, the passages on history as truth rather than eulogy seem an evident parody of Conyers Middleton's preface to his *Life of Cicero* (1741), a work Fielding had already ridiculed in *Shamela*. The grave rhetorical patterns of serious history provide the heroic pattern for his mock-heroic. He is moreover a master of mock-epic inflations and deflations, and of satirical references to the ancients. He can pitch plebeian arguments and quarrels at the level of learned and philosophical discourses. At the same time the dialogue is marvellously spirited in the low comedy, in, for example, Bagshot's and Blueskin's rejoinders to Wild (I. viii; III. xiv), and above all in the wonderful 'dialogue matrimonial' between Jonathan and Lætitia (III. viii) and the colloquy between Jonathan and the Ordinary (IV. xiii). Fielding's stage experience lies behind the comic vernacular here. His strength of mind shows itself in aphoristic condensations and in an almost physical impact of strongly phrased ideas and feelings. The discomfort some readers feel is due, no doubt, as much to the sheer force of statement as to the ironic urgency. Yet however vehement the feeling, however trenchant the irony, many a touch is very funny indeed. To quote James Ralph's prologue to Fieldings' *Temple Beau* (1730),

> The Comick Muse, in Smiles severely gay,
> Shall scoff at Vice, and laugh its Crimes away.

At the climax, the chapter of its hero's execution, *Jonathan Wild* reaches an almost unique manner of comedy, at once fiercely relentless and highly diverting.

The vocabulary is strongest when Fielding's moral feelings are most engaged, as they are, for instance, in attacking martial heroics. The irony is never a disguise to his opinions. No one could mistake his intentions; not only the court-jail equation but selfishness and rapacity of all sorts, swindling and scandalmongering in all ranks, and 'the world''s hypocrisies about 'honour' are relentlessly exposed. Against these are ranged the integrity, the religious faith, the charity and honest principles of the Heartfrees, Friendly and the good magistrate. Though these bulk much less largely than the account of villainy (the book, after all, is Wild's), and though the ironic depreciation of Heartfree unfortunately damages his importance, Fielding has expressed as far as the circumstances allowed the devotion he feels to goodness and

truth, a devotion reflected in the capitalized printing of Mrs
Heartfree's concluding moral (IV. xi). As he was to remark
in *The Case of Elizabeth Canning*, 'there is something within
myself which rouses me to the protection of injured innocence'. Those 'comforts which a good conscience suggests to
a Christian philosopher' were always his moral positives, as
his own faith was always the charitable tolerance Heartfree
urges against the Ordinary (and Adams against Barnabas in
Joseph Andrews). If the general tenor of the book suggests,
like that of *The Pilgrim's Progress*, the loneliness of the
persecuted good amidst a hostile world, that is due not to
sectarianism or despair of mankind at large but to the
passionate conviction that wrongs will be rectified only
when the eyes of the world are opened wide to them.

Like *Jonathan Wild*, the *Voyage to Lisbon*, posthumously
published in 1755, exists in two forms. One version, issued in
February, is shorter than the other, issued in December. It
leaves out some reflections on living persons, though it adds
a complimentary reference to the ship's captain, derived
from a letter Fielding sent to his half-brother Sir John, who
probably made the changes to safeguard the book's reception. Possibly the fuller version was printed but held back
lest it should give offence, the shorter being substituted for
it. But the sudden curiosity about Lisbon caused by the
great earthquake of November—an event which lastingly
disturbed the fashionable doctrines of optimism—may have
prompted the issue of the withheld edition, regardless of
precautions. It is, at any rate, this, the fuller version, which
has remained the received text since Arthur Murphy and
Andrew Millar used it in the collected edition of Fielding's
works in 1762.

The *Voyage*—'stoical, gay, self-deriding, eminently
considerate and extremely censorious'[1]—is the charac-
teristically gallant outcome of circumstances which would
have reduced most men to gloom. Deprived of the company
he cherished because his wife and her companions were ill
during a storm off the Downs, oppressed by a combination
of diseases, cooped up conversationless over a small bowl of
punch with his deaf septuagenarian captain, he thought of
writing his travels, and later reflects that some of its most
amusing pages 'were possibly the production of the most

[1] The phrase is from P. N. Furbank, introduction to the Penguin
edition of *Joseph Andrews*.

disagreeable hours which ever haunted the author'. As his editor Arthur Murphy observed, 'by difficulties his resolution was never subdued; on the contrary, they only aroused him to struggle through them with a peculiar spirit and magnanimity'.

This superiority to circumstances is deeply moving. The account of the illnesses and hardships which drove him to seek relief in Portugal is heartrending—or would be, were the relation less frank and manly. He is touchingly appreciative of the physicians who tried, with only transient success, to relieve him. He records his distresses stoically, his passing alleviations with heartfelt gratitude. It is true that not all of the book is magnanimous; Fielding never suffered fools or villains gladly, and there is a Swiftian fierceness when he comments on the gangs whose extirpation cost him his chances of recovery, a harshness, even bellicosity, when he relates the inhumanities he met with on the journey. He remains as uncompromising against brutality as he had always been. But all this is on grounds not of personal resentment but of social good. If his power to castigate is undiminished, as it is when he reflects on the criminals he suppressed, the public which neglected him, the watermen who derided his sufferings, the exactions imposed on him, or the tyrannies of nautical command, the castigations proceed not from petulance. As Boswell wrote of Johnson, 'his mind was turned to resolution, and never to whining or complaint'. What stands out from the background of censure is his rich appreciativeness—his love of his family, his affection for friends and benefactors, his delight in fine weather and nautical scenes, his exultation in Britain's mercantile strength, his pleasure in sailing, his enthusiasm for fine scenes—the shores of the Thames, Greenwich Hospital, moonlit nights, the sea prospect from Ryde, the verdure of the Isle of Wight, the sunset near Cape Finisterre. His illness seems to augment rather than diminish his sense of physical pleasures; this is the Fielding of whom his cousin, Lady Mary Wortley Montagu, remarked that 'no man enjoyed life more than he did. He was so formed for happiness it is a pity he was not immortal'. He records with infectious satisfaction the meal in the barn at Ryde, the 'clouted' cream, fresh bread, and cider of Devon, the john dory with which he 'gloriously regaled' himself, 'washing it down with some good claret with my wife and her friend', and 'the sweet and comfortable nap' at Brixham which followed his tapping for dropsy the previous day. The zest with which he likes whatever can be liked, the vigour of his disquisitions and the vitality of his portrayals, recall the kindred qualities in the novels. His praise of the common sailor at sea is as striking as his just indignation at the inhuman watermen of the Thames or the callous shore dwellers of the Channel coast. His formidable representation of Mrs Francis at Ryde and her nonentity of a husband is as entertaining in one vein as is that of the captain's 'very pretty fellow' of a nephew in quite another, and the visiting Swiss captain in another again. But the triumph of the book is Captain Veal (his name, and that of his ship *The Queen of Portugal*, are recorded not in the book but in a letter from Fielding to his brother)—a character excellently rendered in the balance of considerations between, on the one hand, his imperious and impetuous temper, enforced with rough manners and violent voice, and on the other his bravery, solicitude for his men and ships, and tenderness for his kitten. The old sea-dog, swaggering in cockade, scarlet coat and outsize sword, combining the finicalness of Sir Courtly Nice with the roughness of Surly, but reduced to trepidation by his passenger's threat of legal action, is an unforgettable portrait. Whatever its faults—the discourses are sometimes too long, the sentences sometimes stiff, the sense not always clear—the *Voyage* offers human interest rich enough to provide that 'real and valuable knowledge of men and things' which, Fielding asserts in his preface, is the only justification for books of travel.

A. R. HUMPHREYS.

1973.

SELECT BIBLIOGRAPHY

EDITIONS AND WORKS

THE most comprehensive modern editions of Fielding are those by Leslie Stephen (10 vols., 1882) and W. E. Henley (16 vols., 1903). There are collected editions of the novels by George Saintsbury (12 vols., 1893), Edmund Gosse (12 vols., 1898–9), and G. H. Maynadier (12 vols., 1905), and in the Shakespeare Head edition (10 vols., 1926). The Wesleyan edition, in progress under W. B. Coley, is setting high standards in annotation and textual authority; *Joseph Andrews* has appeared, edited by Martin C. Battestin (1967), and *Miscellanies* (vol. i), edited by Henry Knight Miller (1972). Most reprints of *Jonathan Wild* follow the 1754 version; that of 1743 is, however, reprinted in the Shakespeare Head and World's Classics editions. The two texts are compared in detail in Aurélien Digeon's *Le Texte des Romans de Fielding* (1923).

NOVELS. *The Adventures of Joseph Andrews, and of his Friend Mr Abraham Adams*, 2 vols., 1742; *The Life of Mr Jonathan Wild the Great* and *A Journey from This World to the Next* (in *Miscellanies*, 3 vols.), 1743; *Tom Jones*, 6 vols., 1749; *Amelia*, 4 vols., 1752.

PLAYS. *Love in Several Masques*, 1728; *The Temple Beau*, 1730; *The Author's Farce; and the Pleasures of the Town*, 1730 (revised 1734); *Tom Thumb*, 1730 (revised and enlarged as *The Tragedy of Tragedies*, 1731); *Rape upon Rape*, 1730 (reissued as *The Coffee-House Politician*, 1730); *The Welsh Opera*, 1731 (reworked as *The Grub-Street Opera*, 1731); *The Letter-Writers*, 1731; *The Lottery*, 1732; *The Modern Husband*, 1732; *The Covent-Garden Tragedy*, 1732; *The Old Debauchees*, 1732; *The Mock Doctor*, 1732; *The Miser*, 1733; *Deborah*, 1733; *The Intriguing Chambermaid*, 1734; *Don Quixote in England*, 1734; *An Old Man Taught Wisdom*, 1735; *The Universal Gallant*, 1735; *Pasquin*, 1736; *Tumble-Down Dick: or, Phaeton in the Suds*, 1736; *Eurydice*, 1737; *The Historical Register for the Year 1736*, 1737; *Eurydice Hiss'd*, 1737; *Miss Lucy in Town*, 1742; *The Wedding-Day*, 1743; *The Fathers: or, The Good-Natur'd Man*, 1778.

PERIODICALS. *The Champion: or, British Mercury*, 2 vols., 15 Nov. 1739–19 June 1742; *The True Patriot: and The History of our Own Times*, 5 Nov. 1745–17 June 1746; *The Jacobite's Journal*, 5 Dec. 1747–5 Nov. 1748; *The Covent-Garden Journal*, 4 Jan.–25 Nov. 1752.

OTHER WRITINGS. *The Masquerade, a Poem*, 1728; *Of True Greatness*, 1741; *The Vernoniad*, 1741; *An Apology for the Life of Mrs Shamela Andrews*, 1741; *The Crisis: A Sermon on Revel. xiv. 9–11*, 1741; *The Opposition, A Vision*, 1742; *A Full Vindication of the Dutchess Dowager of Marlborough*, 1742; *Plutus, the God of Riches* (translated from Aristophanes), 1742; *Concerning the Terrestrial Chrysippus*, 1743; *Miscellanies*, 3 vols., 1743; *A Serious Address to the People of Great Britain*, 1745; *A Dialogue between the Devil, the Pope, and the Pretender*, 1745; *The History of the Present Rebellion in Scotland*, 1745; *A Dialogue between a gentleman of London . . . And an Honest Alderman of the Country Party*, 1747; *A Proper Answer to a Late Scurrilous Libel*, 1747; *Ovid's Art of Love paraphrased, and adapted to the present Time, Book 1*, 1747; *A True State of the Case of Bosavern Penlez*, 1749; *A Charge delivered to the Grand Jury, at the Sessions, the 29th of June 1749*, 1749; *An Enquiry into the Causes of the late Increase of Robbers*, 1751; *A Plan of the Universal Register Office*, 1752 (with John Fielding); *Examples of the Interposition of Providence in the Detection and Punishment of Murder*, 1752; *A Proposal for Making an Effectual Provision for the Poor*, 1753; *A Clear State of the Case of Elizabeth Canning*, 1753; *The Journal of a Voyage to Lisbon*, 1755.

BIOGRAPHY AND CRITICISM

AMONG earlier appreciations of Fielding those by his contemporary and first editor, Arthur Murphy ('An Essay on the Life and Genius of Henry Fielding, Esq.', in *The Works of Henry Fielding*, vol. i, 1762), Hazlitt (in *The English Comic Writers*, 1819), Scott (in *Lives of the Novelists*, 1821), Leslie Stephen (in *Hours in a Library*, third series, 1879, and the introduction to his edition of Fielding's *Works*, 1882), and Austin Dobson (*Fielding*, 1883) compensate in good sense and liberal spirit for any lack of critical subtlety. Among later appreciations Aurélien Digeon's *Les Romans de Fielding* (1923, translated as *The Novels of Fielding*, 1925) is a humane, well-judged work for the general reader: the chapter on *Jonathan Wild* is reprinted, abridged, in *Fielding: a Collection of Critical Essays*, edited by Ronald Paulson (1962), which also reprints 'Fielding's Irony: its Methods and Effects' by A. R. Humphreys, dealing mainly with *Jonathan Wild*.

The most detailed accounts of Fielding's life and work are those by W. L. Cross—*The History of Henry Fielding* (3 vols., 1918)—and F. Homes Dudden—*Henry Fielding; his Life, Works, and Times* (2 vols., 1952). Both abound in biographical material set very fully in the context of contemporary life and thought.

The political references of *Jonathan Wild* are explained in 'Fielding's Political Purpose in *Jonathan Wild*', by J. E. Wells (*PMLA*, xxviii, 1913). W. R. Irwin's *The Making of 'Jonathan Wild'* (1941) examines the criminal as well as the political history of the time, Fielding's use of the Wild material, and his role as moral adjudicator. Ronald Paulson's *Satire and the Novel in Eighteenth-Century England* (1967), referring briefly to *Jonathan Wild*, points out how Wild's prestige is undercut by ignominy. This theme recurs in C. J. Rawson's 'Fielding and Smollett' (in 'Dryden to Johnson', edited by Roger Lonsdale, vol. iv of *A History of Literature in the English Language*, 1971) and is fully developed in Rawson's important study, *Henry Fielding and the Augustan Ideal under Stress* (1972); this deals substantially with *Jonathan Wild*. With other studies—Allan Wendt's 'The Moral Allegory of *Jonathan Wild*' (*ELH*, xxiv, 1970) and Leo Braudy's *Narrative Form in History and Fiction* (1970)—it also points out the inadequacy of the Heartfrees' passive goodness.

The ironic critique of 'greatness' has been much discussed. J. Preston, in 'The Ironic Mode; a Comparison of *Jonathan Wild* and *The Beggar's Opera*' (in *Essays in Criticism*, edited by F. W. Bateson, xvi, 1966), shows the relative poverty of the ironic technique as against the more complex subversiveness of Gay's satire. B. R. Levine, in *Henry Fielding and the Dry Mock* (1967), makes a useful study of ironic procedures. Rawson's two studies (see above) discuss the irony as energetic but limited. Fielding's manipulation of language to caricature Wild is examined in Humphreys, 'Fielding's Irony' (see above), and Leo Braudy, *Narrative Form* (see above); Braudy closely examines the puppet-like delusions of corrupt power. Glenn W. Hatfield's *Henry Fielding and the Language of Irony* (1968), though turning only occasionally to *Jonathan Wild*, offers an admirable analysis of a subject relevant to it, the linguistic corruptions (a kind of hypocrisy of language) by which virtuous terms disguise vicious actions.

The Journal of a Voyage to Lisbon is acknowledged in many accounts of Fielding's work as a characteristic and notable work, but criticism of it amounts to little more than brief appreciation (in, for instance, Austin Dobson's *Eighteenth-Century Vignettes*, first series, 1892, and his introduction to the work in Henley's edition, vol. xvi, and Elizabeth Jenkins's *Henry Fielding*, 1947). Harold E. Pagliaro's introduction to the Nardon Press Edition, New York, 1963, has more substance than these others, but it is hard to find in Great Britain. Cross and Dudden (see above) give the fullest accounts, largely retailing the contents of the book but adding useful details of biography and publication.

THE TEXT

Fielding considerably revised the 1743 text of *Jonathan Wild*, in the third volume of *Miscellanies*, for separate publication in 1754. The revised version is the basis of most reprints, including this one, which inserts before the text an extract from Fielding's Preface to the *Miscellanies* and contains also the 'Advertisement from the Publisher to the Reader' prefixed to the 1754 edition. This latter, despite the heading, shows every sign of being Fielding's own work.

The Journal of a Voyage to Lisbon appeared in a shortened, edited version in February 1755, and a full-length version, largely as Fielding had left it, in December 1755. The present reprint follows the full text. A few misprints and other apparent slips have been silently amended. Missing or erroneous dates have been added or corrected within square brackets: on page 278, however, the entry '[*Tuesday's*]' is already so printed in the original text. Prefixed to both 1755 versions, and included here, is the 'Dedication to the Public', not by Fielding, probably by Arthur Murphy, the friend who issued Fielding's collected works in 1762.

EXTRACT FROM FIELDING'S PREFACE TO THE *MISCELLANIES*
[1743]

I come now to the third and last volume, which contains the history of Jonathan Wild. And here it will not, I apprehend, be necessary to acquaint my reader, that my design is not to enter the lists with that excellent historian, who from authentic papers and records, etc., hath already given so satisfactory an account of the life and actions of this great man. I have not indeed the least intention to depreciate the veracity and impartiality of that history; nor do I pretend to any of those lights, not having, to my knowledge, ever seen a single paper relating to my hero, save some short memoirs, which about the time of his death were published in certain chronicles called newspapers, the authority of which hath been sometimes questioned, and in the Ordinary of Newgate his account, which generally contains a more particular relation of what the heroes are to suffer in the next world, than of what they did in this.

To confess the truth, my narrative is rather of such actions which he might have performed, or would, or should have performed, than what he really did; and may, in reality, as well suit any other such great man, as the person himself whose name it bears.

A second caution I would give my reader is, that as it is not a very faithful portrait of Jonathan Wild himself, so neither is it intended to represent the features of any other person. Roguery, and not a rogue, is my subject; and as I have been so far from endeavouring to particularize any individual, that I have with my utmost art avoided it; so will any such application be unfair in my reader, especially if he knows much of the great world, since he must then be acquainted, I believe, with more than one on whom he can fix the resemblance.

In the third place, I solemnly protest, I do by no means intend in the character of my hero to represent human nature in general. Such insinuations must be attended with very dreadful conclusions; nor do I see any other tendency they can naturally have, but to encourage and soothe men in their villainies, and to make every well-disposed man disclaim his own species, and curse the hour of his birth into such a society. For my part, I understand those writers who describe human nature in this depraved character, as speaking only of such persons as Wild and his gang; and I think it may be justly inferred, that they do not find in their own bosoms any deviation from the general rule. Indeed it would

xviii

be an insufferable vanity in them to conceive themselves as the only exception to it.

But without considering Newgate as no other human than nature with its mask off, which some very shameless writers have done, a thought which no price should purchase me to entertain, I think we may be excused for suspecting, that the splendid palaces of the great are often no other than Newgate with the mask on. Nor do I know any thing which can raise an honest man's indignation higher than that the same morals should be in one place attended with all imaginable misery and infamy, and in the other, with the highest luxury and honour. Let any impartial man in his senses be asked, for which of these two places a composition of cruelty, lust, avarice, rapine, insolence, hypocrisy, fraud and treachery, was best fitted, surely his answer must be certain and immediate; and yet I am afraid all these ingredients glossed over with wealth and a title, have been treated with the highest respect and veneration in the one, while one or two of them have been condemned to the gallows in the other.

If there are then any men of such morals who dare to call themselves great, and are so reputed, or called at least, by the deceived multitude, surely a little private censure by the few is a very moderate tax for them to pay, provided no more was to be demanded. But I fear this is not the case. However the glare of riches, and awe of title, may dazzle and terrify the vulgar; nay, however hypocrisy may deceive the more discerning, there is still a judge in every man's breast, which none can cheat nor corrupt, though perhaps it is the only uncorrupt thing about him. And yet, inflexible and honest as this judge is (however polluted the bench be on which he sits), no man can, in my opinion, enjoy any applause which is not thus adjudged to be his due.

Nothing seems to me more preposterous than that, while the way to true honour lies so open and plain, men should seek false by such perverse and rugged paths: that while it is so easy and safe, and truly honourable, to be good, men should wade through difficulty and danger, and real infamy, to be *great*, or, to use a synonimous word, *villains*.

Nor hath goodness less advantage in the article of pleasure, than of honour over this kind of greatness. The same righteous judge always annexes a bitter anxiety to the purchases of guilt, whilst it adds a double sweetness to the enjoyments of innocence and virtue: for fear, which all the wise agree is the most wretched of human evils, is, in some degree, always attending on the former, and never can in any manner molest the happiness of the latter.

This is the doctrine which I have endeavoured to inculcate in this history, confining myself at the same time within the rules of probability. (For except in one chapter, which is visibly meant as a burlesque on the extravagant accounts of travellers, I believe I have not exceeded it.) And though perhaps it sometimes happens, contrary to the instances I have given, that the villain succeeds in his pursuit, and acquires some transitory imperfect honour or pleasure to himself for his iniquity; yet I believe he oftener shares the fate of my hero, and suffers the punishment, without obtaining the reward.

As I believe it is not easy to teach a more useful lesson than this, if I have been able to add the pleasant to it, I might flatter myself with having carried every point.

But perhaps some apology may be required of me, for having used the world *Greatness*, to which the world have affixed such honourable ideas, in so disgraceful and contemptuous a light. Now if the fact be, that the greatness which is commonly worshipped is really of that kind which I have here represented, the fault seems rather to lie in those who have ascribed it to those honours, to which it hath not in reality the least claim.

The truth, I apprehend, is, we often confound the ideas of goodness and greatness together, or rather include the former in our idea of the latter. If this be so, it is surely a great error, and no less than a mistake of the capacity for the will. In reality, no qualities can be more distinct: for as it cannot be doubted but that benevolence, honour, honesty, and charity, make a good man; and that parts, courage, are the efficient qualities of a great man, so must it be confessed, that the ingredients which compose the former of these characters, bear no analogy to, nor dependence on, those which constitute the latter. A man may therefore be great without being good, or good without being great.

However, though the one bear no necessary dependence on the other, neither is there any absolute repugnancy among them which may totally prevent their union so that they may, though not of necessity, assemble in the same mind, as they actually did, and all in the highest degree, in those of Socrates and Brutus, and perhaps in some among us. I at least know one to whom nature could have added no one great or good quality more than she hath bestowed on him.

Here then appear three distinct characters; the great, the good, and the great and good.

The last of these is the *true sublime* in human nature. That elevation by which the soul of man, raising and extending itself above the order of this creation, and brightened with a certain ray of divinity, looks down on the condition of mortals. This is indeed a glorious object, on which we can never gaze with too much praise and admiration. A perfect work! the *Iliad* of Nature! ravishing and astonishing, and which at once fills us with love, wonder, and delight.

The second falls greatly short of this perfection, and yet hath its merit. Our wonder ceases; our delight is lessened; but our love remains; of which passion, goodness hath always appeared to me the only true and proper object. On this head I think proper to observe, that I do not conceive my good man to be absolutely a fool or a coward; but that he often partakes too little of parts or courage, to have any pretensions to greatness.

Now as to that greatness which is totally devoid of goodness, it seems to me in Nature to resemble the *false sublime* in poetry; whose bombast is, by the ignorant and ill-judging vulgar, often mistaken for solid wit and eloquence, whilst it is in effect the very reverse. Thus pride, ostentation, insolence, cruelty, and every kind of villainy, are often construed into true greatness of mind, in which we always include an idea of goodness.

This bombast greatness then is the character I intend to expose; and the more this prevails in and deceives the world, taking to itself not only riches and power, but often honour, or at least the shadow of it, the more necessary is it to strip the monster of these false colours, and show it in its native deformity: for by suffering vice to possess the reward of virtue, we do a double injury to society, by encouraging the former, and taking away the chief incentive to the latter. Nay, though it is, I believe, impossible to give vice a true relish of honour and glory, or though we give it riches and power, to give it the enjoyment of them, yet it contaminates the food it can't taste, and sullies the robe which neither fits nor becomes it, 'till virtue disdains them both.

ADVERTISEMENT FROM THE PUBLISHER TO THE READER
[1754]

The following pages are the corrected edition of a book which was first published in the year 1743.

That any personal application could have ever been possibly drawn from them, will surprise all who are not deeply versed in the black art (for so it seems most properly to be called), of deciphering men's meaning when couched in obscure, ambiguous, or allegorical expressions: this art hath been exercised more than once on the author of our little book, who hath contracted a considerable degree of odium from having had the scurrility of others imputed to him. The truth is, as a very corrupt state of morals is here represented, the scene seems very properly to have been laid in Newgate; nor do I see any reason for introducing any allegory at all; unless we will agree that there are without those walls, some other bodies of men of worse morals than those within; and who have, consequently, a right to change places with its present inhabitants.

To such persons, if any such there be, I would particularly recommend the perusal of the third chapter of the fourth book of the following history, and more particularly still the speech of the grave man in pages 195, 196 of that book [pages 133-4 of the present edition].

CONTENTS

THE HISTORY OF THE LIFE OF THE LATE MR. JONATHAN WILD THE GREAT

BOOK I

BOOK II

CONTENTS

BOOK III

BOOK IV

THE JOURNAL OF A VOYAGE TO LISBON

THE HISTORY OF THE LIFE
OF THE LATE MR. JONATHAN WILD
THE GREAT

Shewing the wholesome uses drawn from recording the achievements of those wonderful productions of nature called GREAT MEN

As it is necessary that all great and surprising events, the designs of which are laid, conducted, and brought to perfection by the utmost force of human invention and art, should be produced by great and eminent men, so the lives of such may be justly and properly styled the quintessence of history. In these, when delivered to us by sensible writers, we are not only most agreeably entertained, but most usefully instructed; for, besides the attaining hence a consummate knowledge of human nature in general; of its secret springs, various windings, and perplexed mazes; we have here before our eyes lively examples of whatever is amiable or detestable, worthy of admiration or abhorrence, and are consequently taught, in a manner infinitely more effectual than by precept, what we are eagerly to imitate or carefully to avoid.

But besides the two obvious advantages of surveying, as it were in a picture, the true beauty of virtue and deformity of vice, we may moreover learn from Plutarch, Nepos, Suetonius, and other biographers, this useful lesson, not too hastily, nor in the gross, to bestow either our praise or censure; since we shall often find such a mixture of good and evil in the same character that it may require a very accurate judgment and a very elaborate inquiry to determine on which side the balance turns, for though we sometimes meet with an Aristides or a Brutus, a Lysander or a Nero, yet far the greater number are of the mixt kind, neither totally good nor bad; their greatest virtues being obscured and allayed by their vices, and those again softened and coloured over by their virtues.

Of this kind was the illustrious person whose history we now undertake; to whom, though nature had given the greatest and most shining endowments, she had not given them absolutely pure and without allay. Though he had much of the admirable in his character, as much perhaps as is usually to be found in a hero, I will not yet venture to affirm that he was entirely free from all defects, or that the sharp eyes of censure could not spy out some little blemishes lurking amongst his many great perfections.

We would not therefore be understood to affect giving the reader a perfect or consummate pattern of human excellence, but rather, by faithfully recording some little imperfections which shadowed over the lustre of those great qualities which we shall here record, to teach the lesson we have above mentioned, to induce our reader with us to lament the frailty of human nature, and to convince him that no mortal, after a thorough scrutiny, can be a proper object of our adoration.

But before we enter on this great work we must endeavour to remove some errors of opinion which mankind have, by the disingenuity of writers, contracted: for these, from their fear of contradicting the obsolete and absurd doctrines of a set of simple fellows, called, in derision, sages or philosophers, have endeavoured, as much as possible, to confound the ideas of greatness and goodness; whereas no two things can possibly be more distinct from each other, for greatness consists in bringing all manner of mischief on mankind, and goodness in removing it from them. It seems therefore very unlikely that the same person should possess them both; and yet nothing is more usual with writers, who find many instances of greatness in their favourite hero, than to make him a compliment of goodness into the bargain; and this, without considering that by such means they destroy the great perfection called uniformity of character. In the histories of Alexander and Cæsar we are frequently, and indeed impertinently, reminded of their benevolence and generosity, of their clemency and kindness. When the former had with fire and sword overrun a vast empire, had destroyed the lives of an immense number of innocent wretches, had scattered ruin and desolation like a whirlwind we are told, as an example of his clemency, that he did not cut the throat of an old woman, and ravish her daughters, but was content with only undoing them. And when the mighty Cæsar, with wonderful greatness of mind, had destroyed the liberties of his country, and with all the means of fraud and force had placed himself at the head of his equals, had corrupted and enslaved the greatest people whom the sun ever saw, we are reminded, as an evidence of his generosity, of his largesses to his followers and tools, by whose means he had accomplished his purpose, and by whose assistance he was to establish it.

Now, who doth not see that such sneaking qualities as these are rather to be bewailed as imperfections than admired as ornaments in these great men; rather obscuring their glory, and holding them back in their race to greatness, indeed unworthy the end for which they seem to have come into the world, viz. of perpetrating vast and mighty mischief?

We hope our reader will have reason justly to acquit us of any such confounding ideas in the following pages; in which, as we are to record the actions of a great man, so we have nowhere mentioned any spark of goodness which had discovered itself either faintly in him, or more glaringly in any other person, but as a meanness and imperfection, disqualifying them for undertakings which lead to honour and esteem among men.

As our hero had as little as perhaps is to be found of that meanness, indeed only enough to make him partaker of the imperfection of humanity, instead of the perfection of diabolism, we have ventured to call him *The Great*; nor do we doubt but our reader, when he hath perused his story, will concur with us in allowing him that title.

CHAPTER II

Giving an account of as many of our hero's ancestors as can be gathered out of the rubbish of antiquity, which hath been carefully sifted for that purpose

It is the custom of all biographers, at their entrance into their work, to step a little backwards (as far, indeed, generally as they are able) and to trace up their hero, as the ancients did the River Nile, till an incapacity of proceeding higher puts an end to their search.

What first gave rise to this method is somewhat difficult to determine. Sometimes I have thought that the hero's

ancestors have been introduced as foils to himself. Again,
I have imagined it might be to obviate a suspicion that
such extraordinary personages were not produced in the
ordinary course of nature, and may have proceeded from
the author's fear that, if we were not told who their fathers
were, they might be in danger, like Prince Prettyman, of
being supposed to have had none. Lastly, and perhaps
more truly, I have conjectured that the design of the
biographer hath been no more than to shew his great
learning and knowledge of antiquity. A design to which
the world hath probably owed many notable discoveries,
and indeed most of the labours of our antiquarians.

But whatever original this custom had, it is now too well
established to be disputed. I shall therefore conform to
it in the strictest manner.

Mr. Jonathan Wild, or Wyld, then (for he himself did
not always agree in one method of spelling his name), was
descended from the great Wolfstan Wild, who came over
with Hengist, and distinguished himself very eminently at
that famous festival, where the Britons were so treacherously
murdered by the Saxons; for when the word was given, i.e.
Nemet eour Saxes, take out your swords, this gentleman,
being a little hard of hearing, mistook the sound for *Nemet
her sacs, take out their purses*; instead therefore of applying
to the throat, he immediately applied to the pocket of his
guest, and contented himself with taking all that he had,
without attempting his life.

The next ancestor of our hero who was remarkably
eminent was Wild, surnamed Langfanger, or Longfinger.
He flourished in the reign of Henry III, and was strictly
attached to Hubert de Burgh, whose friendship he was
recommended to by his great excellence in an art of which
Hubert was himself the inventor; he could, without the
knowledge of the proprietor, with great ease and dexterity,
draw forth a man's purse from any part of his garment
where it was deposited, and hence he derived his surname.
This gentleman was the first of his family who had the
honour to suffer for the good of his country: on whom a
wit of that time made the following epitaph:

> O shame o' justice! Wild is hang'd,
> For thatten he a pocket fang'd,
> While safe old Hubert, and his gang,
> Doth pocket o' the nation fang.

Langfanger left a son named Edward, whom he had carefully instructed in the art for which he himself was so famous. This Edward had a grandson, who served as a volunteer under the famous Sir John Falstaff, and by his gallant demeanour so recommended himself to his captain, that he would have certainly been promoted by him, had Harry the Fifth kept his word with his old companion.

After the death of Edward the family remained in some obscurity down to the reign of Charles the First, when James Wild distinguished himself on both sides the question in the civil wars, passing from one to t' other, as Heaven seemed to declare itself in favour of either party. At the end of the war, James not being rewarded according to his merits, as is usually the case of such impartial persons, he associated himself with a brave man of those times, whose name was Hind, and declared open war with both parties. He was successful in several actions, and spoiled many of the enemy: till at length, being overpowered and taken, he was, contrary to the law of arms, put basely and cowardly to death by a combination between twelve men of the enemy's party, who, after some consultation, unanimously agreed on the said murder.

This Edward took to wife Rebecca, the daughter of the above-mentioned John Hind, Esq., by whom he had issue John, Edward, Thomas, and Jonathan, and three daughters, namely, Grace, Charity, and Honour. John followed the fortunes of his father, and, suffering with him, left no issue. Edward was so remarkable for his compassionate temper that he spent his life in soliciting the causes of the distressed captives in Newgate, and is reported to have held a strict friendship with an eminent divine who solicited the spiritual causes of the said captives. He married Editha, daughter and co-heiress of Geoffry Snap, gent., who long enjoyed an office under the High Sheriff of London and Middlesex, by which, with great reputation, he acquired a handsome fortune: by her he had no issue. Thomas went very young abroad to one of our American colonies, and hath not been since heard of. As for the daughters, Grace was married to a merchant of Yorkshire who dealt in horses. Charity took to husband an eminent gentleman, whose name I cannot learn, but who was famous for so friendly a disposition that he was bail for above a hundred persons in one year. He had likewise the remarkable humour of walking in Westminster Hall with a straw in his shoe. Honour, the youngest, died unmarried: she lived many years in this town, was a great frequenter of plays, and used to be remarkable for distributing oranges to all who would accept of them.

Jonathan married Elizabeth, daughter of Scragg Hollow, of Hockley-in-the-Hole, Esq.; and by her had Jonathan, who is the illustrious subject of these memoirs.

CHAPTER III

The birth, parentage, and education of Mr. Jonathan Wild the Great

IT is observable that Nature seldom produces any one who is afterwards to act a notable part on the stage of life, but she gives some warning of her intention; and, as the dramatic poet generally prepares the entry of every considerable character with a solemn narrative, or at least a great flourish of drums and trumpets, so doth this our Alma Mater by some shrewd hints pre-admonish us of her intention, giving us warning, as it were, and crying:

——Venienti occurrite morbo.

Thus Astyages, who was the grandfather of Cyrus, dreamt that his daughter was brought to bed of a vine, whose branches overspread all Asia; and Hecuba, while big with Paris, dreamt that she was delivered of a firebrand that set all Troy in flames; so did the mother of our great man, while she was with child of him, dream that she was enjoyed in the night by the gods Mercury and Priapus. This dream puzzled all the learned astrologers of her time, seeming to imply in it a contradiction; Mercury being the god of ingenuity, and Priapus the terror of those who practised it. What made this dream the more wonderful, and perhaps the true cause of its being remembered, was a very extraordinary circumstance, sufficiently denoting something preternatural in it; for though she had never heard even the name of either of these gods, she repeated these very words in the morning, with only a small mistake of the quantity of the latter, which she chose to call *Priăpus* instead of *Priāpus*; and her husband swore that, though he might possibly have named Mercury to her (for he had heard of such an heathen god), he never in his life could anywise have put her in mind of that other deity, with whom he had no acquaintance.

Another remarkable incident was, that during her whole pregnancy she constantly longed for everything she saw; nor could be satisfied with her wish unless she enjoyed it clandestinely; and as nature, by true and accurate observers, is remarked to give us no appetites without furnishing us with the means of gratifying them; so had she at this time a most marvellous glutinous quality attending her fingers, to which, as to birdlime, everything closely adhered that she handled.

To omit other stories, some of which may be perhaps the growth of superstition, we proceed to the birth of our hero, who made his first appearance on this great theatre the very day when the plague first broke out in 1665. Some say his mother was delivered of him in an house of an orbicular or round form in Covent Garden; but of this we are not certain. He was some years afterwards baptized by the famous Mr. Titus Oates.

Nothing very remarkable passed in his years of infancy, save that, as the letters *th* are the most difficult of pronunciation, and the last which a child attains to the utterance of, so they were the first that came with any readiness from young Master Wild. Nor must we omit the early indications which he gave of the sweetness of his temper; for though he was by no means to be terrified into compliance, yet might he, by a sugar-plum, be brought to your purpose: indeed, to say the truth, he was to be bribed to anything, which made many say he was certainly born to be a great man.

He was scarce settled at school before he gave marks of his lofty and aspiring temper; and was regarded by all his schoolfellows with that deference which men generally pay to those superior geniuses who will exact it of them. If an orchard was to be robbed Wild was consulted, and, though he was himself seldom concerned in the execution of the design, yet was he always concerter of it, and treasurer of the booty, some little part of which he would now and then, with wonderful generosity, bestow on those who took it. He was generally very secret on these occasions; but if any offered to plunder of his own head, without acquainting Master Wild, and making a deposit of the booty, he was sure to have an information against him lodged with the schoolmaster, and to be severely punished for his pains.

He discovered so little attention to school-learning that his master, who was a very wise and worthy man, soon gave over all care and trouble on that account, and, acquainting his parents that their son proceeded extremely well in his studies, he permitted his pupil to follow his own inclinations, perceiving they led him to nobler pursuits than the sciences, which are generally acknowledged to be a very unprofitable study, and indeed greatly to hinder the advancement of men in the world; but though Master Wild was not esteemed the readiest at making his exercise, he was universally allowed to be the most dexterous at stealing it of all his schoolfellows, being never detected in such furtive compositions, nor indeed in any other exercitations of his great talents, which all inclined the same way, but once, when he had laid violent hands on a book called *Gradus ad Parnassum*, i.e. *A Step towards Parnassus*; on which account his master, who was a man of most wonderful wit and sagacity, is said to have told him he wished it might not prove in the event *Gradus ad Patibulum*, i.e. *A step towards the gallows*.

But, though he would not give himself the pains requisite to acquire a competent sufficiency in the learned languages, yet did he readily listen with attention to others, especially when they translated the classical authors to him; nor was he in the least backward, at all such times, to express his approbation. He was wonderfully pleased with that passage in the eleventh Iliad where Achilles is said to have bound two sons of Priam upon a mountain, and afterwards to have released them for a sum of money. This was, he said, alone sufficient to refute those who affected a contempt for the wisdom of the ancients, and an undeniable testimony of the great antiquity of priggism.[1] He was ravished with the account which Nestor gives in the same book of the rich booty which he bore off (i.e. stole) from the Eleans. He was desirous of having this often repeated to him, and at the end of every repetition he constantly fetched a deep sigh, and said *it was a glorious booty*.

When the story of Cacus was read to him out of the

[1] This word, in the cant language, signifies thievery.

eighth Æneid he generously pitied the unhappy fate of that great man, to whom he thought Hercules much too severe: one of his schoolfellows commending the dexterity of drawing the oxen backward by their tails into his den, he smiled, and with some disdain said, *He could have taught him a better way*.

He was a passionate admirer of heroes, particularly of Alexander the Great, between whom and the late King of Sweden he would frequently draw parallels. He was much delighted with the accounts of the Czar's retreat from the latter, who carried off the inhabitants of great cities to people his own country. *This*, he said, *was not once thought of by* Alexander; *but* added, *perhaps he did not want them*.

Happy had it been for him if he had confined himself to this sphere; but his chief, if not only blemish, was, that he would sometimes, from an humility in his nature too pernicious to true greatness, condescend to an intimacy with inferior things and persons. Thus the *Spanish Rogue* was his favourite book, and the *Cheats of Scapin* his favourite play.

The young gentleman being now at the age of seventeen, his father, from a foolish prejudice to our universities, and out of a false as well as excessive regard to his morals, brought his son to town, where he resided with him till he was of an age to travel. Whilst he was here, all imaginable care was taken of his instruction, his father endeavouring his utmost to inculcate principles of honour and gentility into his son.

CHAPTER IV

Mr. Wild's first entrance into the world. His acquaintance with Count la Ruse

An accident soon happened after his arrival in town which almost saved the father his whole labour on this head, and provided Master Wild a better tutor than any after-care or expense could have furnished him with. The old gentleman, it seems, was a FOLLOWER of the fortunes of Mr. Snap, son of Mr. Geoffry Snap, whom we have before mentioned to have enjoyed a reputable office under the

Sheriff of London and Middlesex, the daughter of which
Geoffry had intermarried with the Wilds. Mr. Snap the
younger, being thereto well warranted, had laid violent
hands on, or, as the vulgar express it, arrested one Count
la Ruse, a man of considerable figure in those days, and had
confined him to his own house till he could find two seconds
who would in a formal manner give their words that the
count should, at a certain day and place appointed, answer
all that one Thomas Thimble, a taylor, had to say to him;
which Thomas Thimble, it seems, alleged that the count
had, according to the law of the realm, made over his body
to him as a security for some suits of clothes to him delivered
by the said Thomas Thimble. Now as the count, though
perfectly a man of honour, could not immediately find
these seconds, he was obliged for some time to reside at
Mr. Snap's house: for it seems the law of the land is, that
whoever owes another £10, or indeed £2, may be, on the
oath of that person, immediately taken up and carried
away from his own house and family, and kept abroad till
he is made to owe £50, whether he will or no; for which
he is perhaps afterwards obliged to lie in gaol; and all
these without any trial had, or any other evidence of the
debt than the abovesaid oath, which if untrue, as it often
happens, you have no remedy against the perjurer; he
was, forsooth, mistaken.

But though Mr. Snap would not (as perhaps by the nice
rules of honour he was obliged) discharge the count on his
parole, yet did he not (as by the strict rules of law he was
enabled) confine him to his chamber. The count had his
liberty of the whole house, and Mr. Snap, using only the
precaution of keeping his doors well locked and barred,
took his prisoner's word that he would not go forth.

Mr. Snap had by his second lady two daughters, who
were now in the bloom of their youth and beauty. These
young ladies, like damsels in romance, compassionated the
captive count, and endeavoured by all means to make his
confinement less irksome to him; which, though they were
both very beautiful, they could not attain by any other way
so effectually as by engaging with him at cards, in which
contentions, as will appear hereafter, the count was greatly
skilful.

As whisk and swabbers was the game then in the chief
vogue, they were obliged to look for a fourth person in

order to make up their parties. Mr. Snap himself would sometimes relax his mind from the violent fatigues of his employment by these recreations; and sometimes a neighbouring young gentleman or lady came in to their assistance: but the most frequent guest was young Master Wild, who had been educated from his infancy with the Miss Snaps, and was, by all the neighbours, allotted for the husband of Miss Tishy, or Lætitia, the younger of the two; for though, being his cousin-german, she was perhaps, in the eye of a strict conscience, somewhat too nearly related to him, yet the old people on both sides, though sufficiently scrupulous in nice matters, agreed to overlook this objection.

Men of great genius as easily discover one another as freemasons can. It was, therefore, no wonder that the count soon conceived an inclination to an intimacy with our young hero, whose vast abilities could not be concealed from one of the count's discernment; for though this latter was so expert at his cards that he was proverbially said to *play the whole game*, he was no match for Master Wild, who, inexperienced as he was, notwithstanding all the art, the dexterity, and often the fortune of his adversary, never failed to send him away from the table with less in his pocket than he brought to it, for indeed Langfanger himself could not have extracted a purse with more ingenuity than our young hero.

His hands made frequent visits to the count's pocket before the latter had entertained any suspicion of him, imputing the several losses he sustained rather to the innocent and sprightly frolic of Miss Doshy, or Theodosia, with which, as she indulged him with little innocent freedoms about her person in return, he thought himself obliged to be contented; but one night, when Wild imagined the count asleep, he made so unguarded an attack upon him, that the other caught him in the fact: however, he did not think proper to acquaint him with the discovery he had made, but, preventing him from any booty at that time, he only took care for the future to button his pockets, and to pack the cards with double industry.

So far was this detection from causing any quarrel between these two prigs,[1] that in reality it recommended them to each other; for a wise man, that is to say a rogue, considers a trick in life as a gamester doth a trick at play.

[1] Thieves.

It sets him on his guard, but he admires the dexterity of him who plays it. These, therefore, and many other such instances of ingenuity, operated so violently on the count, that, notwithstanding the disparity which age, title, and above all, dress, had set between them, he resolved to enter into an acquaintance with Wild. This soon produced a perfect intimacy, and that a friendship, which had a longer duration than is common to that passion between persons who only propose to themselves the common advantages of eating, drinking, whoring, or borrowing money; which ends, as they soon fail, so doth the friendship founded upon them. Mutual interest, the greatest of all purposes, was the cement of this alliance, which nothing, of consequence, but superior interest, was capable of dissolving.

CHAPTER V

A dialogue between young Master Wild and Count la Ruse, which, having extended to the rejoinder, had a very quiet, easy, and natural conclusion

ONE evening, after the Miss Snaps were retired to rest, the count thus addressed himself to young Wild: "You cannot, I apprehend, Mr. Wild, be such a stranger to your own great capacity, as to be surprised when I tell you I have often viewed, with a mixture of astonishment and concern, your shining qualities confined to a sphere where they can never reach the eyes of those who would introduce them properly into the world, and raise you to an eminence where you may blaze out to the admiration of all men. I assure you I am pleased with my captivity, when I reflect I am likely to owe to it an acquaintance, and I hope friendship, with the greatest genius of my age; and, what is still more, when I indulge my vanity with a prospect of drawing from obscurity (pardon the expression) such talents as were, I believe, never before like to have been buried in it: for I make no question but, at my discharge from confinement, which will now soon happen, I shall be able to introduce you into company, where you may reap the advantage of your superior parts.

"I will bring you acquainted, sir, with those who, as they are capable of setting a true value on such qualifica-

tions, so they will have it both in their power and inclination
to prefer you for them. Such an introduction is the only
advantage you want, without which your merit might be
your misfortune; for those abilities which would entitle
you to honour and profit in a superior station may render
you only obnoxious to danger and disgrace in a lower."

Mr. Wild answered: "Sir, I am not insensible of my
obligations to you, as well for the over-value you have set
on my small abilities, as for the kindness you express in
offering to introduce me among my superiors. I must own
my father hath often persuaded me to push myself into
the company of my betters; but, to say the truth, I have
an awkward pride in my nature, which is better pleased
with being at the head of the lowest class than at the
bottom of the highest. Permit me to say, though the
idea may be somewhat coarse, I had rather stand on the
summit of a dunghill than at the bottom of a hill in Paradise. I have always thought it signifies little into what
rank of life I am thrown, provided I make a great figure
therein, and should be as well satisfied with exerting my
talents well at the head of a small party or gang, as in the
command of a mighty army; for I am far from agreeing
with you, that great parts are often lost in a low situation;
on the contrary, I am convinced it is impossible they
should be lost. I have often persuaded myself that there
were not fewer than a thousand in Alexander's troops
capable of performing what Alexander himself did.

"But, because such spirits were not elected or destined
to an imperial command, are we therefore to imagine they
came off without a booty? or that they contented themselves with the share in common with their comrades?
Surely, no. In civil life, doubtless, the same genius, the
same endowments, have often composed the statesman
and the prig, for so we call what the vulgar name a thief.
The same parts, the same actions, often promote men to
the head of superior societies, which raise them to the head
of lower; and where is the essential difference if the one
ends on Tower Hill and the other at Tyburn? Hath the
block any preference to the gallows, or the axe to the
halter, but was given them by the ill-guided judgment of
men? You will pardon me, therefore, if I am not so
hastily inflamed with the common outside of things, nor
join the general opinion in preferring one state to another.

A guinea is as valuable in a leathern as in an embroidered purse; and a cod's head is a cod's head still, whether in a pewter or a silver dish."

The count replied as follows: "What you have now said doth not lessen my idea of your capacity, but confirms my opinion of the ill effects of bad and low company. Can any man doubt whether it is better to be a great statesman or a common thief? I have often heard that the devil used to say, where or to whom I know not, that it was better to reign in Hell than to be a valet de chambre in Heaven, and perhaps he was in the right; but sure, if he had had the choice of reigning in either, he would have chosen better. The truth therefore is, that by low conversation we contract a greater awe for high things than they deserve. We decline great pursuits not from contempt but despair. The man who prefers the high road to a more reputable way of making his fortune doth it because he imagines the one easier than the other; but you yourself have asserted, and with undoubted truth, that the same abilities qualify you for undertaking, and the same means will bring you to your end in both journeys—as in music it is the same tune, whether you play it in a higher or a lower key. To instance in some particulars: is it not the same qualification which enables this man to hire himself as a servant, and to get into the confidence and secrets of his master in order to rob him, and that to undertake trusts of the highest nature with a design to break and betray them? Is it less difficult by false tokens to deceive a shopkeeper into the delivery of his goods, which you afterwards run away with, than to impose upon him by outward splendour and the appearance of fortune into a credit by which you gain and he loses twenty times as much? Doth it not require more dexterity in the fingers to draw out a man's purse from his pocket, or to take a lady's watch from her side, without being perceived of any (an excellence in which, without flattery, I am persuaded you have no superior), than to cog a die or to shuffle a pack of cards? Is not as much art, as many excellent qualities, required to make a pimping porter at a common bawdy-house as would enable a man to prostitute his own or his friend's wife or child? Doth it not ask as good a memory, as nimble an invention, as steady a countenance, to forswear yourself in Westminster Hall as would furnish out a complete tool of state, or perhaps a statesman himself? It is needless to particularize every instance; in all we shall find that there is a nearer connexion between high and low life than is generally imagined, and that a highwayman is entitled to more favour with the great than he usually meets with. If, therefore, as I think I have proved, the same parts which qualify a man for eminence in a low sphere, qualify him likewise for eminence in a higher, sure it can be no doubt in which he would choose to exert them. Ambition, without which no one can be a great man, will immediately instruct him, in your own phrase, to prefer a hill in Paradise to a dunghill; nay, even fear, a passion the most repugnant to greatness, will shew him how much more safely he may indulge himself in the free and full exertion of his mighty abilities in the higher than in the lower rank; since experience teaches him that there is a crowd oftener in one year at Tyburn than on Tower Hill in a century." Mr. Wild with much solemnity rejoined, "That the same capacity which qualifies a mill-ken,[1] a bridle-cull,[2] or a buttock-and-file,[3] to arrive at any degree of eminence in his profession, would likewise raise a man in what the world esteem a more honourable calling, I do not deny; nay, in many of your instances it is evident that more ingenuity, more art, are necessary to the lower than the higher proficients. If, therefore, you had only contended that every prig might be a statesman if he pleased, I had readily agreed to it; but when you conclude that it is his interest to be so, that ambition would bid him take that alternative, in a word, that a statesman is greater or happier than a prig, I must deny my assent. But, in comparing these two together, we must carefully avoid being misled by the vulgar erroneous estimation of things, for mankind err in disquisitions of this nature as physicians do who in considering the operations of a disease have not a due regard to the age and complexion of the patient. The same degree of heat which is common in this constitution may be a fever in that; in the same manner that which may be riches or honour to me may be poverty or disgrace to another: for all these things are to be estimated by relation to the person who possesses them. A booty of £10 looks as great in the eye of a bridle-cull, and gives as

---

[1] A housebreaker.   [2] A highwayman.
[3] A shoplifter.   Terms used in the Cant Dictionary.

much real happiness to his fancy, as that of as many thousands to the statesman; and doth not the former lay out his acquisitions in whores and fiddles with much greater joy and mirth than the latter in palaces and pictures? What are the flattery, the false compliments of his gang to the statesman, when he himself must condemn his own blunders, and is obliged against his will to give fortune the whole honour of success? What is the pride resulting from such sham applause, compared to the secret satisfaction which a prig enjoys in his mind in reflecting on a well-contrived and well-executed scheme? Perhaps, indeed, the greater danger is on the prig's side; but then you must remember that the greater honour is so too. When I mention honour, I mean that which is paid them by their gang; for that weak part of the world which is vulgarly called THE WISE see both in a disadvantageous and disgraceful light; and as the prig enjoys (and merits too) the greater degree of honour from his gang, so doth he suffer the less disgrace from the world, who think his misdeeds, as they call them, sufficiently at last punished with a halter, which at once puts an end to his pain and infamy; whereas the other is not only hated in power, but detested and contemned at the scaffold; and future ages vent their malice on his fame, while the other sleeps quiet and forgotten. Besides, let us a little consider the secret quiet of their consciences: how easy is the reflection of having taken a few shillings or pounds from a stranger, without any breach of confidence, or perhaps any great harm to the person who loses it, compared to that of having betrayed a public trust, and ruined the fortunes of thousands, perhaps of a great nation! How much braver is an attack on the highway than at a gaming-table; and how much more innocent the character of a b——dy-house than a c——t pimp!" He was eagerly proceeding, when, casting his eyes on the count, he perceived him to be fast asleep; wherefore, having first picked his pocket of three shillings, then gently jogged him in order to take his leave, and promised to return to him the next morning to breakfast, they separated: the count retired to rest, and Master Wild to a night-cellar.

CHAPTER VI

*Further conferences between the count and Master Wild,
with other matters of the* GREAT *kind*

THE count missed his money the next morning, and very
well knew who had it; but, as he knew likewise how fruitless would be any complaint, he chose to pass it by without
mentioning it. Indeed it may appear strange to some
readers that these gentlemen, who knew each other to be
thieves, should never once give the least hint of this knowledge in all their discourse together, but, on the contrary,
should have the words honesty, honour, and friendship as
often in their mouths as any other men. This, I say, may
appear strange to some; but those who have lived long in
cities, courts, gaols, or such places, will perhaps be able to
solve the seeming absurdity.

When our two friends met the next morning the count
(who, though he did not agree with the whole of his friend's
doctrine, was, however, highly pleased with his argument)
began to bewail the misfortune of his captivity, and the
backwardness of friends to assist each other in their
necessities; but what vexed him, he said, most, was the
cruelty of the fair: for he entrusted Wild with the secret
of his having had an intrigue with Miss Theodosia, the
elder of the Miss Snaps, ever since his confinement, though
he could not prevail with her to set him at liberty. Wild
answered, with a smile: "It was no wonder a woman should
wish to confine her lover where she might be sure of having
him entirely to herself"; but added, he believed he could
tell him a method of certainly procuring his escape. The
count eagerly besought him to acquaint him with it. Wild
told him bribery was the surest means, and advised him
to apply to the maid. The count thanked him, but
returned: "That he had not a farthing left besides one
guinea, which he had then given her to change." To
which Wild said: "He must make it up with promises,
which he supposed he was courtier enough to know how to
put off." The count greatly applauded the advice, and said
he hoped he should be able in time to persuade him to
condescend to be a great man, for which he was so perfectly
well qualified.

This method being concluded on, the two friends sat down to cards, a circumstance which I should not have mentioned but for the sake of observing the prodigious force of habit; for though the count knew if he won ever so much of Mr. Wild he should not receive a shilling, yet could he not refrain from packing the cards; nor could Wild keep his hands out of his friend's pockets, though he knew there was nothing in them.

When the maid came home the count began to put it to her; offered her all he had, and promised mountains *in futuro*; but all in vain—the maid's honesty was impregnable. She said: "She would not break her trust for the whole world; no, not if she could gain a hundred pounds by it." Upon which Wild stepping up and telling her, "She need not fear losing her place, for it would never be found out; that they could throw a pair of sheets into the street, by which it might appear he got out at a window; that he himself would swear he saw him descending; that the money would be so much gains in her pocket; that, besides his promises, which she might depend on being performed, she would receive from him twenty shillings and ninepence in ready money (for she had only laid out threepence in plain Spanish); and lastly, that, besides his honour, the count should leave a pair of gold buttons (which afterwards turned out to be brass) of great value, in her hands, as a further pawn."

The maid still remained inflexible, till Wild offered to lend his friend a guinea more, and to deposit it immediately in her hands. This reinforcement bore down the poor girl's resolution, and she faithfully promised to open the door to the count that evening.

Thus did our young hero not only lend his rhetoric, which few people care to do without a fee, but his money too (a sum which many a good man would have made fifty excuses before he would have parted with), to his friend, and procured him his liberty.

But it would be highly derogatory from the GREAT character of Wild, should the reader imagine he lent such a sum to a friend without the least view of serving himself. As, therefore, the reader may easily account for it in a manner more advantageous to our hero's reputation, by concluding that he had some interested view in the count's enlargement, we hope he will judge with charity, especially as the sequel makes it not only reasonable but necessary to suppose he had some such view.

A long intimacy and friendship subsisted between the count and Mr. Wild, who, being by the advice of the count dressed in good clothes, was by him introduced into the best company. They constantly frequented the assemblies, auctions, gaming-tables, and playhouses; at which last they saw two acts every night, and then retired without paying —this being, it seems, an immemorial privilege which the beaus of the town prescribe for themselves. This, however, did not suit Wild's temper, who called it a cheat, and objected against it as requiring no dexterity, but what every blockhead might put in execution. He said it was a custom very much savouring of the sneaking-budge,[1] but neither so honourable nor so ingenious.

Wild now made a considerable figure, and passed for a gentleman of great fortune in the funds. Women of quality treated him with great familiarity, young ladies began to spread their charms for him, when an accident happened that put a stop to his continuance in a way of life too insipid and inactive to afford employment for those great talents which were designed to make a much more considerable figure in the world than attends the character of a beau or a pretty gentleman.

CHAPTER VII

Master Wild sets out on his travels, and returns home again. A very short chapter, containing infinitely more time and less matter than any other in the whole story

WE are sorry we cannot indulge our reader's curiosity with a full and perfect account of this accident; but as there are such various accounts, one of which only can be true, and possibly and indeed probably none; instead of following the general method of historians, who in such cases set down the various reports, and leave to your own conjecture which you will choose, we shall pass them all over.

Certain it is that, whatever this accident was, it determined our hero's father to send his son immediately abroad for seven years; and, which may seem somewhat remarkable,

[1] Shoplifting.

to His Majesty's plantations in America—that part of the world being, as he said, freer from vices than the courts and cities of Europe, and consequently less dangerous to corrupt a young man's morals. And as for the advantages, the old gentleman thought they were equal there with those attained in the politer climates; for travelling, he said, was travelling in one part of the world as well as another; it consisted in being such a time from home, and in traversing so many leagues; and [he] appealed to experience whether most of our travellers in France and Italy did not prove at their return that they might have been sent as profitably to Norway and Greenland.

According to these resolutions of his father, the young gentleman went aboard a ship, and with a great deal of good company set out for the American hemisphere. The exact time of his stay is somewhat uncertain; most probably longer than was intended. But howsoever long his abode there was, it must be a blank in this history, as the whole story contains not one adventure worthy the reader's notice; being indeed a continued scene of whoring, drinking, and removing from one place to another.

To confess a truth, we are so ashamed of the shortness of this chapter, that we would have done a violence to our history, and have inserted an adventure or two of some other traveller; to which purpose we borrowed the journals of several young gentlemen who have lately made the tour of Europe; but to our great sorrow, could not extract a single incident strong enough to justify the theft to our conscience.

When we consider the ridiculous figure this chapter must make, being the history of no less than eight years, our only comfort is, that the histories of some men's lives, and perhaps of some men who have made a noise in the world, are in reality as absolute blanks as the travels of our hero. As, therefore, we shall make sufficient amends in the sequel for this inanity, we shall hasten on to matters of true importance and immense greatness. At present we content ourselves with setting down our hero where we took him up, after acquainting our reader that he went abroad, stayed seven years, and then came home again.

CHAPTER VIII

An adventure where Wild, in the division of the booty, exhibits an astonishing instance of GREATNESS

THE count was one night very successful at the hazard-table, where Wild, who was just returned from his travels, was then present; as was likewise a young gentleman whose name was Bob Bagshot, an acquaintance of Mr. Wild's, and of whom he entertained a great opinion; taking, therefore, Mr. Bagshot aside, he advised him to provide himself (if he had them not about him) with a case of pistols, and to attack the count in his way home, promising to plant himself near with the same arms, as a *corps de reserve*, and to come up on occasion. This was accordingly executed, and the count obliged to surrender to savage force what he had in so genteel and civil a manner taken at play.

And as it is a wise and philosophical observation, that one misfortune never comes alone, the count had hardly passed the examination of Mr. Bagshot when he fell into the hands of Mr. Snap, who, in company with Mr. Wild the elder and one or two more gentlemen, being, it seems, thereto well warranted, laid hold of the unfortunate count and conveyed him back to the same house from which, by the assistance of his good friend, he had formerly escaped.

Mr. Wild and Mr. Bagshot went together to the tavern, where Mr. Bagshot (generously, as he thought) offered to share the booty, and, having divided the money into two unequal heaps, and added a golden snuff-box to the lesser heap, he desired Mr. Wild to take his choice.

Mr. Wild immediately conveyed the larger share of the ready into his pocket, according to an excellent maxim of his: "First secure what share you can before you wrangle for the rest"; and then, turning to his companion, he asked with a stern countenance whether he intended to keep all that sum to himself? Mr. Bagshot answered, with some surprise, that he thought Mr. Wild had no reason to complain; for it was surely fair, at least on his part, to content himself with an equal share of the booty, who had taken the whole. "I grant you took it," replied Wild;

"but, pray, who proposed or counselled the taking it? Can you say that you have done more than executed my scheme? and might not I, if I had pleased, have employed another, since you well know there was not a gentleman in the room but would have taken the money if he had known how, conveniently and safely, to do it?" "That is very true," returned Bagshot, "but did not I execute the scheme, did not I run the whole risk? Should not I have suffered the whole punishment if I had been taken, and is not the labourer worthy of his hire?" "Doubtless," says Jonathan, "he is so, and your hire I shall not refuse you, which is all that the labourer is entitled to or ever enjoys. I remember when I was at school to have heard some verses which for the excellence of their doctrine made an impression on me, purporting that the birds of the air and the beasts of the field work not for themselves. It is true, the farmer allows fodder to his oxen and pasture to his sheep; but it is for his own service, not theirs. In the same manner the ploughman, the shepherd, the weaver, the builder, and the soldier, work not for themselves but others; they are contented with a poor pittance (the labourer's hire), and permit us, the GREAT, to enjoy the fruits of their labours. Aristotle, as my master told us, hath plainly proved, in the first book of his politics, that the low, mean, useful part of mankind are born slaves to the wills of their superiors, and are indeed as much their property as the cattle. It is well said of us, the higher order of mortals, that we are born only to devour the fruits of the earth; and it may be as well said of the lower class, that they are born only to produce them for us. Is not the battle gained by the sweat and danger of the common soldier? Are not the honour and fruits of the victory the general's who laid the scheme? Is not the house built by the labour of the carpenter and the bricklayer? Is it not built for the profit of the architect and for the use of the inhabitant, who could not easily have placed one brick upon another? Is not the cloth or the silk wrought into its form and variegated with all the beauty of colours by those who are forced to content themselves with the coarsest and vilest part of their work, while the profit and enjoyment of their labours fall to the share of others? Cast your eye abroad, and see who is it lives in the most magnificent buildings, feasts his palate with the most luxurious dainties, his eyes with the most beautiful sculptures and delicate paintings, and clothes himself in the finest and richest apparel; and tell me if all these do not fall to his lot who had not any the least share in producing all these conveniences, nor the least ability so to do? Why then should the state of a prig differ from all others? Or why should you, who are the labourer only, the executor of my scheme, expect a share in the profit? Be advised, therefore; deliver the whole booty to me, and trust to my bounty for your reward." Mr. Bagshot was some time silent, and looked like a man thunderstruck, but at last, recovering himself from his surprise, he thus began: "If you think, Mr. Wild, by the force of your arguments, to get the money out of my pocket, you are greatly mistaken. What is all this stuff to me? D—n me, I am a man of honour, and, though I can't talk as well as you, by G— you shall not make a fool of me; and if you take me for one, I must tell you you are a rascal." At which words he laid his hand to his pistol. Wild, perceiving the little success the great strength of his arguments had met with, and the hasty temper of his friend, gave over his design for the present, and told Bagshot he was only in jest. But this coolness with which he treated the other's flame had rather the effect of oil than of water. Bagshot replied in a rage: "D—n me, I don't like such jests; I see you are a pitiful rascal and a scoundrel." Wild, with a philosophy worthy of great admiration, returned: "As for your abuse, I have no regard to it; but, to convince you I am not afraid of you, let us lay the whole booty on the table, and let the conqueror take it all." And having so said, he drew out his shining hanger, whose glittering so dazzled the eyes of Bagshot, that, in tone entirely altered, he said: "No! he was contented with what he had already; that it was mighty ridiculous in them to quarrel among themselves; that they had common enemies enough abroad, against whom they should unite their common force; that if he had mistaken Wild he was sorry for it; and that as for a jest, he could take a jest as well as another." Wild, who had a wonderful knack of discovering and applying to the passions of men, beginning now to have a little insight into his friend, and to conceive what arguments would make the quickest impression on him, cried out in a loud voice: "That he had bullied him into drawing his hanger, and, since it was

out, he would not put it up without satisfaction." "What satisfaction would you have?" answered the other. "Your money or your blood," said Wild. "Why, look ye, Mr. Wild," said Bagshot, "if you want to borrow a little of my part, since I know you to be a man of honour, I don't care if I lend you; for, though I am not afraid of any man living, yet rather than break with a friend, and as it may be necessary for your occasions——" Wild, who often declared that he looked upon borrowing to be as good a way of taking as any, and, as he called it, the genteelest kind of sneaking-budge, putting up his hanger, and shaking his friend by the hand, told him he had hit the nail on the head; it was really his present necessity only that prevailed with him against his will, for that his honour was concerned to pay a considerable sum the next morning. Upon which, contenting himself with one half of Bagshot's share, so that he had three parts in four of the whole, he took leave of his companion and retired to rest.

CHAPTER IX

Wild pays a visit to Miss Lætitia Snap. A description of that lovely young creature, and the successless issue of Mr. Wild's addresses

THE next morning when our hero waked he began to think of paying a visit to Miss Tishy Snap, a woman of great merit and of as great generosity; yet Mr. Wild found a present was ever most welcome to her, as being a token of respect in her lover. He therefore went directly to a toyshop, and there purchased a genteel snuff-box, with which he waited upon his mistress, whom he found in the most beautiful undress. Her lovely hair hung wantonly over her forehead, being neither white with, nor yet free from, powder; a neat double clout, which seemed to have been worn a few weeks only, was pinned under her chin; some remains of that art with which ladies improve nature shone on her cheeks; her body was loosely attired, without stays or jumps, so that her breasts had uncontrolled liberty to display their beauteous orbs, which they did as low as her girdle; a thin covering of a rumpled muslin handkerchief almost hid them from the eyes, save in a few parts, where a good-natured hole gave opportunity to the naked breast to appear. Her gown was a satin of a whitish colour, with about a dozen little silver spots upon it, so artificially interwoven at great distance, that they looked as if they had fallen there by chance. This, flying open, discovered a fine yellow petticoat, beautifully edged round the bottom with a narrow piece of half gold lace, which was now almost become fringe: beneath this appeared another petticoat stiffened with whalebone, vulgarly called a hoop, which hung six inches at least below the other; and under this again appeared an undergarment of that colour which Ovid intends when he says:

——*Qui color albus erat nunc est contrarius albo.*

She likewise displayed two pretty feet covered with silk and adorned with lace, and tied, the right with a handsome piece of blue ribbon; the left, as more unworthy, with a piece of yellow stuff, which seemed to have been a strip of her upper petticoat. Such was the lovely creature whom Mr. Wild attended. She received him at first with some of that coldness which women of strict virtue, by a commendable though sometimes painful restraint, enjoin themselves to their lovers. The snuff-box, being produced, was at first civilly, and indeed gently, refused; but on a second application accepted. The tea-table was soon called for, at which a discourse passed between these young lovers, which, could we set it down with any accuracy, would be very edifying as well as entertaining to our reader; let it suffice then that the wit, together with the beauty, of this young creature, so inflamed the passion of Wild, which, though an honourable sort of a passion, was at the same time so extremely violent, that it transported him to freedoms too offensive to the nice chastity of Lætitia, who was, to confess the truth, more indebted to her own strength for the preservation of her virtue than to the awful respect or backwardness of her lover: he was indeed so very urgent in his addresses, that, had he not with many oaths promised her marriage, we could scarce have been strictly justified in calling his passion honourable; but he was so remarkably attached to decency, that he never offered any violence to a young lady without the most earnest promises of that kind, these being, he said, a ceremonial due to female modesty, which cost so little, and were so easily pronounced, that the omission could arise from nothing but the mere wantonness of brutality. The lovely Lætitia, either out of prudence, or perhaps from religion, of which she was a liberal professor, was deaf to all his promises, and luckily invincible by his force; for, though she had not yet learnt the art of well clenching her fist, nature had not, however, left her defenceless, for at the ends of her fingers she wore arms, which she used with such admirable dexterity, that the hot blood of Mr. Wild soon began to appear in several little spots on his face, and his fullblown cheeks to resemble that part which modesty forbids a boy to turn up anywhere but in a public school, after some pedagogue, strong of arm, hath exercised his talents thereon. Wild now retreated from the conflict, and the victorious Lætitia with becoming triumph and noble spirit, cried out: "D—n your eyes, if this be your way of shewing your love, I'll warrant I gives you enough on't." She then proceeded to talk of her virtue, which Wild bid her carry to the devil with her, and thus our lovers parted.

CHAPTER X

A discovery of some matters concerning the chaste Lætitia which must wonderfully surprise, and perhaps affect, our reader

Mr. WILD was no sooner departed than the fair conqueress, opening the door of a closet, called forth a young gentleman whom she had there enclosed at the approach of the other. The name of this gallant was Tom Smirk. He was clerk to an attorney, and was indeed the greatest beau and the greatest favourite of the ladies at the end of the town where he lived. As we take dress to be the characteristic or efficient quality of a beau, we shall, instead of giving any character of this young gentleman, content ourselves with describing his dress only to our readers. He wore, then, a pair of white stockings on his legs, and pumps on his feet: his buckles were a large piece of pinchbeck plate, which almost covered his whole foot. His breeches were of red plush, which hardly reached his knees; his waistcoat was a white dimity, richly embroidered with yellow silk, over which he wore a blue plush coat with metal buttons,

a smart sleeve, and a cape reaching half-way down his
back. His wig was of a brown colour, covering almost
half his pate, on which was hung on one side a little laced
hat, but cocked with great smartness. Such was the
accomplished Smirk, who, at his issuing forth from the
closet, was received with open arms by the amiable Lætitia.
She addressed him by the tender name of dear Tommy,
and told him she had dismissed the odious creature whom
her father intended for her husband, and had now nothing
to interrupt her happiness with him.

Here, reader, thou must pardon us if we stop a while to
lament the capriciousness of nature in forming this charming part of the creation designed to complete the happiness
of man; with their soft innocence to allay his ferocity, with
their sprightliness to soothe his cares, and with their
constant friendship to relieve all the troubles and dis-
appointments which can happen to him. Seeing then that
these are the blessings chiefly sought after and generally
found in every wife, how must we lament that disposition
in these lovely creatures which leads them to prefer in their
favour those individuals of the other sex who do not seem
intended by nature as so great a masterpiece! For surely,
however useful they may be in the creation, as we are taught
that nothing, not even a louse, is made in vain, yet these
beaus, even that most splendid and honoured part which
in this our island nature loves to distinguish in red, are not,
as some think, the noblest work of the Creator. For my
own part, let any man choose to himself two beaus, let them
be captains or colonels, as well-dressed men as ever lived,
I would venture to oppose a single Sir Isaac Newton, a
Shakespear, a Milton, or perhaps some few others, to both
these beaus; nay, and I very much doubt whether it had
not been better for the world in general that neither of
these beaus had ever been born than that it should have
wanted the benefit arising to it from the labour of any one
of those persons.

If this be true, how melancholy must be the consideration
that any single beau, especially if he have but half a yard
of ribbon in his hat, shall weigh heavier in the scale of
female affection than twenty Sir Isaac Newtons! How
must our reader, who perhaps had wisely accounted for
the resistance which the chaste Lætitia had made to the
violent addresses of the ravished (or rather ravishing) Wild

from that lady's impregnable virtue—how he must blush,
I say, to perceive her quit the strictness of her carriage,
and abandon herself to those loose freedoms which she
indulged to Smirk! But alas! when we discover all, as
to preserve the fidelity of our history we must, when we
relate that every familiarity had passed between them, and
that the FAIR Lætitia (for we must, in this single instance,
imitate Virgil when he drops the *pius* and the *pater*, and
drop our favourite epithet of *chaste*), the FAIR Lætitia had,
I say, made Smirk as happy as Wild desired to be, what
must then be our reader's confusion! We will, therefore,
draw a curtain over this scene, from that philogyny which
is in us, and proceed to matters which, instead of dishonour-
ing the human species, will greatly raise and ennoble it.

CHAPTER XI

*Containing as notable instances of human greatness as are to
be met with in ancient or modern history. Concluding
with some wholesome hints to the gay part of mankind*

WILD no sooner parted from the chaste Lætitia than,
recollecting that his friend the count was returned to his
lodgings in the same house, he resolved to visit him; for
he was none of those half-bred fellows who are ashamed to
see their friends when they have plundered and betrayed
them; from which base and pitiful temper many monstrous
cruelties have been transacted by men, who have sometimes carried their modesty so far as to the murder or utter
ruin of those against whom their consciences have suggested
to them that they have committed some small trespass,
either by the debauching a friend's wife or daughter,
belying or betraying the friend himself, or some other
such trifling instance. In our hero there was nothing not
truly great: he could, without the least abashment, drink
a bottle with the man who knew he had the moment before
picked his pocket; and, when he had stripped him of
everything he had, never desired to do him any further
mischief; for he carried good-nature to that wonderful and
uncommon height that he never did a single injury to man
ᴏr woman by which he himself did not expect to reap
ᴍe advantage. He would often indeed say that by the

contrary party men often made a bad bargain with the
devil, and did his work for nothing.

Our hero found the captive count, not basely lamenting
his fate nor abandoning himself to despair, but, with due
resignation, employing himself in preparing several packs
of cards for future exploits. The count, little suspecting
that Wild had been the sole contriver of the misfortune
which had befallen him, rose up and eagerly embraced
him, and Wild returned his embrace with equal warmth.
They were no sooner seated than Wild took an occasion,
from seeing the cards lying on the table, to inveigh against
gaming, and, with an usual and highly commendable
freedom, after first exaggerating the distressed circumstances
in which the count was then involved, imputed all his
misfortunes to that cursed itch of play which, he said, he
concluded had brought his present confinement upon him,
and must unavoidably end in his destruction. The other,
with great alacrity, defended his favourite amusement (or
rather employment), and, having told his friend the great
success he had after his unluckily quitting the room,
acquainted him with the accident which followed, and which
the reader, as well as Mr. Wild, hath had some intimation
of before; adding, however, one circumstance not hitherto
mentioned, viz. that he had defended his money with the
utmost bravery, and had dangerously wounded at least
two of the three men that had attacked him. This behaviour Wild, who not only knew the extreme readiness with
which the booty had been delivered, but also the constant
frigidity of the count's courage, highly applauded, and
wished he had been present to assist him. The count then
proceeded to animadvert on the carelessness of the watch,
and the scandal it was to the laws that honest people could
not walk the streets in safety; and, after expatiating some
time on that subject, he asked Mr. Wild if he ever saw so
prodigious a run of luck (for so he chose to call his winning,
though he knew Wild was well acquainted with his having
loaded dice in his pocket). The other answered it was
indeed prodigious, and almost sufficient to justify any
person who did not know him better in suspecting his fair
play. "No man, I believe, dares call that in question,"
replied he. "No, surely," says Wild; "you are well known
to be a man of more honour; but pray, sir," continued he,
"did the rascals rob you of all?" "Every shilling," cries

the other, with an oath; "they did not leave me a single stake."

While they were thus discoursing, Mr. Snap, with a gentleman who followed him, introduced Mr. Bagshot into the company. It seems Mr. Bagshot, immediately after his separation from Mr. Wild, returned to the gaming-table, where having trusted to fortune that treasure which he had procured by his industry, the faithless goddess committed a breach of trust, and sent Mr. Bagshot away with as empty pockets as are to be found in any laced coat in the kingdom. Now, as that gentleman was walking to a certain reputable house or shed in Covent Garden Market he fortuned to meet with Mr. Snap, who had just returned from conveying the count to his lodgings, and was then walking to and fro before the gaming-house door; for you are to know, my good reader, if you have never been a man of wit and pleasure about town, that, as the voracious pike lieth snug under some weed before the mouth of any of those little streams which discharge themselves into a large river, waiting for the small fry which issue thereout, so hourly, before the door or mouth of these gaming-houses, doth Mr. Snap, or some other gentleman of his occupation, attend the issuing forth of the small fry of young gentlemen, to whom they deliver little slips of parchment, containing invitations of the said gentlemen to their houses, together with one Mr. John Doe,[1] a person whose company is in great request. Mr. Snap, among many others of these billets, happened to have one directed to Mr. Bagshot, being at the suit or solicitation of one Mrs. Anne Sample, spinster, at whose house the said Bagshot had lodged several months, and whence he had inadvertently departed without taking a formal leave, on which account Mrs. Anne had taken this method of *speaking with* him.

Mr. Snap's house being now very full of good company, he was obliged to introduce Mr. Bagshot into the count's apartment, it being, as he said, the only chamber he had to *lock up* in. Mr. Wild no sooner saw his friend than he ran eagerly to embrace him, and immediately presented him to the count, who received him with great civility.

[1] This is a fictitious name which is put into every writ; for what purpose the lawyers best know.

CHAPTER XII

Further particulars relating to Miss Tishy, which perhaps may not greatly surprise after the former. The description of a very fine gentleman. And a dialogue between Wild and the count, in which public virtue is just hinted at, with, etc.

MR. SNAP had turned the key a very few minutes before a servant of the family called Mr. Bagshot out of the room, telling him there was a person below who desired to speak with him; and this was no other than Miss Lætitia Snap, whose admirer Mr. Bagshot had long been, and in whose tender breast his passion had raised a more ardent flame than that which any of his rivals had been able to raise. Indeed, she was so extremely fond of this youth, that she often confessed to her female confidents, if she could ever have listened to the thought of living with any one man, Mr. Bagshot was he. Nor was she singular in this inclination, many other young ladies being her rivals in this lover, who had all the great and noble qualifications necessary to form a true gallant, and which nature is seldom so extremely bountiful as to indulge to any one person. We will endeavour, however, to describe them all with as much exactness as possible. He was then six feet high, had large calves, broad shoulders, a ruddy complexion, with brown curled hair, a modest assurance, and clean linen. He had indeed, it must be confessed, some small deficiencies to counterbalance these heroic qualities; for he was the silliest fellow in the world, could neither write nor read, nor had he a single grain or spark of honour, honesty, or good-nature, in his whole composition.

As soon as Mr. Bagshot had quitted the room the count, taking Wild by the hand, told him he had something to communicate to him of very great importance. "I am very well convinced," said he, "that Bagshot is the person who robbed me." Wild started with great amazement at this discovery, and answered, with a most serious countenance: "I advise you to take care how you cast any such reflections on a man of Mr. Bagshot's nice honour, for I am certain he will not bear it." "D——n his honour!" quoth the enraged count; "nor can I bear being robbed; I will apply to a justice of the peace." Wild replied, with great indignation: "Since you dare entertain such a suspicion against my friend, I will henceforth disclaim all acquaintance with you. Mr. Bagshot is a man of honour, and my friend, and consequently it is impossible he should be guilty of a bad action." He added much more to the same purpose, which had not the expected weight with the count; for the latter seemed still certain as to the person, and resolute in applying for justice, which, he said, he thought he owed to the public as well as to himself. Wild then changed his countenance into a kind of derision, and spoke as follows: "Suppose it should be possible that Mr. Bagshot had, in a frolic (for I will call it no other), taken this method of borrowing your money, what will you get by prosecuting him? Not your money again, for you hear he was stripped at the gaming-table (of which Bagshot had during their short confabulation informed them); you will get then an opportunity of being still more out of pocket by the prosecution. Another advantage you may promise yourself is the being blown up at every gaming-house in town, for that I will assure you of; and then much good may it do you to sit down with the satisfaction of having discharged what it seems you owe the public. I am ashamed of my own discernment when I mistook you for a great man. Would it not be better for you to receive part (perhaps all) of your money again by a wise concealment: for, however *seedy* [1] Mr. Bagshot may be now, if he hath really played this frolic with you, you may believe he will play it with others, and when he is in cash you may depend on a restoration; the law will be always in your power, and that is the last remedy which a brave or a wise man would resort to. Leave the affair therefore to me; I will examine Bagshot, and, if I find he hath played you this trick, I will engage my own honour you shall in the end be no loser." The count answered: "If I was sure to be no loser, Mr. Wild, I apprehend you have a better opinion of my understanding than to imagine I would prosecute a gentleman for the sake of the public. These are foolish words of course, which we learn a ridiculous habit of speaking, and will often break from us without any design or meaning. I assure you, all I desire is a reimbursement; and if I can by your means obtain that,

[1] Poor.

the public may——" concluding with a phrase too coarse
to be inserted in a history of this kind.

They were now informed that dinner was ready, and the
company assembled below stairs, whither the reader may,
if he please, attend these gentlemen.

There sat down at the table Mr. Snap, and the two Miss
Snaps his daughters, Mr. Wild the elder, Mr. Wild the
younger, the count, Mr. Bagshot, and a grave gentleman
who had formerly had the honour of carrying arms in a
regiment of foot, and who was now engaged in the office
(perhaps a more profitable one) of assisting or following
Mr. Snap in the execution of the laws of his country.

Nothing very remarkable passed at dinner. The conversation (as is usual in polite company) rolled chiefly on
what they were then eating and what they had lately
eaten. In this the military gentleman, who had served
in Ireland, gave them a very particular account of a new
manner of roasting potatoes, and others gave an account
of other dishes. In short, an indifferent bystander would
have concluded from their discourse that they had all
come into this world for no other purpose than to fill their
bellies; and indeed, if this was not the chief, it is probable
it was the most innocent design nature had in their
formation.

As soon as *the dish* was removed, and the ladies retired,
the count proposed a game at hazard, which was immediately assented to by the whole company, and, the dice
being immediately brought in, the count took up the box
and demanded who would set him: to which no one made
any answer, imagining perhaps the count's pockets to be
more empty than they were; for, in reality, that gentleman
(notwithstanding what he had heartily swore to Mr. Wild)
had, since his arrival at Mr. Snap's, conveyed a piece of
plate to pawn, by which means he had furnished himself
with ten guineas. The count, therefore, perceiving this
backwardness in his friends, and probably somewhat
guessing at the cause of it, took the said guineas out of his
pocket, and threw them on the table; when lo (such is the
force of example), all the rest began to produce their funds,
and immediately, a considerable sum glittering in their
eyes, the game began.

CHAPTER XIII

A chapter of which we are extremely vain, and which indeed we look on as our chef-d'œuvre; *containing a wonderful story concerning the devil, and as nice a scene of honour as ever happened*

MY reader, I believe, even if he be a gamester, would not thank me for an exact relation of every man's success; let it suffice then that they played till the whole money vanished from the table. Whether the devil himself carried it away, as some suspected, I will not determine; but very surprising it was that every person protested he had lost, nor could any one guess who, unless *the devil*, had won.

But though very probable it is that this arch-fiend had some share in the booty, it is likely he had not all; Mr. Bagshot being imagined to be a considerable winner, notwithstanding his assertions to the contrary; for he was seen by several to convey money often into his pocket; and what is still a little stronger presumption is, that the grave gentleman whom we have mentioned to have served his country in two honourable capacities, not being willing to trust alone to the evidence of his eyes, had frequently dived into the said Bagshot's pocket, whence (as he tells us in the apology for his life afterwards published [1]), though he might extract a few pieces, he was very sensible he had left many behind. The gentleman had long indulged his curiosity in this way before Mr. Bagshot, in the heat of gaming, had perceived him; but, as Bagshot was now leaving off play, he discovered this ingenious feat of dexterity; upon which, leaping up from his chair in violent passion, he cried out: "I thought I had been among gentlemen and men of honour, but, d—n me, I find we have a pickpocket in company." The scandalous sound of this word extremely alarmed the whole board, nor did they all shew less surprise than the *Conv——n* (whose not sitting of late is much lamented) would express at hearing there

---

[1] Not in a book by itself, in imitation of some other such persons, but in the ordinary's account, etc., where all the apologies for the lives of rogues and whores which have been published within these twenty years should have been inserted.

was an atheist in the room; but it more particularly affected the gentleman at whom it was levelled, though it was not addressed to him. He likewise started from his chair, and, with a fierce countenance and accent, said: "Do you mean me? D—n your eyes, you are a rascal and a scoundrel!" Those words would have been immediately succeeded by blows had not the company interposed, and with strong arm withheld the two antagonists from each other. It was, however, a long time before they could be prevailed on to sit down; which being at last happily brought about, Mr. Wild the elder, who was a well-disposed old man, advised them to shake hands and be friends; but the gentleman who had received the first affront absolutely refused it, and swore *he would have the villain's blood*. Mr. Snap highly applauded the resolution, and affirmed that the affront was by no means to be put up by any who bore the name of a gentleman, and that unless his friend resented it properly he would never execute another warrant in his company; that he had always looked upon him as a man of honour, and doubted not but he would prove himself so; and that, if it was his own case, nothing should persuade him to put up such an affront without proper satisfaction. The count likewise spoke on the same side, and the parties themselves muttered several short sentences purporting their intentions. At last Mr. Wild, our hero, rising slowly from his seat, and having fixed the attention of all present, began as follows: "I have heard with infinite pleasure everything which the two gentlemen who spoke last have said with relation to honour, nor can any man possibly entertain a higher and nobler sense of that word, nor a greater esteem of its inestimable value, than myself. If we have no name to express it by in our Cant Dictionary, it were well to be wished we had. It is, indeed, the essential quality of a gentleman, and which no man who ever was great in the field or on the road (as others express it) can possibly be without. But alas! gentlemen, what pity is it that a word of such sovereign use and virtue should have so uncertain and various an application that scarce two people mean the same thing by it? Do not some by honour mean good-nature and humanity, which weak minds call virtues? How then! Must we deny it to the great, the brave, the noble; to the sackers of towns, the plunderers of provinces,

and the conquerors of kingdoms! Were not these men of
honour? and yet they scorn those pitiful qualities I have
mentioned. Again, some few (or I am mistaken) include
the idea of honesty in their honour. And shall we then
say that no man who withholds from another what law,
or justice perhaps, calls his own, or who greatly and boldly
deprives him of such property, is a man of honour? Heaven
forbid I should say so in this, or, indeed, in any other good
company! Is honour truth? No; it is not in the lie's
going from us, but in its coming to us, our honour is injured.
Doth it then consist in what the vulgar call cardinal virtues?
It would be an affront to your understandings to suppose
it, since we see every day so many men of honour without
any. In what then doth the word honour consist? Why,
in itself alone. A man of honour is he that is called a man
of honour; and while he is so called he so remains, and no
longer. Think not anything a man commits can forfeit
his honour. Look abroad into the world; the PRIG, while
he flourishes, is a man of honour; when in gaol, at the bar,
or the tree, he is so no longer. And why is this distinction?
Not from his actions; for those are often as well known in
his flourishing estate as they are afterwards; but because
men, I mean those of his own party or gang, call him a
man of honour in the former, and cease to call him so in
the latter condition. Let us see then; how hath Mr.
Bagshot injured the gentleman's honour? Why, he hath
called him a pickpocket; and that, probably, by a severe
construction and a long roundabout way of reasoning,
may seem a little to derogate from his honour, if considered
in a very nice sense. Admitting it, therefore, for argument's
sake, to be some small imputation on his honour, let
Mr. Bagshot give him satisfaction; let him doubly and triply
repair this oblique injury by directly asserting that he
believes he is a man of honour." The gentleman answered
he was content to refer it to Mr. Wild, and whatever
satisfaction he thought sufficient he would accept. "Let
him give me my money again first," said Bagshot, "and
then I will call him a man of honour with all my heart."
The gentleman then protested he had not any, which
Snap seconded, declaring he had his eyes on him all the
while; but Bagshot remained still unsatisfied, till Wild,
rapping out a hearty oath, swore he had not taken a single
farthing, adding that whoever asserted the contrary gave

him the lie, and he would resent it. And now, such was the ascendancy of this great man, that Bagshot immediately acquiesced, and performed the ceremonies required: and thus, by the exquisite address of our hero, this quarrel, which had so fatal an aspect, and which between two persons so extremely jealous of their honour would most certainly have produced very dreadful consequences, was happily concluded.

Mr. Wild was, indeed, a little interested in this affair, as he himself had set the gentleman to work, and had received the greatest part of the booty: and as to Mr. Snap's deposition in his favour, it was the usual height to which the ardour of that worthy person's friendship too frequently hurried him. It was his constant maxim that he was a pitiful fellow who would stick at a little rapping [1] for his friend.

CHAPTER XIV

In which the history of GREATNESS *is continued*

MATTER being thus reconciled, and the gaming over, from reasons before hinted, the company proceeded to drink about with the utmost cheerfulness and friendship; drinking healths, shaking hands, and professing the most perfect affection for each other. All which were not in the least interrupted by some designs which they then agitated in their minds, and which they intended to execute as soon as the liquor had prevailed over some of their understandings. Bagshot and the gentleman intending to rob each other; Mr. Snap and Mr. Wild the elder meditating what other creditors they could find out to charge the gentleman then in custody with; the count hoping to renew the play, and Wild, our hero, laying a design to put Bagshot out of the way, or, as the vulgar express it, to hang him with the first opportunity. But none of these great designs could at present be put in execution, for, Mr. Snap being soon after summoned abroad on business of great moment, which required likewise the assistance of Mr. Wild the elder and his other friend, and as he did not care to trust to the nimbleness of the count's heels, of which

[1] Rapping is a cant word for perjury.

he had already had some experience, he declared he must *lock up* for that evening. Here, reader, if thou pleasest, as we are in no great haste, we will stop and make a simile. As when their lap is finished, the cautious huntsman to their kennel gathers the nimble-footed hounds, they with lank ears and tails slouch sullenly on, whilst he, with his whippers-in, follows close at their heels, regardless of their dogged humour, till, having seen them safe within the door, he turns the key, and then retires to whatever business or pleasure calls him thence; so with louring countenance and reluctant steps mounted the count and Bagshot to their chamber, or rather kennel, whither they were attended by Snap and those who followed him, and where Snap, having seen them deposited, very contentedly locked the door and departed. And now, reader, we will, in imitation of the truly laudable custom of the world, leave these our good friends to deliver themselves as they can, and pursue the thriving fortunes of Wild, our hero, who, with that great aversion to satisfaction and content which is inseparably incident to great minds, began to enlarge his views with his prosperity: for this restless, amiable disposition, this noble avidity which increases with feeding, is the first principle or constituent quality of these our great men; to whom, in their passage on to greatness, it happens as to a traveller over the Alps, or, if this be a too far-fetched simile, to one who travels westward over the hills near Bath, where the simile was indeed made. He sees not the end of his journey at once; but, passing on from scheme to scheme, and from hill to hill, with noble constancy, resolving still to attain the summit on which he hath fixed his eye, however dirty the roads may be through which he struggles, he at length arrives—at some vile inn, where he finds no kind of entertainment nor conveniency for repose. I fancy, reader, if thou hast ever travelled in these roads, one part of my simile is sufficiently apparent (and, indeed, in all these illustrations, one side is generally much more apparent than the other); but, believe me, if the other doth not so evidently appear to thy satisfaction, it is from no other reason than because thou art unacquainted with these great men, and hast not had sufficient instruction, leisure, or opportunity, to consider what happens to those who pursue what is generally understood by GREATNESS: for surely, if thou hadst animadverted, not only on the many perils to which great men are daily liable while they are in their progress, but hadst discerned, as it were through a microscope (for it is invisible to the naked eye), that diminutive speck of happiness which they attain even in the consummation of their wishes, thou wouldst lament with me the unhappy fate of these great men, on whom nature hath set so superior a mark, that the rest of mankind are born for their use and emolument only, and be apt to cry out: "It is pity that THOSE for whose pleasure and profit mankind are to labour and sweat, to be hacked and hewed, to be pillaged, plundered, and every way destroyed, should reap so LITTLE advantage from all the miseries they occasion to others." For my part, I own myself of that humble kind of mortals who consider themselves born for the behoof of some great man or other, and could I behold his happiness carved out of the labour and ruin of a thousand such reptiles as myself, I might with satisfaction exclaim, *Sic, sic juvat*: but when I behold one GREAT MAN starving with hunger and freezing with cold, in the midst of fifty thousand who are suffering the same evils for his diversion; when I see another, whose own mind is a more abject slave to his own greatness, and is more tortured and racked by it, than those of all his vassals; lastly, when I consider whole nations rooted out only to bring tears into the eyes of a GREAT MAN, not indeed because he hath extirpated so many, but because he had no more nations to extirpate, then truly I am almost inclined to wish that Nature had spared us this her MASTER-PIECE, and that no GREAT MAN had ever been born into the world.

But to proceed with our history, which will, we hope, produce much better lessons, and more instructive, than any we can preach: Wild was no sooner retired to a night-cellar than he began to reflect on the sweets he had that day enjoyed from the labours of others, viz. first, from Mr. Bagshot, who had for his use robbed the count; and, secondly, from the gentleman, who, for the same good purpose, had picked the pocket of Bagshot. He then proceeded to reason thus with himself: "The art of policy is the art of multiplication, the degrees of greatness being constituted by those two little words *more* or *less*. Mankind are first properly to be considered under two grand divisions, those that use their own hands, and those who employ the hands of others. The former are the base and rabble; the latter, the genteel part of the creation. The mercantile part of the world, therefore, wisely use the term *employing hands*, and justly prefer each other as they employ more or fewer; for thus one merchant says he is greater than another because he employs more hands. And now, indeed, the merchant should seem to challenge some character of greatness, did we not necessarily come to a second division, viz. of those who employ hands for the use of the community in which they live, and of those who employ hands merely for their own use, without any regard to the benefit of society. Of the former sort are the yeoman, the manufacturer, the merchant, and perhaps the gentleman. The first of these being to manure and cultivate his native soil, and to employ hands to produce the fruits of the earth. The second being to improve them by employing hands likewise, and to produce from them those useful commodities which serve as well for the conveniences as necessaries of life. The third is to employ hands for the exportation of the redundance of our own commodities, and to exchange them with the redundance of foreign nations, that thus every soil and every climate may enjoy the fruits of the whole earth. The gentleman is, by employing hands, likewise to embellish his country with the improvement of arts and sciences, with the making and executing good and wholesome laws for the preservation of property and the distribution of justice, and in several other manners to be useful to society. Now we come to the second part of this division, viz. of those who employ hands for their own use only; and this is that noble and great part who are generally distinguished into *conquerors*, *absolute princes*, *statesmen*, and *prigs*.[1] Now all these differ from each other in greatness only—they employ *more* or *fewer* hands. And Alexander the Great was only *greater* than a captain of one of the Tartarian or Arabian hordes, as he was at the head of a larger number. In what then is a single *prig* inferior to any other great man, but because he employs his own hands only; for he is not on that account to be levelled with the base and vulgar, because he employs his hands for his own use only. Now, suppose a *prig* had as many tools as any prime minister ever had, would he not be as great as any prime minister

[1] Thieves.

whatsoever? Undoubtedly he would. What then have I to do in the pursuit of greatness but to procure a gang, and to make the use of this gang centre in myself? This gang shall rob for me only, receiving very moderate rewards for their actions; out of this gang I will prefer to my favour the boldest and most iniquitous (as the vulgar express it); the rest I will, from time to time, as I see occasion, transport and hang at my pleasure; and thus (which I take to be the highest excellence of a *prig*) convert those laws which are made for the benefit and protection of society to my single use."

Having thus preconceived his scheme, he saw nothing wanting to put it in immediate execution but that which is indeed the beginning as well as the end of all human devices: I mean money. Of which commodity he was possessed of no more than sixty-five guineas, being all that remained from the double benefits he had made of Bagshot, and which did not seem sufficient to furnish his house, and every other convenience necessary for so grand an undertaking. He resolved, therefore, to go immediately to the gaming-house, which was then sitting, not so much with an intention of trusting to fortune as to play the surer card of attacking the winner in his way home. On his arrival, however, he thought he might as well try his success at the dice, and reserve the other resource as his last expedient. He accordingly sat down to play; and as Fortune, no more than others of her sex, is observed to distribute her favours with strict regard to great mental endowments, so our hero lost every farthing in his pocket. This loss, however, he bore with great constancy of mind, and with as great composure of aspect. To say truth, he considered the money as only lent for a short time, or rather indeed as deposited with a banker. He then resolved to have immediate recourse to his surer stratagem; and, casting his eyes round the room, he soon perceived a gentleman sitting in a disconsolate posture, who seemed a proper instrument or tool for his purpose. In short (to be as concise as possible in these least shining parts of our history), Wild accosted this man, sounded him, found him fit to execute, proposed the matter, received a ready assent, and, having fixed on the person who seemed that evening the greatest favourite of Fortune, they posted themselves in the most proper place to surprise the enemy as he was retiring to his quarters, where he was soon attacked, subdued, and plundered; but indeed of no considerable booty; for it seems this gentleman played on a common stock, and had deposited his winnings at the scene of action, nor had he any more than two shillings in his pocket when he was attacked.

This was so cruel a disappointment to Wild, and so sensibly affects us, as no doubt it will the reader, that, as it must disqualify us both from proceeding any farther at present, we will now take a little breath, and therefore we shall here close this book.

BOOK II

CHAPTER I

*Characters of silly people, with the proper uses for which
such are designed*

ONE reason why we chose to end our first book, as we did,
with the last chapter, was, that we are now obliged to
produce two characters of a stamp entirely different from
what we have hitherto dealt in. These persons are of that
pitiful order of mortals who are in contempt called good-
natured; being indeed sent into the world by nature with
the same design with which men put little fish into a
pike-pond, in order to be devoured by that voracious
water-hero.

But to proceed with our history: Wild, having shared
the booty in much the same manner as before, i.e. taken
three-fourths of it, amounting to eighteenpence, was now
retiring to rest, in no very happy mood, when by accident
he met with a young fellow who had formerly been his
companion, and indeed intimate friend, at school. It
hath been thought that friendship is usually nursed by
similitude of manners, but the contrary had been the case
between the lads; for whereas Wild was rapacious and
intrepid, the other had always more regard for his skin
than his money; Wild, therefore, had very generously compassionated this defect in his schoolfellow, and had brought
him off from many scrapes, into most of which he had
first drawn him, by taking the fault and whipping to
himself. He had always indeed been well paid on such
occasions; but there are a sort of people who, together with
the best of the bargain, will be sure to have the obligation
too on their side; so it had happened here: for this poor
lad had considered himself in the highest degree obliged
to Mr. Wild, and had contracted a very great esteem and
friendship for him; the traces of which an absence of many
years had not in the least effaced in his mind. He no

sooner knew Wild, therefore, than he accosted him in the most friendly manner, and invited him home with him to breakfast (it being now near nine in the morning), which invitation our hero with no great difficulty consented to. This young man, who was about Wild's age, had some time before set up in the trade of a jeweller, in the materials or stock for which he had laid out the greatest part of a little fortune, and had married a very agreeable woman for love, by whom he then had two children. As our reader is to be more acquainted with this person, it may not be improper to open somewhat of his character, especially as it will serve as a kind of foil to the noble and great disposition of our hero, and as the one seems sent into this world as a proper object on which the talents of the other were to be displayed with a proper and just success.

Mr. Thomas Heartfree then (for that was his name) was of an honest and open disposition. He was of that sort of men whom experience only, and not their own natures, must inform that there are such things as deceit and hypocrisy in the world, and who, consequently, are not at five-and-twenty so difficult to be imposed upon as the oldest and most subtle. He was possessed of several great weaknesses of mind, being good-natured, friendly, and generous to a great excess. He had, indeed, too little regard to common justice, for he had forgiven some debts to his acquaintance only because they could not pay him, and had entrusted a bankrupt, on his setting up a second time, from having been convinced that he had dealt in his bankruptcy with a fair and honest heart, and that he had broke through misfortune only, and not from neglect or imposture. He was withal so silly a fellow that he never took the least advantage of the ignorance of his customers, and contented himself with very moderate gains on his goods; which he was the better enabled to do, notwithstanding his generosity, because his life was extremely temperate, his expenses being solely confined to the cheerful entertainment of his friends at home, and now and then a moderate glass of wine, in which he indulged himself in the company of his wife, who, with an agreeable person, was a mean-spirited, poor, domestic, low-bred animal, who confined herself mostly to the care of her family, placed her happiness in her husband and her children, followed no expensive fashions or diversions, and indeed rarely went abroad, unless to return the visits of a few plain neighbours, and twice a year afforded herself, in company with her husband, the diversion of a play, where she never sat in a higher place than the pit.

To this silly woman did this silly fellow introduce the GREAT WILD, informing her at the same time of their school acquaintance and the many obligations he had received from him. This simple woman no sooner heard her husband had been obliged to her guest than her eyes sparkled on him with a benevolence which is an emanation from the heart, and of which great and noble minds, whose hearts never swell but with an injury, can have no very adequate idea; it is, therefore, no wonder that our hero should misconstrue, as he did, the poor, innocent, and simple affection of Mrs. Heartfree towards her husband's friend, for that great and generous passion, which fires the eyes of a modern heroine, when the colonel is so kind as to indulge his city creditor with partaking of his table to-day, and of his bed to-morrow. Wild, therefore, instantly returned the compliment as he understood it, with his eyes, and presently after bestowed many encomiums on her beauty, with which perhaps she, who was a woman, though a good one, and misapprehended the design, was not displeased any more than the husband.

When breakfast was ended, and the wife retired to her household affairs, Wild, who had a quick discernment into the weaknesses of men, and who, besides the knowledge of his good (or foolish) disposition when a boy, had now discovered several sparks of goodness, friendship, and generosity in his friend, began to discourse over the accidents which had happened in their childhood, and took frequent occasions of reminding him of those favours which we have before mentioned his having conferred on him; he then proceeded to the most vehement professions of friendship, and to the most ardent expressions of joy in this renewal of their acquaintance. He at last told him, with great seeming pleasure, that he believed he had an opportunity of serving him by the recommendation of a gentleman to his custom, who was then on the brink of marriage. "And, if he be not already engaged, I will," says he, "endeavour to prevail on him to furnish his lady with jewels at your shop."

Heartfree was not backward in thanks to our hero, and,

after many earnest solicitations to dinner, which were refused, they parted for the first time.

But here, as it occurs to our memory that our readers may be surprised (an accident which sometimes happens in histories of this kind) how Mr. Wild the elder, in his present capacity, should have been able to maintain his son at a reputable school, as this appears to have been, it may be necessary to inform him that Mr. Wild himself was then a tradesman in good business, but, by misfortunes in the world, to wit, extravagance and gaming, he had reduced himself to that honourable occupation which we have formerly mentioned.

Having cleared up this doubt, we will now pursue our hero, who forthwith repaired to the count, and, having first settled preliminary articles concerning distributions, he acquainted him with the scheme which he had formed against Heartfree; and after consulting proper methods to put it in execution, they began to concert measures for the enlargement of the count; on which the first, and indeed only point to be considered, was to raise money, not to pay his debts, for that would have required an immense sum, and was contrary to his inclination or intention, but to procure him bail; for as to his escape, Mr. Snap had taken such precautions that it appeared absolutely impossible.

CHAPTER II

Great examples of GREATNESS *in Wild, shewn as well by his behaviour to Bagshot as in a scheme laid, first, to impose on Heartfree by means of the count, and then to cheat the count of the booty*

WILD undertook, therefore, to extract some money from Bagshot, who, notwithstanding the depredations made on him, had carried off a pretty considerable booty from their engagement at dice the preceding day. He found Mr. Bagshot in expectation of his bail, and, with a countenance full of concern, which he could at any time, with wonderful art, put on, told him that all was discovered; that the count knew him, and intended to prosecute him for the robbery, "had not I exerted (said he) my utmost interest, and with great difficulty prevailed on him in case you refund the money——" "Refund the money!" cried Bagshot, "that is in your power: for you know what an inconsiderable part of it fell to my share." "How!" replied Wild, "is this your gratitude to me for saving your life? For your own conscience must convince you of your guilt, and with how much certainty the gentleman can give evidence against you." "Marry come up!" quoth Bagshot; "I believe my life alone will not be in danger. I know those who are as guilty as myself. Do you tell me of conscience?" "Yes, sirrah!" answered our hero, taking him by the collar; "and since you dare threaten me I will shew you the difference between committing a robbery and conniving at it, which is all I can charge myself with. I own indeed I suspected, when you shewed me a sum of money, that you had not come honestly by it." "How!" says Bagshot, frightened out of one half of his wits, and amazed out of the other, "can you deny?" "Yes, you rascal," answered Wild, "I do deny everything; and do you find a witness to prove it: and, to shew you how little apprehension I have of your power to hurt me, I will have you apprehended this moment."—At which words he offered to break from him; but Bagshot laid hold of his skirts, and, with an altered tone and manner, begged him not to be so impatient. "Refund then, sirrah," cries Wild, "and perhaps I may take pity on you." "What must I refund?" answered Bagshot. "Every farthing in your pocket," replied Wild; "then I may have some compassion on you, and not only save your life, but, out of an excess of generosity, may return you something." At which words Bagshot seeming to hesitate, Wild pretended to make to the door, and rapt out an oath of vengeance with so violent an emphasis, that his friend no longer presumed to balance, but suffered Wild to search his pockets and draw forth all he found, to the amount of twenty-one guineas and a half, which last piece our generous hero returned him again, telling him he might now sleep secure, but advised him for the future never to threaten his friends.

Thus did our hero execute the greatest exploits with the utmost ease imaginable, by means of those transcendent qualities which nature had indulged him with, viz. a bold heart, a thundering voice, and a steady countenance.

Wild now returned to the count, and informed him that

he had got ten guineas of Bagshot; for, with great and commendable prudence, he sunk the other eleven into his own pocket, and told him with that money he would procure him bail, which he after prevailed on his father, and another gentleman of the same occupation, to become, for two guineas each; so that he made lawful prize of six more, making Bagshot debtor for the whole ten; for such were his great abilities, and so vast the compass of his understanding, that he never made any bargain without overreaching (or, in the vulgar phrase, cheating) the person with whom he dealt.

The count being, by these means, enlarged, the first thing they did, in order to procure credit from tradesmen, was the taking a handsome house ready furnished in one of the new streets; in which as soon as the count was settled, they proceeded to furnish him with servants and equipage, and all the *insignia* of a large estate proper to impose on poor Heartfree. These being all obtained, Wild made a second visit to his friend, and with much joy in his countenance acquainted him that he had succeeded in his endeavours, and that the gentleman had promised to deal with him for the jewels which he intended to present to his bride, and which were designed to be very splendid and costly; he therefore appointed him to go to the count the next morning, and carry with him a set of the richest and most beautiful jewels he had, giving him at the same time some hints of the count's ignorance of that commodity, and that he might extort what price of him he pleased; but Heartfree told him, not without some disdain, that he scorned to take any such advantage; and, after expressing much gratitude to his friend for his recommendation, he promised to carry the jewels at the hour and to the place appointed.

I am sensible that the reader, if he hath but the least notion of greatness, must have such a contempt for the extreme folly of this fellow, that he will be very little concerned at any misfortunes which may befal him in the sequel; for to have no suspicion that an old schoolfellow, with whom he had, in his tenderest years, contracted a friendship, and who, on the accidental renewing of their acquaintance, had professed the most passionate regard for him, should be very ready to impose on him; in short, to conceive that a friend should, of his own accord, without any view to his own interest, endeavour to do him a service, must argue such weakness of mind, such ignorance of the world, and such an artless, simple, undesigning heart, as must render the person possessed of it the lowest creature and the properest object of contempt imaginable, in the eyes of every man of understanding and discernment.

Wild remembered that his friend Heartfree's faults were rather in his heart than in his head; that, though he was so mean a fellow that he was never capable of laying a design to injure any human creature, yet was he by no means a fool, nor liable to any gross imposition, unless where his heart betrayed him. He, therefore, instructed the count to take only one of his jewels at the first interview, and reject the rest as not fine enough, and order him to provide some richer. He said this management would prevent Heartfree from expecting ready money for the jewel he brought with him, which the count was presently to dispose of, and by means of that money, and his great abilities at cards and dice, to get together as large a sum as possible, which he was to pay down to Heartfree at the delivery of the set of jewels, who would be thus void of all manner of suspicion, and would not fail to give him credit for the residue.

By this contrivance, it will appear in the sequel that Wild did not only propose to make the imposition on Heartfree, who was (hitherto) void of all suspicion, more certain; but to rob the count himself of this sum. This double method of cheating the very tools who are our instruments to cheat others is the superlative degree of greatness, and is probably, as far as any spirit crusted over with clay can carry it, falling little short of diabolism itself.

This method was immediately put in execution, and the count the first day took only a single brilliant, worth about three hundred pounds, and ordered a necklace, earrings, and solitaire, of the value of three thousand more, to be prepared by that day sevennight.

The interval was employed by Wild in prosecuting his scheme of raising a gang, in which he met with such success, that within a few days he had levied several bold and resolute fellows, fit for any enterprise, how dangerous or great soever.

We have before remarked that the truest mark of greatness is insatiability. Wild had covenanted with the count to receive three-fourths of the booty, and had, at the same time, covenanted with himself to secure the other fourth part likewise, for which he had formed a very great and noble design; but he now saw with concern that sum which was to be received in hand by Heartfree in danger of being absolutely lost. In order, therefore, to possess himself of that likewise, he contrived that the jewels should be brought in the afternoon, and that Heartfree should be detained before the count could see him; so that the night should overtake him in his return, when two of his gang were ordered to attack and plunder him.

CHAPTER III

Containing scenes of softness, love, and honour, all in the great style

THE count had disposed of his jewel for its full value, and this he had by dexterity raised to a thousand pounds; this sum, therefore, he paid down to Heartfree, promising him the rest within a month. His house, his equipage, his appearance, but, above all, a certain plausibility in his voice and behaviour would have deceived any, but one whose great and wise heart had dictated to him something within, which would have secured him from any danger of imposition from without. Heartfree, therefore, did not in the least scruple giving him credit; but, as he had in reality procured those jewels of another, his own little stock not being able to furnish anything so valuable, he begged the count would be so kind to give his note for the money, payable at the time he mentioned; which that gentleman did not in the least scruple; so he paid him the thousand pound in specie, and gave his note for two thousand eight hundred pounds more to Heartfree, who burnt with gratitude to Wild for the noble customer he had recommended to him.

As soon as Heartfree was departed, Wild, who waited in another room, came in and received the casket from the count, it having been agreed between them that this should be deposited in his hands, as he was the original contriver of the scheme, and was to have the largest share. Wild, having received the casket, offered to meet the count late that evening to come to a division, but such was the latter's confidence in the honour of our hero, that he said, if it was any inconvenience to him, the next morning would do altogether as well. This was more agreeable to Wild, and accordingly, an appointment being made for that purpose, he set out in haste to pursue Heartfree to the place where the two gentlemen were ordered to meet and attack him. Those gentlemen with noble resolution executed their purpose; they attacked and spoiled the enemy of the whole sum he had received from the count.

As soon as the engagement was over, and Heartfree left sprawling on the ground, our hero, who wisely declined trusting the booty in his friends' hands, though he had good experience of their honour, made off after the conquerors: at length, they being all at a place of safety, Wild, according to a previous agreement, received nine-tenths of the booty: the subordinate heroes did indeed profess some little unwillingness (perhaps more than was strictly consistent with honour) to perform their contract; but Wild, partly by argument, but more by oaths and threatenings, prevailed with them to fulfil their promise.

Our hero having thus, with wonderful address, brought this great and glorious action to a happy conclusion, resolved to relax his mind after his fatigue, in the conversation of the fair. He therefore set forwards to his lovely Lætitia; but in his way accidentally met with a young lady of his acquaintance, Miss Molly Straddle, who was taking the air in Bridges Street. Miss Molly, seeing Mr. Wild, stopped him, and with a familiarity peculiar to a genteel town education, tapped, or rather slapped him on the back, and asked him to treat her with a pint of wine at a neighbouring tavern. The hero, though he loved the chaste Lætitia with excessive tenderness, was not of that low snivelling breed of mortals who, as it is generally expressed, *tie themselves to a woman's apron-strings*; in a word, who are tainted with that mean, base, low vice, or virtue as it is called, of constancy; therefore he immediately consented, and attended her to a tavern famous for excellent wine, known by the name of the Rummer and Horseshoe, where they retired to a room by themselves. Wild was very vehement in his addresses, but to no purpose; the young lady declared she would grant no favour till he had made her a present; this was immediately complied with, and the lover made as happy as he could desire.

The immoderate fondness which Wild entertained for his dear Lætitia would not suffer him to waste any considerable time with Miss Straddle. Notwithstanding, therefore, all the endearments and caresses of that young lady, he soon made an excuse to go downstairs, and thence immediately set forward to Lætitia without taking any formal leave of Miss Straddle, or indeed of the drawer, with whom the lady was afterwards obliged to come to an account for the reckoning.

Mr. Wild, on his arrival at Mr. Snap's, found only Miss Doshy at home, that young lady being employed alone, in imitation of Penelope, with her thread or worsted, only with this difference, that whereas Penelope unravelled by night what she had knit or wove or spun by day, so what our young heroine unravelled by day she knit again by night. In short, she was mending a pair of blue stockings with red clocks; a circumstance which perhaps we might have omitted, had it not served to shew that there are still some ladies of this age who imitate the simplicity of the ancients.

Wild immediately asked for his beloved, and was informed that she was not at home. He then inquired where she was to be found, and declared he would not depart till he had seen her, nay, not till he had married her; for, indeed, his passion for her was truly honourable; in other words, he had so ungovernable a desire for her person, that he would go any length to satisfy it. He then pulled out the casket, which he swore was full of the finest jewels, and that he would give them all to her, with other promises, which so prevailed on Miss Doshy, who had not the common failure of sisters in envying, and often endeavouring to disappoint, each other's happiness, that she desired Mr. Wild to sit down a few minutes, whilst she endeavoured to find her sister and to bring her to him. The lover thanked her, and promised to stay till her return; and Miss Doshy, leaving Mr. Wild to his meditations, fastened him in the kitchen by barring the door (for most of the doors in this mansion were made to be bolted on the outside), and then, slapping to the door of the house with great violence, without going out at it, she stole softly upstairs where Miss Lætitia was engaged in close conference with Mr. Bagshot. Miss Letty, being informed by her sister in a whisper of what Mr. Wild had said, and what he had produced, told Mr. Bagshot that a young lady was below to visit her whom she would dispatch with all imaginable haste and return to him. She desired him, therefore, to stay with patience for her in the meantime, and that she would leave the door unlocked, though her papa would never forgive her if he should discover it. Bagshot promised on his honour not to step without his chamber; and the two young ladies went softly downstairs, when, pretending first to make their entry into the house, they repaired to the kitchen, where not even the presence of the chaste Lætitia could restore that harmony to the countenance of her lover which Miss Theodosia had left him possessed of; for, during her absence, he had discovered the absence of a purse containing bank-notes for £900, which had been taken from Mr. Heartfree, and which, indeed, Miss Straddle had, in the warmth of his amorous caresses, unperceived drawn from him. However, as he had that perfect mastery of his temper, or rather of his muscles, which is as necessary to the forming a great character as to the personating it on the stage, he soon conveyed a smile into his countenance, and, concealing as well his misfortune as his chagrin at it, began to pay honourable addresses to Miss Letty. This young lady, among many other good ingredients, had three very predominant passions; to wit, vanity, wantonness, and avarice. To satisfy the first of these she employed Mr. Smirk and company; to the second, Mr. Bagshot and company; and our hero had the honour and happiness of solely engrossing the third. Now, these three sorts of lovers she had very different ways of entertaining. With the first she was all gay and coquette; with the second all fond and rampant; and with the last all cold and reserved. She, therefore, told Mr. Wild, with a most composed aspect, that she was glad he had repented of his manner of treating her at their last interview, where his behaviour was so monstrous that she had resolved never to see him any more; that she was afraid her own sex would hardly pardon her the weakness she was guilty of in receding from that resolution, which she was persuaded he never should have brought herself to, had not her sister, who was there to confirm what she said (as she did with many oaths), betrayed her into his company, by pretending it was another person to visit her: but, however, as he now thought proper to give her more convincing proofs of his affections (for he had now the casket in his hand), and since she perceived his designs were no longer against her virtue, but were such as a woman of honour might listen to, she must own—— and then she feigned an hesitation, when Theodosia began: "Nay, sister, I am resolved you shall counterfeit no longer. I assure you, Mr. Wild, she hath the most violent passion for you in the world; and indeed, dear Tishy, if you offer to go back, since I plainly see Mr. Wild's designs are honourable, I will betray all you have ever said." "How, sister!" answered Lætitia; "I protest you will drive me out of the room: I did not expect this usage from you." Wild then fell on his knees, and, taking hold of her hand, repeated a speech, which, as the reader may easily suggest it to himself, I shall not here set down. He then offered her the casket, but she gently rejected it; and on a second offer, with a modest countenance and voice, desired to know what it contained. Wild then opened it, and took forth (with sorrow I write it, and with sorrow will it be read) one of those beautiful necklaces with which, at the fair of Bartholomew, they deck the well-bewhitened neck of Thalestris Queen of Amazons, Anna Bullen, Queen Elizabeth, or some other high princess in Drollic story. It was indeed composed of that paste which Derdæus Magnus, an ingenious toy-man, doth at a very moderate price dispense of to the second-rate beaus of the metropolis. For, to open a truth, which we ask our reader's pardon for having concealed from him so long, the sagacious count, wisely fearing lest some accident might prevent Mr. Wild's return at the appointed time, had carefully conveyed the jewels which Mr. Heartfree had brought with him into his own pocket, and in their stead had placed in the casket these artificial stones, which, though of equal value to a philosopher, and perhaps of a much greater to a true admirer of the compositions of art, had not, however, the same charms in the eyes of Miss Letty, who had indeed some knowledge of jewels; for Mr. Snap, with great reason, considering how valuable a part of a lady's education it would be to be well instructed in these things, in an age when young ladies learn little more than how to dress themselves, had in her youth placed Miss Letty as the handmaid (or housemaid as the vulgar call it) of an eminent pawnbroker. The lightning, therefore, which should have flashed from the jewels, flashed from her eyes, and thunder immediately followed from her voice. She be-knaved, be-rascalled, be-rogued the unhappy hero, who stood silent, confounded with astonishment, but more with shame and indignation, at being thus outwitted and overreached. At length he recovered his spirits, and, throwing down the casket in a rage, he snatched the key from the table, and, without making any answer to the ladies, who both very plentifully opened upon him, and without taking any leave of them, he flew out at the door, and repaired with the utmost expedition to the count's habitation.

CHAPTER IV

In which Wild, after many fruitless endeavours to discover his friend, moralizes on his misfortune in a speech, which may be of use (if rightly understood) to some other considerable speech-makers

NOT the highest-fed footman of the highest-bred woman of quality knocks with more impetuosity than Wild did at the count's door, which was immediately opened by a well-drest liveryman, who answered that his master was not at home. Wild, not satisfied with this, searched the house, but to no purpose; he then ransacked all the gaming-houses in town, but found no count: indeed, that gentleman had taken leave of his house the same instant Mr. Wild had turned his back, and, equipping himself with boots and a post-horse, without taking with him either servant, clothes, or any necessaries for the journey of a great man, made such mighty expedition that he was now upwards of twenty miles on his way to Dover.

Wild, finding his search ineffectual, resolved to give it over for that night; he then retired to his seat of contemplation, a night-cellar, where, without a single farthing in his pocket, he called for a sneaker of punch, and, placing himself on a bench by himself, he softly vented the following soliloquy:

"How vain is human GREATNESS! What avail superior abilities, and a noble defiance of those narrow rules and bounds which confine the vulgar, when our best-concerted schemes are liable to be defeated! How unhappy is the state of PRIGGISM! How impossible for human prudence to foresee and guard against every circumvention! It is even as a game of chess, where, while the rook, or knight, or bishop, is busied in forecasting some great enterprise, a worthless pawn interposes and disconcerts his scheme. Better had it been for me to have observed the simple laws of friendship and morality than thus to ruin my friend for the benefit of others. I might have commanded his purse to any degree of moderation: I have now disabled him from the power of serving me. Well! but that was not my design. If I cannot arraign my own conduct, why should I, like a woman or a child, sit down and lament the disappointment of chance? But can I acquit myself of all neglect? Did I not misbehave in putting it into the power of others to outwit me? But that is impossible to be avoided. In this a *prig* is more unhappy than any other: a cautious man may, in a crowd, preserve his own pockets by keeping his hand in them; but while the *prig* employs his hands in another's pocket, how shall he be able to defend his own? Indeed, in this light, what can be imagined more miserable than a *prig*? How dangerous are his acquisitions! how unsafe, how unquiet his possessions! Why then should any man wish to be a *prig*, or where is his greatness? I answer, in his mind: 'tis the inward glory, the secret consciousness of doing great and wonderful actions, which can alone support the truly GREAT man, whether he be a CONQUEROR, a TYRANT, a STATESMAN, or a PRIG. These must bear him up against the private curse and public imprecation, and, while he is hated and detested by all mankind, must make him inwardly satisfied with himself. For what but some such inward satisfaction as this could inspire men possessed of power, wealth, of every human blessing which pride, avarice, or luxury could desire, to forsake their homes, abandon ease and repose, and at the expense of riches and pleasures, at the price of labour and hardship, and at the hazard of all that fortune hath liberally given them, could send them at the head of a multitude of *prigs*, called an army, to molest their neighbours; to introduce rape, rapine, bloodshed, and every kind of misery among their own species? What but some such glorious appetite of mind could inflame princes, endowed with the greatest honours, and enriched with the most plentiful revenues, to desire maliciously to rob those subjects of their liberties who are content to sweat for the luxury, and to bow down their knees to the pride, of those very princes? What but this can inspire them to destroy one half of their subjects, in order to reduce the rest to an absolute dependence on their own wills, and on those of their brutal successors? What other motive could seduce a subject, possessed of great property in his community, to betray the interest of his fellow-subjects, of his brethren, and his posterity, to the wanton disposition of such princes? Lastly, what less inducement could persuade the *prig* to forsake the methods of acquiring a safe, an honest, and a plentiful livelihood, and, at the hazard of even life itself, and what is mistakenly called dishonour, to break openly and bravely through the laws of his country, for uncertain, unsteady, and unsafe gain? Let me then hold myself contented with this reflection, that I have been wise though unsuccessful, and am a GREAT though an unhappy man."

His soliloquy and his punch concluded together; for he had at every pause comforted himself with a sip. And now it came first into his head that it would be more difficult to pay for it than it was to swallow it; when, to his great pleasure, he beheld at another corner of the room one of the gentlemen whom he had employed in the attack on Heartfree, and who, he doubted not, would readily lend him a guinea or two; but he had the mortification, on applying to him, to hear that the gaming-table had stript him of all the booty which his own generosity had left in his possession. He was, therefore, obliged to pursue his usual method on such occasions: so, cocking his hat fiercely, he marched out of the room without making any excuse, or any one daring to make the least demand.

CHAPTER V

Containing many surprising adventures, which our hero,
with GREAT GREATNESS, *achieved*

WE will now leave our hero to take a short repose, and return to Mr. Snap's, where, at Wild's departure, the fair Theodosia had again betaken herself to her stocking, and Miss Letty had retired upstairs to Mr. Bagshot; but that gentleman had broken his parole, and, having conveyed himself below stairs behind a door, he took the opportunity of Wild's sally to make his escape. We shall only observe that Miss Letty's surprise was the greater, as she had, notwithstanding her promise to the contrary, taken the precaution to turn the key; but, in her hurry, she did it ineffectually. How wretched must have been the situation of this young creature, who had not only lost a lover on whom her tender heart perfectly doted, but was exposed to the rage of an injured father, tenderly jealous of his honour, which was deeply engaged to the Sheriff of London and Middlesex for the safe custody of the said Bagshot, and for which two very good responsible friends had given not only their words but their bonds.

But let us remove our eyes from this melancholy object, and survey our hero, who, after a successless search for Miss Straddle, with wonderful greatness of mind and steadiness of countenance went early in the morning to visit his friend Heartfree, at a time when the common herd of friends would have forsaken and avoided him. He entered the room with a cheerful air, which he presently changed into surprise on seeing his friend in a nightgown, with his wounded head bound about with linen, and looking extremely pale from a great effusion of blood. When Wild was informed by Heartfree what had happened he first expressed great sorrow, and afterwards suffered as violent agonies of rage against the robbers to burst from him. Heartfree, in compassion to the deep impression his misfortunes seemed to make on his friend, endeavoured to lessen it as much as possible, at the same time exaggerating the obligation he owed to Wild, in which his wife likewise seconded him, and they breakfasted with more comfort than was reasonably to be expected after such an accident; Heartfree expressing great satisfaction that he had put the count's note in another pocket-book; adding, that such a loss would have been fatal to him; "for, to confess the truth to you, my dear friend," said he, "I have had some losses lately which have greatly perplexed my affairs; and though I have many debts due to me from people of great fashion, I assure you I know not where to be certain of getting a shilling." Wild greatly felicitated him on the lucky accident of preserving his note, and then proceeded, with much acrimony, to inveigh against the barbarity of people of fashion, who kept tradesmen out of their money.

While they amused themselves with discourses of this kind, Wild meditating within himself whether he should borrow or steal from his friend, or indeed whether he could not effect both, the apprentice brought a bank-note of £500 in to Heartfree, which he said a gentlewoman in the shop, who had been looking at some jewels, desired him to exchange. Heartfree, looking at the number, immediately recollected it to be one of those he had been robbed of. With this discovery he acquainted Wild, who, with the notable presence of mind and unchanged complexion so essential to a great character, advised him to proceed cautiously; and offered (as Mr. Heartfree himself was, he said, too much flustered to examine the woman with sufficient art) to take her into a room in his house alone. He would, he said, personate the master of the shop, would pretend to shew her some jewels, and would undertake to get sufficient information out of her to secure the rogues, and most probably all their booty. This proposal was readily and thankfully accepted by Heartfree. Wild went immediately upstairs into the room appointed, whither the apprentice, according to appointment, conducted the lady.

The apprentice was ordered downstairs the moment the lady entered the room; and Wild, having shut the door, approached her with great ferocity in his looks, and began to expatiate on the complicated baseness of the crime she had been guilty of; but though he uttered many good lessons of morality, as we doubt whether from a particular reason they may work any very good effect on our reader, we shall omit his speech, and only mention his conclusion, which was by asking her what mercy she could now expect from him? Miss Straddle, for that was the young lady, who had had a good education, and had been more than once present at the Old Bailey, very confidently denied the whole charge, and said she had received the note from a friend. Wild then, raising his voice, told her she should be immediately committed, and she might depend on being convicted; "but," added he, changing his tone, "as I have a violent affection for thee, my dear Straddle, if you will follow my advice, I promise you, on my honour, to forgive you, nor shall you be ever called in question on this account." "Why, what would you have me to do,

Mr. Wild?" replied the young lady, with a pleasanter aspect. "You must know then," said Wild, "the money you picked out of my pocket (nay, by G—d you did, and if you offer to flinch you shall be convicted of it) I won at play of a fellow who it seems robbed my friend of it; you must, therefore, give an information on oath against one Thomas Fierce, and say that you received the note from him, and leave the rest to me. I am certain, Molly, you must be sensible of your obligations to me, who return good for evil to you in this manner." The lady readily consented, and advanced to embrace Mr. Wild, who stepped a little back and cried, "Hold, Molly; there are two other notes of £200 each to be accounted for—where are they?" The lady protested with the most solemn asseverations that she knew of no more; with which, when Wild was not satisfied, she cried: "I will stand search." "That you shall," answered Wild, "and stand strip too." He then proceeded to tumble and search her, but to no purpose, till at last she burst into tears, and declared she would tell the truth (as indeed she did); she then confessed that she had disposed of the one to Jack Swagger, a great favourite of the ladies, being an Irish gentleman, who had been bred clerk to an attorney, afterwards whipt out of a regiment of dragoons, and was then a Newgate solicitor, and a bawdyhouse bully; and, as for the other, she had laid it all out that very morning in brocaded silks and Flanders lace. With this account Wild, who indeed knew it to be a very probable one, was forced to be contented: and now, abandoning all further thoughts of what he saw was irretrievably lost, he gave the lady some further instructions, and then, desiring her to stay a few minutes behind him, he returned to his friend, and acquainted him that he had discovered the whole roguery; that the woman had confessed from whom she had received the note, and promised to give an information before a justice of peace; adding, he was concerned he could not attend him thither, being obliged to go to the other end of the town to receive thirty pounds, which he was to pay that evening. Heartfree said that should not prevent him of his company, for he could easily lend him such a trifle. This was accordingly done and accepted, and Wild, Heartfree, and the lady went to the justice together.

The warrant being granted, and the constable being

acquainted by the lady, who received her information from Wild, of Mr. Fierce's haunts, he was easily apprehended, and, being confronted by Miss Straddle, who swore positively to him, though she had never seen him before, he was committed to Newgate, where he immediately conveyed an information to Wild of what had happened, and in the evening received a visit from him.

Wild affected great concern for his friend's misfortune, and as great surprise at the means by which it was brought about. However, he told Fierce that he must certainly be mistaken in that point of his having had no acquaintance with Miss Straddle: but added, that he would find her out, and endeavour to take off her evidence, which, he observed, did not come home enough to endanger him; besides, he would secure him witnesses of an alibi, and five or six to his character; so that he need be under no apprehension, for his confinement till the sessions would be his only punishment.

Fierce, who was greatly comforted by these assurances of his friend, returned him many thanks, and, both shaking each other very earnestly by the hand, with a very hearty embrace they separated.

The hero considered with himself that the single evidence of Miss Straddle would not be sufficient to convict Fierce, whom he resolved to hang, as he was the person who had principally refused to deliver him the stipulated share of the booty; he therefore went in quest of Mr. James Sly, the gentleman who had assisted in the exploit, and found and acquainted him with the apprehending of Fierce. Wild then, intimating his fear least Fierce should impeach Sly, advised him to be beforehand, to surrender himself to a justice of peace and offer himself as an evidence. Sly approved Mr. Wild's opinion, went directly to a magistrate, and was by him committed to the Gate House, with a promise of being admitted evidence against his companion.

Fierce was in a few days brought to his trial at the Old Bailey, where, to his great confusion, his old friend Sly appeared against him, as did Miss Straddle. His only hopes were now in the assistances which our hero had promised him. These unhappily failed him: so that, the evidence being plain against him, and he making no defence, the jury convicted him, the court condemned him, and Mr. Ketch executed him.

With such infinite address did this truly great man know how to play with the passions of men, to set them at variance with each other, and to work his own purposes out of those jealousies and apprehensions which he was wonderfully ready at creating by means of those great arts which the vulgar call treachery, dissembling, promising, lying, falsehood, etc., but which are by great men summed up in the collective name of policy, or politics, or rather pollitrics; an art of which, as it is the highest excellence of human nature, perhaps our great man was the most eminent master.

CHAPTER VI

Of hats

WILD had now got together a very considerable gang, composed of undone gamesters, ruined bailiffs, broken tradesmen, idle apprentices, attorneys' clerks, and loose and disorderly youths, who, being born to no fortune, nor bred to any trade or profession, were willing to live luxuriously without labour. As these persons wore different *principles*, i.e. *hats*, frequent dissensions grew among them. There were particularly two parties, viz. those who wore hats *fiercely* cocked, and those who preferred the *nab* or trencher hat, with the brim flapping over their eyes. The former were called *cavaliers* and *tory rory ranter boys*, etc.; the latter went by the several names of *wags*, roundheads, shakebags, oldnolls, and several others. Between these, continual jars arose, insomuch that they grew in time to think there was something essential in their differences, and that their interests were incompatible with each other, whereas, in truth, the difference lay only in the fashion of their hats. Wild, therefore, having assembled them all at an alehouse on the night after Fierce's execution, and perceiving evident marks of their misunderstanding, from their behaviour to each other, addressed them in the following gentle, but forcible manner [1]: "Gentlemen, I am

---

[1] There is something very mysterious in this speech, which probably that chapter written by Aristotle on this subject, which is mentioned by a French author, might have given some light into; but that is unhappily among the lost works of that philosopher. It is remarkable that *galerus*, which is Latin for a hat, signifies likewise a dog-fish, as

ashamed to see men embarked in so great and glorious an undertaking, as that of robbing the public, so foolishly and weakly dissenting among themselves. Do you think the first inventors of hats, or at least of the distinctions between them, really conceived that one form of hats should inspire a man with divinity, another with law, another with learning, or another with bravery? No, they meant no more by these outward signs than to impose on the vulgar, and, instead of putting great men to the trouble of acquiring or maintaining the substance, to make it sufficient that they condescend to wear the type or shadow of it. You do wisely, therefore, when in a crowd, to amuse the mob by quarrels on such accounts, that while they are listening to your jargon you may with the greater ease and safety pick their pockets: but surely to be in earnest, and privately to keep up such a ridiculous contention among yourselves, must argue the highest folly and absurdity. When you know you are all *prigs*, what difference can a broad or a narrow brim create? Is a *prig* less a *prig* in one hat than in another? If the public should be weak enough to interest themselves in your quarrels, and to prefer one pack to the other, while both are aiming at their purses, it is your business to laugh at, not imitate their folly. What can be more ridiculous than for gentlemen to quarrel about hats, when there is not one among you whose hat is worth a farthing? What is the use of a hat farther than to keep the head warm, or to hide a bald crown from the public? It is the mark of a gentleman to move his hat on every occasion; and in courts and noble assemblies no man ever wears one. Let me hear no more, therefore, of this childish disagreement, but all toss up your hats together with one

the Greek word κυνέη doth the skin of that animal; of which I suppose the hats or helmets of the ancients were composed, as ours at present are of the beaver or rabbit. Sophocles, in the latter end of his *Ajax*, alludes to a method of cheating in hats, and the scholiast on the place tells us of one Crephontes, who was a master of the art. It is observable likewise that Achilles, in the first Iliad of Homer, tells Agamemnon, in anger, that he had dog's eyes. Now, as the eyes of a dog are handsomer than those of almost any other animal, this could be no term of reproach. He must, therefore, mean that he had a hat on, which, perhaps, from the creature it was made of, or from some other reason, might have been a mark of infamy. This superstitious opinion may account for that custom, which hath descended through all nations, of shewing respect by pulling off this covering, and that no man is esteemed fit to converse with his superiors with it on. I shall conclude this learned note with remarking that the term old hat is at present used by the vulgar in no very honourable sense.

accord, and consider that hat as the best, which will contain the largest booty." He thus ended his speech, which was followed by a murmuring applause, and immediately all present tossed their hats together as he had commanded them.

CHAPTER VII

Shewing the consequence which attended Heartfree's adventures with Wild; all natural and common enough to little wretches who deal with GREAT MEN; *together with some precedents of letters, being the different methods of answering a dun*

LET us now return to Heartfree, to whom the count's note, which he had paid away, was returned, with an account that the drawer was not to be found, and that, on inquiring after him, they had heard he had run away, and consequently the money was now demanded of the endorser. The apprehension of such a loss would have affected any man of business, but much more one whose unavoidable ruin it must prove. He expressed so much concern and confusion on this occasion, that the proprietor of the note was frightened, and resolved to lose no time in securing what he could. So that in the afternoon of the same day Mr. Snap was commissioned to pay Heartfree a visit, which he did with his usual formality, and conveyed him to his own house.

Mrs. Heartfree was no sooner informed of what had happened to her husband than she raved like one distracted; but after she had vented the first agonies of her passion in tears and lamentations she applied herself to all possible means to procure her husband's liberty. She hastened to beg her neighbours to secure bail for him. But, as the news had arrived at their houses before her, she found none of them at home, except an honest Quaker, whose servants durst not tell a lie. However, she succeeded no better with him, for unluckily he had made an affirmation the day before that he would never be bail for any man. After many fruitless efforts of this kind she repaired to her husband, to comfort him at least with her presence. She found him sealing the last of several letters, which he was despatching to his friends and creditors. The moment he saw her a sudden joy sparkled in his eyes, which, however, had a very short duration; for despair soon closed them again; nor could he help bursting into some passionate expressions of concern for her and his little family, which she, on her part, did her utmost to lessen, by endeavouring to mitigate the loss, and to raise in him hopes from the count, who might, she said, be possibly only gone into the country. She comforted him likewise with the expectation of favour from his acquaintance, especially from those whom he had in a particular manner obliged and served. Lastly, she conjured him, by all the value and esteem he professed for her, not to endanger his health, on which alone depended her happiness, by too great an indulgence of grief; assuring him that no state of life could appear unhappy to her with him, unless his own sorrow or discontent made it so.

In this manner did this weak poor-spirited woman attempt to relieve her husband's pains, which it would have rather become her to aggravate, by not only painting out his misery in the liveliest colours imaginable, but by upbraiding him with that folly and confidence which had occasioned it, and by lamenting her own hard fate in being obliged to share his sufferings.

Heartfree returned this goodness (as it is called) of his wife with the warmest gratitude, and they passed an hour in a scene of tenderness too low and contemptible to be recounted to our great readers. We shall, therefore, omit all such relations, as they tend only to make human nature low and ridiculous.

Those messengers who had obtained any answers to his letters now returned. We shall here copy a few of them, as they may serve for precedents to others who have an occasion, which happens commonly enough in genteel life, to answer the impertinence of a dun.

LETTER I

MR. HEARTFREE,—My lord commands me to tell you he is very much surprised at your assurance in asking for money which you know hath been so little while due; however, as he intends to deal no longer at your shop, he hath ordered me to pay you as soon as I shall have cash in hand, which, considering many disbursements for bills long due, etc., can't possibly promise any time, etc., at present. And am your humble servant, ROGER MORECRAFT.

LETTER II

DEAR SIR,—The money, as you truly say, hath been three years due, but upon my soul I am at present incapable of paying a farthing; but as I doubt not, very shortly not only to content that small bill, but likewise to lay out very considerable further sums at your house, hope you will meet with no inconvenience by this short delay in, dear sir, your most sincere humble servant,

CHA. COURTLY.

LETTER III

MR. HEARTFREE,—I beg you would not acquaint my husband of the trifling debt between us; for, as I know you to be a very good-natured man, I will trust you with a secret; he gave me the money long since to discharge it, which I had the ill luck to lose at play. You may be assured I will satisfy you the first opportunity, and am, sir, your very humble servant,

CATH. RUBBERS.

Please to present my compliments to Mrs. Heartfree.

LETTER IV

MR. THOMAS HEARTFREE, Sir,—Yours received: but as to sum mentioned therein, doth not suit at present. Your humble servant,   PETER POUNCE.

LETTER V

SIR,—I am sincerely sorry it is not at present possible for me to comply with your request, especially after so many obligations received on my side, of which I shall always entertain the most grateful memory. I am very greatly concerned at your misfortunes, and would have waited upon you in person, but am not at present very well, and besides, am obliged to go this evening to Vauxhall. I am. sir, your most obliged humble servant.   CHA. EASY.

P.S.—I hope good Mrs. Heartfree and the dear little ones are well.

There were more letters to much the same purpose; but we proposed giving our readers a taste only. Of all these, the last was infinitely the most grating to poor Heartfree, as it came from one to whom, when in distress, he had himself lent a considerable sum, and of whose present flourishing circumstances he was well assured.

CHAPTER VIII

In which our hero carries GREATNESS *to an immoderate height*

LET us remove, therefore, as fast as we can, this detestable picture of ingratitude, and present the much more agreeable portrait of that assurance to which the French very properly annex the epithet of good. Heartfree had scarce done reading his letters when our hero appeared before his eyes; not with that aspect with which a pitiful parson meets his patron after having opposed him at an election, or which a doctor wears when sneaking away from a door when he is informed of his patient's death; not with that downcast countenance which betrays the man who, after a strong conflict between virtue and vice, hath surrendered his mind to the latter, and is discovered in his first treachery; but with that noble, bold, great confidence with which a prime minister assures his dependent that the place he promised him was disposed of before. And such concern and uneasiness as he expresses in his looks on those occasions did Wild testify on the first meeting of his friend. And as the said prime minister chides you for neglect of your interest in not having asked in time, so did our hero attack Heartfree for his giving credit to the count; and, without suffering him to make any answer, proceeded in a torrent of words to overwhelm him with abuse, which, however friendly its intention might be, was scarce to be outdone by an enemy. By these means Heartfree, who might perhaps otherwise have vented some little concern for that recommendation which Wild had given him to the count, was totally prevented from any such endeavour; and, like an invading prince, when attacked in his own dominions, forced to recall his whole strength to defend himself at home. This indeed he did so well, by insisting on the figure and outward appearance of the count and his equipage, that Wild at length grew a little more gentle, and with a sigh said: "I confess I have the least reason of all mankind to censure another for an imprudence of this nature, as I am myself the most easy to be imposed upon, and indeed have been so by this count, who, if he be insolvent, hath cheated me of five hundred pounds. But, for my own part," said he, "I will not yet despair, nor would I have you. Many men have found it convenient to retire or abscond for a while, and afterwards have paid their debts, or at least handsomely compounded them. This I am certain of, should a composition take place, which is the worst I think that can be apprehended, I shall be the only loser; for I shall think myself obliged in honour to repair your loss, even though you must confess it was principally owing to your own folly. Z—ds! had I imagined it necessary, I would have cautioned you, but I thought the part of the town where he lived sufficient caution not to trust him. And such a sum!—The devil must have been in you certainly!"

This was a degree of impudence beyond poor Mrs. Heartfree's imagination. Though she had before vented the most violent execrations on Wild, she was now thoroughly satisfied of his innocence, and begged him not to insist any longer on what he perceived so deeply affected her husband. She said trade could not be carried on without credit, and surely he was sufficiently justified in giving it to such a person as the count appeared to be. Besides, she said, reflections on what was past and irretrievable would be of little service; that their present business was to consider how to prevent the evil consequences which threatened, and first to endeavour to procure her husband his liberty. "Why doth he not procure bail?" said Wild. "Alas! sir," said she, "we have applied to many of our acquaintance in vain; we have met with excuses even where we could least expect them." "Not bail!" answered Wild, in a passion; "he shall have bail, if there is any in the world. It is now very late, but trust me to procure him bail to-morrow morning."

Mrs. Heartfree received these professions with tears, and told Wild he was a friend indeed. She then proposed to stay that evening with her husband, but he would not permit her on account of his little family, whom he would not agree to trust to the care of servants in this time of confusion.

A hackney-coach was then sent for, but without success; for these, like hackney-friends, always offer themselves in the sunshine, but are never to be found when you want them. And as for a chair, Mr. Snap lived in a part of the town which chairmen very little frequent. The good woman was, therefore, obliged to walk home, whither the gallant Wild offered to attend her as a protector. This favour was thankfully accepted, and, the husband and wife having taken a tender leave of each other, the former was locked in and the latter locked out by the hands of Mr. Snap himself.

As this visit of Mr. Wild's to Heartfree may seem one of those passages in history which writers, Drawcansir-like, introduce only *because they dare*; indeed, as it may seem somewhat contradictory to the greatness of our hero, and may tend to blemish his character with an imputation of that kind of friendship which savours too much of weakness and imprudence, it may be necessary to account for this visit, especially to our more sagacious readers, whose satisfaction we shall always consult in the most especial manner. They are to know then that at the first interview with Mrs Heartfree Mr. Wild had conceived that passion, or affection, or friendship, or desire, for that handsome creature, which the gentlemen of this our age agreed to call LOVE, and which is indeed no other than that kind of affection which, after the exercise of the dominical day is over, a lusty divine is apt to conceive for the well-drest sirloin or handsome buttock which the well-edified squire in gratitude sets before him, and which, so violent is his love, he devours in imagination the moment he sees it. Not less ardent was the hungry passion of our hero, who, from the moment he had cast his eyes on that charming dish, had cast about in his mind by what method he might come at it. This, as he perceived, might most easily be effected after the ruin of Heartfree, which, for other considerations, he had intended. So he postponed all endeavours for this purpose till he had first effected what, by order of time, was regularly to precede this latter design; with such regularity did this our hero conduct all his schemes, and so truly superior was he to all the efforts of passion, which so often disconcert and disappoint the noblest views of others.

CHAPTER IX

More GREATNESS *in Wild. A low scene between Mrs. Heart-free and her children, and a scheme of our hero worthy the highest admiration, and even astonishment*

WHEN first Wild conducted his flame (or rather his dish, to continue our metaphor) from the proprietor, he had projected a design of conveying her to one of those eating-houses in Covent Garden, where female flesh is deliciously drest and served up to the greedy appetites of young gentlemen; but, fearing lest she should not come readily enough into his wishes, and that, by too eager and hasty a pursuit, he should frustrate his future expectations, and luckily at the same time a nobler hint suggesting itself to him, by which he might almost inevitably secure his pleasure, together with his profit, he contented himself with waiting on Mrs. Heartfree home, and, after many protestations of friendship and service to her husband, took his leave, and promised to visit her early in the morning, and to conduct her back to Mr. Snap's.

Wild now retired to a night-cellar, where he found several of his acquaintance, with whom he spent the remaining part of the night in revelling; nor did the least compassion for Heartfree's misfortunes disturb the pleasure of his cups. So truly great was his soul, that it was absolutely composed, save that an apprehension of Miss Tishy's making some discovery (as she was then in no good temper towards him) a little ruffled and disquieted the perfect serenity he would otherwise have enjoyed. As he had, therefore, no opportunity of seeing her that evening, he wrote her a letter full of ten thousand protestations of honourable love, and (which he more depended on) containing as many promises, in order to bring the young lady into good humour, without acquainting her in the least with his suspicion, or giving her any caution; for it was his constant maxim never to put it into any one's head to do you a mischief by acquainting him that it is in his power.

We must now return to Mrs. Heartfree, who passed a sleepless night in as great agonies and horror for the absence of her husband as a fine well-bred woman would feel at the return of hers from a long voyage or journey. In the morning the children being brought to her, the eldest asked where dear papa was? At which she could not refrain from bursting into tears. The child, perceiving it, said: "Don't cry, mamma; I am sure papa would not stay abroad if he could help it." At these words she caught the child in her arms, and, throwing herself into the chair in an agony of passion, cried out: "No, my child; nor shall all the malice of hell keep us long asunder."

These are circumstances which we should not, for the amusement of six or seven readers only, have inserted, had they not served to shew that there are weaknesses in vulgar life to which great minds are so entirely strangers that they have not even an idea of them; and, secondly, by exposing the folly of this low creature, to set off and elevate that greatness of which we endeavour to draw a true portrait in this history.

Wild, entering the room, found the mother with one child in her arms, and the other at her knee. After paying her his compliments, he desired her to dismiss the children and servant, for that he had something of the greatest moment to impart to her.

She immediately complied with his request, and, the door being shut, asked him with great eagerness if he had succeeded in his intentions of procuring the bail. He answered he had not endeavoured at it yet, for a scheme had entered into his head by which she might certainly preserve her husband, herself, and her family. In order to which he advised her instantly to remove with the most valuable jewels she had to Holland, before any statute of bankruptcy issued to prevent her; that he would himself attend her thither and place her in safety, and then return to deliver her husband, who would be thus easily able to satisfy his creditors. He added that he was that instant come from Snap's, where he had communicated the scheme to Heartfree, who had greatly approved of it, and desired her to put it in execution without delay, concluding that a moment was not to be lost.

The mention of her husband's approbation left no doubt in this poor woman's breast; she only desired a moment's time to pay him a visit in order to take her leave. But Wild peremptorily refused; he said by every moment's delay she risked the ruin of her family; that she would be absent only a few days from him, for that the moment he had lodged her safe in Holland he would return, procure her husband his liberty, and bring him to her. "I have been the unfortunate, the innocent cause of all my dear Tom's calamity, madam," said he, "and I will perish with him or see him out of it." Mrs. Heartfree overflowed with acknowledgments of his goodness, but still begged for the shortest interview with her husband. Wild declared that a minute's delay might be fatal; and added, though with the voice of sorrow rather than of anger, that if she had not resolution enough to execute the commands he brought her from her husband, his ruin would lie at her door; and, for his own part, he must give up any farther meddling in his affairs.

She then proposed to take her children with her; but Wild would not permit it, saying they would only retard their flight, and that it would be properer for her husband to bring them. He at length absolutely prevailed on this poor woman, who immediately packed up the most valuable effects she could find, and, after taking a tender leave of her infants, earnestly recommended them to the care of a very faithful servant. Then they called a hackney-coach, which conveyed them to an inn, where they were furnished with a chariot and six, in which they set forward for Harwich.

Wild rode with an exulting heart, secure, as he now thought himself, of the possession of that lovely woman, together with a rich cargo. In short, he enjoyed in his mind all the happiness which unbridled lust and rapacious avarice could promise him. As to the poor creature who was to satisfy these passions, her whole soul was employed in reflecting on the condition of her husband and children. A single word scarce escaped her lips, though many a tear gushed from her brilliant eyes, which, if I may use a coarse expression, served only as delicious sauce to heighten the appetite of Wild.

CHAPTER X

Sea-adventures very new and surprising

WHEN they arrived at Harwich they found a vessel, which had put in there, just ready to depart for Rotterdam. So they went immediately on board, and sailed with a fair wind; but they had hardly proceeded out of sight of land when a sudden and violent storm arose and drove them to the south-west; insomuch that the captain apprehended it impossible to avoid the Goodwin Sands, and he and all his crew gave themselves up for lost. Mrs. Heartfree, who had no other apprehensions from death but those of leaving her dear husband and children, fell on her knees to beseech the Almighty's favour, when Wild, with a contempt of danger truly great, took a resolution as worthy to be admired perhaps as any recorded of the bravest hero, ancient or modern; a resolution which plainly proved him to have these two qualifications so necessary to a hero, to be superior to all the energies of fear or pity. He saw the tyrant death ready to rescue from him his intended prey, which he had yet devoured only in imagination. He, therefore, swore he would prevent him, and immediately attacked the poor wretch, who was in the utmost agonies of despair, first with solicitation, and afterwards with force.

Mrs. Heartfree, the moment she understood his meaning, which, in her present temper of mind, and in the opinion she held of him, she did not immediately, rejected him with all the repulses which indignation and horror could animate: but when he attempted violence she filled the cabin with her shrieks, which were so vehement that they reached the ears of the captain, the storm at this time luckily abating. This man, who was a brute rather from his education and the element he inhabited than from nature, ran hastily down to her assistance, and, finding her struggling on the ground with our hero, he presently rescued her from her intended ravisher, who was soon obliged to quit the woman, in order to engage with her lusty champion, who spared neither pains nor blows in the assistance of his fair passenger.

When the short battle was over, in which our hero, had he not been overpowered with numbers, who came down on their captain's side, would have been victorious, the captain rapped out a hearty oath, and asked Wild, if he had no more Christianity in him than to ravish a woman in a storm? To which the other greatly and sullenly answered: "It was very well; but d——n him if he had not satisfaction the moment they came on shore." The captain with great scorn replied: "Kiss ——" etc., and then, forcing Wild out of the cabin, he, at Mrs. Heartfree's request, locked her into it, and returned to the care of his ship.

The storm was now entirely ceased, and nothing remained

but the usual ruffling of the sea after it, when one of the sailors spied a sail at a distance, which the captain wisely apprehended might be a privateer (for we were then engaged in a war with France), and immediately ordered all the sail possible to be crowded; but his caution was in vain, for the little wind which then blew was directly adverse, so that the ship bore down upon them, and soon appeared to be what the captain had feared, a French privateer. He was in no condition of resistance, and immediately struck on her firing the first gun. The captain of the Frenchman, with several of his hands, came on board the English vessel, which they rifled of everything valuable, and, amongst the rest, of poor Mrs. Heartfree's whole cargo; and then taking the crew, together with the two passengers, aboard his own ship, he determined, as the other would be only a burthen to him, to sink her, she being very old and leaky, and not worth going back with to Dunkirk. He preserved, therefore, nothing but the boat, as his own was none of the best, and then, pouring a broadside into her, he sent her to the bottom.

The French captain, who was a very young fellow, and a man of gallantry, was presently enamoured to no small degree with his beautiful captive; and imagining Wild, from some words he dropt, to be her husband, notwithstanding the ill affection towards him which appeared in her looks, he asked her if she understood French. She answered in the affirmative, for indeed she did perfectly well. He then asked her how long she and that gentleman (pointing to Wild) had been married. She answered, with a deep sigh and many tears, that she was married indeed, but not to that villain, who was the sole cause of all her misfortunes. That appellation raised a curiosity in the captain, and he importuned her in so pressing but gentle a manner to acquaint him with the injuries she complained of, that she was at last prevailed on to recount to him the whole history of her afflictions. This so moved the captain, who had too little notions of greatness, and so incensed him against our hero, that he resolved to punish him; and, without regard to the laws of war, he immediately ordered out his shattered boat, and, making Wild a present of half a dozen biscuits to prolong his misery, he put him therein, and then, committing him to the mercy of the sea, proceeded on his cruise.

CHAPTER XI

*The great and wonderful behaviour of our hero
in the boat*

IT is probable that a desire of ingratiating himself with
his charming captive, or rather conqueror, had no little
share in promoting this extraordinary act of illegal justice;
for the Frenchman had conceived the same sort of passion
or hunger which Wild himself had felt, and was almost as
much resolved, by some means or other, to satisfy it. We
will leave him, however, at present in the pursuit of his
wishes, and attend our hero in his boat, since it is in circumstances of distress that true greatness appears most
wonderful. For that a prince in the midst of his courtiers,
all ready to compliment him with his favourite character
or title, and indeed with everything else, or that a conqueror, at the head of a hundred thousand men, all prepared
to execute his will, how ambitious, wanton, or cruel soever,
should, in the giddiness of their pride, elevate themselves
many degrees above those their tools, seems not difficult
to be imagined, or indeed accounted for. But that a man
in chains, in prison, nay, in the vilest dungeon, should,
with persevering pride and obstinate dignity, discover that
vast superiority in his own nature over the rest of mankind,
who to a vulgar eye seem much happier than himself;
nay, that he should discover heaven and providence (whose
peculiar care, it seems, he is) at that very time at work
for him; this is among the arcana of greatness, to be
perfectly understood only by an adept in that science.

What could be imagined more miserable than the situation of our hero at this season, floating in a little boat on
the open sea, without oar, without sail, and at the mercy
of the first wave to overwhelm him? nay, this was indeed
the fair side of his fortune, as it was a much more eligible
fate than that alternative which threatened him with
almost unavoidable certainty, viz. starving with hunger,
the sure consequence of a continuance of the calm.

Our hero, finding himself in this condition, began to
ejaculate a round of blasphemies, which the reader, without
being over-pious, might be offended at seeing repeated.
He then accused the whole female sex, and the passion of

love (as he called it), particularly that which he bore to Mrs. Heartfree, as the unhappy occasion of his present sufferings. At length, finding himself descending too much into the language of meanness and complaint, he stopped short, and soon after broke forth as follows: "D—n it, a man can die but once! what signifies it? Every man must die, and when it is over it is over. I never was afraid of anything yet, nor I won't begin now; no, d—n me, won't I. What signifies fear? I shall die whether I am afraid or not: who 's afraid then, d—n me?" At which words he looked extremely fierce, but, recollecting that no one was present to see him, he relaxed a little the terror of his countenance, and, pausing a while, repeated the word, "D—n!" "Suppose I should be d—ned at last," cries he, "when I never thought a syllable of the matter? I have often laughed and made a jest about it, and yet it may be so, for anything which I know to the contrary. If there should be another world it will go hard with me, that is certain. I shall never escape for what I have done to Heartfree. The devil must have me for that undoubtedly. The devil! Pshaw! I am not such a fool to be frightened at him neither. No, no; when a man 's dead there 's an end of him. I wish I was certainly satisfied of it though: for there are some men of learning, as I have heard, of a different opinion. It is but a bad chance, methinks, I stand. If there be no other world, why I shall be in no worse condition than a block or a stone: but if there should— d—n me I will think no longer about it.—Let a pack of cowardly rascals be afraid of death, I dare look him in the face. But shall I stay and be starved?—No, I will eat up the biscuits the French son of a whore bestowed on me, and then leap into the sea for drink, since the unconscionable dog hath not allowed me a single dram." Having thus said, he proceeded immediately to put his purpose in execution, and, as his resolution never failed him, he had no sooner dispatched the small quantity of provision which his enemy had with no vast liberality presented him, than he cast himself headlong into the sea.

CHAPTER XII

The strange and yet natural escape of our hero

OUR hero, having with wonderful resolution thrown himself into the sea, as we mentioned at the end of the last chapter, was miraculously within two minutes after replaced in his boat; and this without the assistance of a dolphin or a seahorse, or any other fish or animal, who are always as ready at hand when a poet or historian pleases to call for them to carry a hero through the sea, as any chairman at a coffee-house door near St. James's to convey a beau over a street, and preserve his white stockings. The truth is, we do not choose to have any recourse to miracles, from the strict observance we pay to that rule of Horace:

Nec Deus intersit, nisi dignus vindice nodus.

The meaning of which is, do not bring in a supernatural agent when you can do without him; and indeed we are much deeper read in natural than supernatural causes. We will, therefore, endeavour to account for this extraordinary event from the former of these; and in doing this it will be necessary to disclose some profound secrets to our reader, extremely well worth his knowing, and which may serve him to account for many occurrences of the phenomenous kind which have formerly appeared in this our hemisphere.

Be it known then that the great Alma Mater, Nature, is of all other females the most obstinate, and tenacious of her purpose. So true is that observation:

Naturam expellas furca licet, usque recurret.

Which I need not render in English, it being to be found in a book which most fine gentlemen are forced to read. Whatever Nature, therefore, purposes to herself, she never suffers any reason, design, or accident to frustrate. Now, though it may seem to a shallow observer that some persons were designed by Nature for no use or purpose whatever, yet certain it is that no man is born into the world without his particular allotment, viz. some to be kings, some statesmen, some embassadors, some bishops, some generals, and so on. Of these there be two kinds; those to whom Nature is so generous to give some endowment qualifying them for the parts she intends them afterwards to act on this stage, and those whom she uses as instances of her unlimited power, and for whose preferment to such and such stations Solomon himself could have invented no other reason than that Nature designed them so. These latter some great philosophers have, to shew them to be the favourites of Nature, distinguished by the honourable appellation of NATURALS. Indeed, the true reason of the general ignorance of mankind on this head seems to be this; that, as Nature chooses to execute these her purposes by certain second causes, and as many of these second causes seem so totally foreign to her design, the wit of man, which, like his eye, sees best directly forward, and very little and imperfectly what is oblique, is not able to discern the end by the means. Thus, how a handsome wife or daughter should contribute to execute her original designation of a general, or how flattery or half a dozen houses in a borough-town should denote a judge, or a bishop, he is not capable of comprehending. And, indeed, we ourselves, wise as we are, are forced to reason *ab effectu*; and if we had been asked what Nature had intended such men for, before she herself had by the event demonstrated her purpose, it is possible we might sometimes have been puzzled to declare; for it must be confessed that at first sight, and to a mind uninspired, a man of vast natural capacity and much acquired knowledge may seem by Nature designed for power and honour, rather than one remarkable only for the want of these, and indeed all other qualifications; whereas daily experience convinces us of the contrary, and drives us as it were into the opinion I have here disclosed.

Now, Nature having originally intended our great man for that final exaltation which, as it is the most proper and becoming end of all great men, it were heartily to be wished they might all arrive at, would by no means be diverted from her purpose. She, therefore, no sooner spied him in the water than she softly whispered in his ear to attempt the recovery of his boat, which call he immediately obeyed, and, being a good swimmer, and it being a perfect calm, with great facility accomplished it.

Thus we think this passage in our history, at first so

greatly surprising, is very naturally accounted for, and our relation rescued from the Prodigious, which, though it often occurs in biography, is not to be encouraged nor much commended on any occasion, unless when absolutely necessary to prevent the history's being at an end. Secondly, we hope our hero is justified from that imputation of want of resolution which must have been fatal to the greatness of his character.

CHAPTER XIII

The conclusion of the boat adventure, and the end of the second book

OUR hero passed the remainder of the evening, the night, and the next day, in a condition not much to be envied by any passion of the human mind, unless by ambition; which, provided it can only entertain itself with the most distant music of fame's trumpet, can disdain all the pleasures of the sensualist, and those more solemn, though quieter comforts, which a good conscience suggests to a Christian philosopher.

He spent his time in contemplation, that is to say, in blaspheming, cursing, and sometimes singing and whistling. At last, when cold and hunger had almost subdued his native fierceness, it being a good deal past midnight and extremely dark, he thought he beheld a light at a distance, which the cloudiness of the sky prevented his mistaking for a star: this light, however, did not seem to approach him, at least it approached by such imperceptible degrees that it gave him very little comfort, and at length totally forsook him. He then renewed his contemplation as before, in which he continued till the day began to break, when, to his inexpressible delight, he beheld a sail at a very little distance, and which luckily seemed to be making towards him. He was likewise soon espied by those in the vessel, who wanted no signals to inform them of his distress, and, as it was almost a calm, and their course lay within five hundred yards of him, they hoisted out their boat and fetched him aboard.

The captain of this ship was a Frenchman; she was laden with deal from Norway, and had been extremely shattered in the late storm. This captain was of that kind of men who are actuated by general humanity, and whose compassion can be raised by the distress of a fellow-creature, though of a nation whose king hath quarrelled with the monarch of their own. He, therefore, commiserating the circumstances of Wild, who had dressed up a story proper to impose upon such a silly fellow, told him that, as himself well knew, he must be a prisoner on his arrival in France, but that he would endeavour to procure his redemption; for which our hero greatly thanked him. But, as they were making very slow sail (for they had lost their mainmast in the storm), Wild saw a little vessel at a distance, they being within a few leagues of the English shore, which, on enquiry, he was informed was probably an English fishing-boat. And, it being then perfectly calm, he proposed that, if they would accommodate him with a pair of scullers, he could get within reach of the boat, at least near enough to make signals to her; and he preferred any risk to the certain fate of being a prisoner. As his courage was somewhat restored by the provisions (especially brandy) with which the Frenchmen had supplied him, he was so earnest in his entreaties, that the captain, after many persuasions, at length complied, and he was furnished with scullers, and with some bread, pork, and a bottle of brandy. Then, taking leave of his preservers, he again betook himself to his boat, and rowed so heartily that he soon came within the sight of the fisherman, who immediately made towards him and took him aboard.

No sooner was Wild got safe on board the fisherman than he begged him to make the utmost speed into Deal, for that the vessel which was still in sight was a distressed Frenchman, bound for Havre de Grace, and might easily be made a prize if there was any ship ready to go in pursuit of her. So nobly and greatly did our hero neglect all obligations conferred on him by the enemies of his country, that he would have contributed all he could to the taking his benefactor, to whom he owed both his life and his liberty.

The fisherman took his advice, and soon arrived at Deal, where the reader will, I doubt not, be as much concerned as Wild was, that there was not a single ship prepared to go on the expedition.

Our hero now saw himself once more safe on terra firma,

but unluckily at some distance from that city where men of ingenuity can most easily supply their wants without the assistance of money, or rather can most easily procure money for the supply of their wants. However, as his talents were superior to every difficulty, he framed so dextrous an account of his being a merchant, having been taken and plundered by the enemy, and of his great effects in London, that he was not only heartily regaled by the fisherman at his house, but made so handsome a booty by way of borrowing, a method of taking which we have before mentioned to have his approbation, that he was enabled to provide himself with a place in the stage-coach; which (as God permitted it to perform the journey) brought him at the appointed time to an inn in the metropolis.

And now, reader, as thou canst be in no suspense for the fate of our great man, since we have returned him safe to the principal scene of his glory, we will a little look back on the fortunes of Mr. Heartfree, whom we left in no very pleasant situation; but of this we shall treat in the next book.

BOOK III

CHAPTER I

*The low and pitiful behaviour of Heartfree; and the
foolish conduct of his apprentice*

His misfortunes did not entirely prevent Heartfree from
closing his eyes. On the contrary, he slept several hours
the first night of his confinement. However, he perhaps
paid too severely dear both for his repose and for a sweet
dream which accompanied it, and represented his little
family in one of those tender scenes which had frequently
passed in the days of his happiness and prosperity, when
the provision they were making for the future fortunes of
their children used to be one of the most agreeable topics
of discourse with which he and his wife entertained themselves. The pleasantness of this vision, therefore, served
only, on his awaking, to set forth his present misery with
additional horror, and to heighten the dreadful ideas which
now crowded on his mind.

He had spent a considerable time after his first rising
from the bed on which he had, without undressing, thrown
himself, and now began to wonder at Mrs. Heartfree's long
absence; but as the mind is desirous (and perhaps wisely
too) to comfort itself with drawing the most flattering conclusions from all events, so he hoped the longer her stay
was the more certain was his deliverance. At length his
impatience prevailed, and he was just going to dispatch a
messenger to his own house when his apprentice came to
pay him a visit, and on his enquiry informed him that his
wife had departed in company with Mr. Wild many hours
before, and had carried all his most valuable effects with
her; adding at the same time that she had herself positively
acquainted him she had her husband's express orders for
so doing, and that she was gone to Holland.

It is the observation of many wise men, who have studied
the anatomy of the human soul with more attention than
our young physicians generally bestow on that of the

body, that great and violent surprise hath a different effect from that which is wrought in a good housewife by perceiving any disorders in her kitchen; who, on such occasions, commonly spreads the disorder, not only over her whole family, but over the whole neighbourhood.—Now, these great calamities, especially when sudden, tend to stifle and deaden all the faculties, instead of rousing them; and accordingly Herodotus tells us a story of Crœsus, King of Lydia, who, on beholding his servants and courtiers led captive, wept bitterly, but, when he saw his wife and children in that condition, stood stupid and motionless; so stood poor Heartfree on this relation of his apprentice, nothing moving but his colour, which entirely forsook his countenance.

The apprentice, who had not in the least doubted the veracity of his mistress, perceiving the surprise which too visibly appeared in his master, became speechless likewise, and both remained silent some minutes, gazing with astonishment and horror at each other. At last Heartfree cried out in an agony: "My wife deserted me in my misfortunes!" "Heaven forbid, sir!" answered the other. "And what is become of my poor children?" replied Heartfree. "They are at home, sir," said the apprentice. "Heaven be praised! She hath forsaken them too!" cries Heartfree: "fetch them hither this instant. Go, my dear Jack, bring hither my little all which remains now: fly, child, if thou dost not intend likewise to forsake me in my afflictions." The youth answered he would die sooner than entertain such a thought, and, begging his master to be comforted, instantly obeyed his orders.

Heartfree, the moment the young man was departed, threw himself on his bed in an agony of despair; but, recollecting himself after he had vented the first sallies of his passion, he began to question the infidelity of his wife as a matter impossible. He ran over in his thoughts the uninterrupted tenderness which she had always shewn him, and, for a minute, blamed the rashness of his belief against her; till the many circumstances of her having left him so long, and neither writ nor sent to him since her departure with all his effects and with Wild, of whom he was not before without suspicion, and, lastly and chiefly, her false pretence to his commands, entirely turned the scale, and convinced him of her disloyalty.

While he was in these agitations of mind the good apprentice, who had used the utmost expedition, brought his children to him. He embraced them with the most passionate fondness, and imprinted numberless kisses on their little lips. The little girl flew to him with almost as much eagerness as he himself exprest at her sight, and cried out: "O papa, why did you not come home to poor mamma all this while! I thought you would not have left your little Nancy so long." After which he asked her for her mother, and was told she had kissed them both in the morning, and cried very much for his absence. All which brought a flood of tears into the eyes of this weak, silly man, who had not greatness sufficient to conquer these low efforts of tenderness and humanity.

He then proceeded to enquire of the maidservant, who acquainted him that she knew no more than that her mistress had taken leave of her children in the morning with many tears and kisses, and had recommended them in the most earnest manner to her care; she said she had promised faithfully to take care of them, and would, while they were entrusted to her, fulfil her promise. For which profession Heartfree expressed much gratitude to her, and, after indulging himself with some little fondnesses which we shall not relate, he delivered his children into the good woman's hands, and dismissed her.

CHAPTER II

A soliloquy of Heartfree's, full of low and base ideas, without a syllable of GREATNESS

BEING now alone, he sat some short time silent, and then burst forth into the following soliloquy:

"What shall I do? Shall I abandon myself to a dispirited despair, or fly in the face of the Almighty? Surely both are unworthy of a wise man; for what can be more vain than weakly to lament my fortune if irretrievable, or, if hope remains, to offend that Being who can most strongly support it? but are my passions then voluntary? Am I so absolutely their master that I can resolve with myself, so far only will I grieve? Certainly no. Reason, however we flatter ourselves, hath not such despotic empire in our minds, that it can, with imperial voice, hush all our sorrow in a moment. Where then is its use? For either it is an empty sound, and we are deceived in thinking we have reason, or it is given us to some end, and hath a part assigned it by the all-wise Creator. Why, what can its office be other than justly to weigh the worth of all things, and to direct us to that perfection of human wisdom which proportions our esteem of every object by its real merit, and prevents us from over or undervaluing whatever we hope for, we enjoy, or we lose. It doth not foolishly say to us, Be not glad, or, Be not sorry, which would be as vain and idle as to bid the purling river cease to run, or the raging wind to blow. It prevents us only from exulting, like children, when we receive a toy, or from lamenting when we are deprived of it. Suppose then I have lost the enjoyments of this world, and my expectation of future pleasure and profit is for ever disappointed, what relief can my reason afford? What, unless it can shew me I had fixed my affections on a toy; that what I desired was not, by a wise man, eagerly to be affected, nor its loss violently deplored? for there are toys adapted to all ages, from the rattle to the throne; and perhaps the value of all is equal to their several possessors; for if the rattle pleases the ear of the infant, what can the flattery of sycophants give more to the prince? The latter is as far from examining into the reality and source of his pleasure as the former; for if both did, they must both equally despise it. And surely, if we consider them seriously, and compare them together, we shall be forced to conclude all those pomps and pleasures of which men are so fond, and which, through so much danger and difficulty, with such violence and villainy, they pursue, to be as worthless trifles as any exposed to sale in a toyshop. I have often noted my little girl viewing, with eager eyes, a jointed baby; I have marked the pains and solicitations she hath used till I have been prevailed on to indulge her with it. At her first obtaining it, what joy hath sparkled in her countenance! with what raptures hath she taken possession! but how little satisfaction hath she found in it! What pains to work out her amusement from it! Its dress must be varied; the tinsel ornaments which first caught her eyes produce no longer pleasure; she endeavours to make it stand and walk in vain, and is constrained herself to supply it with conversation. In a day's time it is thrown by and neglected, and some less costly toy preferred to it. How like the situation of this child is that of every man! What difficulties in the pursuit of his desires! what inanity in the possession of most, and satiety in those which seem more real and substantial! The delights of most men are as childish and as superficial as that of my little girl; a feather or a fiddle are their pursuits and their pleasures through life, even to their ripest years, if such men may be said to attain any ripeness at all. But let us survey those whose understandings are of a more elevated and refined temper; how empty do they soon find the world of enjoyments worth their desire or attaining! How soon do they retreat to solitude and contemplation, to gardening and planting, and such rural amusements, where their trees and they enjoy the air and the sun in common, and both vegetate with very little difference between them. But suppose (which neither truth nor wisdom will allow) we could admit something more valuable and substantial in these blessings, would not the uncertainty of their possession be alone sufficient to lower their price? How mean a tenure is that at the will of fortune, which chance, fraud, and rapine are every day so likely to deprive us of, and often the more likely by how much the greater worth our possessions are of! Is it not to place our affections on a bubble in the water, or on a picture in the clouds! What madman would build a fine house or frame a beautiful garden on land in which he held so uncertain an interest? But again, was all this less undeniable, did Fortune, the lady of our manor, lease to us for our lives, of how little consideration must even this term appear! For, admitting that these pleasures were not liable to be torn from us, how certainly must we be torn from them! Perhaps to-morrow—nay, or even sooner; for as the excellent poet says:

> Where is to-morrow?—In the other world.
> To thousands this is true, and the reverse
> Is sure to none.

But if I have no further hope in this world, can I have none beyond it? Surely those laborious writers, who have taken such infinite pains to destroy or weaken all the proofs of futurity, have not so far succeeded as to exclude us from hope. That active principle in man which with such boldness pushes us on through every labour and difficulty, to attain the most distant and most improbable event in this world, will not surely deny us a little flattering prospect of those beautiful mansions which, if they could be thought chimerical, must be allowed the loveliest which can entertain the eye of man; and to which the road, if we understand it rightly, appears to have so few thorns and briars in it, and to require so little labour and fatigue from those who shall pass through it, that its ways are truly said to be ways of pleasantness, and all its paths to be those of peace. If the proofs of Christianity be as strong as I imagine them, surely enough may be deduced from that ground only, to comfort and support the most miserable man in his afflictions. And this I think my reason tells me, that, if the professors and propagators of infidelity are in the right, the losses which death brings to the virtuous are not worth their lamenting; but if these are, as certainly they seem, in the wrong, the blessings it procures them are not sufficiently to be coveted and rejoiced at.

"On my own account, then, I have no cause for sorrow, but on my children's!—Why, the same Being to whose goodness and power I entrust my own happiness is likewise as able and as willing to procure theirs. Nor matters it what state of life is allotted for them, whether it be their fate to procure bread with their own labour, or to eat it at the sweat of others. Perhaps, if we consider the case with proper attention, or resolve it with due sincerity, the former is much the sweeter. The hind may be more happy than the lord, for his desires are fewer, and those such as are attended with more hope and less fear. I will do my utmost to lay the foundations of my children's happiness, I will carefully avoid educating them in a station superior to their fortune, and for the event trust to that Being in whom whoever rightly confides, must be superior to all worldly sorrows."

In this low manner did this poor wretch proceed to argue, till he had worked himself up into an enthusiasm which by degrees soon became invulnerable to every human attack; so that when Mr. Snap acquainted him with the return of the writ, and that he must carry him to Newgate, he received the message as Socrates did the news of the ship's arrival, and that he was to prepare for death.

CHAPTER III

Wherein our hero proceeds in the road to GREATNESS

BUT we must not detain our reader too long with these low characters. He is doubtless as impatient as the audience at the theatre till the principal figure returns on the stage; we will therefore indulge his inclination, and pursue the actions of the Great Wild.

There happened to be in the stage-coach in which Mr. Wild travelled from Dover a certain young gentleman who had sold an estate in Kent, and was going to London to receive the money. There was likewise a handsome young woman who had left her parents at Canterbury, and was proceeding to the same city, in order (as she informed her fellow-travellers) to make her fortune. With this girl the young spark was so much enamoured that he publicly acquainted her with the purpose of his journey, and offered her a considerable sum in hand and a settlement if she would consent to return with him into the country, where she would be at a safe distance from her relations. Whether she accepted this proposal or no we are not able with any tolerable certainty to deliver: but Wild, the moment he heard of this money, began to cast about in his mind by what means he might become master of it. He entered into a long harangue about the methods of carrying money safely on the road, and said: "He had at that time two bank-bills of a hundred pounds each sewed in his coat; which," added he, "is so safe a way, that it is almost impossible I should be in any danger of being robbed by the most cunning highwayman."

The young gentleman, who was no descendant of Solomon, or, if he was, did not, any more than some other descendants of wise men, inherit the wisdom of his ancestor, greatly approved Wild's ingenuity, and, thanking him for his information, declared he would follow his example when he returned into the country; by which means he proposed to save the premium commonly taken for the remittance. Wild had then no more to do but to inform himself rightly of the time of the gentleman's journey, which he did with great certainty before they separated.

At his arrival in town he fixed on two whom he regarded

as the most resolute of his gang for this enterprise; and, accordingly, having summoned the principal, or most desperate, as he imagined him, of these two (for he never chose to communicate in the presence of more than one), he proposed to him the robbing and murdering this gentleman.

Mr. Marybone (for that was the gentleman's name to whom he applied) readily agreed to the robbery, but he hesitated at the murder. He said, as to robbery, he had, on much weighing and considering the matter, very well reconciled his conscience to it; for, though that noble kind of robbery which was executed on the highway was, from the cowardice of mankind, less frequent, yet the baser and meaner species, sometimes called cheating, but more commonly known by the name of robbery within the law, was in a manner universal. He did not, therefore, pretend to the reputation of being so much honester than other people; but could by no means satisfy himself in the commission of murder, which was a sin of the most heinous nature, and so immediately prosecuted by God's judgment that it never passed undiscovered or unpunished.

Wild, with the utmost disdain in his countenance, answered as follows: "Art thou he whom I have selected out of my whole gang for this glorious undertaking, and dost thou cant of God's revenge against murder? You have, it seems, reconciled your conscience (a pretty word) to robbery, from its being so common. Is it then the novelty of murder which deters you? Do you imagine that guns, and pistols, and swords, and knives, are the only instruments of death? Look into the world and see the numbers whom broken fortunes and broken hearts bring untimely to the grave. To omit those glorious heroes who, to their immortal honour, have massacred whole nations, what think you of private persecution, treachery, and slander, by which the very souls of men are in a manner torn from their bodies? Is it not more generous, nay, more good-natured, to send a man to his rest, than, after having plundered him of all he hath, or from malice or malevolence deprived him of his character, to punish him with a languishing death, or, what is worse, a languishing life? Murder, therefore, is not so uncommon as you weakly conceive it, though, as you said of robbery, that more noble kind which lies within the paw of the law may be so. But this is the most innocent in him who doth it, and the most eligible to him who is to suffer it. Believe me, lad, the tongue of a viper is less hurtful than that of a slanderer, and the gilded scales of a rattlesnake less dreadful than the purse of the oppressor. Let me, therefore, hear no more of your scruples; but consent to my proposal without further hesitation, unless, like a woman, you are afraid of blooding your clothes, or, like a fool, are terrified with the apprehensions of being hanged in chains. Take my word for it, you had better be an honest man than half a rogue. Do not think of continuing in my gang without abandoning yourself absolutely to my pleasure; for no man shall ever receive a favour at my hands who sticks at anything, or is guided by any other law than that of my will."

Wild then ended his speech, which had not the desired effect on Marybone: he agreed to the robbery, but would not undertake the murder, as Wild (who feared that, by Marybone's demanding to search the gentleman's coat, he might hazard suspicion himself) insisted. Marybone was immediately entered by Wild in his black-book, and was presently after impeached and executed as a fellow on whom his leader could not place sufficient dependence; thus falling, as many rogues do, a sacrifice, not to his roguery, but to his conscience.

CHAPTER IV

In which a young hero, of wonderful good promise, makes his first appearance, with many other GREAT MATTERS

OUR hero next applied himself to another of his gang, who instantly received his orders, and, instead of hesitating at a single murder, asked if he should blow out the brains of all the passengers, coachman and all. But Wild, whose moderation we have before noted, would not permit him; and, therefore, having given him an exact description of the devoted person, with his other necessary instructions, he dismissed him, with the strictest orders to avoid, if possible, doing hurt to any other person.

The name of this youth, who will hereafter make some figure in this history, being the Achates of our Æneas, or rather the Hephæstion of our Alexander, was Fireblood.

He had every qualification to make a second-rate GREAT MAN; or, in other words, he was completely equipped for the tool of a real or first-rate GREAT MAN. We shall therefore (which is the properest way of dealing with this kind of GREATNESS) describe him negatively, and content ourselves with telling our reader what qualities he had not; in which number were humanity, modesty, and fear, not one grain of any of which was mingled in his whole composition.

We will now leave this youth, who was esteemed the most promising of the whole gang, and whom Wild often declared to be one of the prettiest lads he had ever seen, of which opinion, indeed, were most other people of his acquaintance; we will, however, leave him at his entrance on this enterprise, and keep our attention fixed on our hero, whom we shall observe taking large strides towards the summit of human glory.

Wild, immediately at his return to town, went to pay a visit to Miss Lætitia Snap; for he had that weakness of suffering himself to be enslaved by women, so naturally incident to men of heroic disposition; to say the truth, it might more properly be called a slavery to his own appetite; for, could he have satisfied that, he had not cared three farthings what had become of the little tyrant for whom he professed so violent a regard. Here he was informed that Mr. Heartfree had been conveyed to Newgate the day before, the writ being then returnable. He was somewhat concerned at this news; not from any compassion for the misfortunes of Heartfree, whom he hated with such inveteracy that one would have imagined he had suffered the same injuries from him which he had done towards him. His concern, therefore, had another motive; in fact, he was uneasy at the place of Mr. Heartfree's confinement, as it was to be the scene of his future glory, and where consequently he should be frequently obliged to see a face which hatred, and not shame, made him detest the sight of.

To prevent this, therefore, several methods suggested themselves to him. At first he thought of removing him out of the way by the ordinary method of murder, which he doubted not but Fireblood would be very ready to execute; for that youth had, at their last interview, sworn, D——n his eyes, he thought there was no better pastime than blowing a man's brains out. But, besides the danger of this method, it did not look horrible nor barbarous enough for the last mischief which he should do to Heartfree. Considering, therefore, a little farther with himself, he at length came to a resolution to hang him, if possible, the very next session.

Now, though the observation—how apt men are to hate those they injure, or how unforgiving they are of the injuries they do themselves, be common enough, yet I do not remember to have ever seen the reason of this strange phenomenon as at first it appears. Know, therefore, reader, that with much and severe scrutiny we have discovered this hatred to be founded on the passion of fear, and to arise from an apprehension that the person whom we have ourselves greatly injured will use all possible endeavours to revenge and retaliate the injuries we have done him. An opinion so firmly established in bad and great minds (and those who confer injuries on others have seldom very good or mean ones) that no benevolence, nor even beneficence, on the injured side, can eradicate it. On the contrary, they refer all these acts of kindness to imposture and design of lulling their suspicion, till an opportunity offers of striking a surer and severer blow; and thus, while the good man who hath received it hath truly forgotten the injury, the evil mind which did it hath it in lively and fresh remembrance.

As we scorn to keep any discoveries secret from our readers, whose instruction, as well as diversion, we have greatly considered in this history, we have here digressed somewhat to communicate the following short lesson to those who are simple and well inclined: though as a Christian thou art obliged, and we advise thee, to forgive thy enemy, NEVER TRUST THE MAN WHO HATH REASON TO SUSPECT THAT YOU KNOW HE HATH INJURED YOU.

CHAPTER V

More and more GREATNESS, *unparalleled in history or romance*

IN order to accomplish this great and noble scheme, which the vast genius of Wild had contrived, the first necessary step was to regain the confidence of Heartfree. But, however necessary this was, it seemed to be attended with such insurmountable difficulties, that even our hero for some time despaired of success. He was greatly superior to all mankind in the steadiness of his countenance, but this undertaking seemed to require more of that noble quality than had ever been the portion of a mortal. However, at last he resolved to attempt it, and from his success I think we may fairly assert that what was said by the Latin poet of labour, that it conquers all things, is much more true when applied to impudence.

When he had formed his plan he went to Newgate, and burst resolutely into the presence of Heartfree, whom he eagerly embraced and kissed; and then, first arraigning his own rashness, and afterwards lamenting his unfortunate want of success, he acquainted him with the particulars of what had happened; concealing only that single incident of his attack on the other's wife, and his motive to the undertaking, which, he assured Heartfree, was a desire to preserve his effects from a statute of bankruptcy.

The frank openness of this declaration, with the composure of countenance with which it was delivered; his seeming only ruffled by the concern for his friend's misfortune; the probability of truth attending it, joined to the boldness and disinterested appearance of this visit, together with his many professions of immediate service at a time when he could not have the least visible motive from self-love; and above all, his offering him money, the last and surest token of friendship, rushed with such united force on the well-disposed heart, as it is vulgarly called, of this simple man, that they instantly staggered and soon subverted all the determination he had before made in prejudice of Wild, who, perceiving the balance to be turning in his favour, presently threw in a hundred imprecations on his own folly and ill-advised forwardness to serve his friend, which had thus unhappily produced his ruin; he added as many curses on the count, whom he vowed to pursue with revenge all over Europe; lastly, he cast in some grains of comfort, assuring Heartfree that his wife was fallen into the gentlest hands, that she would be carried no farther than Dunkirk, whence she might very easily be redeemed.

Heartfree, to whom the lightest presumption of his wife's fidelity would have been more delicious than the absolute restoration of all his jewels, and who, indeed, had with the utmost difficulty been brought to entertain the slightest suspicion of her inconstancy, immediately abandoned all distrust of both her and his friend, whose sincerity (luckily for Wild's purpose) seemed to him to depend on the same evidence. He then embraced our hero, who had in his countenance all the symptoms of the deepest concern, and begged him to be comforted; saying that the intentions, rather than the actions of men, conferred obligations; that as to the event of human affairs, it was governed either by chance or some superior agent; that friendship was concerned only in the direction of our designs; and suppose these failed of success, or produced an event never so contrary to their aim, the merit of a good intention was not in the least lessened, but was rather entitled to compassion.

Heartfree, however, was soon curious enough to inquire how Wild had escaped the captivity which his wife then suffered. Here, likewise, he recounted the whole truth, omitting only the motive to the French captain's cruelty, for which he assigned a very different reason, namely, his attempt to secure Heartfree's jewels. Wild, indeed, always kept as much truth as was possible in everything; and this he said was turning the cannon of the enemy upon themselves.

Wild, having thus with admirable and truly laudable conduct achieved the first step, began to discourse on the badness of the world, and particularly to blame the severity of creditors, who seldom or never attended to any unfortunate circumstances, but without mercy inflicted confinement on the debtor, whose body the law, with very unjustifiable rigour, delivered into their power. He added, that for his part, he looked on this restraint to be as heavy a punishment as any appointed by law for the greatest offenders. That the loss of liberty was, in his opinion, equal to, if not worse, than the loss of life; that he had always determined, if by any accident or misfortune he had been subjected to the former, he would run the greatest risk of the latter to rescue himself from it; which he said, if men did not want resolution, was always enough; for that it was ridiculous to conceive that two or three men could confine two or three hundred, unless the prisoners were either fools or cowards, especially when they were neither chained nor fettered. He went on in this manner till, perceiving the utmost attention in Heartfree, he ventured to propose to him an endeavour to make his escape, which he said might easily be executed; that he would himself raise a party in the prison, and that, if a murder or two should happen in the attempt, he (Heartfree) might keep free from any share either in the guilt or in the danger.

There is one misfortune which attends all great men and their schemes, viz. that, in order to carry them into execution, they are obliged, in proposing their purpose to their tools, to discover themselves to be of that disposition in which certain little writers have advised mankind to place no confidence; an advice which hath been sometimes taken. Indeed, many inconveniences arise to the said great men from these scribblers publishing without restraint their hints or alarms to society; and many great and glorious schemes have been thus frustrated; wherefore it were to be wished that in all well-regulated governments such liberties should be by some wholesome laws restrained, and all writers inhibited from venting any other instructions to the people than what should be first approved and licensed by the said great men, or their proper instruments or tools; by which means nothing would ever be published but what made for the advancing their most noble projects.

Heartfree, whose suspicions were again raised by this advice, viewing Wild with inconceivable disdain, spoke as follows: "There is one thing the loss of which I should deplore infinitely beyond that of liberty and of life also; I mean that of a good conscience; a blessing which he who possesses can never be thoroughly unhappy; for the bitterest potion of life is by this so sweetened, that it soon becomes palatable; whereas, without it, the most delicate enjoyments quickly lose all their relish, and life itself grows insipid, or rather nauseous, to us. Would you then lessen my misfortunes by robbing me of what hath been my only comfort under them, and on which I place my dependence of being relieved from them? I have read that Socrates refused to save his life by breaking the laws of his country, and departing from his prison when it was open. Perhaps my virtue would not go so far; but heaven forbid liberty should have such charms to tempt me to the perpetration of so horrid a crime as murder! As to the poor evasion of committing it by other hands, it might be useful indeed to those who seek only the escape from temporal punishment, but can be of no service to excuse me to that Being whom I chiefly fear offending; nay, it would greatly aggravate my guilt by so impudent an endeavour to impose upon Him, and by so wickedly involving others in my crime. Give me, therefore, no more advice of this kind; for this is my great comfort in all my afflictions, that it is in the power of no enemy to rob me of my conscience, nor will I ever be so much my own enemy as to injure it."

Though our hero heard all this with proper contempt, he made no direct answer, but endeavoured to evade his proposal as much as possible, which he did with admirable dexterity: this method of getting tolerably well off, when you are repulsed in your attack on a man's conscience, may be styled the art of retreating, in which the politician, as well as the general, hath sometimes a wonderful opportunity of displaying his great abilities in his profession.

Wild, having made this admirable retreat, and argued away all design of involving his friend in the guilt of murder, concluded, however, that he thought him rather too scrupulous in not attempting his escape; and then, promising to use all such means as the other would permit in his service, took his leave for the present. Heartfree, having indulged himself an hour with his children, repaired to rest, which he enjoyed quiet and undisturbed; whilst Wild, disdaining repose, sat up all night, consulting how he might bring about the final destruction of his friend, without being beholden to any assistance from himself, which he now despaired of procuring. With the result of these consultations we shall acquaint our reader in good time, but at present we have matters of much more consequence to relate to him.

CHAPTER VI

The event of Fireblood's adventure; and a treaty of marriage, which might have been concluded either at Smithfield or St. James's

FIREBLOOD returned from his enterprise unsuccessful. The gentleman happened to go home another way than he had intended; so that the whole design miscarried. Fireblood had indeed robbed the coach, and had wantonly discharged a pistol into it, which slightly wounded one of the passengers in the arm. The booty he met with was not very considerable, though much greater than that with which he acquainted Wild; for of eleven pounds in money, two silver watches, and a wedding-ring, he produced no more than two guineas and the ring, which he protested with numberless oaths was his whole booty. However, when an advertisement of the robbery was published, with a reward promised for the ring and the watches, Fireblood was obliged to confess the whole, and to acquaint our hero where he had pawned the watches; which Wild, taking the full value of them for his pains, restored to the right owner.

He did not fail catechizing his young friend on this occasion. He said he was sorry to see any of his gang guilty of a breach of honour; that without honour *priggery* was at an end; that if a *prig* had but honour he would overlook every vice in the world. "But, nevertheless," said he, "I will forgive you this time, as you are a hopeful lad; and I hope never afterwards to find you delinquent in this great point."

Wild had now brought his gang to great regularity: he was obeyed and feared by them all. He had likewise established an office, where all men who were robbed, paying the value only (or a little more) of their goods, might have them again. This was of notable use to several persons who had lost pieces of plate they had received from their grandmothers; to others who had a particular value for certain rings, watches, heads of canes, snuff-boxes, etc., for which they would not have taken twenty times as much as they were worth, either because they had them a little while or a long time, or that somebody else had had them before, or from some other such excellent reason, which often stamps a greater value on a toy than the great Bubble-boy himself would have the impudence to set upon it.

By these means he seemed in so promising a way of procuring a fortune, and was regarded in so thriving a light by all the gentlemen of his acquaintance, as by the keeper and turnkeys of Newgate, by Mr. Snap, and others of his occupation, that Mr. Snap one day, taking Mr. Wild the elder aside, very seriously proposed what they had often lightly talked over, a strict union between their families, by marrying his daughter Tishy to our hero.

This proposal was very readily accepted by the old gentleman, who promised to acquaint his son with it.

On the morrow on which this message was delivered, our hero, little dreaming of the happiness which, of its own accord, was advancing so near towards him, had called Fireblood to him; and, after informing that youth of the violence of his passion for the young lady, and assuring him what confidence he reposed in him and his honour, he dispatched him to Miss Tishy with the following letter; which we here insert, not only as we take it to be extremely curious, but to be a much better pattern for that epistolary kind of writing which is generally called love-letters than any to be found in the *academy of compliments*, and which we challenge all the beaus of our time to excel either in matter or spelling.

MOST DEIVINE and ADWHORABLE CRETURE,—I doubt not but those IIs, briter than the son, which have kindled such a flam in my hart, have likewise the faculty of seeing it. It would be the hiest preassumption to imagin you eggnorant of my loav. No, madam, I sollemly purtest, that of all the butys in the unaversal glob, there is none kapable of hateracting my IIs like you. Corts and pallaces would be to me deserts without your kumpany, and with it a wilderness would have more charms than haven itself. For I hope you will beleve me when I sware every place in the univarse is a haven with you. I am konvinced you must be sinsibel of my violent passion for you, which, if I endevored to hid it, would be as impossible as for you, or the son, to hid your buty's. I assure you I have not slept a wink since I had the hapness of seeing you last; therefore hop you will, out of Kumpassion, let me have the honour of seeing you this afternune; for I am, with the greatest adwhoration,

Most deivine creeture,
Iour most pessionate amirer,
Adwhorer, and slave,
JOHANATAN WYLD.

If the spelling of this letter be not so strictly orthographical, the reader will be pleased to remember that such a defect might be worthy of censure in a low and scholastic character, but can be no blemish in that sublime greatness of which we endeavour to raise a complete idea in this history. In which kind of composition spelling, or indeed any kind of human literature, hath never been thought a necessary ingredient; for if these sort of great personages can but complot and contrive their noble schemes, and hack and hew mankind sufficiently, there

will never be wanting fit and able persons who can spell
to record their praises. Again, if it should be observed
that the style of this letter doth not exactly correspond
with that of our hero's speeches, which we have here
recorded, we answer, it is sufficient if in these the historian
adheres faithfully to the matter, though he embellishes
the diction with some flourishes of his own eloquence,
without which the excellent speeches recorded in ancient
historians (particularly in Sallust) would have scarce been
found in their writings. Nay, even amongst the moderns,
famous as they are for elocution, it may be doubted whether
those inimitable harangues published in the monthly
magazines came literally from the mouths of the HURGOS,
etc., as they are there inserted, or whether we may not
rather suppose some historian of great eloquence hath
borrowed the matter only, and adorned it with those
rhetorical flowers for which many of the said HURGOS are
not so extremely eminent.

CHAPTER VII

*Matters preliminary to the marriage between
Mr. Jonathan Wild and the chaste Lætitia*

BUT to proceed with our history; Fireblood, having received
this letter, and promised on his honour, with many voluntary asseverations, to discharge his embassy faithfully,
went to visit the fair Lætitia. The lady, having opened
the letter and read it, put on an air of disdain, and told
Mr. Fireblood she could not conceive what Mr. Wild meant
by troubling her with his impertinence; she begged him to
carry the letter back again, saying, had she known from
whom it came, she would have been d—d before she had
opened it. "But with you, young gentleman," says she,
"I am not in the least angry. I am rather sorry that so
pretty a young man should be employed in such an errand."
She accompanied these words with so tender an accent and
so wanton a leer, that Fireblood, who was no backward
youth, began to take her by the hand, and proceeded so
warmly, that, to imitate his actions with the rapidity of
our narration, he in a few minutes ravished this fair creature,

or at least would have ravished her, if she had not, by a timely compliance, prevented him.

Fireblood, after he had ravished as much as he could, returned to Wild, and acquainted him, as far as any wise man would, with what had passed; concluding with many praises of the young lady's beauty, with whom, he said, if his honour would have permitted him, he should himself have fallen in love; but, d—n him if he would not sooner be torn in pieces by wild horses than even think of injuring his friend. He asserted indeed, and swore so heartily, that, had not Wild been so thoroughly convinced of the impregnable chastity of the lady, he might have suspected his success; however, he was, by these means, entirely satisfied of his friend's inclination towards his mistress.

Thus constituted were the love affairs of our hero, when his father brought him Mr. Snap's proposal. The reader must know very little of love, or indeed of anything else, if he requires any information concerning the reception which this proposal met with. *Not guilty* never sounded sweeter in the ears of a prisoner at the bar, nor the sound of a reprieve to one at the gallows, than did ever word of the old gentleman in the ears of our hero. He gave his father full power to treat in his name, and desired nothing more than expedition.

The old people now met, and Snap, who had information from his daughter of the violent passion of her lover, endeavoured to improve it to the best advantage, and would have not only declined giving her any fortune himself, but have attempted to cheat her of what she owed to the liberality of her relations, particularly of a pint silver caudle-cup, the gift of her grandmother. However, in this the young lady herself afterwards took care to prevent him. As to the old Mr. Wild, he did not sufficiently attend to all the designs of Snap, as his faculties were busily employed in designs of his own, to overreach (or, as others express it, to cheat) the said Mr. Snap, by pretending to give his son a whole number for a chair, when in reality he was entitled to a third only.

While matters were thus settling between the old folks the young lady agreed to admit Mr. Wild's visits, and, by degrees, began to entertain him with all the shew of affection which the great natural reserve of her temper, and the greater artificial reserve of her education, would permit. At length, everything being agreed between their parents, settlements made, and the lady's fortune (to wit, seventeen pounds and nine shillings in money and goods) paid down, the day for their nuptials was fixed, and they were celebrated accordingly.

Most private histories, as well as comedies, end at this period; the historian and the poet both concluding they have done enough for their hero when they have married him; or intimating rather that the rest of his life must be a dull calm of happiness, very delightful indeed to pass through, but somewhat insipid to relate; and matrimony in general must, I believe, without any dispute, be allowed to be this state of tranquil felicity, including so little variety, that, like Salisbury Plain, it affords only one prospect, a very pleasant one it must be confessed, but the same.

Now there was all the probability imaginable that this contract would have proved of such happy note, both from the great accomplishments of the young lady, who was thought to be possessed of every qualification necessary to make the marriage state happy, and from the truly ardent passion of Mr. Wild; but, whether it was that nature and fortune had great designs for him to execute, and would not suffer his vast abilities to be lost and sunk in the arms of a wife, or whether neither nature nor fortune had any hand in the matter, is a point I will not determine. Certain it is that this match did not produce that serene state we have mentioned above, but resembled the most turbulent and ruffled, rather than the most calm sea.

I cannot here omit a conjecture, ingenious enough, of a friend of mine, who had a long intimacy in the Wild family. He hath often told me he fancied one reason of the dissatisfactions which afterwards fell out between Wild and his lady, arose from the number of gallants to whom she had, before marriage, granted favours; for, says he, and indeed very probable it is too, the lady might expect from her husband what she had before received from several, and, being angry not to find one man as good as ten, she had, from that indignation, taken those steps which we cannot perfectly justify.

From this person I received the following dialogue, which he assured me he had overheard and taken down verbatim. It passed on the day fortnight after they were married.

CHAPTER VIII

A dialogue matrimonial, which passed between Jonathan Wild, Esq., and Lætitia his wife, on the morning of the day fortnight on which his nuptials were celebrated; which concluded more amicably than those debates generally do

JONATHAN. My dear, I wish you would lie a little longer in bed this morning.

Lætitia. Indeed I cannot; I am engaged to breakfast with Jack Strongbow.

Jonathan. I don't know what Jack Strongbow doth so often at my house. I assure you I am uneasy at it; for, though I have no suspicion of your virtue, yet it may injure your reputation in the opinion of my neighbours.

Lætitia. I don't trouble my head about my neighbours; and they shall no more tell me what company I am to keep than my husband shall.

Jonathan. A good wife would keep no company which made her husband uneasy.

Lætitia. You might have found one of those good wives, sir, if you had pleased; I had no objection to it.

Jonathan. I thought I had found one in you.

Lætitia. You did! I am very much obliged to you for thinking me so poor-spirited a creature; but I hope to convince you to the contrary. What, I suppose you took me for a raw senseless girl, who knew nothing what other married women do!

Jonathan. No matter what I took you for; I have taken you for better and worse.

Lætitia. And at your own desire too; for I am sure you never had mine. I should not have broken my heart if Mr. Wild had thought proper to bestow himself on any other more happy woman. Ha, ha!

Jonathan. I hope, madam, you don't imagine that was not in my power, or that I married you out of any kind of necessity.

Lætitia. O no, sir; I am convinced there are silly women enough. And far be it from me to accuse you of any necessity for a wife. I believe you could have been very well contented with the state of a bachelor; I have no reason to complain of your necessities; but that, you know, a woman cannot tell beforehand.

Jonathan. I can't guess what you would insinuate, for I believe no woman had ever less reason to complain of her husband's want of fondness.

Lætitia. Then some, I am certain, have great reason to complain of the price they give for them. But I know better things. (*These words were spoken with a very great air, and toss of the head.*)

Jonathan. Well, my sweeting, I will make it impossible for you to wish me more fond.

Lætitia. Pray, Mr. Wild, none of this nauseous behaviour, nor those odious words. I wish you were fond! I assure you, I don't know what you would pretend to insinuate of me. I have no wishes which misbecome a virtuous woman. No, nor should not, if I had married for love. And especially now, when nobody, I am sure, can suspect me of any such thing.

Jonathan. If you did not marry for love why did you marry?

Lætitia. Because it was convenient, and my parents forced me.

Jonathan. I hope, madam, at least, you will not tell me to my face you have made your convenience of me.

Lætitia. I have made nothing of you; nor do I desire the honour of making anything of you.

Jonathan. Yes, you have made a husband of me.

Lætitia. No, you made yourself so; for I repeat once more it was not my desire, but your own.

Jonathan. You should think yourself obliged to me for that desire.

Lætitia. La, sir! you was not so singular in it. I was not in despair. I have had other offers, and better too.

Jonathan. I wish you had accepted them with all my heart.

Lætitia. I must tell you, Mr. Wild, this is a very brutish manner in treating a woman to whom you have such obligations; but I know how to despise it, and to despise you too for shewing it me. Indeed, I am well enough paid for the foolish preference I gave to you. I flattered myself that I should at least have been used with good manners. I thought I had married a gentleman; but I find you every way contemptible and below my concern.

Jonathan. D—n you, madam, have I not the more reason to complain when you tell me you married for your convenience only?

Lætitia. Very fine truly. Is it behaviour worthy a man to swear at a woman? Yet why should I mention what comes from a wretch whom I despise?

Jonathan. Don't repeat that word so often. I despise you as heartily as you can me. And, to tell you a truth, I married you for my convenience likewise, to satisfy a passion which I have now satisfied, and you may be d—d for anything I care.

Lætitia. The world shall know how barbarously I am treated by such a villain.

Jonathan. I need take very little pains to acquaint the world what a b—ch you are, your actions will demonstrate it.

Lætitia. Monster! I would advise you not to depend too much on my sex, and provoke me too far; for I can do you a mischief, and will, if you dare use me so, you villain!

Jonathan. Begin whenever you please, madam; but assure yourself, the moment you lay aside the woman, I will treat you as such no longer; and if the first blow is yours, I promise you the last shall be mine.

Lætitia. Use me as you will; but d—n me if ever you shall use me as a woman again; for may I be cursed if ever I enter into your bed more.

Jonathan. May I be cursed if that abstinence be not the greatest obligation you can lay upon me; for I assure you faithfully your person was all I had ever any regard for; and that I now loathe and detest as much as ever I liked it.

Lætitia. It is impossible for two people to agree better; for I always detested your person; and as for any other regard, you must be convinced I never could have any for you.

Jonathan. Why, then, since we are come to a right understanding, as we are to live together, suppose we agreed, instead of quarrelling and abusing, to be civil to each other.

Lætitia. With all my heart.

Jonathan. Let us shake hands then, and henceforwards never live like man and wife; that is, never be loving nor ever quarrel.

Lætitia. Agreed. But pray, Mr. Wild, why b—ch? Why did you suffer such a word to escape you?

Jonathan. It is not worth your remembrance.

Lætitia. You agree I shall converse with whomsoever I please?

Jonathan. Without control? And I have the same liberty?

Lætitia. When I interfere may every curse you can wish attend me!

Jonathan. Let us now take a farewell kiss, and may I be hanged if it is not the sweetest you ever gave me.

Lætitia. But why b—ch? Methinks I should be glad to know why b—ch?

At which words he sprang from the bed, d—ing her temper heartily. She returned it again with equal abuse, which was continued on both sides while he was dressing. However, they agreed to continue steadfast in this new resolution; and the joy arising on that occasion at length dismissed them pretty cheerfully from each other, though Lætitia could not help concluding with the words, "Why b—ch?"

CHAPTER IX

Observations on the foregoing dialogue, together with a base design on our hero, which must be detested by every lover of GREATNESS

THUS did this dialogue (which, though we have termed it matrimonial, had indeed very little savour of the sweets of matrimony in it) produce at last a resolution more wise than strictly pious, and which, if they could have rigidly adhered to it, might have prevented some unpleasant moments as well to our hero as to his serene consort; but their hatred was so very great and unaccountable that they never could bear to see the least composure in one another's countenance without attempting to ruffle it. This set them on so many contrivances to plague and vex one another, that, as their proximity afforded them such frequent opportunities of executing their malicious purposes, they seldom passed one easy or quiet day together.

And this, reader, and no other, is the cause of those many inquietudes which thou must have observed to disturb the repose of some married couples who mistake implacable hatred for indifference; for why should Corvinus, who lives in a round of intrigue, and seldom doth, and never willingly would, dally with his wife, endeavour to prevent her from the satisfaction of an intrigue in her turn? Why doth Camilla refuse a more agreeable invitation abroad, only to expose her husband at his own table at home? In short, to mention no more instances, whence can all the quarrels, and jealousies, and jars proceed in people who have no love for each other, unless from that noble passion above mentioned, that desire, according to my Lady Betty Modish, of *curing each other of a smile*.

We thought proper to give our reader a short taste of the domestic state of our hero, the rather to shew him that great men are subject to the same frailties and inconveniences in ordinary life with little men, and that heroes are really of the same species with other human creatures, notwithstanding all the pains they themselves or their flatterers take to assert the contrary; and that they differ chiefly in the immensity of their greatness, or, as the vulgar erroneously call it, villainy. Now, therefore, that we may not dwell too long on low scenes in a history of the sublime kind, we shall return to actions of a higher note and more suitable to our purpose.

When the boy Hymen had, with his lighted torch, driven the boy Cupid out of doors, that is to say, in common phrase, when the violence of Mr. Wild's passion (or rather appetite) for the chaste Lætitia began to abate, he returned to visit his friend Heartfree, who was now in the liberties of the Fleet, and had appeared to the commission of bankruptcy against him. Here he met with a more cold reception than he himself had apprehended. Heartfree had long entertained suspicions of Wild, but these suspicions had from time to time been confounded with circumstances, and principally smothered with that amazing confidence which was indeed the most striking virtue in our hero. Heartfree was unwilling to condemn his friend without certain evidence, and laid hold on every probable semblance to acquit him; but the proposal made at his last visit had so totally blackened his character in this poor man's opinion, that it entirely fixed the wavering scale, and he no longer doubted but that our hero was one of the greatest villains in the world.

Circumstances of great improbability often escape men who devour a story with greedy ears; the reader, therefore, cannot wonder that Heartfree, whose passions were so variously concerned, first for the fidelity, and secondly for the safety of his wife; and, lastly, who was so distracted with doubt concerning the conduct of his friend, should at this relation pass unobserved the incident of his being committed to the boat by the captain of the privateer, which he had at the time of his telling so lamely accounted for; but now, when Heartfree came to reflect on the whole, and with a high prepossession against Wild, the absurdity of this fact glared in his eyes and struck him in the most sensible manner. At length a thought of great horror suggested itself to his imagination, and this was, whether the whole was not a fiction, and Wild, who was, as he had learned from his own mouth, equal to any undertaking how black soever, had not spirited away, robbed, and murdered his wife.

Intolerable as this apprehension was, he not only turned it round and examined it carefully in his own mind, but acquainted young Friendly with it at their next interview. Friendly, who detested Wild (from that envy probably with which these GREAT CHARACTERS naturally inspire low fellows), encouraged these suspicions so much, that Heartfree resolved to attach our hero and carry him before a magistrate.

This resolution had been some time taken, and Friendly, with a warrant and a constable, had with the utmost diligence searched several days for our hero; but, whether it was that in compliance with modern custom he had retired to spend the honeymoon with his bride, the only moon indeed in which it is fashionable or customary for the married parties to have any correspondence with each other; or perhaps his habitation might for particular reasons be usually kept a secret, like those of some few great men whom unfortunately the law hath left out of that reasonable as well as honourable provision which it hath made for the security of the persons of other great men.

But Wild resolved to perform works of supererogation in the way of honour, and, though, no hero is obliged to answer the challenge of my lord chief justice, or indeed of any other magistrate, but may with unblemished reputation slide away from it, yet such was the bravery, such the greatness, the magnanimity of Wild, that he appeared in person to it.

Indeed envy may say one thing, which may lessen the glory of this action, namely, that the said Mr. Wild knew nothing of the said warrant or challenge; and as thou mayest be assured, reader, that the malicious fury will omit nothing which can anyways sully so great a character, so she hath endeavoured to account for this second visit of our hero to his friend Heartfree from a very different motive than that of asserting his own innocence.

CHAPTER X

Mr. Wild with unprecedented generosity visits his friend Heartfree, and the ungrateful reception he met with

IT hath been said then that Mr. Wild, not being able on the strictest examination to find in a certain spot of human nature called his own heart the least grain of that pitiful low quality called honesty, had resolved, perhaps a little too generally, that there was no such thing. He, therefore, imputed the resolution with which Mr. Heartfree had so positively refused to concern himself in murder, either to a fear of bloodying his hands or the apprehension of a ghost, or lest he should make an additional example in that excellent book called *God's Revenge against Murder*; and doubted not but he would (at least in his present necessity) agree without scruple to a simple robbery, especially where any considerable booty should be proposed, and the safety of the attack plausibly made appear; which if he could prevail on him to undertake, he would immediately afterwards get him impeached, convicted, and hanged. He no sooner, therefore, had discharged his duties to Hymen, and heard that Heartfree had procured himself the liberties of the Fleet, than he resolved to visit him, and to propose a robbery with all the allurements of profit, ease, and safety.

This proposal was no sooner made than it was answered by Heartfree in the following manner:

"I might have hoped the answer which I gave to your

former advice would have prevented me from the danger of receiving a second affront of this kind. An affront I call it, and surely, if it be so to call a man a villain, it can be no less to shew him you suppose him one. Indeed, it may be wondered how any man can arrive at the boldness, I may say impudence, of first making such an overture to another; surely it is seldom done, unless to those who have previously betrayed some symptoms of their own baseness. If I have therefore shewn you any such, these insults are more pardonable; but I assure you, if such appear, they discharge all their malignance outwardly, and reflect not even a shadow within; for to me baseness seems inconsistent with this rule, OF DOING NO OTHER PERSON AN INJURY FROM ANY MOTIVE OR ON ANY CONSIDERATION WHATEVER. This, sir, is the rule by which I am determined to walk, nor can that man justify disbelieving me who will not own he walks not by it himself. But, whether it be allowed to me or no, or whether I feel the good effects of its being practised by others, I am resolved to maintain it; for surely no man can reap a benefit from my pursuing it equal to the comfort I myself enjoy: for what a ravishing thought, how replete with ecstasy, must the consideration be, that Almighty Goodness is by its own nature engaged to reward me! How indifferent must such a persuasion make a man to all the occurrences of this life! What trifles must he represent to himself both the enjoyments and the afflictions of this world! How easily must he acquiesce under missing the former, and how patiently will he submit to the latter, who is convinced that his failing of a transitory imperfect reward here is a most certain argument of his obtaining one permanent and complete hereafter! Dost thou think then, thou little, paltry, mean animal (with such language did he treat our truly great man), that I will forego such comfortable expectations for any pitiful reward which thou canst suggest or promise to me; for that sordid lucre for which all pains and labour are undertaken by the industrious, and all barbarities and iniquities committed by the vile; for a worthless acquisition, which such as thou art can possess, can give, or can take away?" The former part of this speech occasioned much yawning in our hero, but the latter roused his anger; and he was collecting his rage to answer, when Friendly and the constable, who had been summoned by Heartfree on Wild's first appearance, entered the room, and seized the great man just as his wrath was bursting from his lips.

The dialogue which now ensued is not worth relating: Wild was soon acquainted with the reason of this rough treatment, and presently conveyed before a magistrate.

Notwithstanding the doubts raised by Mr. Wild's lawyer on his examination, he insisting that the proceeding was improper, for that a *writ de homine replegiando* should issue, and on the return of that a *capias in withernam*, the justice inclined to commitment, so that Wild was driven to other methods for his defence. He, therefore, acquainted the justice that there was a young man likewise with him in the boat, and begged that he might be sent for, which request was accordingly granted, and the faithful Achates (Mr. Fireblood) was soon produced to bear testimony for his friend, which he did with so much becoming zeal, and went through his examination with such coherence (though he was forced to collect his evidence from the hints given him by Wild in the presence of the justice and the accusers), that, as here was direct evidence against mere presumption, our hero was most honourably acquitted, and poor Heartfree was charged by the justice, the audience, and all others who afterwards heard the story, with the blackest ingratitude, in attempting to take away the life of a man to whom he had such eminent obligations.

Lest so vast an effort of friendship as this of Fireblood's should too violently surprise the reader in this degenerate age, it may be proper to inform him that, beside the ties of engagement in the same employ, another nearer and stronger alliance subsisted between our hero and this youth, which latter was just departed from the arms of the lovely Lætitia when he received her husband's message; an instance which may also serve to justify those strict intercourses of love and acquaintance which so commonly subsist in modern history between the husband and gallant, displaying the vast force of friendship contracted by this more honourable than legal alliance, which is thought to be at present one of the strongest bonds of amity between great men, and the most reputable as well as easy way to their favour.

Four months had now passed since Heartfree's first confinement, and his affairs had begun to wear a more benign aspect; but they were a good deal injured by this

attempt on Wild (so dangerous is any attack on a GREAT
MAN), several of his neighbours, and particularly one or
two of his own trade, industriously endeavouring, from
their bitter animosity against such kind of iniquity, to
spread and exaggerate his ingratitude as much as possible;
not in the least scrupling, in the violent ardour of their
indignation, to add some small circumstances of their own
knowledge of the many obligations conferred on Heartfree
by Wild. To all these scandals he quietly submitted,
comforting himself in the consciousness of his own innocence, and confiding in time, the sure friend of justice,
to acquit him.

CHAPTER XI

*A scheme so deeply laid, that it shames all the politics of
this our age; with digression and subdigression*

WILD having now, to the hatred he bore Heartfree on
account of those injuries he had done him, an additional
spur from this injury received (for so it appeared to him,
who, no more than the most ignorant, considered how truly
he deserved it), applied his utmost industry to accomplish
the ruin of one whose very name sounded odious in his
ears; when luckily a scheme arose in his imagination which
not only promised to effect it securely, but (which pleased
him most) by means of the mischief he had already done
him; and which would at once load him with the imputation of having committed what he himself had done to
him, and would bring on him the severest punishment for
a fact of which he was not only innocent, but had already
so greatly suffered by. And this was no other than to
charge him with having conveyed away his wife, with his
most valuable effects, in order to defraud his creditors.

He no sooner started this thought than he immediately
resolved on putting it in execution. What remained to
consider was only the *quomodo*, and the person or tool to
be employed; for the stage of the world differs from that
in Drury Lane principally in this—that whereas, on the
latter, the hero or chief figure is almost continually before
your eyes, whilst the under-actors are not seen above once
in an evening; now, on the former, the hero or great man

is always behind the curtain, and seldom or never appears
or doth anything in his own person. He doth indeed, in
this GRAND DRAMA, rather perform the part of the prompter,
and doth instruct the well-drest figures, who are strutting
in public on the stage, what to say and do. To say the
truth, a puppet-show will illustrate our meaning better,
where it is the master of the show (the great man) who
dances and moves everything, whether it be the King of
Muscovy or whatever other potentate *alias* puppet which
we behold on the stage; but he himself keeps wisely out
of sight: for, should he once appear, the whole motion
would be at an end. Not that any one is ignorant of his
being there, or supposes that the puppets are not mere
sticks of wood, and he himself the sole mover; but as this
(though every one knows it) doth not appear visibly, i.e.
to their eyes, no one is ashamed of consenting to be imposed
upon; of helping on the drama, by calling the several sticks
or puppets by the names which the master hath allotted
to them, and by assigning to each the character which the
great man is pleased they shall move in, or rather in which
he himself is pleased to move them.

It would be to suppose thee, gentle reader, one of very
little knowledge in this world, to imagine thou hast never
seen some of these puppet-shows which are so frequently
acted on the great stage; but though thou shouldst have
resided all thy days in those remote parts of this island
which great men seldom visit, yet, if thou hast any penetra-
tion, thou must have had some occasions to admire both
the solemnity of countenance in the actor and the gravity
in the spectator, while some of those farces are carried on
which are acted almost daily in every village in the kingdom.
He must have a very despicable opinion of mankind indeed
who can conceive them to be imposed on as often as they
appear to be so. The truth is, they are in the same situation with the readers of romances; who, though they know
the whole to be one entire fiction, nevertheless agree to be
deceived; and, as these find amusement, so do the others
find ease and convenience in this concurrence. But, this
being a subdigression, I return to my digression.

A GREAT MAN ought to do his business by others; to
employ hands, as we have before said, to his purposes, and
keep himself as much behind the curtain as possible; and
though it must be acknowledged that two very great men,

whose names will be both recorded in history, did in these latter times come forth themselves on the stage, and did hack and hew and lay each other most cruelly open to the diversion of the spectators, yet this must be mentioned rather as an example of avoidance than imitation, and is to be ascribed to the number of those instances which serve to evince the truth of these maxims: *Nemo mortalium omnibus horis sapit. Ira furor brevis est*, etc.

CHAPTER XII

New instances of Friendly's folly, etc.

To return to my history, which, having rested itself a little, is now ready to proceed on its journey: Fireblood was the person chosen by Wild for this service. He had, on a late occasion, experienced the talents of this youth for a good round perjury. He immediately, therefore, found him out, and proposed it to him; when, receiving his instant assent, they consulted together, and soon framed an evidence, which, being communicated to one of the most bitter and severe creditors of Heartfree, by him laid before a magistrate, and attested by the oath of Fireblood, the justice granted his warrant; and Heartfree was accordingly apprehended and brought before him.

When the officers came for this poor wretch they found him meanly diverting himself with his little children, the younger of whom sat on his knees, and the elder was playing at a little distance from him with Friendly. One of the officers, who was a very good sort of a man, but one very laudably severe in his office, after acquainting Heartfree with his errand, bade him come along and be d—d, and leave those little bastards, for so, he said, he supposed they were, for a legacy to the parish. Heartfree was much surprised at hearing there was a warrant for felony against him; but he shewed less concern than Friendly did in his countenance. The elder daughter, when she saw the officer lay hold on her father, immediately quitted her play, and, running to him and bursting into tears, cried out: "You shall not hurt poor papa." One of the other ruffians offered to take the little one rudely from his knees; but Heartfree started up, and, catching the fellow by the collar, dashed his head so violently against the wall, that, had he had any brains, he might possibly have lost them by the blow.

The officer, like most of those heroic spirits who insult men in adversity, had some prudence mixt with his zeal for justice. Seeing, therefore, this rough treatment of his companion, he began to pursue more gentle methods, and very civilly desired Mr. Heartfree to go with him, seeing he was an officer, and obliged to execute his warrant; that he was sorry for his misfortune, and hoped he would be acquitted. The other answered: "He should patiently submit to the laws of his country, and would attend him whither he was ordered to conduct him"; then, taking leave of his children with a tender kiss, he recommended them to the care of Friendly, who promised to see them safe home, and then to attend him at the justice's, whose name and abode he had learned of the constable.

Friendly arrived at the magistrate's house just as that gentleman had signed the mittimus against his friend; for the evidence of Fireblood was so clear and strong, and the justice was so incensed against Heartfree, and so convinced of his guilt, that he would hardly hear him speak in his own defence, which the reader perhaps, when he hears the evidence against him, will be less inclined to censure; for this witness deposed: "That he had been, by Heartfree himself, employed to carry the orders of embezzling to Wild, in order to be delivered to his wife; that he had been afterwards present with Wild and her at the inn when they took coach for Harwich, where she shewed him the casket of jewels, and desired him to tell her husband that she had fully executed his command"; and this he swore to have been done after Heartfree had notice of the commission, and, in order to bring it within that time, Fireblood, as well as Wild, swore that Mrs. Heartfree lay several days concealed at Wild's house before her departure for Holland.

When Friendly found the justice obdurate, and that all he could say had no effect, nor was it any way possible for Heartfree to escape being committed to Newgate, he resolved to accompany him thither; where, when they arrived, the turnkey would have confined Heartfree (he having no money) amongst the common felons; but Friendly would not permit it, and advanced every shilling he had in his pocket, to procure a room in the press-yard for his friend, which indeed, through the humanity of the keeper, he did at a cheap rate.

They spent that day together, and in the evening the prisoner dismissed his friend, desiring him, after many thanks for his fidelity, to be comforted on his account. "I know not," says he, "how far the malice of my enemy may prevail; but whatever my sufferings are, I am convinced my innocence will somewhere be rewarded. If, therefore, any fatal accident should happen to me (for he who is in the hands of perjury may apprehend the worst), my dear Friendly, be a father to my poor children"; at which words the tears gushed from his eyes. The other begged him not to admit any such apprehensions, for that he would employ his utmost diligence in his service, and doubted not but to subvert any villainous design laid for his destruction, and to make his innocence appear to the world as white as it was in his own opinion.

We cannot help mentioning a circumstance here, though we doubt it will appear very unnatural and incredible to our reader; which is, that, notwithstanding the former character and behaviour of Heartfree, this story of his embezzling was so far from surprising his neighbours, that many of them declared they expected no better from him. Some were assured he could pay forty shillings in the pound if he would. Others had overheard hints formerly pass between him and Mrs. Heartfree which had given them suspicions. And what is most astonishing of all is, that many of those who had before censured him for an extravagant, heedless fool, now no less confidently abused him for a cunning, tricking, avaricious knave.

CHAPTER XIII

Something concerning Fireblood which will surprise; and somewhat touching one of the Miss Snaps, which will greatly concern the reader

HOWEVER, notwithstanding all these censures abroad, and in despite of all his misfortunes at home, Heartfree in Newgate enjoyed a quiet, undisturbed repose; while our hero, nobly disdaining rest, lay sleepless all night, partly from the apprehensions of Mrs. Heartfree's return before he had executed his scheme, and partly from a suspicion lest Fireblood should betray him; of whose infidelity he had, nevertheless, no other cause to maintain any fear, but from his knowing him to be an accomplished rascal, as the vulgar term it, a complete GREAT MAN in our language. And indeed, to confess the truth, these doubts were not without some foundation; for the very same thought unluckily entered the head of that noble youth, who considered whether he might not possibly sell himself for some advantage to the other side, as he had yet no promise from Wild; but this was, by the sagacity of the latter, prevented in the morning with a profusion of promises, which shewed him to be of the most generous temper in the world, with which Fireblood was extremely well satisfied, and made use of so many protestations of his faithfulness that he convinced Wild of the justice of his suspicions.

At this time an accident happened, which, though it did not immediately affect our hero, we cannot avoid relating, as it occasioned great confusion in his family, as well as in the family of Snap. It is indeed a calamity highly to be lamented, when it stains untainted blood, and happens to an honourable house—an injury never to be repaired—a blot never to be wiped out—a sore never to be healed. To detain my reader no longer, Miss Theodosia Snap was now safely delivered of a male infant, the product of an amour which that beautiful (O that I could say virtuous!) creature had with the count.

Mr. Wild and his lady were at breakfast when Mr. Snap, with all the agonies of despair both in his voice and countenance, brought them this melancholy news. Our hero, who had (as we have said) wonderful good-nature when his greatness or interest was not concerned, instead of reviling his sister-in-law, asked with a smile: "Who was the father?" But the chaste Lætitia, we repeat the chaste, for well did she now deserve that epithet, received it in another manner. She fell into the utmost fury at the relation, reviled her sister in the bitterest terms, and vowed she would never see nor speak to her more; then burst into tears and lamented over her father that such dishonour should ever happen to him and herself. At length she fell severely on her husband for the light treatment which he gave this fatal accident. She told him he was unworthy of the honour he enjoyed of marrying into a chaste family. That she looked on it as an affront to her virtue. That if he had married one of the naughty hussies of the town he could have behaved to her in no other manner. She concluded with desiring her father to make an example of the slut, and to turn her out of doors; for that she would not otherwise enter his house, being resolved never to set her foot within the same threshold with the trollop, whom she detested so much the more because (which was perhaps true) she was her own sister.

So violent, and indeed so outrageous, was this chaste lady's love of virtue, that she could not forgive a single slip (indeed the only one Theodosia had ever made) in her own sister, in a sister who loved her, and to whom she owed a thousand obligations.

Perhaps the severity of Mr. Snap, who greatly felt the injury done to the honour of his family, would have relented, had not the parish-officers been extremely pressing on this occasion, and for want of security, conveyed the unhappy young lady to a place, the name of which, for the honour of the Snaps, to whom our hero was so nearly allied, we bury in eternal oblivion; where she suffered so much correction for her crime, that the good-natured reader of the male kind may be inclined to compassionate her, at least to imagine she was sufficiently punished for a fault which, with submission to the chaste Lætitia and all other strictly virtuous ladies, it should be either less criminal in a woman to commit, or more so in a man to solicit her to it.

But to return to our hero, who was a living and strong instance that human greatness and happiness are not always inseparable. He was under a continual alarm of frights, and fears, and jealousies. He thought every man he beheld wore a knife for his throat, and a pair of scissors for his purse. As for his own gang particularly, he was thoroughly convinced there was not a single man amongst them who would not, for the value of five shillings, bring him to the gallows. These apprehensions so constantly broke his rest, and kept him so assiduously on his guard to frustrate and circumvent any designs which might be formed against him, that his condition, to any other than the glorious eye of ambition, might seem rather deplorable than the object of envy or desire.

CHAPTER XIV

*In which our hero makes a speech well worthy to be celebrated;
and the behaviour of one of the gang, perhaps more
unnatural than any other part of this history*

THERE was in the gang a man named Blueskin, one of those
merchants who trade in dead oxen, sheep, etc., in short,
what the vulgar call a butcher. This gentleman had two
qualities of a great man, viz. undaunted courage, and an
absolute contempt of those ridiculous distinctions of *meum*
and *tuum*, which would cause endless disputes did not the
law happily decide them by converting both into *suum*.
The common form of exchanging property by trade seemed
to him too tedious; he, therefore, resolved to quit the
mercantile profession, and, falling acquainted with some of
Mr. Wild's people, he provided himself with arms, and
enlisted of the gang; in which he behaved for some time
with great decency and order, and submitted to accept
such share of the booty with the rest as our hero allotted him.

But this subserviency agreed ill with his temper; for
we should have before remembered a third heroic quality,
namely, ambition, which was no inconsiderable part of his
composition. One day, therefore, having robbed a gentleman at Windsor of a gold watch, which, on its being
advertised in the newspapers, with a considerable reward,
was demanded of him by Wild, he peremptorily refused to
deliver it.

"How, Mr. Blueskin!" says Wild; "you will not deliver
the watch?" "No, Mr. Wild," answered he; "I have
taken it, and will keep it; or, if I dispose of it, I will dispose
of it myself, and keep the money for which I sell it."
"Sure," replied Wild, "you have not the assurance to
pretend you have any property or right in this watch?"
"I am certain," returned Blueskin, "whether I have any
right in it or no, you can prove none." "I will undertake,"
cries the other, "to shew I have an absolute right to it, and
that by the laws of our gang, of which I am providentially
at the head." "I know not who put you at the head of it,"
cries Blueskin; "but those who did certainly did it for their
own good, that you might conduct them the better in their
robberies, inform them of the richest booties, prevent

surprises, pack juries, bribe evidence, and so contribute to
their benefit and safety; and not to convert all their labour
and hazard to your own benefit and advantage." "You
are greatly mistaken, sir," answered Wild; "you are talking
of a legal society, where the chief magistrate is always
chosen for the public good, which, as we see in all the
legal societies of the world, he constantly consults, daily
contributing, by his superior skill, to their prosperity, and
not sacrificing their good to his own wealth, or pleasure,
or humour: but in an illegal society or gang, as this of ours,
it is otherwise; for who would be at the head of a gang,
unless for his own interest? And without a head, you know,
you cannot subsist. Nothing but a head, and obedience
to that head, can preserve a gang a moment from destruction. It is absolutely better for you to content yourselves
with a moderate reward, and enjoy that in safety at the
disposal of your chief, than to engross the whole with the
hazard to which you will be liable without his protection.
And surely there is none in the whole gang who hath less
reason to complain than you; you have tasted of my
favours; witness that piece of ribbon you wear in your hat,
with which I dubbed you captain. Therefore pray, captain,
deliver the watch." "D—n your cajoling," says Blueskin: "do you think I value myself on this bit of ribbon,
which I could have bought myself for sixpence, and have
worn without your leave? Do you imagine I think myself
a captain because you, whom I know not empowered to
make one, call me so? The name of captain is but a
shadow: the men and the salary are the substance; and
I am not to be bubbled with a shadow. I will be called
captain no longer, and he who flatters me by that name
I shall think affronts me, and I will knock him down,
I assure you." "Did ever man talk so unreasonably?"
cries Wild. "Are you not respected as a captain by the
whole gang since my dubbing you so? But it is the
shadow only, it seems; and you will knock a man down
for affronting you who calls you captain! Might not a
man as reasonably tell a minister of state: *Sir, you have
given me the shadow only? The ribbon or the bauble that you
gave me implies that I have either signalized myself, by some
great action, for the benefit and glory of my country, or at
least that I am descended from those who have done so. I
know myself to be a scoundrel, and so have been those few*

*ancestors I can remember, or have ever heard of. Therefore
I am resolved to knock the first man down who calls me sir or
right honourable.* But all great and wise men think themselves sufficiently repaid by what procures them honour
and precedence in the gang, without enquiring into substance; nay, if a title or a feather be equal to this purpose,
they are substance, and not mere shadows. But I have
not time to argue with you at present, so give me the
watch without any more deliberation." "I am no more a
friend to deliberation than yourself," answered Blueskin,
"and so I tell you, once for all, by G— I will never give
you the watch, no, nor will I ever hereafter surrender any
part of my booty. I won it, and I will wear it. Take
your pistols yourself, and go out on the highway and
don't lazily think to fatten yourself with the dangers and
pains of other people." At which words he departed in
a fierce mood, and repaired to the tavern used by the gang,
where he had appointed to meet some of his acquaintance,
whom he informed of what had passed between him and
Wild, and advised them all to follow his example; which
they all readily agreed to, and Mr. Wild's d—tion was the
universal toast; in drinking bumpers to which they had
finished a large bowl of punch, when a constable, with a
numerous attendance, and Wild at their head, entered the
room and seized on Blueskin, whom his companions, when
they saw our hero, did not dare attempt to rescue. The
watch was found upon him, which, together with Wild's
information, was more than sufficient to commit him to
Newgate.

In the evening Wild and the rest of those who had been
drinking with Blueskin met at the tavern, where nothing
was to be seen but the profoundest submission to their
leader. They vilified and abused Blueskin, as much as
they had before abused our hero, and now repeated the
same toast, only changing the name of Wild into that of
Blueskin; all agreeing with Wild that the watch found in
his pocket, and which must be a fatal evidence against
him, was a just judgment on his disobedience and revolt.

Thus did this great man by a resolute and timely example
(for he went directly to the justice when Blueskin left him)
quell one of the most dangerous conspiracies which could
possibly arise in a gang, and which, had it been permitted
one day's growth, would inevitably have ended in his

destruction; so much doth it behove all great men to be eternally on their guard, and expeditious in the execution of their purposes; while none but the weak and honest can indulge themselves in remissness or repose.

The Achates, Fireblood, had been present at both these meetings; but, though he had a little too hastily concurred in cursing his friend, and in vowing his perdition, yet now he saw all that scheme dissolved he returned to his integrity, of which he gave an incontestable proof, by informing Wild of the measures which had been concerted against him, in which he said he had pretended to acquiesce, in order the better to betray them; but this, as he afterwards confessed on his deathbed at Tyburn, was only a copy of his countenance; for that he was, at that time, as sincere and hearty in his opposition to Wild as any of his companions.

Our hero received Fireblood's information with a very placid countenance. He said, as the gang had seen their errors, and repented, nothing was more noble than forgiveness. But, though he was pleased modestly to ascribe this to his lenity, it really arose from much more noble and political principles. He considered that it would be dangerous to attempt the punishment of so many; besides, he flattered himself that fear would keep them in order: and indeed Fireblood had told him nothing more than he knew before, viz. that they were all complete prigs, whom he was to govern by their fears, and in whom he was to place no more confidence than was necessary, and to watch them with the utmost caution and circumspection: for a rogue, he wisely said, like gunpowder, must be used with caution; since both are altogether as liable to blow up the party himself who uses them as to execute his mischievous purpose against some other person or animal.

We will now repair to Newgate, it being the place where most of the great men of this history are hastening as fast as possible; and, to confess the truth, it is a castle very far from being an improper or misbecoming habitation for any great man whatever. And as this scene will continue during the residue of our history, we shall open it with a new book, and shall therefore take this opportunity of closing our third.

BOOK IV

CHAPTER I

*A sentiment of the ordinary's, worthy to be written in letters
of gold; a very extraordinary instance of folly in Friendly,
and a dreadful accident which befell our hero*

HEARTFREE had not been long in Newgate before his
frequent conversation with his children, and other instances
of a good heart, which betrayed themselves in his actions
and conversation, created an opinion in all about him that
he was one of the silliest fellows in the universe. The
ordinary himself, a very sagacious as well as very worthy
person, declared that he was a cursed rogue, but no
conjurer.

What indeed might induce the former, i.e. the roguish
part of this opinion in the ordinary, was a wicked sentiment
which Heartfree one day disclosed in conversation, and
which we, who are truly orthodox, will not pretend to
justify, that he believed a sincere Turk would be saved.
To this the good man, with becoming zeal and indignation,
answered, "I know not what may become of a sincere
Turk; but, if this be your persuasion, I pronounce it impossible you should be saved. No, sir; so far from a sincere
Turk's being within the pale of salvation, neither will
any sincere Presbyterian, Anabaptist, nor Quaker whatever,
be saved."

But neither did the one nor the other part of this character
prevail on Friendly to abandon his old master. He spent
his whole time with him, except only those hours when he
was absent for his sake, in procuring evidence for him
against his trial, which was now shortly to come on. Indeed
this young man was the only comfort, besides a clear
conscience and the hopes beyond the grave, which this poor
wretch had; for the sight of his children was like one of
those alluring pleasures which men in some diseases indulge
themselves often fatally in, which at once flatter and
heighten their malady.

Friendly being one day present while Heartfree was, with tears in his eyes, embracing his eldest daughter, and lamenting the hard fate to which he feared he should be obliged to leave her, spoke to him thus: "I have long observed with admiration the magnanimity with which you go through your own misfortunes, and the steady countenance with which you look on death. I have observed that all your agonies arise from the thoughts of parting with your children, and of leaving them in a distrest condition; now, though I hope all your fears will prove ill grounded, yet, that I may relieve you as much as possible from them, be assured that, as nothing can give me more real misery than to observe so tender and loving a concern in a master, to whose goodness I owe so many obligations, and whom I so sincerely love, so nothing can afford me equal pleasure with my contributing to lessen or to remove it. Be convinced, therefore, if you can place any confidence in my promise, that I will employ my little fortune, which you know to be not entirely inconsiderable, in the support of this your little family. Should any misfortune, which I pray Heaven avert, happen to you before you have better provided for these little ones, I will be myself their father, nor shall either of them ever know distress if it be any way in my power to prevent it. Your younger daughter I will provide for, and as for my little prattler, your elder, as I never yet thought of any woman for a wife, I will receive her as such at your hands; nor will I ever relinquish her for another." Heartfree flew to his friend, and embraced him with raptures of acknowledgment. He vowed to him that he had eased every anxious thought of his mind but one, and that he must carry with him out of the world. "O Friendly!" cried he, "it is my concern for that best of women, whom I hate myself for having ever censured in my opinion. O Friendly! thou didst know her goodness; yet, sure, her perfect character none but myself was ever acquainted with. She had every perfection, both of mind and body, which Heaven hath indulged to her whole sex, and possessed all in a higher excellence than nature ever indulged to another in any single virtue. Can I bear the loss of such a woman? Can I bear the apprehensions of what mischiefs that villain may have done to her, of which death is perhaps the lightest?" Friendly gently interrupted him as soon as he saw any opportunity, endeavouring to comfort him on this head likewise, by magnifying every circumstance which could possibly afford any hopes of his seeing her again.

By this kind of behaviour, in which the young man exemplified so uncommon an height of friendship, he had soon obtained in the castle the character of as odd and silly a fellow as his master. Indeed they were both the byword, laughing-stock, and contempt of the whole place.

The sessions now came on at the Old Bailey. The grand jury at Hicks's Hall had found the bill of indictment against Heartfree, and on the second day of the session he was brought to his trial; where, notwithstanding the utmost efforts of Friendly and the honest old female servant, the circumstances of the fact corroborating the evidence of Fireblood, as well as that of Wild, who counterfeited the most artful reluctance at appearing against his old friend Heartfree, the jury found the prisoner guilty.

Wild had now accomplished his scheme; for as to what remained, it was certainly unavoidable, seeing that Heartfree was entirely void of interest with the great, and was besides convicted on a statute the infringers of which could hope no pardon.

The catastrophe to which our hero had reduced this wretch was so wonderful an effort of greatness, that it probably made Fortune envious of her own darling; but whether it was from this envy, or only from that known inconstancy and weakness so often and judiciously remarked in that lady's temper, who frequently lifts men to the summit of human greatness, only

ut lapsu graviore ruant ;

certain it is, she now began to meditate mischief against Wild, who seems to have come to that period at which all heroes have arrived, and which she was resolved they never should transcend. In short, there seems to be a certain measure of mischief and iniquity which every great man is to fill up, and then Fortune looks on him of no more use than a silkworm whose bottom is spun, and deserts him. Mr. Blueskin was convicted the same day of robbery, by our hero, an unkindness which, though he had drawn on himself, and necessitated him to, he took greatly amiss: as Wild, therefore, was standing near him, with that disregard and indifference which great men are too carelessly inclined to have for those whom they have ruined, Blue-skin, privily drawing a knife, thrust the same into the body of our hero with such violence, that all who saw it concluded he had done his business. And, indeed, had not Fortune, not so much out of love to our hero as from a fixed resolution to accomplish a certain purpose, of which we have formerly given a hint, carefully placed his guts out of the way, he must have fallen a sacrifice to the wrath of his enemy, which, as he afterwards said, he did not deserve; for, had he been contented to have robbed and only submitted to give him the booty, he might have still continued safe and unimpeached in the gang; but, so it was, that the knife, missing those noble parts (the noblest of many) the guts, perforated only the hollow of his belly, and caused no other harm than an immoderate effusion of blood, of which, though it at present weakened him, he soon after recovered.

This accident, however, was in the end attended with worse consequences: for, as very few people (those greatest of all men, absolute princes, excepted) attempt to cut the thread of human life, like the fatal sisters, merely out of wantonness and for their diversion, but rather by so doing propose to themselves the acquisition of some future good, or the avenging some past evil; and as the former of these motives did not appear probable, it put inquisitive persons on examining into the latter. Now, as the vast schemes of Wild, when they were discovered, however great in their nature, seemed to some persons, like the projects of most other such persons, rather to be calculated for the glory of the great man himself than to redound to the general good of society, designs began to be laid by several of those who thought it principally their duty to put a stop to the future progress of our hero; and a learned judge particularly, a great enemy to this kind of greatness, procured a clause in an Act of Parliament as a trap for Wild, which he soon after fell into. By this law it was made capital in a prig to steal with the hands of other people. A law so plainly calculated for the destruction of all priggish greatness, that it was indeed impossible for our hero to avoid it.

CHAPTER II

A short hint concerning popular ingratitude. Mr. Wild's arrival in the castle, with other occurrences to be found in no other history

IF we had any leisure we would here digress a little on that ingratitude which so many writers have observed to spring up in the people in all free governments towards their great men; who, while they have been consulting the good of the public, by raising their own greatness, in which the whole body (as the kingdom of France thinks itself in the glory of their grand monarch) was so deeply concerned, have been sometimes sacrificed by those very people for whose glory the said great men were so industriously at work: and this from a foolish zeal for a certain ridiculous imaginary thing called liberty, to which great men are observed to have a great animosity.

This law had been promulgated a very little time when Mr. Wild, having received from some dutiful members of the gang a valuable piece of goods, did, for a consideration somewhat short of its original price, re-convey it to the right owner; for which fact, being ungratefully informed against by the said owner, he was surprised in his own house, and, being overpowered by numbers, was hurried before a magistrate, and by him committed to that castle, which, suitable as it is to greatness, we do not choose to name too often in our history, and where many great men at this time happened to be assembled.

The governor, or, as the law more honourably calls him, keeper of this castle, was Mr. Wild's old friend and acquaintance. This made the latter greatly satisfied with the place of his confinement, as he promised himself not only a kind reception and handsome accommodation there, but even to obtain his liberty from him if he thought it necessary to desire it: but, alas! he was deceived; his old friend knew him no longer, and refused to see him, and the lieutenant-governor insisted on as high garnish for fetters, and as exorbitant a price for lodging, as if he had had a fine gentleman in custody for murder, or any other genteel crime.

To confess a melancholy truth, it is a circumstance much

to be lamented, that there is no absolute dependence on the friendship of great men; an observation which hath been frequently made by those who have lived in courts, or in Newgate, or in any other place set apart for the habitation of such persons.

The second day of his confinement he was greatly surprised at receiving a visit from his wife; and much more so, when, instead of a countenance ready to insult him, the only motive to which he could ascribe her presence, he saw the tears trickling down her lovely cheeks. He embraced her with the utmost marks of affection, and declared he could hardly regret his confinement, since it had produced such an instance of the happiness he enjoyed in her, whose fidelity to him on this occasion would, he believed, make him the envy of most husbands, even in Newgate. He then begged her to dry her eyes, and be comforted; for that matters might go better with him than she expected. "No, no," says she, "I am certain you would be found guilty. *Death.* I knew what it would always come to. I told you it was impossible to carry on such a trade long; but you would not be advised, and now you see the consequence—now you repent when it is too late. All the comfort I shall have when you are *nubbed* [1] is, that I gave you a good advice. If you had always gone out by yourself, as I would have had you, you might have robbed on to the end of the chapter; but you was wiser than all the world, or rather lazier, and see what your laziness is come to—to the *cheat,* [2] for thither you will go now, that's infallible. And a just judgment on you for following your headstrong will; I am the only person to be pitied; poor I, who shall be scandalized for your fault. *There goes she whose husband was hanged:* methinks I hear them crying so already." At which words she burst into tears. He could not then forbear chiding her for this unnecessary concern on his account, and begged her not to trouble him any more. She answered with some spirit: "On your account, and be d—d to you! No, if the old cull of a justice had not sent me hither, I believe it would have been long enough before I should have come hither to see after you; d—n me, I am committed for the *filing-lay,* [3] man, and we shall be both *nubbed* together. I' faith, my dear, it almost makes me amends for being *nubbed* myself,

---

[1] The cant word for hanging.   [2] The gallows.   [3] Picking pockets.

to have the pleasure of seeing thee *nubbed* too." "Indeed, my dear," answered Wild, "it is what I have long wished for thee; but I do not desire to bear thee company, and I have still hopes to have the pleasure of seeing you go without me; at least I will have the pleasure to be rid of you now." And so saying, he seized her by the waist, and with strong arm flung her out of the room; but not before she had with her nails left a bloody memorial on his cheek: and thus this fond couple parted.

Wild had scarce recovered himself from the uneasiness into which this unwelcome visit, proceeding from the disagreeable fondness of his wife, had thrown him, than the faithful Achates appeared. The presence of this youth was indeed a cordial to his spirits. He received him with open arms, and expressed the utmost satisfaction in the fidelity of his friendship, which so far exceeded the fashion of the times, and said many things which we have forgot on the occasion; but we remember they all tended to the praise of Fireblood, whose modesty, at length, put a stop to the torrent of compliments, by asserting he had done no more than his duty, and that he should have detested himself could he have forsaken his friend in his adversity; and, after many protestations that he came the moment he heard of his misfortune, he asked him if he could be of any service. Wild answered, since he had so kindly proposed that question, he must say he should be obliged to him if he could lend him a few guineas; for that he was very *seedy*. Fireblood replied that he was greatly unhappy in not having it then in his power, adding many hearty oaths that he had not a farthing of money in his pocket, which was, indeed, strictly true; for he had only a bank-note, which he had that evening purloined from a gentleman in the playhouse passage. He then asked for his wife, to whom, to speak truly, the visit was intended, her confinement being the misfortune of which he had just heard; for, as for that of Mr. Wild himself, he had known it from the first minute, without ever intending to trouble him with his company. Being informed, therefore, of the visit which had lately happened, he reproved Wild for his cruel treatment of that good creature; then taking as sudden a leave as he civilly could of the gentleman, he hastened to comfort his lady, who received him with great kindness.

CHAPTER III

Curious anecdotes relating to the history of Newgate

THERE resided in the castle at the same time with Mr. Wild one Roger Johnson, a very GREAT MAN, who had long been at the head of all the *prigs* in Newgate, and had raised contributions on them. He examined into the nature of their defence, procured and instructed their evidence, and made himself, at least in their opinion, so necessary to them, that the whole fate of Newgate seemed entirely to depend upon him.

Wild had not been long in confinement before he began to oppose this man. He represented him to the *prigs* as a fellow who, under the plausible pretence of assisting their causes, was in reality undermining THE LIBERTIES OF NEWGATE. He at first threw out certain sly hints and insinuations; but, having by degrees formed a party against Roger, he one day assembled them together, and spoke to them in the following florid manner:

"Friends and fellow-citizens,—The cause which I am to mention to you this day is of such mighty importance, that when I consider my own small abilities, I tremble with an apprehension lest your safety may be rendered precarious by the weakness of him who hath undertaken to represent to you your danger. Gentlemen, the liberty of Newgate is at stake; your privileges have been long undermined, and are now openly violated by one man; by one who hath engrossed to himself the whole conduct of your trials, under colour of which he exacts what contributions on you he pleases; but are those sums appropriated to the uses for which they are raised? Your frequent convictions at the Old Bailey, those depredations of justice, must too sensibly and sorely demonstrate the contrary. What evidence doth he ever produce for the prisoner which the prisoner himself could not have provided, and often better instructed? How many noble youths have there been lost when a single *alibi* would have saved them! Should I be silent, nay, could your own injuries want a tongue to remonstrate, the very breath which by his neglect hath been stopped at the *cheat* would cry out loudly against him. Nor is the exorbitancy of his plunders visible only in the dreadful consequences it hath produced to the *prigs*, nor glares it only in the miseries brought on them: it blazes forth in the more desirable effects it hath wrought for himself, in the rich perquisites acquired by it: witness that silk nightgown, that robe of shame, which, to his eternal dishonour, he publicly wears; that gown which I will not scruple to call the winding-sheet of the liberties of Newgate. Is there a *prig* who hath the interest and honour of Newgate so little at heart that he can refrain from blushing when he beholds that trophy, purchased with the breath of so many *prigs*? Nor is this all. His waistcoat embroidered with silk, and his velvet cap, bought with the same price, are ensigns of the same disgrace. Some would think the rags which covered his nakedness when first he was committed hither well exchanged for these gaudy trappings; but in my eye no exchange can be profitable when dishonour is the condition. If, therefore, Newgate——" Here the only copy which we could procure of this speech breaks off abruptly; however, we can assure the reader, from very authentic information, that he concluded with advising the *prigs* to put their affairs into other hands. After which, one of his party, as had been before concerted, in a very long speech recommended him (Wild himself) to their choice.

Newgate was divided into parties on this occasion, the *prigs* on each side representing their chief or great man to be the only person by whom the affairs of Newgate could be managed with safety and advantage. The *prigs* had indeed very incompatible interests; for, whereas the supporters of Johnson, who was in possession of the plunder of Newgate, were admitted to some share under their leader, so the abettors of Wild had, on his promotion, the same views of dividing some part of the spoil among themselves. It is no wonder, therefore, they were both so warm on each side. What may seem more remarkable was, that the debtors, who were entirely unconcerned in the dispute, and who were the destined plunder of both parties, should interest themselves with the utmost violence, some on behalf of Wild, and others in favour of Johnson. So that all Newgate resounded with WILD *for ever*, JOHNSON *for ever*. And the poor debtors re-echoed *the liberties of Newgate*, which, in the cant language, signifies *plunder*, as loudly as the thieves themselves. In short, such quarrels and animosities happened between them, that they seemed rather the people of two countries long at war with each other than the inhabitants of the same castle.

Wild's party at length prevailed, and he succeeded to the place and power of Johnson, whom he presently stripped of all his finery; but, when it was proposed that he should sell it and divide the money for the good of the whole, he waived that motion, saying it was not yet time, that he should find a better opportunity, that the clothes wanted cleaning, with many other pretences, and within two days, to the surprise of many, he appeared in them himself; for which he vouchsafed no other apology than that they fitted him much better than they did Johnson, and that they became him in a much more elegant manner.

This behaviour of Wild greatly incensed the debtors, particularly those by whose means he had been promoted. They grumbled extremely, and vented great indignation against Wild; when one day a very grave man, and one of much authority among them, bespake them as follows:

"Nothing sure can be more justly ridiculous than the conduct of those who should lay the lamb in the wolf's way, and then should lament his being devoured. What a wolf is in a sheepfold, a great man is in society. Now, when one wolf is in possession of a sheepfold, how little would it avail the simple flock to expel him and place another in his stead! Of the same benefit to us is the overthrowing one *prig* in favour of another. And for what other advantage was your struggle? Did you not all know that Wild and his followers were *prigs*, as well as Johnson and his? What then could the contention be among such but that which you have now discovered it to have been? Perhaps some would say, Is it then our duty tamely to submit to the rapine of the *prig* who now plunders us for fear of an exchange? Surely no: but I answer, It is better to shake the plunder off than to exchange the plunderer. And by what means can we effect this but by a total change in our manners? Every *prig* is a slave. His own *priggish* desires, which enslave him, themselves betray him to the tyranny of others. To preserve, therefore, the liberty of Newgate is to change the manners of Newgate. Let us, therefore, who are confined here for debt only, separate ourselves entirely from the *prigs*; neither drink with them nor converse with them. Let us at the same time separate ourselves farther from *priggism* itself. Instead of being ready, on every opportunity, to pillage each other, let us be content with our honest share of the common bounty, and with the acquisition of our own industry. When we separate from the *prigs*, let us enter into a closer alliance with one another. Let us consider ourselves all as members of one community, to the public good of which we are to sacrifice our private views; not to give up the interest of the whole for every little pleasure or profit which shall accrue to ourselves. Liberty is consistent with no degree of honesty inferior to this, and the community where this abounds no *prig* will have the impudence or audaciousness to endeavour to enslave; or if he should, his own destruction would be the only consequence of his attempt. But while one man pursues his ambition, another his interest, another his safety; while one hath a roguery (a *priggism* they here call it) to commit, and another a roguery to defend; they must naturally fly to the favour and protection of those who have power to give them what they desire, and to defend them from what they fear; nay, in this view it becomes their interest to promote this power in their patrons. Now, gentlemen, when we are no longer *prigs*, we shall no longer have these fears or these desires. What remains, therefore, for us but to resolve bravely to lay aside our *priggism*, our roguery, in plainer words, and preserve our liberty, or to give up the latter in the preservation and preference of the former?'

This speech was received with much applause; however, Wild continued as before to levy contributions among the prisoners, to apply the garnish to his own use, and to strut openly in the ornaments which he had stripped from Johnson. To speak sincerely, there was more bravado than real use or advantage in these trappings. As for the nightgown, its outside indeed made a glittering tinsel appearance, but it kept him not warm, nor could the finery of it do him much honour, since every one knew it did not properly belong to him; as to the waistcoat, it fitted him very ill, being infinitely too big for him; and the cap was so heavy that it made his head ache. Thus these clothes, which perhaps (as they presented the idea of their misery more sensibly to the people's eyes) brought him more envy, hatred, and detraction, than all his deeper impositions and more real advantages, afforded very little use or honour to the wearer; nay, could scarce serve to amuse his own vanity when this was cool enough to reflect with the least seriousness. And, should I speak in the language of a man who estimated human happiness without regard to that greatness, which we have so laboriously endeavoured to paint in this history, it is probable he never took (i.e. robbed the prisoners of) a shilling, which he himself did not pay too dear for.

CHAPTER IV

The dead-warrant arrives for Heartfree; on which occasion Wild betrays some human weakness

THE dead-warrant, as it is called, now came down to Newgate for the execution of Heartfree among the rest of the prisoners. And here the reader must excuse us, who profess to draw natural, not perfect characters, and to record the truths of history, not the extravagances of romance, while we relate a weakness in Wild of which we are ourselves ashamed, and which we would willingly have concealed, could we have preserved at the same time that strict attachment to truth and impartiality, which we have professed in recording the annals of this great man. Know then, reader, that this dead-warrant did not affect Heartfree, who was to suffer a shameful death by it, with half the concern it gave Wild, who had been the occasion of it. He had been a little struck the day before on seeing the children carried away in tears from their father. This sight brought the remembrance of some slight injuries he had done the father to his mind, which he endeavoured as much as possible to obliterate; but, when one of the keepers (I should say lieutenants of the castle) repeated Heartfree's name among those of the malefactors who were to suffer within a few days, the blood forsook his countenance, and in a cold still stream moved heavily to his heart, which had scarce strength enough left to return it through his veins. In short, his body so visibly demonstrated the pangs of his mind, that to escape observation he retired to his room, where he sullenly gave vent to such bitter agonies, that even the injured Heartfree, had not the apprehension of what his wife had suffered shut every avenue of compassion, would have pitied him.

When his mind was thoroughly fatigued, and worn out with the horrors which the approaching fate of the poor wretch, who lay under a sentence which he had iniquitously brought upon him, had suggested, sleep promised him relief; but this promise was, alas! delusive. This certain friend to the tired body is often the severest enemy to the oppressed mind. So at least it proved to Wild, adding visionary to real horrors, and tormenting his imagination with phantoms too dreadful to be described. At length, starting from these visions, he no sooner recovered his waking senses, than he cried out: "I may yet prevent this catastrophe. It is not too late to discover the whole." He then paused a moment; but greatness, instantly returning to his assistance, checked the base thought, as it first offered itself to his mind. He then reasoned thus coolly with himself: "Shall I, like a child, or a woman, or one of those mean wretches whom I have always despised, be frightened by dreams and visionary phantoms to sully that honour which I have so difficultly acquired and so gloriously maintained? Shall I, to redeem the worthless life of this silly fellow, suffer my reputation to contract a stain which the blood of millions cannot wipe away? Was it only that the few, the simple part of mankind, should call me a rogue, perhaps I could submit; but to be for ever contemptible to the PRIGS, as a wretch who wanted spirit to execute my undertaking, can never be digested. What is the life of a single man? Have not whole armies and nations been sacrificed to the honour of ONE GREAT MAN? Nay, to omit that first class of greatness, the conquerors of mankind, how often have numbers fallen by a fictitious plot only to satisfy the spleen, or perhaps exercise the ingenuity, of a member of that second order of greatness the ministerial! What have I done then? Why, I have ruined a family, and brought an innocent man to the gallows. I ought rather to weep with Alexander that I have ruined no more, than to regret the little I have done." He at length, therefore, bravely resolved to consign over Heartfree to his fate, though it cost him more struggling than may easily be believed, utterly to conquer his reluctance, and to banish away every degree of humanity from his mind, these little sparks of which composed one of those weaknesses which we lamented in the opening of our history.

But, in vindication of our hero, we must beg leave to observe that Nature is seldom so kind as those writers who draw characters absolutely perfect. She seldom creates any man so completely great, or completely low, but that some sparks of humanity will glimmer in the former, and some sparks of what the vulgar call evil will dart forth in the latter: utterly to extinguish which will give some pain, and uneasiness to both; for I apprehend no mind was ever yet formed entirely free from blemish, unless per-adventure that of a sanctified hypocrite, whose praises some well-fed flatterer hath gratefully thought proper to sing forth.

CHAPTER V

Containing various matters

THE day was now come when poor Heartfree was to suffer an ignominious death. Friendly had in the strongest manner confirmed his assurance of fulfilling his promise of becoming a father to one of his children and a husband to the other. This gave him inexpressible comfort, and he had, the evening before, taken his last leave of the little wretches with a tenderness which drew a tear from one of the keepers, joined to a magnanimity which would have pleased a stoic. When he was informed that the coach which Friendly had provided for him was ready, and that the rest of the prisoners were gone, he embraced that faithful friend with great passion, and begged that he would leave him here; but the other desired leave to accompany him to his end, which at last he was forced to comply with. And now he was proceeding towards the coach when he found his difficulties were not yet over; for now a friend arrived of whom he was to take a harder and more tender leave than he had yet gone through. This friend, reader, was no other than Mrs. Heartfree herself, who ran to him with a look all wild, staring, and frantic, and having reached his arms, fainted away in them without uttering a single syllable. Heartfree was, with great difficulty, able to preserve his own senses in such a surprise at such a season. And, indeed, our good-natured reader will be rather inclined to wish this miserable couple had, by dying in each other's arms, put a final period to their woes, than have survived to taste those bitter moments which were to be their portion, and which the unhappy wife, soon recovering from the short intermission of being, now began to suffer. When she became first mistress of her voice she burst forth into the following accents: "O my husband! Is this the condition in which I find you after our cruel separation? Who hath done this? Cruel Heaven! What is the occasion? I know thou canst deserve no ill. Tell me, somebody who can speak, while I have my senses left to understand, what is the matter?" At which words several laughed, and one answered: "The matter! Why no great matter. The gentleman is not the first, nor won't be the last: the worst of the matter is, that is we are to stay all the morning here I shall lose my dinner." Heartfree, pausing a moment and recollecting himself, cried out: "I will bear all with patience." And then, addressing himself to the commanding officer, begged he might only have a few minutes by himself with his wife, whom he had not seen before since his misfortunes. The great man answered: "He had compassion on him, and would do more than he could answer; but he supposed he was too much a gentleman not to know that something was due for such civility." On this hint, Friendly, who was himself half dead, pulled five guineas out of his pocket, which the great man took, and said he would be so generous to give him ten minutes; on which one observed that many a gentleman had bought ten minutes with a woman dearer, and many other facetious remarks were made, unnecessary to be here related. Heartfree was now suffered to retire into a room with his wife, the commander informing him at his entrance that he must be expeditious, for that the rest of the good company would be at the tree before him, and he supposed he was a gentleman of too much breeding to make them wait.

This tender wretched couple were now retired for these few minutes, which the commander without carefully measured with his watch; and Heartfree was mustering all his resolution to part with what his soul so ardently doted on, and to conjure her to support his loss for the sake of her poor infants, and to comfort her with the promise of Friendly on their account; but all his design was frustrated. Mrs. Heartfree could not support the shock, but again fainted away, and so entirely lost every symptom of life that Heartfree called vehemently for assistance. Friendly rushed first into the room, and was soon followed by many others, and, what was remarkable, one who had unmoved beheld the tender scene between these parting lovers was touched to the quick by the pale looks of the woman, and ran up and down for water, drops, etc., with the utmost hurry and confusion. The ten minutes were expired, which the commander now hinted; and seeing nothing offered for the renewal of the term (for indeed Friendly had unhappily emptied his pockets), he began to grow very importunate, and at last told Heartfree he should be ashamed not to act more like a man. Heartfree begged his pardon, and said he would make him wait no longer. Then, with the deepest sigh, cried: "Oh, my angel!" and, embracing his wife with the utmost eagerness, kissed her pale lips with more fervency than ever bridegroom did the blushing cheeks of his bride. He then cried: "The Almighty bless thee! and, if it be His pleasure, restore thee to life; if not, I beseech Him we may presently meet again in a better world than this." He was breaking from her, when, perceiving her sense returning, he could not forbear renewing his embrace, and again pressing her lips, which now recovered life and warmth so fast that he begged one ten minutes more to tell her what her swooning had prevented her hearing. The worthy commander, being perhaps a little touched at this tender scene, took Friendly aside, and asked him what he would give if he would suffer his friend to remain half an hour? Friendly answered, anything; that he had no more money in his pocket, but he would certainly pay him that afternoon. "Well, then, I'll be moderate," said he; "twenty guineas." Friendly answered: "It is a bargain." The commander, having exacted a firm promise, cried: "Then I don't care if they stay a whole hour together; for what signifies hiding good news? the gentleman is reprieved"; of which he had just before received notice in a whisper. It would be very impertinent to offer at a description of the joy this occasioned to the two friends, or to Mrs. Heartfree, who was now again recovered. A surgeon, who was happily present, was employed to bleed them all. After which the commander, who had his promise of the money again confirmed to him, wished Heartfree joy, and, shaking him very friendly by the hands, cleared the room of all the company, and left the three friends together.

CHAPTER VI

In which the foregoing happy incident is accounted for

BUT here, though I am convinced my good-natured reader may almost want the surgeon's assistance also, and that there is no passage in this whole story which can afford him equal delight, let, lest our reprieve should seem to resemble that in the *Beggar's Opera*, I shall endeavour to shew him that this incident, which is indoubtedly true, is at least as natural as delightful; for we assure him we would rather have suffered half mankind to be hanged, than have saved one contrary to the strictest rules of writing and probability.

Be it known, then (a circumstance which I think highly credible), that the great Fireblood had been, a few days before, taken in the fact of a robbery, and carried before the same justice of peace who had, on his evidence, committed Heartfree to prison. This magistrate, who did indeed no small honour to the commission he bore, duly considered the weighty charge committed to him, by which he was entrusted with decisions affecting the lives, liberties, and properties of his countrymen. He, therefore, examined always with the utmost diligence and caution into every minute circumstance. And, as he had a good deal balanced, even when he committed Heartfree, on the excellent character given him by Friendly and the maid; and as he was much staggered on finding that, of the two persons on whose evidence alone Heartfree had been committed, and had been since convicted, one was in Newgate for a felony, and the other was now brought before him for a robbery, he thought proper to put the matter very home to Fireblood at this time. The young Achates was taken, as we have said, in the fact; so that denial he saw was in vain. He, therefore, honestly confessed what he knew must be proved; and desired, on the merit of the discoveries he made, to be admitted as an evidence against his accomplices.

This afforded the happiest opportunity to the justice to satisfy his conscience in relation to Heartfree. He told Fireblood that, if he expected the favour he solicited, it must be on condition that he revealed the whole truth to him concerning the evidence which he had lately given against a bankrupt, and which some circumstances had induced a suspicion of; that he might depend on it the truth would be discovered by other means, and gave some oblique hints (a deceit entirely justifiable) that Wild himself had offered such a discovery. The very mention of Wild's name immediately alarmed Fireblood, who did not in the least doubt the readiness of that GREAT MAN to hang any of the gang when his own interest seemed to require it. He, therefore, hesitated not a moment; but, having obtained a promise from the justice that he should be accepted as an evidence, he discovered the whole falsehood, and declared that he had been seduced by Wild to depose as he had done.

The justice, having thus luckily and timely discovered this scene of villainy, *alias* greatness, lost not a moment in using his utmost endeavours to get the case of the unhappy convict represented to the sovereign, who immediately granted him that gracious reprieve which caused such happiness to the persons concerned; and which we hope we have now accounted for to the satisfaction of the reader.

The good magistrate, having obtained this reprieve for Heartfree, thought it incumbent on him to visit him in the prison, and to sound, if possible, the depth of this affair, that, if he should appear as innocent as he now began to conceive him, he might use all imaginable methods to obtain his pardon and enlargement.

The next day, therefore, after that when the miserable scene above described had passed, he went to Newgate, where he found those three persons, namely, Heartfree, his wife, and Friendly, sitting together. The justice informed the prisoner of the confession of Fireblood, with the steps which he had taken upon it. The reader will easily conceive the many outward thanks, as well as inward gratitude, which he received from all three; but those were of very little consequence to him compared with the secret satisfaction he felt in his mind from reflecting on the preservation of innocence, as he soon after very clearly perceived was the case.

When he entered the room Mrs. Heartfree was speaking

with some earnestness; as he perceived, therefore, he had
interrupted her, he begged she would continue her discourse,
which, if he prevented by his presence, he desired to depart;
but Heartfree would not suffer it. He said she had been
relating some adventures which perhaps might entertain
him to hear, and which she the rather desired he would
hear, as they might serve to illustrate the foundation on
which this falsehood had been built, which had brought
on her husband all his misfortunes.

The justice very gladly consented, and Mrs. Heartfree,
at her husband's desire, began the relation from the first
renewal of Wild's acquaintance with him; but, though this
recapitulation was necessary for the information of our
good magistrate, as it would be useless, and perhaps tedious,
to the reader, we shall only repeat that part of her story
to which he only is a stranger, beginning with what happened
to her after Wild had been turned adrift in the boat by the
captain of the French privateer.

CHAPTER VII

Mrs. Heartfree relates her adventures

MRS. HEARTFREE proceeded thus: "The vengeance which
the French captain exacted on that villain (our hero)
persuaded me that I was fallen into the hands of a man of
honour and justice; nor indeed was it possible for any
person to be treated with more respect and civility than
I now was; but if this could not mitigate my sorrows when
I reflected on the condition in which I had been betrayed to
leave all that was dear to me, much less could it produce
such an effect when I discovered, as I soon did, that I owed
it chiefly to a passion which threatened me with great
uneasiness, as it quickly appeared to be very violent, and
as I was absolutely in the power of the person who possessed
it, or was rather possessed by it. I must, however, do
him the justice to say my fears carried my suspicions farther
than I afterwards found I had any reason to carry them:
he did indeed very soon acquaint me with his passion, and
used all those gentle methods which frequently succeed
with our sex to prevail with me to gratify it; but never once
threatened, nor had the least recourse to force. He did

not even once insinuate to me that I was totally in his power, which I myself sufficiently saw, and whence I drew the most dreadful apprehensions, well knowing that, as there are some dispositions so brutal that cruelty adds a zest and savour to their pleasures, so there are others whose gentler inclinations are better gratified when they win us by softer methods to comply with their desires; yet that even these may be often compelled by an unruly passion to have recourse at last to the means of violence, when they despair of success from persuasion; but I was happily the captive of a better man. My conqueror was one of those over whom vice hath a limited jurisdiction; and, though he was too easily prevailed on to sin, he was proof against any temptation to villainy.

"We had been two days almost totally becalmed, when, a brisk gale rising as we were in sight of Dunkirk, we saw a vessel making full sail towards us. The captain of the privateer was so strong that he apprehended no danger but from a man-of-war, which the sailors discerned this not to be. He, therefore, struck his colours, and furled his sails as much as possible, in order to lie by and expect her, hoping she might be a prize." (Here Heartfree smiling, his wife stopped and inquired the cause. He told her it was from her using the sea-terms so aptly: she laughed, and answered he would wonder less at this when he heard the long time she had been on board; and then proceeded.) "This vessel now came alongside of us, and hailed us, having perceived that on which we were aboard to be of her own country; they begged us not to put into Dunkirk, but to accompany them in their pursuit of a large English merchantman, whom we should easily overtake, and both together as easily conquer. Our captain immediately consented to this proposition, and ordered all his sail to be crowded. This was most unwelcome news to me; however, he comforted me all he could by assuring me I had nothing to fear, that he would be so far from offering the least rudeness to me himself, that he would, at the hazard of his life, protect me from it. This assurance gave me all the consolation which my present circumstances and the dreadful apprehensions I had on your dear account would admit." (At which words the tenderest glances passed on both sides between the husband and wife.)

"We sailed near twelve hours, when we came in sight of

the ship we were in pursuit of, and which we should probably have soon come up with had not a very thick mist
ravished her from our eyes. This mist continued several
hours, and when it cleared up we discovered our companion
at a great distance from us; but what gave us (I mean the
captain and his crew) the greatest uneasiness was the sight
of a very large ship within a mile of us, which presently
saluted us with a gun, and now appeared to be a third-rate
English man-of-war. Our captain declared the impossibility of either fighting or escaping, and accordingly struck
without waiting for the broadside which was preparing for
us, and which perhaps would have prevented me from the
happiness I now enjoy." This occasioned Heartfree to
change colour; his wife therefore passed hastily to circumstances of a more smiling complexion.

"I greatly rejoiced at this event, as I thought it would
not only restore me to the safe possession of my jewels,
but to what I value beyond all the treasure in the universe.
My expectation, however, of both these was somewhat
crossed for the present: as to the former, I was told they
should be carefully preserved; but that I must prove my
right to them before I could expect their restoration,
which, if I mistake not, the captain did not very eagerly
desire I should be able to accomplish: and as to the latter,
I was acquainted that I should be put on board the first
ship which they met on her way to England, but that they
were proceeding to the West Indies.

"I had not been long on board the man-of-war before
I discovered just reason rather to lament than rejoice at
the exchange of my captivity; for such I concluded my
present situation to be. I had now another lover in the
captain of this Englishman, and much rougher and less
gallant than the Frenchman had been. He used me with
scarce common civility, as indeed he shewed very little to
any other person, treating his officers little better than a
man of no great good-breeding would exert to his meanest
servant, and that too on some very irritating provocation.
As for me, he addressed me with the insolence of a bashaw
to a Circassian slave; he talked to me with the loose licence
in which the most profligate libertines converse with harlots,
and which women abandoned only in a moderate degree
detest and abhor. He often kissed me with very rude
familiarity, and one day attempted further brutality; when

a gentleman on board, and who was in my situation, that is, had been taken by a privateer and was retaken, rescued me from his hands, for which the captain confined him, though he was not under his command, two days in irons: when he was released (for I was not suffered to visit him in his confinement) I went to him and thanked him with the utmost acknowledgment for what he had done and suffered on my account. The gentleman behaved to me in the handsomest manner on this occasion; told me he was ashamed of the high sense I seemed to entertain of so small an obligation if an action to which his duty as a Christian and his honour as a man obliged him. From this time I lived in great familiarity with this man, whom I regarded as my protector, which he professed himself ready to be on all occasions, expressing the utmost abhorrence of the captain's brutality, especially that shewn towards me, and the tenderness of a parent for the preservation of my virtue, for which I was not myself more solicitous than he appeared. He was, indeed, the only man I had hitherto met since my unhappy departure who did not endeavour by all his looks, words, and actions, to assure me he had a liking to my unfortunate person; the rest seeming desirous of sacrificing the little beauty they complimented to their desires, without the least consideration of the ruin which I earnestly represented to them they were attempting to bring on me and on my future repose.

"I now passed several days pretty free from the captain's molestation, till one fatal night." Here, perceiving Heartfree grew pale, she comforted him by an assurance that Heaven had preserved her chastity, and again had restored her unsullied to his arms. She continued thus: "Perhaps I give it a wrong epithet in the word fatal; but a wretched night I am sure I may call it, for no woman who came off victorious was, I believe, ever in greater danger. One night, I say, having drank his spirits high with punch, in company with the purser, who was the only man in the ship he admitted to his table, the captain sent for me into his cabin; whither, though unwilling, I was obliged to go. We were no sooner alone together than he seized me by the hand, and, after affronting my ears with discourse which I am unable to repeat, he swore a great oath that his passion was to be dallied with no longer; that I must not expect to treat him in the manner to which a set of blockhead land-men submitted. 'None of your coquette airs, therefore, with me, madam,' said he, 'for I am resolved to have you this night. No struggling nor squalling, for both will be impertinent. The first man who offers to come in here, I will have his skin flea'd off at the gangway.' He then attempted to pull me violently towards his bed. I threw myself on my knees, and with tears and entreaties besought his compassion; but this was, I found, to no purpose: I then had recourse to threats, and endeavoured to frighten him with the consequence; but neither had this, though it seemed to stagger him more than the other method, sufficient force to deliver me. At last a stratagem came into my head, of which my perceiving him reel gave me the first hint. I entreated a moment's reprieve only, when, collecting all the spirits I could muster, I put on a constrained air of gaiety, and told him, with an affected laugh, he was the roughest lover I had ever met with, and that I believed I was the first woman he had ever paid his addresses to. 'Addresses,' said he; 'd—n your dresses! I want to undress you.' I then begged him to let us drink some punch together; for that I loved a can as well as himself, and never would grant the favour to any man till I had drank a hearty glass with him. 'Oh!' said he, 'if that be all, you shall have punch enough to drown yourself in.' At which words he rung the bell, and ordered in a gallon of that liquor. I was in the meantime obliged to suffer his nauseous kisses, and some rudenesses which I had great difficulty to restrain within moderate bounds. When the punch came in he took up the bowl and drank my health ostentatiously, in such a quantity that it considerably advanced my scheme. I followed him with bumpers as fast as possible, and was myself obliged to drink so much that at another time it would have staggered my own reason, but at present it did not affect me. At length, perceiving him very far gone, I watched an opportunity, and ran out of the cabin, resolving to seek protection of the sea if I could find no other; but Heaven was now graciously pleased to relieve me; for in his attempt to pursue me he reeled backwards, and, falling down the cabin stairs, he dislocated his shoulder and so bruised himself that I was not only preserved that night from any danger of my intended ravisher, but the accident threw him into a fever which endangered his life, and whether he ever recovered or no I am not certain; for during his delirious fits the eldest lieutenant commanded the ship. This was a virtuous and a brave fellow, who had been twenty-five years in that post without being able to obtain a ship, and had seen several boys, the bastards of noblemen, put over his head. One day while the ship remained under his command an English vessel bound to Cork passed by; myself and my friend, who had formerly lain two days in irons on my account, went on board this ship with the leave of the good lieutenant, who made us such presents as he was able of provisions, and, congratulating me on my delivery from a danger to which none of the ship's crew had been strangers, he kindly wished us both a safe voyage."

CHAPTER VIII

In which Mrs. Heartfree continues the relation of her adventures

"THE first evening after we were aboard this vessel, which was a brigantine, we being then at no very great distance from the Madeiras, the most violent storm arose from the north-west, in which we presently lost both our masts; and indeed death now presented itself as inevitable to us: I need not tell my Tommy what were then my thoughts. Our danger was so great that the captain of the ship, a professed atheist, betook himself to prayers, and the whole crew, abandoning themselves for lost, fell with the utmost eagerness to the emptying a cask of brandy, not one drop of which, they swore, should be polluted with salt water. I observed here my old friend displayed less courage than I expected from him. He seemed entirely swallowed up in despair. But Heaven be praised! we were all at last preserved. The storm, after above eleven hours' continuance, began to abate, and by degrees entirely ceased, but left us still rolling at the mercy of the waves, which carried us at their own pleasure to the south-east a vast number of leagues. Our crew were all dead drunk with the brandy which they had taken such care to preserve from the sea; but, indeed, had they been awake, their labour would have been of very little service, as we had lost all our rigging, our brigantine being reduced to a naked hulk only. In this condition we floated above thirty hours, till in the midst of a very dark night we spied a light, which seeming to approach us, grew so large that our sailors concluded it to be the lantern of a man-of-war; but when we were cheering ourselves with the hopes of our deliverance from this wretched situation, on a sudden, to our great concern, the light entirely disappeared, and left us in despair increased by the remembrance of those pleasing imaginations with which we had entertained our minds during its appearance. The rest of the night we passed in melancholy conjectures on the light which had deserted us, which the major part of the sailors concluded to be a meteor. In this distress we had one comfort, which was a plentiful store of provisions; this so supported the spirits of the sailors, that they declared had they but a sufficient quantity of brandy they cared not whether they saw land for a month to come; but indeed we were much nearer it than we imagined, as we perceived at break of day. One of the most knowing of the crew declared we were near the continent of Africa; but when we were within three leagues of it a second violent storm arose from the north, so that we again gave over all hopes of safety. This storm was not quite so outrageous as the former, but of much longer continuance, for it lasted near three days, and drove us an immense number of leagues to the south. We were within a league of the shore, expecting every moment our ship to be dashed in pieces, when the tempest ceased all on a sudden; but the waves still continued to roll like mountains, and before the sea recovered its calm motion, our ship was thrown so near the land, that the captain ordered out his boat, declaring he had scarce any hopes of saving her; and indeed we had not quitted her many minutes before we saw the justice of his apprehensions, for she struck against a rock and immediately sunk. The behaviour of the sailors on this occasion very much affected me; they beheld their ship perish with the tenderness of a lover or a parent; they spoke of her as the fondest husband would of his wife; and many of them, who seemed to have no tears in their composition, shed them plentifully at her sinking. The captain himself cried out: 'Go thy way, charming Molly, the sea never devoured a lovelier morsel. If I have fifty vessels I shall never love another like thee. Poor slut! I shall remember thee to my dying day.' Well, the boat now conveyed us all safe to shore, where we landed with very little difficulty. It was now about noon, and the rays of the sun, which descended almost perpendicularly on our heads, were extremely hot and troublesome. However, we travelled through this extreme heat about five miles over a plain. This brought us to a vast wood, which extended itself as far as we could see, both to the right and left, and seemed to me to put an entire end to our progress. Here we decreed to rest and dine on the provision which we had brought from the ship, of which we had sufficient for very few meals; our boat being so overloaded with people that we had very little room for luggage of any kind. Our repast was salt pork broiled, which the keenness of hunger made so delicious to my companions that they fed very heartily upon it. As for myself, the fatigue of my body and the vexation of my mind had so thoroughly weakened me, that I was almost entirely deprived of appetite; and the utmost dexterity of the most accomplished French cook would have been ineffectual had he endeavoured to tempt me with delicacies. I thought myself very little a gainer by my late escape from the tempest, by which I seemed only to have exchanged the element in which I was presently to die. When our company had sufficiently, and indeed very plentifully feasted themselves, they resolved to enter the wood and endeavour to pass it, in expectation of finding some inhabitants, at least some provision. We proceeded therefore in the following order: one man in the front with a hatchet, to clear our way, and two others followed him with guns, to protect the rest from wild beasts; then walked the rest of our company, and last of all the captain himself, being armed likewise with a gun, to defend us from any attack behind—in the rear, I think you call it. And thus our whole company, being fourteen in number, travelled on till night overtook us, without seeing anything unless a few birds and some very insignificant animals. We rested all night under the covert of some trees, and indeed we very little wanted shelter at that season, the heat in the day being the only inclemency we had to combat with in this climate. I cannot help telling you my old friend lay still nearest me on the ground, and declared he would be my protector should any of the sailors offer rudeness; but I can acquit them of any such attempt; nor was I ever affronted by any one, more than with a coarse expression, proceeding rather from the roughness and ignorance of their education than from any abandoned principle, or want of humanity.

"We had now proceeded very little way on our next day's march when one of the sailors, having skipt nimbly up a hill, with the assistance of a speaking trumpet informed us that he saw a town a very little way off. This news so comforted me, and gave me such strength, as well as spirits, that, with the help of my old friend and another, who suffered me to lean on them, I, with much difficulty, attained the summit; but was so absolutely overcome in climbing it, that I had no longer sufficient strength to support my tottering limbs, and was obliged to lay myself again on the ground; nor could they prevail on me to undertake descending through a very thick wood into a plain, at the end of which indeed appeared some houses, or rather huts, but at a much greater distance than the sailor assured us; the little way, as he had called it, seeming to me full twenty miles, nor was it, I believe, much less."

CHAPTER IX

Containing incidents very surprising

"THE captain declared he would, without delay, proceed to the town before him; in which resolution he was seconded by all the crew; but when I could not be persuaded, nor was I able to travel any farther before I had rested myself, my old friend protested he would not leave me, but would stay behind as my guard; and, when I had refreshed myself with a little repose, he would attend me to the town, which the captain promised he would not leave before he had seen us.

"They were no sooner departed than (having first thanked my protector for his care of me) I resigned myself to sleep, which immediately closed my eyelids, and would probably have detained me very long in his gentle dominions, had I not been awaked with a squeeze by the hand of my guard, which I at first thought intended to alarm me with the danger of some wild beast; but I soon perceived it arose from a softer motive, and that a gentle swain was the only wild beast I had to apprehend. He began now to disclose his passion in the strongest manner imaginable, indeed with a warmth rather beyond that of both my former lovers, but as yet without any attempt of absolute force. On my side remonstrances were made in more bitter exclamations and revilings than I had used to any, that villain Wild excepted. I told him he was the basest and most treacherous wretch alive; that his having cloaked his iniquitous designs under the appearance or virtue and friendship added an ineffable degree of horror to them; that I detested him of all mankind the most, and could I be brought to yield to prostitution, he should be the last to enjoy the ruins of my honour. He suffered himself not to be provoked by this language, but only changed his manner of solicitation from flattery to bribery. He unript the lining of his waistcoat, and pulled forth several jewels; these, he said, he had preserved from infinite danger to the happiest purpose, if I could be won by them. I rejected them often with the utmost indignation, till at last, casting my eye, rather by accident than design, on a diamond necklace, a thought, like lightning, shot through my mind, and, in an instant, I remembered that this was the very necklace you had sold the cursed count, the cause of all our misfortunes. The confusion of ideas into which this surprise hurried me prevented my reflecting on the villain who then stood before me; but the first recollection presently told me it could be no other than the count himself, the wicked tool of Wild's barbarity. Good heavens! what was then my condition! How shall I describe the tumult of passions which then laboured in my breast? However, as I was happily unknown to him, the least suspicion on his side was altogether impossible. He imputed, therefore, the eagerness with which I gazed on the jewels to a very wrong cause, and endeavoured to put as much additional softness into his countenance as he was able. My fears were a little quieted, and I was resolved to be very liberal of promises, and hoped so thoroughly to persuade him of my venality that he might, without any doubt, be drawn in to wait the captain and crew's return, who would, I was very certain, not only preserve me from his violence, but secure the restoration of what you had been so cruelly robbed of. But, alas! I was mistaken."

Mrs. Heartfree, again perceiving symptoms of the utmos disquietude in her husband's countenance, cried out, "My dear, don't you apprehend any harm.—But, to deliver you as soon as possible from your anxiety—when he perceived I declined the warmth of his addresses he begged me to consider; he changed at once his voice and features, and, in a very different tone from what he had hitherto affected, he swore I should not deceive him as I had the captain; that fortune had kindly thrown an opportunity in his way which he was resolved not foolishly to lose; and concluded with a violent oath that he was determined to enjoy me that moment, and therefore I knew the consequences of resistance. He then caught me in his arms, and began such rude attempts, that I screamed out with all the force I could, though I had so little hopes of being rescued, when there suddenly rushed forth from a thicket a creature which, at his first appearance, and in the hurry of spirits I then was, I did not take for a man; but, indeed, had he been the fiercest of wild beasts, I should have rejoiced at his devouring us both. I scarce perceived he had a musket in his hand before he struck my ravisher such a blow with it that he felled him at my feet. He then advanced with a gentle air towards me, and told me in French he was extremely glad he had been luckily present to my assistance. He was naked, except his middle and his feet, if I can call a body so which was covered with hair almost equal to any beast whatever. Indeed, his appearance was so horrid in my eyes, that the friendship he had shewn me, as well as his courteous behaviour, could not entirely remove the dread I had conceived from his figure. I believe he saw this very visibly; for he begged me not to be frightened, since, whatever accident had brought me thither, I should have reason to thank Heaven for meeting him, at whose hands I might assure myself of the utmost civility and protection. In the midst of all this consternation, I had spirits enough to take up the casket of jewels which the villain, in falling, had dropped out of his hands, and conveyed it into my pocket. My deliverer, telling me that I seemed extremely weak and faint, desired me to refresh myself at his little hut, which, he said, was hard by. If his demeanour had been less kind and obliging, my desperate situation must have lent me confidence; for sure the alternative could not be doubtful, whether I should rather trust this man, who, notwithstanding his savage outside, expressed so much devotion to serve me, which at least I was not certain of the falsehood of, or should abide with one whom I so perfectly well knew to be an accomplished villain. I, therefore, committed myself to his guidance, though with tears in my eyes, and begged him to have compassion on my innocence, which was absolutely in his power. He said, the treatment he had been witness of, which he supposed was from one who had broken his trust towards me, sufficiently justified my suspicion; but begged me to dry my eyes, and he would soon convince me that I was with a man of different sentiments. The kind accents which accompanied these words gave me some comfort, which was assisted by the repossession of our jewels by an accident so strongly savouring of the disposition of Providence in my favour.

"We left the villain weltering in his blood, though beginning to recover a little motion, and walked together to his hut, or rather cave, for it was underground, on the side of a hill; the situation was very pleasant, and from its mouth we overlooked a large plain and the town I had before seen. As soon as I entered it, he desired me to sit down on a bench of earth, which served him for chairs, and then laid before me some fruits, the wild product of that country, one or two of which had an excellent flavour. He likewise produced some baked flesh, a little resembling that of venison. He then brought forth a bottle of brandy, which he said had remained with him ever since his settling there, now above thirty years, during all which time he had never opened it, his only liquor being water; that he had reserved this bottle as a cordial in sickness; but, he thanked Heaven, he had never yet had occasion for it. He then acquainted me that he was a hermit, that he had been formerly cast away on that coast, with his wife, whom he dearly loved, but could not preserve from perishing; on which account he had resolved never to return to France, which was his native country, but to devote himself to prayer and a holy life, placing all his hopes in the blessed expectation of meeting that dear woman again in heaven, where, he was convinced, she was now a saint and an interceder for him. He said he had exchanged a watch with the king of that country, whom he described to be a very just and good man, for a gun, some powder, shot, and ball, with which he sometimes provided himself food, but more generally used it in defending himself against wild beasts; so that his diet was chiefly of the vegetable kind. He told me many more circumstances, which I may relate to you hereafter: but, to be as concise as possible at present, he at length greatly comforted me by promising to conduct me to a seaport, where I might have an opportunity to meet with some vessels trafficking for slaves; and whence I might once more commit myself to that element which, though I had already suffered so much on it, I must again trust to put me in possession of all I loved.

"The character he gave me of the inhabitants of the town we saw below us, and of their king, made me desirous of being conducted thither; especially as I very much wished to see the captain and sailors, who had behaved very kindly to me, and with whom, notwithstanding all the civil behaviour of the hermit, I was rather easier in my mind than alone with this single man; but he dissuaded me greatly from attempting such a walk till I had recreated my spirits with rest, desiring me to repose myself on his couch or bank, saying that he himself would retire without the cave, where he would remain as my guard. I accepted this kind proposal, but it was long before I could procure any slumber; however, at length, weariness prevailed over my fears, and I enjoyed several hours' sleep. When I awaked I found my faithful sentinel on his post and ready at my summons. This behaviour infused some confidence into me, and I now repeated my request that he would go with me to the town below; but he answered, I would be better advised to take some repast before I undertook the journey, which I should find much longer than it appeared. I consented, and he set forth a greater variety of fruits than before, of which I ate very plentifully. My collation being ended, I renewed the mention of my walk, but he still persisted in dissuading me, telling me that I was not yet strong enough; that I could repose myself nowhere with greater safety than in his cave; and that, for his part, he could have no greater happiness than that of attending me, adding, with a sigh, it was a happiness he should envy any other more than all the gifts of fortune. You may imagine I began now to entertain suspicions; but he presently removed all doubt by throwing himself at my feet and expressing the warmest passion for me. I should have now sunk with despair had he not accompanied these professions with the most vehement protestations that he would never offer me any other force but that of entreaty, and that he would rather die the most cruel death by my coldness than gain the highest bliss by becoming the occasion of a tear of sorrow to these bright eyes, which he said were stars, under whose benign influence alone he could enjoy, or indeed suffer life." She was repeating many more compliments he made her, when a horrid uproar, which alarmed the whole gate, put a stop to her narration at present. It is impossible for me to give the reader a better idea of the noise which now arose than by desiring him to imagine I had the hundred tongues the poet once wished for, and was vociferating from them all at once, by hollowing, scolding, crying, swearing, bellowing, and, in short, by every different articulation which is within the scope of the human organ.

CHAPTER X

A horrible uproar in the gate

BUT however great an idea the reader may hence conceive of this uproar, he will think the occasion more than adequate to it when he is informed that our hero (I blush to name it) had discovered an injury done to his honour, and that in the tenderest point. In a word, reader (for thou must know it, though it give thee the greatest horror imaginable), he had caught Fireblood in the arms of his lovely Lætitia.

As the generous bull, who, having long depastured among a number of cows, and thence contracted an opinion that these cows are all his own property, if he beholds another bull bestride a cow within his walks, he roars aloud, and threatens instant vengeance with his horns, till the whole parish are alarmed with his bellowing; not with less noise nor less dreadful menaces did the fury of Wild burst forth and terrify the whole gate. Long time did rage render his voice inarticulate to the hearer; as when, at a visiting day, fifteen or sixteen or perhaps twice as many females, of delicate but shrill pipes, ejaculate all at once on different subjects, all is sound only, the harmony entirely melodious indeed, but conveys no idea to our ears; but at length, when reason began to get the better of his passion, which latter, being deserted by his breath, began a little to retreat, the following accents leapt over the hedge of his teeth, or rather the ditch of his gums, whence those hedgestakes had long since by a batten been displaced in battle with an amazon of Drury.

[1] ". . . Man of honour! doth this become a friend? Could I have expected such a breach of all the laws of honour from thee, whom I had taught to walk in its paths? Hadst thou chosen any other way to injure my confidence I could have forgiven it; but this is a stab in the tenderest part, a wound never to be healed, an injury never to be repaired; for it is not only the loss of an agreeable companion, of the affection of a wife dearer to my soul than life itself, it is not this loss alone I lament; this loss is accompanied with disgrace and with dishonour. The blood of the Wilds, which hath run with such uninterrupted purity through so many generations, this blood is fouled, contaminated: hence flow my tears, hence arises my grief. This is the injury never to be redressed, nor ever to be with honour forgiven." "My —— in a bandbox!" answered Fireblood; "here is a noise about your honour! If the mischief done to your blood be all you complain of, I am sure you complain of nothing; for my blood is as good as yours." "You have no conception," replied Wild, "of the tenderness of honour; you know not how nice and delicate it is in both sexes; so delicate that the least breath of air which rudely blows on it destroys it." "I will prove from your own words," says Fireblood, "I have not wronged your honour. Have you not often told me that the honour of a man consisted in receiving no affront from his own sex, and that of woman in receiving no kindness from ours? Now, sir, if I have given you no affront, how have I injured your honour?" "But doth not everything," cried Wild, "of the wife belong to the husband? A married man, therefore, hath his wife's honour as well as his own, and by injuring hers you injure his. How cruelly you have hurt me in this tender part I need not repeat; the whole gate knows it, and the world shall. I will apply to Doctors' Commons for my redress against her; I will shake off as much of my dishonour as I can by parting with her; and as for you, expect to hear of me in Westminster

[1] The beginning of this speech is lost.

Hall; the modern method of repairing these breaches and of resenting this affront." "D—n your eyes!" cries Fireblood; "I fear you not, nor do I believe a word you say." "Nay, if you affront me personally," says Wild, "another sort of resentment is prescribed." At which word, advancing to Fireblood, he presented him with a box on the ear, which the youth immediately returned; and now our hero and his friend fell to boxing, though with some difficulty, both being encumbered with the chains which they wore between their legs: a few blows passed on both sides before the gentlemen who stood by stept in and parted the combatants; and now both parties having whispered each other, that, if they outlived the ensuing sessions and escaped the tree, one should give and the other should receive satisfaction in single combat, they separated and the gate soon recovered its former tranquillity.

Mrs. Heartfree was then desired by the justice and her husband both, to conclude her story, which she did in the words of the next chapter.

CHAPTER XI

The conclusion of Mrs. Heartfree's adventures

"If I mistake not, I was interrupted just as I was beginning to repeat some of the compliments made me by the hermit." "Just as you had finished them, I believe, madam," said the justice. "Very well, sir," said she; "I am sure I have no pleasure in the repetition. He concluded then with telling me, though I was in his eyes the most charming woman in the world, and might tempt a saint to abandon the ways of holiness, yet my beauty inspired him with a much tenderer affection towards me than to purchase any satisfaction of his own desires with my misery; if, therefore, I could be so cruel to him to reject his honest and sincere address, nor could submit to a solitary life with one who would endeavour by all possible means to make me happy, I had no force to dread; for that I was as much at my liberty as if I was in France, or England, or any other free country. I repulsed him with the same civility with which he advanced; and told him that, as he professed great regard to religion, I was convinced he would cease from all

further solicitation when I informed him that, if I had no
other objection, my own innocence would not admit of my
hearing him on this subject, for that I was married. He
started a little at that word, and was for some time silent;
but, at length recovering himself, he began to urge the
uncertainty of my husband's being alive, and the probability of the contrary. He then spoke of marriage as of
a civil policy only, on which head he urged many arguments
not worth repeating, and was growing so very eager and
importunate that I know not whither his passion might
have hurried him had not three of the sailors, well armed,
appeared at that instant in sight of the cave. I no sooner
saw them than, exulting with the utmost inward joy,
I told him my companions were come for me, and that
I must now take my leave of him; assuring him that I would
always remember, with the most grateful acknowledgment,
the favours I had received at his hands. He fetched a
very heavy sigh, and, squeezing me tenderly by the hand,
he saluted my lips with a little more eagerness than the
European salutations admit of, and told me he should
likewise remember my arrival at his cave to the last day
of his life, adding, O that he could there spend the whole
in the company of one whose bright eyes had kindled—but
I know you will think, sir, that we women love to repeat
the compliments made us, I will therefore omit them. In
a word, the sailors being now arrived, I quitted him with
some compassion for the reluctance with which he parted
from me, and went forward with my companions.

"We had proceeded but a very few paces before one of
the sailors said to his comrades: 'D—n me, Jack, who
knows whether yon fellow hath not some good flip in his
cave?' I innocently answered: 'The poor wretch hath
only one bottle of brandy.' 'Hath he so?' cries the sailor;
''fore George, we will taste it'; and so saying they immediately returned back, and myself with them. We found
the poor man prostrate on the ground, expressing all the
symptoms of misery and lamentation. I told him in
French (for the sailors could not speak that language) what
they wanted. He pointed to the place where the bottle was
deposited, saying they were welcome to that and whatever
else he had, and adding he cared not if they took his life
also. The sailors searched the whole cave, where finding
nothing more which they deemed worth their taking, they

walked off with the bottle, and, immediately emptying it without offering me a drop, they proceeded with me towards the town.

"In our way I observed one whisper another, while he kept his eye steadfastly fixed on me. This gave me some uneasiness; but the other answered: 'No, d—n me, the captain will never forgive us: besides, we have enough of it among the black women, and, in my mind, one colour is as good as another.' This was enough to give me violent apprehensions; but I heard no more of that kind till we came to the town, where, in about six hours, I arrived in safety.

"As soon as I came to the captain he enquired what was become of my friend, meaning the villainous count. When he was informed by me of what had happened, he wished me heartily joy of my delivery, and, expressing the utmost abhorrence of such baseness, swore if ever he met him he would cut his throat; but, indeed, we both concluded that he had died of the blow which the hermit had given him.

"I was now introduced to the chief magistrate of this country, who was desirous of seeing me. I will give you a short description of him. He was chosen (as is the custom there) for his superior bravery and wisdom. His power is entirely absolute during its continuance; but, on the first deviation from equity and justice, he is liable to be deposed and punished by the people, the elders of whom, once a year, assemble to examine into his conduct. Besides the danger which these examinations, which are very strict, expose him to, his office is of such care and trouble that nothing but that restless love of power so predominant in the mind of man could make it the object of desire, for he is indeed the only slave of all the natives of this country. He is obliged, in time of peace, to hear the complaint of every person in his dominions and to render him justice; for which purpose every one may demand an audience of him, unless during the hour which he is allowed for dinner, when he sits alone at the table, and is attended in the most public manner with more than European ceremony. This is done to create an awe and respect towards him in the eye of the vulgar; but lest it should elevate him too much in his own opinion, in order to his humiliation he receives every evening in private, from a kind of beadle, a gentle kick on his posteriors; besides which he wears a ring in his nose, somewhat resembling that we ring our pigs with, and a chain round his neck not unlike that worn by our aldermen; both which I suppose to be emblematical, but heard not the reasons of either assigned. There are many more particularities among these people which, when I have an opportunity, I may relate to you. The second day after my return from court one of his officers, whom they call SCHACH PIMPACH, waited upon me, and, by a French interpreter who lives here, informed me that the chief magistrate liked my person, and offered me an immense present if I would suffer him to enjoy it (this is, it seems, their common form of making love). I rejected the present, and never heard any further solicitations; for, as it is no shame for women here to consent at the first proposal, so they never receive a second.

"I had resided in this town a week when the captain informed me that a number of slaves, who had been taken captives in war, were to be guarded to the seaside, where they were to be sold to the merchants who traded in them to America; that if I would embrace this opportunity I might assure myself of finding a passage to America, and thence to England; acquainting me at the same time that he himself intended to go with them. I readily agreed to accompany him. The chief, being advertised of our designs, sent for us both to court, and, without mentioning a word of love to me, having presented me with a very rich jewel, of less value, he said, than my chastity, took a very civil leave, recommending me to the care of Heaven, and ordering us a large supply of provisions for our journey.

"We were provided with mules for ourselves and what we carried with us, and in nine days reached the seashore, where we found an English vessel ready to receive both us and the slaves. We went aboard it, and sailed the next day with a fair wind for New England, where I hoped to get an immediate passage to the Old: but Providence was kinder than my expectation; for the third day after we were at sea we met an English man-of-war homeward bound; the captain of it was a very good-natured man, and agreed to take me on board. I accordingly took my leave of my old friend, the master of the shipwrecked vessel, who went on to New England, whence he intended to pass to Jamaica, where his owners lived. I was now treated with great civility, had a little cabin assigned me, and dined every day at the captain's table, who was indeed a very gallant man, and, at first, made me a tender of his affections; but, when he found me resolutely bent to preserve myself pure and entire for the best of husbands, he grew cooler in his addresses, and soon behaved in a manner very pleasing to me, regarding my sex only so far as to pay me a deference, which is very agreeable to us all.

"To conclude my story; I met with no adventure in this passage at all worth relating, till my landing at Gravesend, whence the captain brought me in his own boat to the Tower. In a short hour after my arrival we had that meeting which, however dreadful at first, will, I now hope, by the good offices of the best of men, whom Heaven for ever bless, end in our perfect happiness, and be a strong instance of what I am persuaded is the surest truth, THAT PROVIDENCE WILL SOONER OR LATER PROCURE THE FELICITY OF THE VIRTUOUS AND INNOCENT."

Mrs. Heartfree thus ended her speech, having before delivered to her husband the jewels which the count had robbed him of, and that presented her by the African chief, which last was of immense value. The good magistrate was sensibly touched at her narrative, as well on the consideration of the sufferings she had herself undergone as for those of her husband, which he had himself been innocently the instrument of bringing upon him. That worthy man, however, much rejoiced in what he had already done for his preservation, and promised to labour with his utmost interest and industry to procure the absolute pardon, rather of his sentence than of his guilt, which he now plainly discovered was a barbarous and false imputation.

CHAPTER XII

The history returns to the contemplation of GREATNESS

BUT we have already, perhaps, detained our reader too long in this relation from the consideration of our hero, who daily gave the most exalted proofs of greatness in cajoling the *prigs*, and in exactions on the debtors; which latter now grew so great, i.e. corrupted in their morals, that they spoke with the utmost contempt of what the vulgar call honesty. The greatest character among them was that of a pickpocket, or, in truer language, a *file*; and the only censure was want of dexterity. As to virtue, goodness, and such like, they were the objects of mirth and derision, and all Newgate was a complete collection of *prigs*, every man being desirous to pick his neighbour's pocket, and every one was as sensible that his neighbour was as ready to pick his: so that (which is almost incredible) as great roguery was daily committed within the walls of Newgate as without.

The glory resulting from these actions of Wild probably animated the envy of his enemies against him. The day of his trial now approached; for which, as Socrates did, he prepared himself; but not weakly and foolishly, like that philosopher, with patience and resignation, but with a good number of false witnesses. However, as success is not always proportioned to the wisdom of him who endeavours to attain it, so are we more sorry than ashamed to relate that our hero was, notwithstanding his utmost caution and prudence, convicted, and sentenced to a death which, when we consider not only the great men who have suffered it, but the much larger number of those whose highest honour it hath been to merit it, we cannot call otherwise than honourable. Indeed, those who have unluckily missed it seem all their days to have laboured in vain to attain an end which Fortune, for reasons only known to herself, hath thought proper to deny them. Without any further preface then, our hero was sentenced to be hanged by the neck: but, whatever was to be now his fate, he might console himself that he had perpetrated what

——Nec Judicis ira, nec ignis,
Nec poterit ferrum, nec edax abolere vetustas.

For my own part, I confess, I look on this death of hanging to be as proper for a hero as any other; and I solemnly declare that had Alexander the Great been hanged it would not in the least have diminished my respect to his memory. Provided a hero in his life doth but execute a sufficient quantity of mischief; provided he be but well and heartily cursed by the widow, the orphan, the poor, and the oppressed (the sole rewards, as many authors have bitterly lamented both in prose and verse, of greatness, i.e. *priggism*), I think it avails little of what nature his death be, whether it be by the axe, the halter, or the sword. Such names will be always sure of living to posterity, and of enjoying that fame which they so gloriously and eagerly coveted; for, according to a GREAT dramatic poet:

> Fame
> Not more survives from good than evil deeds.
> Th' aspiring youth that fired th' Ephesian dome
> Outlives in fame the pious fool who rais'd it.

Our hero now suspected that the malice of his enemies would overpower him. He, therefore, betook himself to that true support of greatness in affliction, a bottle; by means of which he was enabled to curse, swear, and bully, and brave his fate. Other comfort indeed he had not much, for not a single friend ever came near him. His wife, whose trial was deferred to the next sessions, visited him but once, when she plagued, tormented, and upbraided so cruelly, that he forbade the keeper ever to admit her again. The ordinary of Newgate had frequent conferences with him, and greatly would it embellish our history could we record all which that good man delivered on these occasions; but unhappily we could procure only the substance of a single conference, which was taken down in shorthand by one who overheard it. We shall transcribe it, therefore, exactly in the same form and words we received it; nor can we help regarding it as one of the most curious pieces which either ancient or modern history hath recorded.

CHAPTER XIII

A dialogue between the ordinary of Newgate and Mr. Jonathan Wild the Great; in which the subjects of death, immortality, and other grave matters, are very learnedly handled by the former

ORDINARY. Good morrow to you, sir; I hope you rested well last night.

Jonathan. D—n'd ill, sir. I dreamt so confoundedly of hanging, that it disturbed my sleep.

Ordinary. Fie upon it! You should be more resigned. I wish you would make a little better use of those instructions which I have endeavoured to inculcate into you, and particularly last Sunday, and from these words: *Those who do evil shall go into everlasting fire, prepared for the devil and his angels.* I undertook to shew you, first, what is meant by EVERLASTING FIRE; and, secondly, who were THE DEVIL AND HIS ANGELS. I then proceeded to draw some inferences from the whole [1]; in which I am mightily deceived if I did not convince you that you yourself was one of those ANGELS, and, consequently, must expect EVERLASTING FIRE to be your portion in the other world.

Jonathan. Faith, doctor, I remember very little of your inferences; for I fell asleep soon after your naming your text. But did you preach this doctrine then, or do you repeat it now in order to comfort me?

Ordinary. I do it in order to bring you to a true sense of your manifold sins, and, by that means, to induce you to repentance. Indeed, had I the eloquence of Cicero, or of Tully, it would not be sufficient to describe the pains of hell or the joys of heaven. The utmost that we are taught is, *that ear hath not heard, nor can heart conceive.* Who then would, for the pitiful consideration of the riches and pleasures of this world, forfeit such inestimable happiness! such joys! such pleasures! such delights? Or who would run the venture of such misery, which, but to think on, shocks the human understanding? Who, in his senses, then, would prefer the latter to the former?

Jonathan. Ay, who indeed? I assure you, doctor, I had much rather be happy than miserable. But [2] * * * * * * * *

Ordinary. Nothing can be plainer. St. * * * * * * * * *

Jonathan. * * * * * If once convinced * * * * * * no man * * lives of * * * * * * whereas sure the clergy * * opportunity * better informed * * * * all manner of vice * * *

Ordinary. * are * atheist. * * deist * ari * * cinian * hanged * * burnt * * oiled * oasted. * * * dev * * his an * * * ell fire * * ternal da * * * tion.

Jonathan. You * * * to frighten me out of my wits.

---

[1] He pronounced this word HULL, and perhaps would have spelt it so.
[2] This part was so blotted that it was illegible.

But the good * * * is, I doubt not, more merciful than his wicked * * If I should believe all you say, I am sure I should die in inexpressible horror.

Ordinary. Despair is sinful. You should place your hopes in repentance and grace; and though it is most true that you are in danger of the judgment, yet there is still room for mercy; and no man, unless excommunicated, is absolutely without hopes of a reprieve.

Jonathan. I am not without hopes of a reprieve from the cheat yet. I have pretty good interest; but if I cannot obtain it, you shall not frighten me out of my courage. I will not die like a pimp. D—n me, what is death? It is nothing but to be with Platos and with Cæsars, as the poet says, and all the other great heroes of antiquity. * * *

Ordinary. Ay, all this is very true; but life is sweet for all that; and I had rather live to eternity than go into the company of any such heathens, who are, I doubt not, in hell with the devil and his angels; and, as little as you seem to apprehend it, you may find yourself there before you expect it. Where, then, will be your tauntings and your vauntings, your boastings and your braggings? You will then be ready to give more for a drop of water than you ever gave for a bottle of wine.

Jonathan. Faith, doctor! well minded. What say you to a bottle of wine?

Ordinary. I will drink no wine with an atheist. I should expect the devil to make a third in such company, for, since he knows you are his, he may be impatient to have his due.

Jonathan. It is your business to drink with the wicked, in order to amend them.

Ordinary. I despair of it; and so I consign you over to the devil, who is ready to receive you.

Jonathan. You are more unmerciful to me than the judge, doctor. He recommended my soul to heaven; and it is your office to shew me the way thither.

Ordinary. No: the gates are barred against all revilers of the clergy.

Jonathan. I revile only the wicked ones, if any such are, which cannot affect you, who, if men were preferred in the church by merit only, would have long since been a bishop. Indeed, it might raise any good man's indignation to observe one of your vast learning and abilities obliged to exert them in so low a sphere, when so many of your inferiors wallow in wealth and preferment.

Ordinary. Why, it must be confessed that there are bad men in all orders; but you should not censure too generally. I must own I might have expected higher promotion; but I have learnt patience and resignation; and I would advise you to the same temper of mind; which if you can attain, I know you will find mercy. Nay, I do now promise you you will. It is true you are a sinner; but your crimes are not of the blackest dye: you are no murderer, nor guilty of sacrilege. And, if you are guilty of theft, you make some atonement by suffering for it, which many others do not. Happy is it indeed for those few who are detected in their sins, and brought to exemplary punishment for them in this world. So far, therefore, from repining at your fate when you come to the tree, you should exult and rejoice in it; and, to say the truth, I question whether, to a wise man, the catastrophe of many of those who die by a halter is not more to be envied than pitied. Nothing is so sinful as sin, and murder is the greatest of all sins. It follows, that whoever commits murder is happy in suffering for it. If, therefore, a man who commits murder is so happy in dying for it, how much better must it be for you, who have committed a less crime!

Jonathan. All this is very true; but let us take a bottle of wine to cheer our spirits.

Ordinary. Why wine? Let me tell you, Mr. Wild, there is nothing so deceitful as the spirits given us by wine. If you must drink, let us have a bowl of punch—a liquor I the rather prefer, as it is nowhere spoken against in Scripture, and as it is more wholesome for the gravel, a distemper with which I am grievously afflicted.

Jonathan (*having called for a bowl*). I ask your pardon, doctor; I should have remembered that punch was your favourite liquor. I think you never taste wine while there is any punch remaining on the table?

Ordinary. I confess I look on punch to be the more eligible liquor, as well for the reasons I have before mentioned as likewise for one other cause, viz. it is the properest for a DRAUGHT. I own I took it a little unkind of you to mention wine, thinking you knew my palate.

Jonathan. You are in the right; and I will take a swinging cup to your being made a bishop.

Ordinary. And I will wish you a reprieve in as large a draught. Come, don't despair; it is yet time enough to think of dying; you have good friends, who very probably may prevail for you. I have known many a man reprieved who had less reason to expect it.

Jonathan. But if I should flatter myself with such hopes, and be deceived—what then would become of my soul?

Ordinary. Pugh! Never mind your soul—leave that to me; I will render a good account of it, I warrant you. I have a sermon in my pocket which may be of some use to you to hear. I do not value myself on the talent of preaching, since no man ought to value himself for any gift in this world. But perhaps there are not many such sermons. But to proceed, since we have nothing else to do till the punch comes. My text is the latter part of a verse only:

———To the Greeks FOOLISHNESS.

The occasion of these words was principally that philosophy of the Greeks which at that time had overrun great part of the heathen world, had poisoned, and, as it were, puffed up their minds with pride, so that they disregarded all kinds of doctrine in comparison of their own; and, however safe and however sound the learning of the others might be, yet, if it anywise contradicted their own laws, customs, and received opinions, *away with it—it is not for us.* It was to the Greeks FOOLISHNESS.

In the former part, therefore, of my discourse on these words, I shall principally confine myself to the laying open and demonstrating the great emptiness and vanity of this philosophy, with which these idle and absurd sophists were so proudly blown up and elevated.

And here I shall do two things: First, I shall expose the matter; and, secondly, the manner of this absurd philosophy.

And first, for the first of these, namely, the matter. Now here we may retort the unmannerly word which our adversaries have audaciously thrown in our faces; for what was all this mighty matter of philosophy, this heap of knowledge, which was to bring such large harvests of honour to those who sowed it, and so greatly and nobly to enrich the ground on which it fell; what was it but FOOLISHNESS? An inconsistent heap of nonsense, of absurdities and contradictions, bringing no ornament to the mind in its theory, nor exhibiting any usefulness to the body in its practice. What were all the sermons and the sayings, the fables and the morals of all these wise men, but, to use the word mentioned in my text once more, FOOLISHNESS? What was their great master Plato, or their other great light Aristotle? Both fools, mere quibblers and sophists, idly and vainly attached to certain ridiculous notions of their own, founded neither on truth nor on reason. Their whole works are a strange medley of the greatest falsehoods, scarce covered over with the colour of truth: their precepts are neither borrowed from nature nor guided by reason; mere fictions, serving only to evince the dreadful height of human pride; in one word, FOOLISHNESS. It may be perhaps expected of me that I should give some instances from their works to prove this charge; but, as to transcribe every passage to my purpose would be to transcribe their whole works, and as in such a plentiful crop it is difficult to choose; instead of trespassing on your patience, I shall conclude this first head with asserting what I have so fully proved, and what may indeed be inferred from the text, that the philosophy of the Greeks was FOOLISHNESS.

Proceed we now, in the second place, to consider the manner in which this inane and simple doctrine was propagated. And here—— But here the punch by entering waked Mr. Wild, who was fast asleep, and put an end to the sermon; nor could we obtain any further account of the conversation which passed at this interview.

CHAPTER XIV

Wild proceeds to the highest consummation of human
GREATNESS

THE day now drew nigh when our great man was to exemplify the last and noblest act of greatness by which any hero can signalize himself. This was the day of execution, or consummation, or apotheosis (for it is called by different names), which was to give our hero an opportunity of facing death and damnation, without any fear in his heart, or, at least, without betraying any symptoms of it in his countenance. A completion of greatness which is heartily to be wished to every great man; nothing being more worthy of lamentation than when Fortune, like a lazy poet, winds up her catastrophe awkwardly, and, bestowing too little care on her fifth act, dismisses the hero with a sneaking and private exit, who had in the former part of the drama performed such notable exploits as must promise to every good judge among the spectators a noble, public, and exalted end.

But she was resolved to commit no such error in this instance. Our hero was too much and too deservedly her favourite to be neglected by her in his last moments; accordingly all efforts for a reprieve were vain, and the name of Wild stood at the head of those who were ordered for execution.

From the time he gave over all hopes of life, his conduct was truly great and admirable. Instead of shewing any marks of dejection or contrition, he rather infused more confidence and assurance into his looks. He spent most of his hours in drinking with his friends and with the good man above commemorated. In one of these compotations, being asked whether he was afraid to die, he answered: "D—n me, it is only a dance without music." Another time, when one expressed some sorrow for his misfortune, as he termed it, he said with great fierceness: "A man can die but once." Again, when one of his intimate acquaintance hinted his hopes, that he would die like a man, he cocked his hat in defiance, and cried out greatly: "Zounds! who's afraid?"

Happy would it have been for posterity, could we have retrieved any entire conversation which passed at this season, especially between our hero and his learned comforter; but we have searched many pasteboard records in vain.

On the eve of his apotheosis, Wild's lady desired to see him, to which he consented. This meeting was at first very tender on both sides; but it could not continue so, for unluckily, some hints of former miscarriages intervening, as particularly when she asked him how he could have used her so barbarously once as calling her b—, and whether such language became a man, much less a gentleman, Wild flew into a violent passion, and swore she was the vilest of b—s to upbraid him at such a season with an unguarded word spoke long ago. She replied, with many tears, she was well enough served for her folly in visiting such a brute; but she had one comfort, however, that it would be the last time he could ever treat her so; that indeed she had some obligation to him, for that his cruelty to her would reconcile her to the fate he was to-morrow to suffer; and, indeed, nothing but such brutality could have made the consideration of his shameful death (so this weak woman called hanging), which was now inevitable, to be borne even without madness. She then proceeded to a recapitulation of his faults in an exacter order, and with more perfect memory, than one would have imagined her capable of; and it is probable would have rehearsed a complete catalogue had not our hero's patience failed him, so that with the utmost fury and violence he caught her by the hair and kicked her, as heartily as his chains would suffer him, out of the room.

At length the morning came which Fortune at his birth had resolutely ordained for the consummation of our hero's GREATNESS: he had himself indeed modestly declined the public honour she intended him, and had taken a quantity of laudanum, in order to retire quietly off the stage; but we have already observed, in the course of our wonderful history, that to struggle against this lady's decrees is vain and impotent; and whether she hath determined you shall be hanged or be a prime minister, it is in either case lost labour to resist. Laudanum, therefore, being unable to stop the breath of our hero, which the fruit of hemp-seed, and not the spirit of poppy-seed, was to overcome, he was at the usual hour attended by the proper gentleman appointed for that purpose, and acquainted that the cart was ready. On this occasion he exerted that greatness of courage which hath been so much celebrated in other heroes; and, knowing it was impossible to resist, he gravely declared he would attend them. He then descended to that room where the fetters of great men are knocked off in a most solemn and ceremonious manner. Then shaking hands with his friends (to wit, those who were conducting him to the tree), and drinking their healths in a bumper of brandy, he ascended the cart, where he was no sooner seated than he received the acclamations of the multitude, who were highly ravished with his GREATNESS.

The cart now moved slowly on, being preceded by a troop of horse-guards bearing javelins in their hands, through streets lined with crowds all admiring the great behaviour of our hero, who rode on, sometimes sighing, sometimes swearing, sometimes singing or whistling, as his humour varied.

When he came to the tree of glory, he was welcomed with an universal shout of the people, who were there assembled in prodigious numbers to behold a sight much more rare in populous cities than one would reasonably imagine it should be, viz. the proper catastrophe of a great man.

But though envy was, through fear, obliged to join the general voice in applause on this occasion, there were not wanting some who maligned this completion of glory, which was now about to be fulfilled to our hero, and endeavoured to prevent it by knocking him on the head as he stood under the tree, while the ordinary was performing his last office. They therefore began to batter the cart with stones, brickbats, dirt, and all manner of mischievous weapons, some of which, erroneously playing on the robes of the ecclesiastic, made him so expeditious in his repetition, that with wonderful alacrity he had ended almost in an instant, and conveyed himself into a place of safety in a hackney-coach, where he waited the conclusion with a temper of mind described in these verses:

> *Suave mari magno, turbantibus æquora ventis,*
> *E terra alterius magnum spectare laborem.*

We must not, however, omit one circumstance, as it serves to shew the most admirable conservation of character in our hero to his last moment, which was, that, whilst the ordinary was busy in his ejaculations, Wild, in the midst of the shower of stones, etc., which played upon him, applied his hands to the parson's pocket, and emptied it of his bottle-screw, which he carried out of the world in his hand.

The ordinary being now descended from the cart, Wild had just opportunity to cast his eyes around the crowd, and to give them a hearty curse, when immediately the horses moved on, and with universal applause our hero swung out of this world.

Thus fell Jonathan Wild the GREAT, by a death as glorious as his life had been, and which was so truly agreeable to it, that the latter must have been deplorably maimed and imperfect without the former: a death which hath been alone wanting to complete the characters of several ancient and modern heroes, whose histories would then have been read with much greater pleasure by the wisest in all ages. Indeed we could almost wish that whenever Fortune seems wantonly to deviate from her purpose, and leaves her work imperfect in this particular, the historian would indulge himself in the licence of poetry and romance, and even do a violence to truth, to oblige his reader with a page which must be the most delightful in all his history, and which could never fail of producing an instructive moral.

Narrow minds may possibly have some reason to be ashamed of going this way out of the world, if their consciences can fly in their faces and assure them they have not merited such an honour; but he must be a fool who is ashamed of being hanged, who is not weak enough to be ashamed of having deserved it.

CHAPTER XV

The character of our hero, and the conclusion of this history

WE will now endeavour to draw the character of this great man; and, by bringing together those several features as it were of his mind which lie scattered up and down in this history, to present our readers with a perfect picture of greatness.

Jonathan Wild had every qualification necessary to form a great man. As his most powerful and predominant passion was ambition, so nature had, with consummate propriety, adapted all his faculties to the attaining those glorious ends to which this passion directed him. He was extremely ingenious in inventing designs, artful in contriving the means to accomplish his purposes, and resolute in executing them: for as the most exquisite cunning and most undaunted boldness qualified him for any undertaking, so was he not restrained by any of those weaknesses which disappoint the views of mean and vulgar souls, and which are comprehended in one general term of honesty, which is a corruption of HONOSTY, a word derived from what the Greeks call an ass. He was entirely free from those low vices of modesty and good-nature, which, as he said, implied a total negation of human greatness, and were the only qualities which absolutely rendered a man incapable of making a considerable figure in the world. His lust was inferior only to his ambition; but, as for what simple people call love, he knew not what it was. His avarice was immense, but it was of the rapacious, not of the tenacious kind; his rapaciousness was indeed so violent, that nothing ever contented him but the whole; for, however considerable the share was which his coadjutors allowed him of a booty, he was restless in inventing means to make himself master of the smallest pittance reserved by them. He said laws were made for the use of *prigs* only, and to secure their property; they were never, therefore, more perverted than when their edge was turned against these; but that this generally happened through their want of sufficient dexterity. The character which he most valued himself upon, and which he principally honoured in others, was that of hypocrisy. His opinion was, that no one could carry *priggism* very far without it; for which reason, he said, there was little greatness to be expected in a man who acknowledged his vices, but always much to be hoped from him who professed great virtues: wherefore, though he would always shun the person whom he discovered guilty of a good action, yet he was never deterred by a good character, which was more commonly the effect of profession than of action: for which reason, he himself was always very liberal of honest professions, and had as much virtue and goodness in his mouth as a saint; never in the least scrupling to swear by his honour, even to those who knew him the best; nay, though he held good-nature and modesty in the highest contempt, he constantly practised the affectation of both, and recommended this to others, whose welfare, on his own account, he wished well to. He laid down several maxims as the certain methods of attaining greatness, to which, in his own pursuit of it, he constantly adhered. As:

1. Never to do more mischief to another than was necessary to the effecting his purpose; for that mischief was too precious a thing to be thrown away.
2. To know no distinction of men from affection; but to sacrifice all with equal readiness to his interest.
3. Never to communicate more of an affair than was necessary to the person who was to execute it.

4. Not to trust him who hath deceived you, nor who knows he hath been deceived by you.

5. To forgive no enemy; but to be cautious and often dilatory in revenge.

6. To shun poverty and distress, and to ally himself as close as possible to power and riches.

7. To maintain a constant gravity in his countenance and behaviour, and to affect wisdom on all occasions.

8. To foment eternal jealousies in his gang, one of another.

9. Never to reward any one equal to his merit; but always to insinuate that the reward was above it.

10. That all men were knaves or fools, and much the greater number a composition of both.

11. That a good name, like money, must be parted with, or at least greatly risked, in order to bring the owner any advantage.

12. That virtues, like precious stones, were easily counterfeited; that the counterfeits in both cases adorned the wearer equally, and that very few had knowledge or discernment sufficient to distinguish the counterfeit jewel from the real.

13. That many men were undone by not going deep enough in roguery; as in gaming any man may be a loser who doth not play the whole game.

14. That men proclaim their own virtues, as shopkeepers expose their goods, in order to profit by them.

15. That the heart was the proper seat of hatred, and the countenance of affection and friendship.

He had many more of the same kind, all equally good with these, and which were after his decease found in his study, as the twelve excellent and celebrated rules were in that of King Charles the First; for he never promulgated them in his lifetime, not having them constantly in his mouth, as some grave persons have the rules of virtue and morality, without paying the least regard to them in their actions: whereas our hero, by a constant and steady adherence to his rules in conforming everything he did to them, acquired at length a settled habit of walking by them, till at last he was in no danger of inadvertently going out of the way; and by these means he arrived at that degree of greatness, which few have equalled; none, we may say, have exceeded: for, though it must be allowed that there have been some few heroes, who have done greater mischiefs to mankind, such as those who have betrayed the liberty of their country to others, or have undermined and overpowered it themselves; or conquerors who have impoverished, pillaged, sacked, burnt, and destroyed the countries and cities of their fellow-creatures, from no other provocation than that of glory, i.e. as the tragic poet calls it,

> a privilege to kill,
> A strong temptation to do bravely ill;

yet, if we consider it in the light wherein actions are placed in this line:

> *Lætius est, quoties magno tibi constat honestum;*

when we see our hero, without the least assistance or pretence, setting himself at the head of a gang, which he had not any shadow of right to govern; if we view him maintaining absolute power, and exercising tyranny over a lawless crew, contrary to all law but that of his own will; if we consider him setting up an open trade publicly, in defiance not only of the laws of his country but of the common sense of his countrymen; if we see him first contriving the robbery of others, and again the defrauding the very robbers of that booty, which they had ventured their necks to acquire, and which without any hazard, they might have retained; here sure he must appear admirable, and we may challenge not only the truth of history, but almost the latitude of fiction, to equal his glory.

Nor had he any of those flaws in his character which, though they have been commended by weak writers, have (as I hinted in the beginning of this history) by the judicious reader been censured and despised. Such was the clemency of Alexander and Cæsar, which nature had so grossly erred in giving them, as a painter would who should dress a peasant in robes of state or give the nose or any other feature of a Venus to a satyr. What had the destroyers of mankind, that glorious pair, one of whom came into the world to usurp the dominion and abolish the constitution of his own country; the other to conquer, enslave, and rule over the whole world, at least as much as was well known to him, and the shortness of his life would give him leave to visit; what had, I say, such as these to do with clemency? Who cannot see the absurdity and contradiction of mixing such an ingredient with those noble and great qualities I have before mentioned? Now, in Wild everything was truly great, almost without alloy, as his imperfections (for surely some small ones he had) were only such as served to denominate him a human creature, of which kind none ever arrived at consummate excellence. But surely his whole behaviour to his friend Heartfree is a convincing proof that the true iron or steel greatness of his heart was not debased by any softer metal. Indeed, while greatness consists in power, pride, insolence, and doing mischief to mankind—to speak out—while a great man and a great rogue are synonymous terms, so long shall Wild stand unrivalled on the pinnacle of GREATNESS. Nor must we omit here, as the finishing of his character, what indeed ought to be remembered on his tomb or his statue, the conformity above mentioned of his death to his life; and that Jonathan Wild the Great, after all his mighty exploits, was, what so few GREAT men can accomplish—hanged by the neck till he was dead.

Having thus brought our hero to his conclusion, it may be satisfactory to some readers (for many, I doubt not, carry their concern no farther than his fate) to know what became of Heartfree. We shall acquaint them, therefore, that his sufferings were now at an end; that the good magistrate easily prevailed for his pardon, nor was contented till he had made him all the reparation he could for his troubles, though the share he had in bringing these upon him was not only innocent but from its motive laudable. He procured the restoration of the jewels from the man-of-war at her return to England, and, above all, omitted no labour to restore Heartfree to his reputation, and to persuade his neighbours, acquaintance, and customers, of his innocence. When the commission of bankruptcy was satisfied, Heartfree had a considerable sum remaining; for the diamond presented to his wife was of prodigious value, and infinitely recompensed the loss of those jewels which Miss Straddle had disposed of. He now set up again in his trade: compassion for his unmerited misfortunes brought him many customers among those who had any regard to humanity; and he hath, by industry joined with parsimony, amassed a considerable fortune. His wife and he are now grown old in the purest love and friendship, but never had another child. Friendly married his elder daughter at the age of nineteen, and became his partner in trade. As to the younger, she never would listen to the addresses of any lover, not even of a young nobleman, who offered to take her with two thousand pounds, which her father would have willingly produced, and indeed did his utmost to persuade her to the match; but she refused absolutely, nor would give any other reason, when Heartfree pressed her, than that she had dedicated her days to his service, and was resolved no other duty should interfere with that which she owed the best of fathers, nor prevent her from being the nurse of his old age.

Thus Heartfree, his wife, his two daughters, his son-in-law, and his grandchildren, of which he hath several, live all together in one house; and that with such amity and affection towards each other, that they are in the neighbourhood called the family of love.

As to all the other persons mentioned in this history in the light of greatness, they had all the fate adapted to it, being every one hanged by the neck, save two, viz. Miss Theodosia Snap, who was transported to America, where she was pretty well married, reformed, and made a good wife; and the count, who recovered of the wound he had received from the hermit and made his escape into France where he committed a robbery, was taken, and broke on the wheel.

Indeed, whoever considers the common fate of great men must allow they well deserve and hardly earn that applause which is given them by the world; for, when we reflect on the labours and pains, the cares, disquietudes, and dangers which attend their road to greatness, we may say with the divine *that a man may go to heaven with half the pains which it costs him to purchase hell*. To say the truth, the world have this reason at least to honour such characters as that of Wild: that, while it is in the power of every man to be perfectly honest, not one in a thousand is capable of being a complete rogue; and few indeed there are who, if they were inspired with the vanity of imitating our hero, would not after much fruitless pains be obliged to own themselves inferior to MR. JONATHAN WILD THE GREAT.

THE JOURNAL OF A VOYAGE
TO LISBON

DEDICATION TO THE PUBLIC

YOUR candour is desired on the perusal of the following
sheets, as they are the product of a genius that has long
been your delight and entertainment. It must be acknowledged that a lamp almost burnt out does not give so
steady and uniform a light as when it blazes in its full
vigour; but yet it is well known that by its wavering, as
if struggling against its own dissolution, it sometimes darts
a ray as bright as ever. In like manner, a strong and lively
genius will, in its last struggles, sometimes mount aloft,
and throw forth the most striking marks of its original
lustre.

Wherever these are to be found, do you, the genuine
patrons of extraordinary capacities, be as liberal in your
applauses of him who is now no more as you were of him
whilst he was yet amongst you. And, on the other hand,
if in this little work there should appear any traces of a
weakened and decayed life, let your own imaginations
place before your eyes a true picture in that of a hand
trembling in almost its latest hour, of a body emaciated
with pains, yet struggling for your entertainment; and let
this affecting picture open each tender heart, and call
forth a melting tear, to blot out whatever failings may be
found in a work begun in pain, and finished almost at the
same period with life.

It was thought proper by the friends of the deceased
that this little piece should come into your hands as it
came from the hands of the author, it being judged that
you would be better pleased to have an opportunity of
observing the faintest traces of a genius you have long
admired, than have it patched by a different hand, by
which means the marks of its true author might have been
effaced.

That the success of the last written, though first published,
volume of the author's posthumous pieces may be attended
with some convenience to those innocents he hath left

behind, will no doubt be a motive to encourage its circulation through the kingdom, which will engage every future genius to exert itself for your pleasure.

The principles and spirit which breathe in every line of the small fragment begun in answer to Lord Bolingbroke will unquestionably be a sufficient apology for its publication, although vital strength was wanting to finish a work so happily begun and so well designed.

AUTHOR'S PREFACE

THERE would not, perhaps, be a more pleasant or profitable study, among those which have their principal end in amusement, than that of travels or voyages, if they were writ, as they might be and ought to be, with a joint view to the entertainment and information of mankind. If the conversation of travellers be so eagerly sought after as it is, we may believe their books will be still more agreeable company, as they will in general be more instructive and more entertaining.

But when I say the conversation of travellers is usually so welcome, I must be understood to mean that only of such as have had good sense enough to apply their peregrinations to a proper use, so as to acquire from them a real and valuable knowledge of men and things, both which are best known by comparison. If the customs and manners of men were everywhere the same, there would be no office so dull as that of a traveller, for the difference of hills, valleys, rivers, in short, the various views in which we may see the face of the earth, would scarce afford him a pleasure worthy of his labour; and surely it would give him very little opportunity of communicating any kind of entertainment or improvement to others.

To make a traveller an agreeable companion to a man of sense, it is necessary, not only that he should have seen much, but that he should have overlooked much of what he hath seen. Nature is not, any more than a great genius, always admirable in her productions, and therefore the traveller, who may be called her commentator, should not expect to find everywhere subjects worthy of his notice.

It is certain, indeed, that one may be guilty of omission, as well as of the opposite extreme; but a fault on that side will be more easily pardoned, as it is better to be hungry than surfeited; and to miss your dessert at the table of a man whose gardens abound with the choicest fruits, than to have your taste affronted with every sort of trash that can be picked up at the green-stall or the wheelbarrow.

If we should carry on the analogy between the traveller and the commentator, it is impossible to keep one's eye a moment off from the laborious much-read Doctor Zachary Gray, of whose redundant notes on *Hudibras* I shall only say that it is, I am confident, the single book extant in which above five hundred authors are quoted, not one of which could be found in the collection of the late Doctor Mead.

As there are few things which a traveller is to record, there are fewer on which he is to offer his observations: this is the office of the reader; and it is so pleasant a one, that he seldom chooses to have it taken from him, under the pretence of lending him assistance. Some occasions, indeed, there are, when proper observations are pertinent, and others when they are necessary; but good sense alone must point them out. I shall lay down only one general rule; which I believe to be of universal truth between relator and hearer, as it is between author and reader; this is, that the latter never forgive any observation of the former which doth not convey some knowledge that they are sensible they could not possibly have attained of themselves.

But all his pains in collecting knowledge, all his judgment in selecting, and all his art in communicating it, will not suffice, unless he can make himself, in some degree, an agreeable as well as an instructive companion. The highest instruction we can derive from the tedious tale of a dull fellow scarce ever pays us for our attention. There is nothing, I think, half so valuable as knowledge, and yet there is nothing which men will give themselves so little trouble to attain; unless it be, perhaps, that lowest degree of it which is the object of curiosity, and which hath therefore that active passion constantly employed in its service. This, indeed, it is in the power of every traveller to gratify; but it is the leading principle in weak minds only.

To render his relation agreeable to the man of sense, it is therefore necessary that the voyager should possess several eminent and rare talents; so rare indeed, that it is almost wonderful to see them ever united in the same person.

And if all these talents must concur in the relator, they are certainly in a more eminent degree necessary to the writer; for here the narration admits of higher ornaments of style, and every fact and sentiment offers itself to the fullest and most deliberate examination.

It would appear, therefore, I think, somewhat strange if such writers as these should be found extremely common; since Nature hath been a most parsimonious distributor of her richest talents, and hath seldom bestowed many on the same person. But, on the other hand, why there should scarce exist a single writer of this kind worthy our regard; and, whilst there is no other branch of history (for this is history) which hath not exercised the greatest pens, why this alone should be overlooked by all men of great genius and erudition, and delivered up to the Goths and Vandals as their lawful property, is altogether as difficult to determine.

And yet that this is the case, with some very few exceptions, is most manifest. Of these I shall willingly admit Burnet and Addison; if the former was not, perhaps, to be considered as a political essayist, and the latter as a commentator on the classics, rather than as a writer of travels; which last title, perhaps, they would both of them have been least ambitious to affect.

Indeed, if these two and two or three more should be removed from the mass, there would remain such a heap of dullness behind, that the appellation of voyage-writer would not appear very desirable.

I am not here unapprised that old Homer himself is by some considered as a voyage-writer; and, indeed, the beginning of his Odyssey may be urged to countenance that opinion, which I shall not controvert. But, whatever species of writing the Odyssey is of, it is surely at the head of that species, as much as the Iliad is of another; and so far the excellent Longinus would allow, I believe, at this day.

But, in reality, the Odyssey, the Telemachus, and all of that kind, are to the voyage-writing I here intend, what romance is to true history, the former being the confounder and corrupter of the latter. I am far from supposing that Homer, Hesiod, and the other ancient poets and mythologists, had any settled design to pervert and confuse the records of antiquity; but it is certain they have effected it; and for my part I must confess I should have honoured and loved Homer more had he written a true history of his own times in humble prose, than those noble poems that have so justly collected the praise of all ages; for, though

I read these with more admiration and astonishment,
I still read Herodotus, Thucydides, and Xenophon with
more amusement and more satisfaction.

The original poets were not, however, without excuse
They found the limits of nature too strait for the immensity of their genius, which they had not room to exert
without extending fact by fiction; and that especially at
a time when the manners of men were too simple to afford
that variety which they have since offered in vain to the
choice of the meanest writers. In doing this they are
again excusable for the manner in which they have done it.

Ut speciosa dehinc miracula promant.

They are not, indeed, so properly said to turn reality into
fiction, as fiction into reality. Their paintings are so bold,
their colours so strong, that everything they touch seems
to exist in the very manner they represent it; their portraits
are so just, and their landscapes so beautiful, that we
acknowledge the strokes of nature in both, without inquiring
whether Nature herself, or her journeyman the poet, formed
the first pattern of the piece.

But other writers (I will put Pliny at their head) have
no such pretensions to indulgence; they lie for lying sake,
or in order insolently to impose the most monstrous
improbabilities and absurdities upon their readers on their
own authority; treating them as some fathers treat children,
and as other fathers do laymen, exacting their belief of
whatever they relate, on no other foundation than their
own authority, without ever taking the pains of adapting
their lies to human credulity, and of calculating them for
the meridian of a common understanding; but, with as
much weakness as wickedness, and with more impudence
often than either, they assert facts contrary to the honour
of God, to the visible order of the creation, to the known
laws of nature, to the histories of former ages, and to the
experience of our own, and which no man can at once
understand and believe.

If it should be objected (and it can nowhere be objected
better than where I now write,[1] as there is nowhere more
pomp of bigotry) that whole nations have been firm
believers in such most absurd suppositions, I reply, the
fact is not true. They have known nothing of the matter,

[1] At Lisbon.

and have believed they knew not what. It is, indeed, with me no matter of doubt but that the Pope and his clergy might teach any of those Christian heterodoxies, the tenets of which are the most diametrically opposite to their own; nay, all the doctrines of Zoroaster, Confucius, and Mahomet, not only with certain and immediate success, but without one Catholic in a thousand knowing he had changed his religion.

What motive a man can have to sit down, and to draw forth a list of stupid, senseless, incredible lies upon paper, would be difficult to determine, did not Vanity present herself so immediately as the adequate cause. The vanity of knowing more than other men is, perhaps, besides hunger, the only inducement to writing, at least to publishing, at all. Why then should not the voyage-writer be inflamed with the glory of having seen what no man ever did or will see but himself? This is the true source of the wonderful in the discourse and writings, and sometimes, I believe, in the actions of men. There is another fault, of a kind directly opposite to this, to which these writers are sometimes liable, when, instead of filling their pages with monsters which nobody hath ever seen, and with adventures which never have, nor possibly could have, happened to them, waste their time and paper with recording things and facts of so common a kind, that they challenge no other right of being remembered than as they had the honour of having happened to the author, to whom nothing seems trivial that in any manner happens to himself. Of such consequence do his own actions appear to one of this kind, that he would probably think himself guilty of infidelity should he omit the minutest thing in the detail of his journal. That the fact is true is sufficient to give it a place there, without any consideration whether it is capable of pleasing or surprising, of diverting or informing, the reader.

I have seen a play (if I mistake not it is one of Mrs. Behn's or of Mrs. Centlivre's) where this vice in a voyage-writer is finely ridiculed. An ignorant pedant, to whose government, for I know not what reason, the conduct of a young nobleman in his travels is committed, and who is sent abroad to shew my lord the world, of which he knows nothing himself, before his departure from a town, calls for his journal to record the goodness of the wine and tobacco, with other articles of the same importance, which are to furnish the materials of a voyage at his return home. The humour, it is true, is here carried very far; and yet, perhaps, very little beyond what is to be found in writers who profess no intention of dealing in humour at all.

Of one or other, or both of these kinds, are, I conceive, all that vast pile of books which pass under the names of voyages, travels, adventures, lives, memoirs, histories, etc., some of which a single traveller sends into the world in many volumes, and others are, by judicious booksellers, collected into vast bodies in folio, and inscribed with their own names, as if they were indeed their own travels: thus unjustly attributing to themselves the merit of others.

Now, from both these faults we have endeavoured to steer clear in the following narrative; which, however the contrary may be insinuated by ignorant, unlearned, and fresh-water critics, who have never travelled either in books or ships, I do solemnly declare doth, in my own impartial opinion, deviate less from truth than any other voyage extant; my Lord Anson's alone being, perhaps, excepted.

Some few embellishments must be allowed to every historian; for we are not to conceive that the speeches in Livy, Sallust, or Thucydides, were literally spoken in the very words in which we now read them. It is sufficient that every fact hath its foundation in truth, as I do seriously aver is the case in the ensuing pages; and when it is so, a good critic will be so far from denying all kind of ornament of style or diction, or even of circumstance, to his author, that he would be rather sorry if he omitted it; for he could hence derive no other advantage than the loss of an additional pleasure in the perusal.

Again, if any merely common incident should appear in this journal, which will seldom, I apprehend, be the case, the candid reader will easily perceive it is not introduced for its own sake, but for some observations and reflections naturally resulting from it; and which, if but little to his amusement, tend directly to the instruction of the reader or to the information of the public; to whom, if I choose to convey such instruction or information with an air of joke and laughter, none but the dullest of fellows will, I believe, censure it; but if they should, I have the authority of more than one passage in Horace to alledge in my defence.

Having thus endeavoured to obviate some censures, to which a man without the gift of foresight, or any fear of the imputation of being a conjurer, might conceive this work would be liable, I might now undertake a more pleasing task, and fall at once to the direct and positive praises of the work itself; of which, indeed, I could say a thousand good things; but the task is so very pleasant that I shall leave it wholly to the reader, and it is all the task that I impose on him. A moderation for which he may think himself obliged to me when he compares it with the conduct of authors, who often fill a whole sheet with their own praises, to which they sometimes set their own real names, and sometimes a fictitious one. One hint, however, I must give the kind reader; which is, that if he should be able to find no sort of amusement in the book, he will be pleased to remember the public utility which will arise from it. If entertainment, as Mr. Richardson observes, be but a secondary consideration in a romance; with which Mr. Addison, I think, agrees, affirming the use of the pastry-cook to be the first; if this, I say, be true of a mere work of invention, sure it may well be so considered in a work founded, like this, on truth; and where the political reflections form so distinguishing a part.

But perhaps I may hear, from some critic of the most saturnine complexion, that my vanity must have made a horrid dupe of my judgment, if it hath flattered me with an expectation of having anything here seen in a grave light, or of conveying any useful instruction to the public, or to their guardians. I answer, with the great man whom I just now quoted, that my purpose is to convey instruction in the vehicle of entertainment; and so to bring about at once, like the revolution in the *Rehearsal*, a perfect reformation of the laws relating to our maritime affairs: an undertaking, I will not say more modest, but surely more feasible, than that of reforming a whole people, by making use of a vehicular story, to wheel in among them worse manners than their own.

AUTHOR'S INTRODUCTION

In the beginning of August 1753, when I had taken the Duke of Portland's medicine, as it is called, near a year, the effects of which had been the carrying off the symptoms of a lingering, imperfect gout, I was persuaded by Mr. Ranby, the king's premier serjeant-surgeon, and the ablest advice, I believe, in all branches of the physical profession, to go immediately to Bath. I accordingly writ that very night to Mrs. Bowden, who, by the next post, informed me she had taken me a lodging for a month certain.

Within a few days after this, whilst I was preparing for my journey, and when I was almost fatigued to death with several long examinations, relating to five different murders, all committed within the space of a week, by different gangs of street-robbers, I received a message from His Grace the Duke of Newcastle, by Mr. Carrington, the king's messenger, to attend His Grace the next morning, in Lincoln's Inn Fields, upon some business of importance; but I excused myself from complying with the message, as, besides being lame, I was very ill with the great fatigues I had lately undergone added to my distemper.

His Grace, however, sent Mr. Carrington, the very next morning, with another summons; with which, though in the utmost distress, I immediately complied; but the duke, happening, unfortunately for me, to be then particularly engaged, after I had waited some time, sent a gentleman to discourse with me on the best plan which could be invented for putting an immediate end to those murders and robberies which were every day committed in the streets; upon which I promised to transmit my opinion, in writing, to His Grace, who, as the gentleman informed me, intended to lay it before the Privy Council.

Though this visit cost me a severe cold, I, notwithstanding, set myself down to work; and in about four days sent the duke as regular a plan as I could form, with all the reasons and arguments I could bring to support it, drawn out in several sheets of paper; and soon received a message from the duke by Mr. Carrington, acquainting me that my plan was highly approved of, and that all the terms of it would be complied with.

The principal and most material of those terms was the immediately depositing six hundred pounds in my hands; at which small charge I undertook to demolish the then reigning gangs, and to put the civil policy into such order, that no such gangs should ever be able, for the future, to form themselves into bodies, or at least to remain any time formidable to the public.

I had delayed my Bath journey for some time, contrary to the repeated advice of my physical acquaintance, and to the ardent desire of my warmest friends, though my distemper was now turned to a deep jaundice; in which case the Bath waters are generally reputed to be almost infallible. But I had the most eager desire of demolishing this gang of villains and cut-throats, which I was sure of accomplishing the moment I was enabled to pay a fellow who had undertaken, for a small sum, to betray them into the hands of a set of thief-takers whom I had enlisted into the service, all men of known and approved fidelity and intrepidity.

After some weeks the money was paid at the treasury, and within a few days after two hundred pounds of it had come to my hands, the whole gang of cut-throats was entirely dispersed, seven of them were in actual custody, and the rest driven, some out of the town, and others out of the kingdom.

Though my health was now reduced to the last extremity, I continued to act with the utmost vigour against these villains; in examining whom, and in taking the depositions against them, I have often spent whole days, nay, sometimes whole nights, especially when there was any difficulty in procuring sufficient evidence to convict them; which is a very common case in street-robberies, even when the guilt of the party is sufficiently apparent to satisfy the most tender conscience. But courts of justice know nothing of a cause more than what is told them on oath by a witness; and the most flagitious villain upon earth is tried in the same manner as a man of the best character who is accused of the same crime.

Meanwhile, amidst all my fatigues and distresses, I had the satisfaction to find my endeavours had been attended with such success that this hellish society were almost utterly extirpated, and that, instead of reading of murders and street-robberies in the news almost every morning, there was, in the remaining part of the month of November, and in all December, not only no such thing as a murder, but not even a street-robbery committed. Some such, indeed, were mentioned in the public papers; but they were all found, on the strictest enquiry, to be false.

In this entire freedom from street-robberies, during the dark months, no man will, I believe, scruple to acknowledge that the winter of 1753 stands unrivalled, during a course of many years; and this may possibly appear the more extraordinary to those who recollect the outrages with which it began.

Having thus fully accomplished my undertaking, I went into the country, in a very weak and deplorable condition, with no fewer or less diseases than a jaundice, a dropsy, and an asthma, altogether uniting their forces in the destruction of a body so entirely emaciated that it had lost all its muscular flesh.

Mine was now no longer what was called a Bath case; nor, if it had been so, had I strength remaining sufficient to go thither, a ride of six miles only being attended with an intolerable fatigue. I now discharged my lodgings at Bath, which I had hitherto kept. I began in earnest to look on my case as desperate, and I had vanity enough to rank myself with those heroes who, of old times, became voluntary sacrifices to the good of the public.

But, lest the reader should be too eager to catch at the word *vanity*, and should be unwilling to indulge me with so sublime a gratification, for I think he is not too apt to gratify me, I will take my key a pitch lower, and will frankly own that I had a stronger motive than the love of the public to push me on: I will therefore confess to him that my private affairs at the beginning of the winter had but a gloomy aspect; for I had not plundered the public or the poor of those sums which men, who are always ready to plunder both as much as they can, have been pleased to suspect me of taking: on the contrary, by composing, instead of inflaming, the quarrels of porters and beggars (which I blush when I say hath not been universally practised), and by refusing to take a shilling from a man who most undoubtedly would not have had another left,

I had reduced an income of about five hundred pounds [1] a year of the dirtiest money upon earth to little more than three hundred pounds; a considerable proportion of which remained with my clerk; and, indeed, if the whole had done so, as it ought, he would be but ill paid for sitting almost sixteen hours in the twenty-four in the most unwholesome, as well as nauseous air in the universe, and which hath in his case corrupted a good constitution without contaminating his morals.

But, not to trouble the reader with anecdotes, contrary to my own rule laid down in my preface, I assure him I thought my family was very slenderly provided for; and that my health began to decline so fast that I had very little more of life left to accomplish what I had thought of too late. I rejoiced, therefore, greatly in seeing an opportunity, as I apprehended, of gaining such merit in the eye of the public, that, if my life were the sacrifice to it, my friends might think they did a popular act in putting my family at least beyond the reach of necessity, which I myself began to despair of doing. And though I disclaim all pretence to that Spartan or Roman patriotism which loved the public so well that it was always ready to become a voluntary sacrifice to the public good, I do solemnly declare I have that love for my family.

After this confession, therefore, that the public was not the principal deity to which my life was offered a sacrifice,

[1] A predecessor of mine used to boast that he made one thousand pounds a year in his office; but how he did this (if indeed he did it) is to me a secret. His clerk, now mine, told me I had more business than he had ever known there; I am sure I had as much as any man could do. The truth is, the fees are so very low, when any are due, and so much is done for nothing, that, if a single justice of peace had business enough to employ twenty clerks, neither he nor they would get much by their labour. The public will not, therefore, I hope, think I betray a secret when I inform them that I received from the Government a yearly pension out of the public service-money; which, I believe, indeed, would have been larger had my great patron been convinced of an error, which I have heard him utter more than once, that he could not indeed say that the acting as a principal justice of peace in Westminster was on all accounts very desirable, but that all the world knew it was a very lucrative office. Now, to have shewn him plainly that a man must be a rogue to make a very little this way, and that he could not make much by being as great a rogue as he could be, would have required more confidence than, I believe, he had in me, and more of his conversation than he chose to allow me; I therefore resigned the office and the farther execution of my plan to my brother, who had long been my assistant. And now, lest the case between me and the reader should be the same in both instances as it was between me and the great man, I will not add another word on the subject.

and when it is farther considered what a poor sacrifice this was, being indeed no other than the giving up what I saw little likelihood of being able to hold much longer, and which, upon the terms I held it, nothing but the weakness of human nature could represent to me as worth holding at all; the world may, I believe, without envy, allow me all the praise to which I have any title.

My aim, in fact, was not praise, which is the last gift they care to bestow; at least, this was not my aim as an end, but rather as a means of purchasing some moderate provision for my family, which, though it should exceed my merit, must fall infinitely short of my service, if I succeeded in my attempt.

To say the truth, the public never act more wisely than when they act most liberally in the distribution of their rewards; and here the good they receive is often more to be considered than the motive from which they receive it. Example alone is the end of all public punishments and rewards. Laws never inflict disgrace in resentment, nor confer honour from gratitude. "For it is very hard, my lord," said a convicted felon at the bar to the late excellent Judge Burnet, "to hang a poor man for stealing a horse." "You are not to be hanged, sir," answered my ever-honoured and beloved friend, "for stealing a horse, but you are to be hanged that horses may not be stolen." In like manner it might have been said to the late Duke of Marlborough, when the Parliament was so deservedly liberal to him, after the Battle of Blenheim: "You receive not these honours and bounties on account of a victory past, but that other victories may be obtained."

I was now, in the opinion of all men, dying of a complication of disorders; and, were I desirous of playing the advocate, I have an occasion fair enough; but I disdain such an attempt. I relate facts plainly and simply as they are; and let the world draw from them what conclusions they please, taking with them the following facts for their instruction: the one is, that the proclamation offering one hundred pounds for the apprehending felons for certain felonies committed in certain places, which I prevented from being revived, had formerly cost the Government several thousand pounds within a single year. Secondly, that all such proclamations, instead of curing the evil, had actually increased it; had multiplied the number of robberies; had propagated the worst and wickedest of perjuries; had laid snares for youth and ignorance which, by the temptation of these rewards, had been sometimes drawn into guilt; and sometimes, which cannot be thought on without the highest horror, had destroyed them without it. Thirdly, that my plan had not put the Government to more than three hundred pound expense, and had produced none of the ill consequences above mentioned; but, lastly, had actually suppressed the evil for a time, and had plainly pointed out the means of suppressing it for ever. This I would myself have undertaken, had my health permitted, at the annual expense of the above-mentioned sum.

After having stood the terrible six weeks which succeeded last Christmas, and put a lucky end, if they had known their own interests, to such numbers of aged and infirm valetudinarians, who might have gasped through two or three mild winters more, I returned to town in February, in a condition less despaired of by myself than by any of my friends. I now became the patient of Dr. Ward, who wished I had taken his advice earlier.

By his advice I was tapped, and fourteen quarts of water drawn from my belly. The sudden relaxation which this caused, added to my enervate, emaciated habit of body, so weakened me that within two days I was thought to be falling into the agonies of death.

I was at the worst on that memorable day when the public lost Mr. Pelham. From that day I began slowly, as it were, to draw my feet out of the grave; till in two months' time I had again acquired some little degree of strength, but was again full of water.

During this whole time I took Mr. Ward's medicines, which had seldom any perceptible operation. Those in particular of the diaphoretic kind, the working of which is thought to require a great strength of constitution to support, had so little effect on me, that Mr. Ward declared it was as vain to attempt sweating me as a deal board.

In this situation I was tapped a second time. I had one quart of water less taken from me now than before; but I bore all the consequences of the operation much better. This I attributed greatly to a dose of laudanum prescribed by my surgeon. It first gave me the most delicious flow of spirits, and afterwards as comfortable a nap.

The month of May, which was now begun, it seemed reasonable to expect would introduce the spring, and drive off that winter which yet maintained its footing on the stage. I resolved, therefore, to visit a little house of mine in the country, which stands at Ealing, in the county of Middlesex, in the best air, I believe, in the whole kingdom, and far superior to that of Kensington Gravel Pits; for the gravel is here much wider and deeper, the place higher and more open towards the south, whilst it is guarded from the north wind by a ridge of hills, and from the smells and smoke of London by its distance; which last is not the fate of Kensington, when the wind blows from any corner of the east.

Obligations to Mr. Ward I shall always confess; for I am convinced that he omitted no care in endeavouring to serve me, without any expectation or desire of fee or reward.

The powers of Mr. Ward's remedies want indeed no unfair puffs of mine to give them credit; and though this distemper of the dropsy stands, I believe, first in the list of those over which he is always certain of triumphing, yet, possibly, there might be something particular in my case capable of eluding that radical force which had healed so many thousands. The same distemper, in different constitutions, may possibly be attended with such different symptoms, that to find an infallible nostrum for the curing any one distemper in every patient may be almost as difficult as to find a panacea for the cure of all.

But even such a panacea one of the greatest scholars and best of men did lately apprehend he had discovered. It is true, indeed, he was no physician; that is, he had not by the forms of his education acquired a right of applying his skill in the art of physic to his own private advantage; and yet, perhaps, it may be truly asserted that no other modern hath contributed so much to make his physical skill useful to the public; at least, that none hath undergone the pains of communicating this discovery in writing to the world. The reader, I think, will scarce need to be informed that the writer I mean is the late Bishop of Cloyne, in Ireland, the discovery that of the virtues of tar-water.

I then happened to recollect, upon a hint given me by the inimitable and shamefully distressed author of the *Female Quixote*, that I had many years before, from curiosity only, taken a cursory view of Bishop Berkeley's treatise on the virtues of tar-water, which I had formerly observed he strongly contends to be that real panacea which Sydenham supposes to have an existence in nature, though it yet remains undiscovered, and perhaps will always remain so.

Upon the reperusal of this book I found the bishop only asserting his opinion that tar-water might be useful in the dropsy, since he had known it to have a surprising success in the cure of a most stubborn anasarca, which is indeed no other than, as the word implies, the dropsy of the flesh; and this was, at that time, a large part of my complaint.

After a short trial, therefore, of a milk diet, which I presently found did not suit with my case, I betook myself to the bishop's prescription, and dosed myself every morning and evening with half a pint of tar-water.

It was no more than three weeks since my last tapping, and my belly and limbs were distended with water. This did not give me the worse opinion of tar-water; for I never supposed there could be any such virtue in tar-water as immediately to carry off a quantity of water already collected. For my delivery from this I well knew I must be again obliged to the trochar; and if the tar-water did me any good at all it must be only by the slowest degrees; and that if it should ever get the better of my distemper it must be by the tedious operation of undermining, and not by a sudden attack and storm.

Some visible effects, however, and far beyond what my most sanguine hopes could with any modesty expect, I very soon experienced; the tar-water having, from the very first, lessened my illness, increased my appetite, and added, though in a very slow proportion, to my bodily strength.

But if my strength had increased a little my water daily increased much more. So that, by the end of May, my belly became again ripe for the trochar, and I was a third time tapped; upon which, two very favourable symptoms appeared. I had three quarts of water taken from me less than had been taken the last time; and I bore the relaxation with much less (indeed with scarce any) faintness.

Those of my physical friends on whose judgment I chiefly depended seemed to think my only chance of life consisted in having the whole summer before me; in which I might hope to gather sufficient strength to encounter the inclemencies of the ensuing winter. But this chance began daily to lessen. I saw the summer mouldering away, or rather, indeed, the year passing away without intending to bring on any summer at all. In the whole month of May the sun scarce appeared three times. So that the early fruits came to the fulness of their growth, and to some appearance of ripeness, without acquiring any real maturity; having wanted the heat of the sun to soften and meliorate their juices. I saw the dropsy gaining rather than losing ground; the distance growing still shorter between the tappings. I saw the asthma likewise beginning again to become more troublesome. I saw the midsummer quarter drawing towards a close. So that I conceived, if the Michaelmas quarter should steal off in the same manner, as it was, in my opinion, very much to be apprehended it would, I should be delivered up to the attacks of winter before I recruited my forces, so as to be anywise able to withstand them.

I now began to recall an intention, which from the first dawnings of my recovery I had conceived, of removing to a warmer climate; and, finding this to be approved of by a very eminent physician, I resolved to put it into immediate execution.

Aix in Provence was the place first thought on; but the difficulties of getting thither were insuperable. The journey by land, beside the expense of it, was infinitely too long and fatiguing; and I could hear of no ship that was likely to set out from London, within any reasonable time, for Marseilles, or any other port in that part of the Mediterranean.

Lisbon was presently fixed on in its room. The air here, as it was near four degrees to the south of Aix, must be more mild and warm, and the winter shorter and less piercing.

It was not difficult to find a ship bound to a place with which we carry on so immense a trade. Accordingly, my brother soon informed me of the excellent accommodations for passengers which were to be found on board a ship that was obliged to sail for Lisbon in three days.

I eagerly embraced the offer, notwithstanding the shortness of the time; and, having given my brother full power to contract for our passage, I began to prepare my family for the voyage with the utmost expedition.

But our great haste was needless; for the captain having twice put off his sailing, I at length invited him to dinner with me at Fordhook, a full week after the time on which he had declared, and that with many asseverations, he must and would weigh anchor.

He dined with me according to his appointment; and when all matters were settled between us, left me with positive orders to be on board the Wednesday following, when he declared he would fall down the river to Gravesend, and would not stay a moment for the greatest man in the world.

He advised me to go to Gravesend by land, and there wait the arrival of his ship, assigning many reasons for this, every one of which was, as I well remember, among those that had before determined me to go on board near the Tower.

THE JOURNAL OF A VOYAGE TO LISBON

WEDNESDAY, *June* 26, 1754. On this day the most melancholy sun I had ever beheld arose, and found me awake at my house at Fordhook. By the light of this sun I was, in my own opinion, last to behold and take leave of some of those creatures on whom I doted with a mother-like fondness, guided by nature and passion, and uncured and unhardened by all the doctrine of that philosophical school where I had learned to bear pains and to despise death.

In this situation, as I could not conquer Nature, I submitted entirely to her, and she made as great a fool of me as she had ever done of any woman whatsoever; under pretence of giving me leave to enjoy, she drew me in to suffer, the company of my little ones during eight hours; and I doubt not whether, in that time, I did not undergo more than in all my distemper.

At twelve precisely my coach was at the door, which was no sooner told me than I kissed my children round, and went into it with some little resolution. My wife, who behaved more like a heroine and philosopher, though at the same time the tenderest mother in the world, and my eldest daughter, followed me; some friends went with us, and others here took their leave; and I heard my behaviour applauded, with many murmurs and praises to which I well knew I had no title; as all other such philosophers may, if they have any modesty, confess on the like occasions.

In two hours we arrived in Redriffe, and immediately went on board, and were to have sailed the next morning; but, as this was the king's Proclamation Day, and consequently a holiday at the custom-house, the captain could not clear his vessel till the Thursday; for these holidays are as strictly observed as those in the popish calendar, and are almost as numerous. I might add that both are opposite to the genius of trade, and consequently *contra bonum publicum*.

To go on board the ship it was necessary first to go into a boat; a matter of no small difficulty, as I had no use of my limbs, and was to be carried by men who, though sufficiently strong for their burthen, were, like Archimedes, puzzled to find a steady footing. Of this, as few of my readers have not gone into wherries on the Thames, they will easily be able to form to themselves an idea. However, by the assistance of my friend Mr. Welch, whom I never think or speak of but with love and esteem, I conquered this difficulty, as I did afterwards that of ascending the ship, into which I was hoisted with more ease by a chair lifted with pulleys. I was soon seated in a great chair in the cabin, to refresh myself after a fatigue which had been more intolerable, in a quarter of a mile's passage from my coach to the ship, than I had before undergone in a land-journey of twelve miles, which I had travelled with the utmost expedition.

This latter fatigue was, perhaps, somewhat heightened by an indignation which I could not prevent arising in my mind. I think, upon my entrance into the boat, I presented a spectacle of the highest horror. The total loss of limbs was apparent to all who saw me, and my face contained marks of a most diseased state, if not of death itself. Indeed, so ghastly was my countenance, that timorous women with child had abstained from my house, for fear of the ill consequences of looking at me. In this condition I ran the gauntlope (so I think I may justly call it) through rows of sailors and watermen, few of whom failed of paying their compliments to me by all manner of insults and jests on my misery. No man who knew me will think I conceived any personal resentment at this behaviour; but it was a lively picture of that cruelty and inhumanity in the nature of men which I have often contemplated with concern, and which leads the mind into a train of very uncomfortable and melancholy thoughts. It may be said that this barbarous custom is peculiar to the English, and of them only to the lowest degree; that it is an excrescence of an uncontrolled licentiousness mistaken for liberty, and never shews itself in men who are polished and refined in such manner as human nature requires to produce that perfection of which it is susceptible, and to purge away that malevolence of disposition of which, at our birth, we partake in common with the savage creation.

This may be said, and this is all that can be said; and it is, I am afraid, but little satisfactory to account for the inhumanity of those who, while they boast of being made after God's own image, seem to bear in their minds a resemblance of the vilest species of brutes; or rather, indeed, of our idea of devils; for I don't know that any brutes can be taxed with such malevolence.

A sirloin of beef was now placed on the table, for which, though little better than carrion, as much was charged by the master of the little paltry ale-house who dressed it as would have been demanded for all the elegance of the King's Arms, or any other polite tavern or eating-house! for, indeed, the difference between the best house and the worst is, that at the former you pay largely for luxury, at the latter for nothing.

Thursday, June 27. This morning the captain, who lay on shore at his own house, paid us a visit in the cabin, and behaved like an angry bashaw, declaring that, had he known we were not to be pleased, he would not have carried us for five hundred pounds. He added many asseverations that he was a gentleman, and despised money; not forgetting several hints of the presents which had been made him for his cabin, of twenty, thirty, and forty guineas, by several gentlemen, over and above the sum for which they had contracted. This behaviour greatly surprised me, as I knew not how to account for it, nothing having happened since we parted from the captain the evening before in perfect good-humour; and all this broke forth on the first moment of his arrival this morning. He did not, however, suffer my amazement to have any long continuance before he clearly shewed me that all this was meant only as an apology to introduce another procrastination (being the fifth) of his weighing anchor, which was now postponed till Saturday, for such was his will and pleasure.

Besides the disagreeable situation in which we then lay, in the confines of Wapping and Redriffe, tasting a delicious mixture of the air of both these sweet places, and enjoying the concord of sweet sounds of seamen, watermen, fish-women, oyster-women, and of all the vociferous inhabitants of both shores, composing altogether a greater variety of harmony than Hogarth's imagination hath brought together in that print of his, which is enough to make a man deaf to look at—I had a more urgent cause to press our departure, which was, that the dropsy, for which I had undergone three tappings, seemed to threaten me with a fourth discharge before I should reach Lisbon, and when I should have nobody on board capable of performing the operation; but I was obliged to hearken to the voice of reason, if I may use the captain's own words, and to rest myself contented. Indeed, there was no alternative within my reach but what would have cost me much too dear.

There are many evils in society from which people of the highest rank are so entirely exempt, that they have not the least knowledge or idea of them; nor indeed of the characters which are formed by them. Such, for instance, is the conveyance of goods and passengers from one place to another. Now there is no such thing as any kind of knowledge contemptible in itself; and, as the particular knowledge I here mean is entirely necessary to the well understanding and well enjoying this journal; and, lastly, as in this case the most ignorant will be those very readers whose amusement we chiefly consult, and to whom we wish to be supported principally to write, we will here enter somewhat largely into the discussion of this matter; the rather, for that no ancient or modern author (if we can trust the catalogue of Doctor Mead's library) hath ever undertaken it, but that it seems (in the style of Don Quixote) a task reserved for my pen alone.

When I first conceived this intention I began to entertain thoughts of enquiring into the antiquity of travelling; and, as many persons have performed in this way (I mean have travelled) at the expense of the public, I flattered myself that the spirit of improving arts and sciences, and of advancing useful and substantial learning, which so eminently distinguishes this age, and hath given rise to more speculative societies in Europe than I at present can recollect the names of—perhaps, indeed, than I or any other, besides their very near neighbours, ever heard mentioned—would assist in promoting so curious a work; a work begun with the same views, calculated for the same purposes, and fitted for the same uses, with the labours which those right honourable societies have so cheerfully undertaken themselves, and encouraged in others; sometimes with the highest honours, even with admission into their colleges, and with enrolment among their members.

From these societies I promised myself all assistance in their power, particularly the communication of such valuable manuscripts and records as they must be supposed to have collected from those obscure ages of antiquity when history yields us such imperfect accounts of the residence, and much more imperfect of the travels, of the human race; unless, perhaps, as a curious and learned member of the young Society of Antiquarians is said to have hinted his conjectures, that their residence and their travels were one and the same; and this discovery (for such it seems to be) he is said to have owed to the lighting by accident on a book, which we shall have occasion to mention presently, the contents of which were then little known to the society.

The King of Prussia, moreover, who, from a degree of benevolence and taste which in either case is a rare production in so northern a climate, is the great encourager of art and science, I was well assured would promote so useful a design, and order his archives to be searched on my behalf.

But after well weighing all these advantages, and much meditation on the order of my work, my whole design was subverted in a moment by hearing of the discovery just mentioned to have been made by the young antiquarian, who, from the most ancient record in the world (though I don't find the society are all agreed on this point), one long preceding the date of the earliest modern collections, either of books or butterflies, none of which pretend to go beyond the flood, shews us that the first man was a traveller, and that he and his family were scarce settled in Paradise before they disliked their own home, and became passengers to another place. Hence it appears that the humour of travelling is as old as the human race, and that it was their curse from the beginning.

By this discovery my plan became much shortened, and I found it only necessary to treat of the conveyance of goods and passengers from place to place; which, not being universally known, seemed proper to be explained before we examined into its original. There are, indeed, two different ways of tracing all things used by the historian and the antiquary; these are upwards and downwards. The former shews you how things are, and leaves to others to discover when they began to be so. The latter shews you how things were, and leaves their present existence to be examined by others. Hence the former is more useful, the latter more curious. The former receives the thanks of mankind; the latter of that valuable part, the virtuosi.

In explaining, therefore, this mystery of carrying goods and passengers from one place to another, hitherto so profound a secret to the very best of our readers, we shall pursue the historical method, and endeavour to shew by what means it is at present performed, referring the more curious enquiry either to some other pen or to some other opportunity.

Now there are two general ways of performing (if God permit) this conveyance, viz. by land and water, both of which have much variety; that by land being performed in different vehicles, such as coaches, caravans, waggons, etc.; and that by water in ships, barges, and boats, of various sizes and denominations. But, as all these methods of conveyance are formed on the same principles, they agree so well together, that it is fully sufficient to comprehend them all in the general view, without descending to such minute particulars as would distinguish one method from another.

Common to all of these is one general principle, that, as the goods to be conveyed are usually the larger, so they are to be chiefly considered in the conveyance; the owner being indeed little more than an appendage to his trunk, or box, or bale, or at best a small part of his own baggage, very little care is to be taken in stowing or packing them up with convenience to himself; for the conveyance is not of passengers and goods, but of goods and passengers.

Secondly, from this conveyance arises a new kind of relation, or rather of subjection, in the society, by which the passenger becomes bound in allegiance to his conveyer. This allegiance is indeed only temporary and local, but the most absolute during its continuance of any known in Great Britain, and, to say truth, scarce consistent with the liberties of a free people, nor could it be reconciled with them, did it not move downwards; a circumstance universally apprehended to be incompatible to all kinds of slavery; for Aristotle in his *Politics* hath proved abundantly to my satisfaction that no men are born to be slaves, except barbarians; and these only to such as are not themselves barbarians; and indeed Mr. Montesquieu hath carried it very little farther in the case of the Africans; the real truth being that no man is born to be a slave, unless to him who is able to make him so.

Thirdly, this subjection is absolute, and consists of a perfect resignation both of body and soul to the disposal of another; after which resignation, during a certain time, his subject retains no more power over his own will than an Asiatic slave, or an English wife, by the laws of both countries, and by the customs of one of them. If I should mention the instance of a stage-coachman, many of my readers would recognize the truth of what I have here observed; all, indeed, that ever have been under the dominion of that tyrant, who in this free country is as absolute as a Turkish bashaw. In two particulars only his power is defective; he cannot press you into his service, and if you enter yourself at one place, on condition of being discharged at a certain time at another, he is obliged to perform his agreement, if God permit, but all the inter-mediate time you are absolutely under his government; he carries you how he will, when he will, and whither he will, provided it be not much out of the road; you have nothing to eat or to drink, but what, and when, and where he pleases. Nay, you cannot sleep unless he pleases you should; for he will order you sometimes out of bed at midnight and hurry you away at a moment's warning: indeed, if you can sleep in his vehicle he cannot prevent it; nay, indeed, to give him his due, this he is ordinarily disposed to encourage: for the earlier he forces you to rise in the morning, the more time he will give you in the heat of the day, sometimes even six hours at an ale-house, or at their doors, where he always gives you the same indul-gence which he allows himself; and for this he is generally very moderate in his demands. I have known a whole bundle of passengers charged no more than half a crown for being suffered to remain quiet at an ale-house for above a whole hour, and that even in the hottest day in summer.

But as this kind of tyranny, though it hath escaped our political writers, hath been I think touched by our dramatic, and is more trite among the generality of readers; and as this and all other kinds of such subjection are alike unknown to my friends, I will quit the passengers by land, and treat of those who travel by water; for whatever is said on this subject is applicable to both alike, and we may bring them together as closely as they are brought in the liturgy, when they are recommended to the prayers of all Christian congregations; and (which I have often thought very remarkable) where they are joined with other miserable wretches, such as women in labour, people in sickness, infants just born, prisoners, and captives.

Goods and passengers are conveyed by water in divers vehicles, the principal of which being a ship, it shall suffice to mention that alone. Here the tyrant doth not derive his title, as the stage-coachman doth, from the vehicle itself in which he stows his goods and passengers, but he is called the captain—a word of such various use and uncertain signification, that it seems very difficult to fix any positive idea to it: if, indeed, there be any general meaning, which may comprehend all its different uses, that of the head or chief of any body of men seems to be most capable of this comprehension; for whether they be a company of soldiers, a crew of sailors, or a gang of rogues, he who is at the head of them is always styled the captain.

The particular tyrant whose fortune it was to stow us aboard laid a further claim to this appellation than the bare command of a vehicle of conveyance. He had been the captain of a privateer, which he chose to call being in the king's service, and thence derived a right of hoisting the military ornament of a cockade over the button of his hat. He likewise wore a sword of no ordinary length by his side, with which he swaggered in his cabin, among the wretches his passengers, whom he had stowed in cupboards on each side. He was a person of a very singular character. He had taken it into his head that he was a gentleman, from those very reasons that proved he was not one; and to shew himself a fine gentleman, by a behaviour which seemed to insinuate he had never seen one. He was, moreover, a man of gallantry; at the age of seventy he had the finicalness of Sir Courtly Nice, with the roughness of Surly; and, while he was deaf himself, had a voice capable of deafening all others.

Now, as I saw myself in danger by the delays of the captain, who was, in reality, waiting for more freight, and as the wind had been long nested, as it were, in the southwest, where it constantly blew hurricanes, I began with great reason to apprehend that our voyage might be long, and that my belly, which began already to be much

extended, would require the water to be let out at a time
when no assistance was at hand; though, indeed, the captain
comforted me with assurances that he had a pretty young
fellow on board who acted as his surgeon, as I found he
likewise did as steward, cook, butler, sailor. In short, he
had as many offices as Scrub in the play, and went through
them all with great dexterity; this of surgeon was, perhaps,
the only one in which his skill was somewhat deficient, at
least that branch of tapping for the dropsy; for he very
ingenuously and modestly confessed he had never seen the
operation performed, nor was possessed of that chirurgical
instrument with which it is performed.

Friday, June 28. By way of prevention, therefore, I this
day sent for my friend Mr. Hunter, the great surgeon and
anatomist of Covent Garden; and, though my belly was
not yet very full and tight, let out ten quarts of water; the
young sea-surgeon attended the operation, not as a per-
former, but as a student.

I was now eased of the greatest apprehension which I
had from the length of the passage; and I told the captain
I was become indifferent as to the time of his sailing. He
expressed much satisfaction in this declaration, and at
hearing from me that I found myself, since my tapping,
much lighter and better. In this, I believe, he was sincere;
for he was, as we shall have occasion to observe more than
once, a very good-natured man; and, as he was a very
brave one too, I found that the heroic constancy with
which I had borne an operation that is attended with
scarce any degree of pain had not a little raised me in his
esteem. That he might adhere, therefore, in the most
religious and rigorous manner to his word, when he had
no longer any temptation from interest to break it, as he
had no longer any hopes of more goods or passengers, he
ordered his ship to fall down to Gravesend on Sunday
morning, and there to wait his arrival.

Sunday, June 30. Nothing worth notice passed till that
morning, when my poor wife, after passing a night in the
utmost torments of the toothache, resolved to have it
drawn. I dispatched therefore a servant into Wapping
to bring in haste the best tooth-drawer he could find. He
soon found out a female of great eminence in the art; but
when he brought her to the boat, at the water-side, they
were informed that the ship was gone; for indeed she had

set out a few minutes after his quitting her; nor did the
pilot, who well knew the errand on which I had sent my
servant, think fit to wait a moment for his return, or to
give me any notice of his setting out, though I had very
patiently attended the delays of the captain four days,
after many solemn promises of weighing anchor every one
of the three last.

But of all the petty bashaws or turbulent tyrants I ever
beheld, this sour-faced pilot was the worst tempered; for
during the time that he had the guidance of the ship, which
was till we arrived in the Downs, he complied with no one's
desires, nor did he give a civil word, or indeed a civil look,
to any on board.

The tooth-drawer, who, as I said before, was one of
great eminence among her neighbours, refused to follow
the ship; so that my man made himself the best of his
way, and with some difficulty came up with us before we
were got under full sail; for after that, as we had both
wind and tide with us, he would have found it impossible
to overtake the ship till she was come to an anchor at
Gravesend.

The morning was fair and bright, and we had a passage
thither, I think, as pleasant as can be conceived: for, take
it with all its advantages, particularly the number of fine
ships you are always sure of seeing by the way, there is
nothing to equal it in all the rivers of the world. The
yards of Deptford and of Woolwich are noble sights, and
give us a just idea of the great perfection to which we are
arrived in building those floating castles, and the figure
which we may always make in Europe among the other
maritime powers.   That of Woolwich, at least, very strongly
imprinted this idea on my mind; for there was now on the
stocks there the *Royal Anne*, supposed to be the largest
ship ever built, and which contains ten carriage-guns more
than had ever yet equipped a first-rate.

It is true, perhaps, that there is more of ostentation than
of real utility in ships of this vast and unwieldy burthen,
which are rarely capable of acting against an enemy; but
if the building such contributes to preserve, among other
nations, the notion of the British superiority in naval
affairs, the expense, though very great, is well incurred,
and the ostentation is laudable and truly political.   Indeed,
I should be sorry to allow that Holland, France, or Spain,

possessed a vessel larger and more beautiful than the largest and most beautiful of ours; for this honour I would always administer to the pride of our sailors, who should challenge it from all their neighbours with truth and success. And sure I am that not our honest tars alone, but every inhabitant of this island, may exult in the comparison, when he considers the King of Great Britain as a maritime prince, in opposition to any other prince in Europe; but I am nôt so certain that the same idea of superiority will result from comparing our land forces with those of many other crowned heads. In number they all far exceed us, and in the goodness and splendour of their troops many nations, particularly the Germans and French, and perhaps the Dutch, cast us at a distance; for, however we may flatter ourselves with the Edwards and Henrys of former ages, the change of the whole art of war since those days, by which the advantage of personal strength is in a manner entirely lost, hath produced a change in military affairs to the advantage of our enemies. As for our successes in later days, if they were not entirely owing to the superior genius of our general, they were not a little due to the superior force of his money. Indeed, if we should arraign Marshal Saxe of ostentation when he shewed his army, drawn up, to our captive general, the day after the Battle of La Val, we cannot say that the ostentation was entirely vain; since he certainly shewed him an army which had not been often equalled, either in the number or goodness of the troops, and which, in those respects, so far exceeded ours, that none can ever cast any reflection on the brave young prince who could not reap the laurels of conquest in that day; but his retreat will be always mentioned as an addition to his glory.

In our marine the case is entirely the reverse, and it must be our own fault if it doth not continue so; for continue so it will as long as the flourishing state of our trade shall support it, and this support it can never want till our legislature shall cease to give sufficient attention to the protection of our trade, and our magistrates want sufficient power, ability, and honesty, to execute the laws; a circumstance not to be apprehended, as it cannot happen till our senates and our benches shall be filled with the blindest ignorance, or with the blackest corruption.

Besides the ships in the docks, we saw many on the

water: the yachts are sights of great parade, and the king's body yacht is, I believe, unequalled in any country for convenience as well as magnificence; both which are consulted in building and equipping her with the most exquisite art and workmanship.

We saw likewise several Indiamen just returned from their voyage. These are, I believe, the largest and finest vessels which are anywhere employed in commercial affairs. The colliers, likewise, which are very numerous, and even assemble in fleets, are ships of great bulk; and if we descend to those used in the American, African, and European trades, and pass through those which visit our own coasts, to the small craft that lie between Chatham and the Tower, the whole forms a most pleasing object to the eye, as well as highly warming to the heart of an Englishman who has any degree of love for his country, or can recognize any effect of the patriot in his constitution.

Lastly, the Royal Hospital at Greenwich, which presents so delightful a front to the water, and doth such honour at once to its builder and the nation, to the great skill and ingenuity of the one, and to the no less sensible gratitude of the other, very properly closes the account of this scene; which may well appear romantic to those who have not themselves seen that, in this one instance, truth and reality are capable, perhaps, of exceeding the power of fiction.

When we had passed by Greenwich we saw only two or three gentlemen's houses, all of very moderate account, till we reached Gravesend: these are all on the Kentish shore, which affords a much drier, wholesomer, and pleasanter situation, than doth that of its opposite, Essex. This circumstance, I own, is somewhat surprising to me, when I reflect on the numerous villas that crowd the river from Chelsea upwards as far as Shepperton, where the narrower channel affords not half so noble a prospect, and where the continual succession of the small craft, like the frequent repetition of all things, which have nothing in them great, beautiful, or admirable, tire the eye, and give us distaste and aversion, instead of pleasure. With some of these situations, such as Barnes, Mortlake, etc., even the shore of Essex might contend, not upon very unequal terms; but on the Kentish borders there are many spots to be chosen by the builder which might justly claim the preference over almost the very finest of those in Middlesex and Surrey.

How shall we account for this depravity in taste? for surely there are none so very mean and contemptible as to bring the pleasure of seeing a number of little wherries, gliding along after one another, in competition with what we enjoy in viewing a succession of ships, with all their sails expanded to the winds, bounding over the waves before us.

And here I cannot pass by another observation on the deplorable want of taste in our enjoyments, which we shew by almost totally neglecting the pursuit of what seems to me the highest degree of amusement; this is, the sailing ourselves in little vessels of our own, contrived only for our ease and accommodation, to which such situations of our villas as I have recommended would be so convenient, and even necessary.

This amusement, I confess, if enjoyed in any perfection, would be of the expensive kind; but such expense would not exceed the reach of a moderate fortune, and would fall very short of the prices which are daily paid for pleasures of a far inferior rate. The truth, I believe, is, that sailing in the manner I have just mentioned is a pleasure rather unknown, or unthought of, than rejected by those who have experienced it; unless, perhaps, the apprehension of danger or sea-sickness may be supposed, by the timorous and delicate, to make too large deductions—insisting that all their enjoyments shall come to them pure and unmixed, and being ever ready to cry out:

——*Nocet empta dolore voluptas.*

This, however, was my present case; for the ease and lightness which I felt from my tapping, the gaiety of the morning, the pleasant sailing with wind and tide, and the many agreeable objects with which I was constantly entertained during the whole way, were all suppressed and overcome by the single consideration of my wife's pain, which continued incessantly to torment her till we came to an anchor, when I dispatched a messenger in great haste for the best reputed operator in Gravesend. A surgeon of some eminence now appeared, who did not decline tooth-drawing, though he certainly would have been offended with the appellation of tooth-drawer no less than his brethren, the members of that venerable body, would be with that of barber, since the late separation between those long-united companies, by which, if the surgeons have gained much, the barbers are supposed to have lost very little.

This able and careful person (for so I sincerely believe he is), after examining the guilty tooth, declared that it was such a rotten shell, and so placed at the very remotest end of the upper jaw, where it was in a manner covered and secured by a large, fine, firm tooth, that he despaired of his power of drawing it.

He said, indeed, more to my wife, and used more rhetoric to dissuade her from having it drawn, than is generally employed to persuade young ladies to prefer a pain of three moments to one of three months' continuance, especially if those young ladies happen to be past forty and fifty years of age, when, by submitting to support a racking torment, the only good circumstance attending which is, it is so short that scarce one in a thousand can cry out "I feel it," they are to do a violence to their charms, and lose one of those beautiful holders with which alone Sir Courtly Nice declares a lady can ever lay hold of his heart.

He said at last so much, and seemed to reason so justly, that I came over to his side, and assisted him in prevailing on my wife (for it was no easy matter) to resolve on keeping her tooth a little longer, and to apply palliatives only for relief. These were opium applied to the tooth, and blisters behind the ears.

Whilst we were at dinner this day in the cabin, on a sudden the window on one side was beat into the room with a crash as if a twenty-pounder had been discharged among us. We were all alarmed at the suddenness of the accident, for which, however, we were soon able to account, for the sash, which was shivered all to pieces, was pursued into the middle of the cabin by the bowsprit of a little ship called a cod-smack, the master of which made us amends for running (carelessly at best) against us, and injuring the ship, in the sea-way; that is to say, by damning us all to hell, and uttering several pious wishes that it had done us much more mischief. All which were answered in their own kind and phrase by our men, between whom and the other crew a dialogue of oaths and scurrility was carried on as long as they continued in each other's hearing.

It is difficult, I think, to assign a satisfactory reason why sailors in general should, of all others, think themselves entirely discharged from the common bands of humanity, and should seem to glory in the language and behaviour of savages! They see more of the world, and have, most of them, a more erudite education than is the portion of landmen of their degree. Nor do I believe that in any country they visit (Holland itself not excepted) they can ever find a parallel to what daily passes on the River Thames. Is it that they think true courage (for they are the bravest fellows upon earth) inconsistent with all the gentleness of a humane carriage, and that the contempt of civil order springs up in minds but little cultivated, at the same time and from the same principles with the contempt of danger and death? Is it——? in short, it is so; and how it comes to be so I leave to form a question in the Robin Hood Society, or to be propounded for solution among the enigmas in the *Woman's Almanac* for the next year.

Monday, July 1. This day Mr. Welch took his leave of me after dinner, as did a young lady of her sister, who was proceeding with my wife to Lisbon. They both set out together in a post-chaise for London.

Soon after their departure our cabin, where my wife and I were sitting together, was visited by two ruffians, whose appearance greatly corresponded with that of the sheriffs, or rather the knight-marshal's bailiffs. One of these especially, who seemed to affect a more than ordinary degree of rudeness and insolence, came in without any kind of ceremony, with a broad gold lace on his hat, which was cocked with much military fierceness on his head. An inkhorn at his button-hole and some papers in his hand sufficiently assured me what he was, and I asked him if he and his companion were not custom-house officers: he answered with sufficient dignity that they were, as an information which he seemed to conclude would strike the hearer with awe, and suppress all further inquiry; but, on the contrary, I proceeded to ask of what rank he was in the custom-house, and, receiving an answer from his companion, as I remember, that the gentleman was a riding surveyor, I replied that he might be a riding surveyor, but could be no gentleman, for that none who had any title to that denomination would break into the presence of a lady without an apology or even moving his hat. He then took his covering from his head and laid it on the table, saying, he asked pardon, and blamed the mate, who should, he said, have informed him if any persons of distinction were below. I told him he might guess by our appearance (which, perhaps, was rather more than could be said with the strictest adherence to truth) that he was before a gentleman and lady, which should teach him to be very civil in his behaviour, though we should not happen to be of that number whom the world calls people of fashion and distinction. However, I said, that, as he seemed sensible of his error, and had asked pardon, the lady would permit him to put his hat on again if he chose it. This he refused with some degree of surliness, and failed not to convince me that, if I should condescend to become more gentle, he would soon grow more rude.

I now renewed a reflection, which I have often seen occasion to make, that there is nothing so incongruous in nature as any kind of power with lowness of mind and of ability, and that there is nothing more deplorable than the want of truth in the whimsical notion of Plato, who tells us that "Saturn, well knowing the state of human affairs, gave us kings and rulers, not of human but divine original; for, as we make not shepherds of sheep, nor oxherds of oxen, nor goatherds of goats, but place some of our own kind over all as being better and fitter to govern them; in the same manner were demons by the divine love set over us as a race of beings of a superior order to men, and who, with great ease to themselves, might regulate our affairs and establish peace, modesty, freedom, and justice, and, totally destroying all sedition, might complete the happiness of the human race. So far, at least, may even now be said with truth, that in all states which are under the government of mere man, without any divine assistance, there is nothing but labour and misery to be found. From what I have said, therefore, we may at least learn, with our utmost endeavours, to imitate the Saturnian institution; borrowing all assistance from our immortal part, while we pay to this the strictest obedience, we should form both our private economy and public policy from its dictates. By this dispensation of our immortal minds we are to establish a law and to call it by that name. But if any government be in the hands of a single person, of the few, or of the many, and such governor or governors shall abandon himself or themselves to the unbridled pursuit of the wildest pleasures or desires, unable to restrain any passion, but possessed with an insatiable bad disease; if such shall attempt to govern, and at the same time to trample on all laws, there can be no means of preservation left for the wretched people."—Plato, *de Leg.*, lib. iv. p. 713, c. 714, edit. Serrani.

It is true that Plato is here treating of the highest or sovereign power in a state, but it is as true that his observations are general and may be applied to all inferior powers; and, indeed, every subordinate degree is immediately derived from the highest; and, as it is equally protected by the same force and sanctified by the same authority, is alike dangerous to the well-being of the subject.

Of all powers, perhaps, there is none so sanctified and protected as this which is under our present consideration. So numerous, indeed, and strong, are the sanctions given to it by many Acts of Parliament, that, having once established the laws of customs on merchandise, it seems to have been the sole view of the legislature to strengthen the hands and to protect the persons of the officers who become established by those laws, many of whom are so far from bearing any resemblance to the Saturnian institution, and to be chosen from a degree of beings superior to the rest of the human race, that they sometimes seem industriously picked out of the lowest and vilest orders of mankind.

There is, indeed, nothing so useful to man in general, nor so beneficial to particular societies and individuals, as trade. This is that Alma Mater at whose plentiful breast all mankind are nourished. It is true, like other parents, she is not always equally indulgent to all her children, but, though she gives to her favourites a vast proportion of redundancy and superfluity, there are very few whom she refuses to supply with the conveniences, and none with the necessaries, of life.

Such a benefactress as this must naturally be beloved by Mankind in general; it would be wonderful, therefore, if her interest was not considered by them, and protected from the fraud and violence of some of her rebellious offspring, who, coveting more than their share or more than she thinks proper to allow them, are daily employed in meditating mischief against her, and in endeavouring to steal from their brethren those shares which this great Alma Mater had allowed them.

At length our governor came on board, and about six in the evening we weighed anchor, and fell down to the Nore, whither our passage was extremely pleasant, the evening being very delightful, the moon just past the full, and both wind and tide favourable to us.

Tuesday, July 2. This morning we again set sail, under all the advantages we had enjoyed the evening before. This day we left the shore of Essex and coasted along Kent, passing by the pleasant island of Thanet, which is an island, and that of Sheppey, which is not an island, and about three o'clock, the wind being now full in our teeth, we came to an anchor in the Downs, within two miles of Deal. My wife, having suffered intolerable pain from her tooth, again renewed her resolution of having it drawn, and another surgeon was sent for from Deal, but with no better success than the former. He likewise declined the operation, for the same reason which had been assigned by the former: however, such was her resolution, backed with pain, that he was obliged to make the attempt, which concluded more in honour of his judgment than of his operation; for, after having put my poor wife to inexpressible torment, he was obliged to leave her tooth *in statu quo*; and she had now the comfortable prospect of a long fit of pain, which might have lasted her whole voyage, without any possibility of relief.

In these pleasing sensations, of which I had my just share, nature, overcome with fatigue, about eight in the evening resigned her to rest—a circumstance which would have given me some happiness, could I have known how to employ those spirits which were raised by it; but, unfortunately for me, I was left in a disposition of enjoying an agreeable hour without the assistance of a companion, which has always appeared to me necessary to such enjoyment; my daughter and her companion were both retired seasick to bed; the other passengers were a rude schoolboy of fourteen years old and an illiterate Portuguese friar, who understood no language but his own, in which I had not the least smattering. The captain was the only person left in whose conversation I might indulge myself; but unluckily, besides a total ignorance of everything in the world but a ship, he had the misfortune of being so deaf, that to make him hear, I will not say understand, my words, I must run the risk of conveying them to the ears of my wife, who, though on another room (called, I think the state-room—being, indeed, a most stately apartment, capable of containing one human body in length, if not very tall, and three bodies in breadth), lay asleep within a yard of me. In this situation necessity and choice were one and the same thing; the captain and I sat down together to a small bowl of punch, over which we both soon fell fast asleep, and so concluded the evening.

Wednesday, July 3. This morning I awaked at four o'clock, for my distemper seldom suffered me to sleep later. I presently got up, and had the pleasure of enjoying the sight of a tempestuous sea for four hours before the captain was stirring; for he loved to indulge himself in morning slumbers, which were attended with a wind-music, much more agreeable to the performers than to the hearers, especially such as have, as I had, the privilege of sitting in the orchestra. At eight o'clock the captain rose, and sent his boat on shore. I ordered my man likewise to go in it, as my distemper was not of that kind which entirely deprives us of appetite. Now, though the captain had well victualled his ship with all manner of salt provisions for the voyage, and had added great quantities of fresh stores, particularly of vegetables, at Gravesend, such as beans and peas, which had been on board only two days, and had possibly not been gathered above two more, I apprehended I could provide better for myself at Deal than the ship's ordinary seemed to promise. I accordingly sent for fresh provisions of all kinds from the shore, in order to put off the evil day of starving as long as possible. My man returned with most of the articles I sent for, and I now thought myself in a condition of living a week on my own provisions. I therefore ordered my own dinner, which I wanted nothing but a cook to dress and a proper fire to dress it at; but those were not to be had, nor indeed any addition to my roast mutton, except the pleasure of the captain's company, with that of the other passengers; for my wife continued the whole day in a state of dozing, and my other females, whose sickness did not abate by the rolling of the ship at anchor, seemed more inclined to empty their stomachs than to fill them. Thus I passed the whole day (except about an hour at dinner) by myself, and the

evening concluded with the captain as the preceding one
had done; one comfortable piece of news he communicated
to me, which was, that he had no doubt of a prosperous
wind in the morning; but as he did not divulge the reasons
of this confidence, and as I saw none myself besides the
wind being directly opposite, my faith in this prophecy
was not strong enough to build any great hopes upon.

Thursday, July 4. This morning, however, the captain
seemed resolved to fulfil his own predictions, whether the
wind would or no; he accordingly weighed anchor, and,
taking the advantage of the tide when the wind was not
very boisterous, he hoisted his sails; and, as if his power
had been no less absolute over Æolus than it was over
Neptune, he forced the wind to blow him on in its own
despite.

But as all men who have ever been at sea well know how
weak such attempts are, and want no authorities of Scripture to prove that the most absolute power of a captain of
a ship is very contemptible in the wind's eye, so did it befall
our noble commander, who, having struggled with the wind
three or four hours, was obliged to give over, and lost in a
few minutes all that he had been so long a-gaining; in short,
we returned to our former station, and once more cast
anchor in the neighbourhood of Deal.

Here, though we lay near the shore, that we might
promise ourselves all the emolument which could be
derived from it, we found ourselves deceived; and that we
might with as much conveniency be out of the sight of
land; for, except when the captain launched forth his own
boat, which he did always with great reluctance, we were
incapable of procuring anything from Deal, but at a price
too exorbitant, and beyond the reach even of modern
luxury—the fare of a boat from Deal, which lay at two
miles' distance, being at least three half-crowns, and, if
we had been in any distress for it, as many half-guineas;
for these good people consider the sea as a large common
appendant to their manor, in which when they find any of
their fellow-creatures impounded, they conclude that they
have a full right of making them pay at their own discretion
for their deliverance: to say the truth, whether it be that
men who live on the seashore are of an amphibious kind,
and do not entirely partake of human nature, or whatever
else may be the reason, they are so far from taking any

share in the distresses of mankind, or of being moved with any compassion for them, that they look upon them as blessings showered down from above, and which the more they improve to their own use, the greater is their gratitude and piety. Thus at Gravesend a sculler requires a shilling for going less way than he would row in London for threepence; and at Deal a boat often brings more profit in a day than it can produce in London in a week, or perhaps in a month; in both places the owner of the boat founds his demand on the necessity and distress of one who stands more or less in absolute want of his assistance, and with the urgency of these always rises in the exorbitancy of his demand, without ever considering that, from these very circumstances, the power or ease of gratifying such demand is in like proportion lessened. Now, as I am unwilling that some conclusions, which may be, I am aware, too justly drawn from these observations, should be imputed to human nature in general, I have endeavoured to account for them in a way more consistent with the goodness and dignity of that nature. However it be, it seems a little to reflect on the governors of such monsters that they do not take some means to restrain these impositions, and prevent them from triumphing any longer in the miseries of those who are, in many circumstances at least, their fellow-creatures, and considering the distresses of a wretched seaman, from his being wrecked to his being barely wind-bound, as a blessing sent among them from above, and calling it by that blasphemous name.

Friday, July 5. This day I sent a servant on board a man-of-war that was stationed here, with my compliments to the captain, to represent to him the distress of the ladies, and to desire the favour of his long-boat to conduct us to Dover, at about seven miles' distance; and at the same time presumed to make use of a great lady's name, the wife of the First Lord Commissioner of the Admiralty, who would, I told him, be pleased with any kindness shewn by him towards us in our miserable condition. And this I am convinced was true, from the humanity of the lady, though she was entirely unknown to me.

The captain returned a verbal answer to a long letter acquainting me that what I desired could not be complied with, it being a favour not in his power to grant. This might be, and I suppose was, true; but it is as true that, if he was able to write, and had pen, ink, and paper on board, he might have sent a written answer, and that it was the part of a gentleman so to have done; but this is a character seldom maintained on the watery element, especially by those who exercise any power on it. Every commander of a vessel here seems to think himself entirely free from all those rules of decency and civility which direct and restrain the conduct of the members of a society on shore; and each, claiming absolute dominion in his little wooden world, rules by his own laws and his own discretion. I do not, indeed, know so pregnant an instance of the dangerous consequences of absolute power, and its aptness to intoxicate the mind, as that of those petty tyrants, who become such in a moment, from very well-disposed and social members of that communion in which they affect no superiority, but live in an orderly state of legal subjection with their fellow-citizens.

Saturday, July 6. This morning our commander, declaring he was sure the wind would change, took the advantage of an ebbing tide, and weighed his anchor. His assurance, however, had the same completion, and his endeavours the same success, with his former trial; and he was soon obliged to return once more to his old quarters. Just before we let go our anchor, a small sloop, rather than submit to yield us an inch of way, ran foul of our ship, and carried off her bowsprit. This obstinate frolic would have cost those aboard the sloop very dear, if our steersman had not been too generous to exert his superiority, the certain consequence of which would have been the immediate sinking of the other. This contention of the inferior with a might capable of crushing it in an instant may seem to argue no small share of folly or madness, as well as of impudence; but I am convinced there is very little danger in it: contempt is a port to which the pride of man submits to fly with reluctance, but those who are within it are always in a place of the most assured security; for whosoever throws away his sword prefers, indeed, a less honourable but much safer means of avoiding danger than he who defends himself with it. And here we shall offer another distinction, of the truth of which much reading and experience have well convinced us, that as in the most absolute governments there is a regular progression of slavery downwards, from the top to the bottom, the mischief of which is seldom felt with any great force and bitterness but by the next immediate degree; so in the most dissolute and anarchical states there is as regular an ascent of what is called rank or condition, which is always laying hold of the head of him who is advanced but one step higher on the ladder, who might, if he did not too much despise such efforts, kick his pursuer headlong to the bottom. We will conclude this digression with one general and short observation, which will, perhaps, set the whole matter in a clearer light than the longest and most laboured harangue. Whereas envy of all things most exposes us to danger from others, so contempt of all things best secures us from them. And thus, while the dung-cart and the sloop are always meditating mischief against the coach and the ship, and throwing themselves designedly in their way, the latter consider only their own security, and are not ashamed to break the road and let the other pass by them.

Monday, July 8. Having passed our Sunday without anything remarkable, unless the catching a great number of whitings in the afternoon may be thought so, we now set sail on Monday at six o'clock, with a little variation of wind; but this was so very little, and the breeze itself so small, that the tide was our best and indeed almost our only friend. This conducted us along the short remainder of the Kentish shore. Here we passed that cliff of Dover which makes so tremendous a figure in Shakespeare, and which whoever reads without being giddy, must, according to Mr. Addison's observation, have either a very good head or a very bad one; but which, whoever contracts any such ideas from the sight of, must have at least a poetic if not a Shakesperian genius. In truth, mountains, rivers, heroes, and gods owe great part of their existence to the poets; and Greece and Italy do so plentifully abound in the former, because they furnish so glorious a number of the latter; who while they bestowed immortality on every little hillock and blind stream, left the noblest rivers and mountains in the world to share the same obscurity with the eastern and western poets, in which they are celebrated.

This evening we beat the sea of Sussex in sight of Dungeness, with much more pleasure than progress; for the weather was almost a perfect calm, and the moon, which was almost at the full, scarce suffered a single cloud to veil her from our sight.

Tuesday, Wednesday, July 9, 10. These two days we had much the same fine weather, and made much the same way; but in the evening of the latter day a pretty fresh gale sprung up at N.N.W., which brought us by the morning in sight of the Isle of Wight.

Thursday, July 11. This gale continued till towards noon; when the east end of the island bore but little ahead of us. The captain swaggered and declared he would keep the sea; but the wind got the better of him, so that about three he gave up the victory, and making a sudden tack stood in for the shore, passed by Spithead and Portsmouth, and came to an anchor at a place called Ryde on the island.

A most tragical incident fell out this day at sea. While the ship was under sail, but making as will appear no great way, a kitten, one of four of the feline inhabitants of the cabin, fell from the window into the water: an alarm was immediately given to the captain, who was then upon deck, and received it with the utmost concern and many bitter oaths. He immediately gave orders to the steersman in favour of the poor thing, as he called it; the sails were instantly slackened, and all hands, as the phrase is, employed to recover the poor animal. I was, I own, extremely surprised at all this; less indeed at the captain's extreme tenderness than at his conceiving any possibility of success; for if puss had had nine thousand instead of nine lives, I concluded they had been all lost. The boatswain, however, had more sanguine hopes, for, having stripped himself of his jacket, breeches, and shirt, he leaped boldly into the water, and to my great astonishment in a few minutes returned to the ship, bearing the motionless animal in his mouth. Nor was this, I observed, a matter of such great difficulty as it appeared to my ignorance, and possibly may seem to that of my fresh-water reader. The kitten was now exposed to air and sun on the deck, where its life, of which it retained no symptoms, was despaired of by all.

The captain's humanity, if I may so call it, did not so totally destroy his philosophy as to make him yield himself up to affliction on this melancholy occasion. Having felt his loss like a man, he resolved to shew he could bear it like one; and, having declared he had rather have lost a cask of rum or brandy, betook himself to threshing at backgammon with the Portuguese friar, in which innocent amusement they had passed about two - thirds of their time.

But as I have, perhaps, a little too wantonly endeavoured to raise the tender passions of my readers in this narrative, I should think myself unpardonable if I concluded it without giving them the satisfaction of hearing that the kitten at last recovered, to the great joy of the good captain, but to the great disappointment of some of the sailors, who asserted that the drowning a cat was the very surest way of raising a favourable wind; a supposition of which, though we have heard several plausible accounts, we will not presume to assign the true original reason.

Friday, July 12. This day our ladies went ashore at Ryde, and drank their afternoon tea at an ale-house there with great satisfaction: here they were regaled with fresh cream, to which they had been strangers since they left the Downs.

Saturday, July 13. The wind seeming likely to continue in the same corner where it had been almost constantly for two months together, I was persuaded by my wife to go ashore and stay at Ryde till we sailed. I approved the motion much; for though I am a great lover of the sea, I now fancied there was more pleasure in breathing the fresh air of the land; but how to get thither was the question; for, being really that dead luggage which I considered all passengers to be in the beginning of this narrative, and incapable of any bodily motion without external impulse, it was in vain to leave the ship, or to determine to do it, without the assistance of others. In one instance, perhaps, the living luggage is more difficult to be moved or removed than an equal or much superior weight of dead matter; which, if of the brittle kind, may indeed be liable to be broken through negligence; but this, by proper care, may be almost certainly prevented; whereas the fractures to which the living lumps are exposed are sometimes by no caution avoidable, and often by no art to be amended.

I was deliberating on the means of conveyance, not so much out of the ship to the boat as out of a little tottering boat to the land; a matter which, as I had already experienced in the Thames, was not extremely easy, when to be performed by any other limbs than your own. Whilst I weighed all that could suggest itself on this head, without strictly examining the merit of the several schemes which were advanced by the captain and sailors, and, indeed, giving no very deep attention even to my wife, who, as well as her friend and my daughter, were exerting their tender concern for my ease and safety, Fortune, for I am convinced she had a hand in it, sent me a present of a buck; a present welcome enough of itself, but more welcome on account of the vessel in which it came, being a large hoy, which in some places would pass for a ship, and many people would go some miles to see the sight. I was pretty easily conveyed on board this hoy; but to get from hence to the shore was not so easy a task; for, however strange it may appear, the water itself did not extend so far; an instance which seems to explain those lines of Ovid:

Omnia pontus erant, deerant quoque littora ponto,

in a less tautological sense than hath generally been imputed to them.

In fact, between the sea and the shore there was, at low water, an impassable gulf, if I may so call it, of deep mud, which could neither be traversed by walking nor swimming; so that for near one half of the twenty-four hours Ryde was inaccessible by friend or foe. But as the magistrates of this place seemed more to desire the company of the former than to fear that of the latter, they had begun to make a small causeway to the low-water mark, so that foot passengers might land whenever they pleased; but as this work was of a public kind, and would have cost a large sum of money, at least ten pounds, and the magistrates, that is to say, the churchwardens, the overseers, constable, and tithing-man, and the principal inhabitants, had every one of them some separate scheme of private interest to advance at the expense of the public, they fell out among themselves; and, after having thrown away one half of the requisite sum, resolved at least to save the other half, and rather be contented to sit down losers themselves than to enjoy any benefit which might bring in a greater profit to another. Thus that unanimity which is so necessary in all public affairs became wanting, and every man, from the fear of being a bubble to another, was, in reality, a bubble to himself.

However, as there is scarce any difficulty to which the strength of men, assisted with the cunning of art, is not equal, I was at last hoisted into a small boat, and, being rowed pretty near the shore, was taken up by two sailors, who waded with me through the mud, and placed me in a chair on the land, whence they afterwards conveyed me a quarter of a mile farther, and brought me to a house which seemed to bid the fairest for hospitality of any in Ryde.

We brought with us our provisions from the ship, so that we wanted nothing but a fire to dress our dinner, and a room in which we might eat it. In neither of these had we any reason to apprehend a disappointment, our dinner consisting only of beans and bacon; and the worst apartment in His Majesty's dominions, either at home or abroad, being fully sufficient to answer our present ideas of delicacy.

Unluckily, however, we were disappointed in both; for when we arrived about four at our inn, exulting in the hopes of immediately seeing our beans smoking on the table, we had the mortification of seeing them on the table indeed, but without the circumstance which would have made the sight agreeable, being in the same state in which we had dispatched them from our ship.

In excuse for this delay, though we had exceeded, almost purposely, the time appointed, and our provision had arrived three hours before, the mistress of the house acquainted us that it was not for want of time to dress them that they were not ready, but for fear of their being cold or overdone before we should come; which she assured us was much worse than waiting a few minutes for our dinner; an observation so very just, that it is impossible to find any objection in it; but, indeed, it was not altogether so proper at this time, for we had given the most absolute orders to have them ready at four, and had been ourselves, not without much care and difficulty, most exactly punctual in keeping to the very minute of our appointment. But tradesmen, innkeepers, and servants never care to indulge us in matters contrary to our true interest, which they always know better than ourselves; nor can any bribes corrupt them to go out of their way whilst they are consulting our good in our own despite.

Our disappointment in the other particular, in defiance of our humility, as it was more extraordinary, was more provoking. In short, Mrs. Francis (for that was the name of the good woman of the house) no sooner received the news of our intended arrival than she considered more the gentility than the humanity of her guests, and applied herself not to that which kindles but to that which extinguishes fire, and, forgetting to put on her pot, fell to washing her house.

As the messenger who had brought my venison was impatient to be dispatched, I ordered it to be brought and laid on the table in the room where I was seated; and the table not being large enough, one side, and that a very bloody one, was laid on the brick floor. I then ordered Mrs. Francis to be called in, in order to give her instructions concerning it; in particular, what I would have roasted and what baked; concluding that she would be highly pleased with the prospect of so much money being spent in her house as she might have now reason to expect, if the wind continued only a few days longer to blow from the same points whence it had blown for several weeks past.

I soon saw good cause, I must confess, to despise my own sagacity. Mrs. Francis, having received her orders, without making any answer, snatched the side from the floor, which remained stained with blood, and, bidding a servant to take up that on the table, left the room with no pleasant countenance, muttering to herself that, "had she known the litter which was to have been made, she would not have taken such pains to wash her house that morning. If this was gentility, much good may it do such gentlefolks; for her part she had no notion of it."

From these murmurs I received two hints. The one, that it was not from a mistake of our inclination that the good woman had starved us, but from wisely consulting her own dignity, or rather perhaps her vanity, to which our hunger was offered up as a sacrifice. The other, that I was now sitting in a damp room, a circumstance, though it had hitherto escaped my notice from the colour of the bricks, which was by no means to be neglected in a valetudinary state.

My wife, who, besides discharging excellently well her own and all the tender offices becoming the female character; who, besides being a faithful friend, an amiable companion, and a tender nurse, could likewise supply the wants of a decrepit husband, and occasionally perform his part, had, before this, discovered the immoderate attention to neatness in Mrs. Francis, and provided against its ill consequences. She had found, though not under the same roof, a very snug apartment belonging to Mr. Francis, and which had escaped the mop by his wife's being satisfied it could not possibly be visited by gentlefolks.

This was a dry, warm, oaken-floored barn, lined on both sides with wheaten straw, and opening at one end into a green field and a beautiful prospect. Here, without hesitation, she ordered the cloth to be laid, and came hastily to snatch me from worse perils by water than the common dangers of the sea.

Mrs. Francis, who could not trust her own ears, or could not believe a footman in so extraordinary a phenomenon, followed my wife, and asked her if she had indeed ordered the cloth to be laid in the barn? She answered in the affirmative; upon which Mrs. Francis declared she would not dispute her pleasure, but it was the first time she believed that quality had ever preferred a barn to a house. She shewed at the same time the most pregnant marks of contempt, and again lamented the labour she had undergone, through her ignorance of the absurd taste of her guests.

At length we were seated in one of the most pleasant spots, I believe, in the kingdom, and were regaled with our beans and bacon, in which there was nothing deficient but the quantity. This defect was, however, so deplorable that we had consumed our whole dish before we had visibly lessened our hunger. We now waited with impatience the arrival of our second course, which necessity, and not luxury, had dictated. This was a joint of mutton which Mrs. Francis had been ordered to provide; but when, being tired with expectation, we ordered our servants *to see for something else*, we were informed that there was nothing else; on which Mrs. Francis, being summoned, declared there was no such thing as mutton to be had at Ryde. When I expressed some astonishment at their having no butcher in a village so situated, she answered they had a very good one, and one that killed all sorts of meat in season, beef two or three times a year, and mutton the whole year round; but that, it being then beans and peas time, he killed no meat, by reason he was sure of not selling it. This she had not thought worthy of communication, any more than that there lived a fisherman at next door, who was then provided with plenty of soles, and whitings, and lobsters, far superior to those which adorn a city feast.

This discovery being made by accident, we completed the best, the pleasantest, and the merriest meal, with more appetite, more real, solid luxury, and more festivity than was ever seen in an entertainment at White's.

It may be wondered at, perhaps, that Mrs. Francis should be so negligent of providing for her guests, as she may seem to be thus inattentive to her own interest; but this was not the case; for, having clapped a poll-tax on our heads at our arrival, and determined at what price to discharge our bodies from her house, the less she suffered any other to share in the levy the clearer it came into her own pocket; and that it was better to get twelve pence in a shilling than ten pence, which latter would be the case if she afforded us fish at any rate.

Thus we passed a most agreeable day owing to good appetites and good humour; two hearty feeders which will devour with satisfaction whatever food you place before them; whereas, without these, the elegance of St. James's, the charde, the perigord-pie, or the ortolan, the venison, the turtle, or the custard, may titillate the throat, but will never convey happiness to the heart or cheerfulness to the countenance.

As the wind appeared still immovable, my wife proposed my lying on shore. I presently agreed, though in defiance of an Act of Parliament, by which persons wandering abroad and lodging in ale-houses are decreed to be rogues and vagabonds; and this too after having been very singularly officious in putting that law in execution.

My wife, having reconnoitred the house, reported that there was one room in which were two beds. It was concluded, therefore, that she and Harriot should occupy one, and myself take possession of the other. She added likewise an ingenious recommendation of this room to one who had so long been in a cabin, which it exactly resembled, as it was sunk down with age on one side, and was in the form of a ship with gunwales too.

For my own part, I make little doubt but this apartment was an ancient temple, built with the materials of a wreck, and probably dedicated to Neptune in honour of THE BLESSING sent by him to the inhabitants; such blessings having in all ages been very common to them. The timber employed in it confirms this opinion, being such as is seldom used by any but shipbuilders. I do not find indeed any mention of this matter in Hearn; but perhaps its antiquity was too modern to deserve his notice. Certain it is that this island of Wight was not an early convert to Christianity; nay, there is some reason to doubt whether it was ever entirely converted. But I have only time to touch slightly on things of this kind, which, luckily for us, we have a society whose peculiar profession it is to discuss and develop.

Sunday, July 19 [i.e. 14]. This morning early I summoned Mrs. Francis, in order to pay her the preceding day's account. As I could recollect only two or three articles I thought there was no necessity of pen and ink. In a single instance only we had exceeded what the law allows gratis to a foot-soldier on his march, viz. vinegar, salt, etc., and dressing his meat. I found, however, I was mistaken in my calculation; for when the good woman attended with her bill it contained as follows:

	£	s.	d.
Bread and beer	0	2	4
Wind	0	2	0
Rum	0	2	0
Dressing dinner	0	3	0
Tea	0	1	6
Firing	0	1	0
Lodging	0	1	6
Servants' lodging	0	0	6
	£0	13	10

Now that five people and two servants should live a day and night at a public-house for so small a sum will appear incredible to any person in London above the degree of a chimney-sweeper; but more astonishing will it seem that these people should remain so long at such a house without tasting any other delicacy than bread, small beer, a teacupful of milk called cream, a glass of rum converted into punch by their own materials, and one bottle of *wind*, of which we only tasted a single glass, though possibly, indeed, our servants drank the remainder of the bottle.

This *wind* is a liquor of English manufacture, and its flavour is thought very delicious by the generality of the English, who drink it in great quantities. Every seventh year is thought to produce as much as the other six. It is then drunk so plentifully that the whole nation are in a manner intoxicated by it; and consequently very little business is carried on at that season.

It resembles in colour the red wine which is imported from Portugal, as it doth in its intoxicating quality; hence, and from this agreement in the orthography, the one is often confounded with the other, though both are seldom esteemed by the same person. It is to be had in every parish of the kingdom, and a pretty large quantity is consumed in the metropolis, where several taverns are set apart solely for the vendition of this liquor, the masters never dealing in any other.

The disagreement in our computation produced some small remonstrance to Mrs. Francis on my side; but this received an immediate answer: "She scorned to overcharge gentlemen; her house had been always frequented by the very best gentry of the island; and she had never had a bill found fault with in her life, though she had lived upwards of forty years in the house, and within that time the greatest gentry in Hampshire had been at it; and that Lawyer Willis never went to any other when he came to those parts. That for her part she did not get her livelihood by travellers, who were gone and away, and she never expected to see them more, but that her neighbours might come again; wherefore, to be sure, they had the only right to complain."

She was proceeding thus, and from her volubility of tongue seemed likely to stretch the discourse to an immoderate length, when I suddenly cut all short by paying the bill.

This morning our ladies went to church, more, I fear, from curiosity than religion; they were attended by the captain in a most military attire, with his cockade in his hat and his sword by his side. So unusual an appearance in this little chapel drew the attention of all present, and probably disconcerted the women, who were in dishabille, and wished themselves drest, for the sake of the curate, who was the greatest of their beholders.

While I was left alone I received a visit from Mr. Francis himself, who was much more considerable as a farmer than as an inn-holder. Indeed, he left the latter entirely to the care of his wife, and he acted wisely, I believe, in so doing.

As nothing more remarkable passed on this day I will close

it with the account of these two characters, as far as a few days' residence could inform me of them. If they should appear as new to the reader as they did to me, he will not be displeased at finding them here.

This amiable couple seemed to border hard on their grand climacteric; nor indeed were they shy of owning enough to fix their ages within a year or two of that time. They appeared to be rather proud of having employed their time well than ashamed of having lived so long; the only reason which I could ever assign why some fine ladies, and fine gentlemen too, should desire to be thought younger than they really are by the contemporaries of their grandchildren. Some, indeed, who too hastily credit appearances, might doubt whether they had made so good a use of their time as I would insinuate, since there was no appearance of anything but poverty, want, and wretchedness, about their house; nor could they produce anything to a customer in exchange for his money but a few bottles of *wind*, and spirituous liquors, and some very bad ale, to drink; with rusty bacon and worse cheese to eat. But then it should be considered, on the other side, that whatever they received was almost as entirely clear profit as the blessing of a wreck itself; such an inn being the very reverse of a coffee-house; for here you can neither sit for nothing nor have anything for your money.

Again, as many marks of want abounded everywhere, so were the marks of antiquity visible. Scarce anything was to be seen which had not some scar upon it, made by the hand of Time; not an utensil, it was manifest, had been purchased within a dozen years last past; so that whatever money had come into the house during that period at least must have remained in it, unless it had been sent abroad for food, or other perishable commodities; but these were supplied by a small portion of the fruits of the farm, in which the farmer allowed he had a very good bargain. In fact, it is inconceivable what sums may be collected by starving only, and how easy it is for a man to die rich if he will but be contented to live miserable.

Nor is there in this kind of starving anything so terrible as some apprehend. It neither wastes a man's flesh nor robs him of his cheerfulness. The famous Cornaro's case well proves the contrary; and so did Farmer Francis, who was of a round stature, had a plump, round face, with a

kind of smile on it, and seemed to borrow an air of wretchedness rather from his coat's age than from his own.

The truth is, there is a certain diet which emaciates men
more than any possible degree of abstinence; though I do
not remember to have seen any caution against it, either
in Cheney, Arbuthnot, or in any other modern writer or
regimen. Nay, the very name is not, I believe, in the
learned Dr. James's *Dictionary*; all which is the more
extraordinary as it is a very common food in this kingdom,
and the college themselves were not long since very liberally
entertained with it by the present attorney and other
eminent lawyers in Lincoln's Inn Hall, and were all made
horribly sick by it.

But though it should not be found among our English
physical writers, we may be assured of meeting with it
among the Greeks; for nothing considerable in nature
escapes their notice, though many things considerable in
them, it is to be feared, have escaped the notice of their
readers. The Greeks, then, to all such as feed too vora-
ciously on this diet, give the name of HEAUTOFAGI, which
our physicians will, I suppose, translate *men that eat
themselves*.

As nothing is so destructive to the body as this kind of
food, so nothing is so plentiful and cheap; but it was
perhaps the only cheap thing the farmer disliked. Probably living much on fish might produce this disgust; for
Diodorus Siculus attributes the same aversion in a people
of Æthiopia to the same cause; he calls them the fish-eaters,
and asserts that they cannot be brought to eat a single
meal with the Heautofagi by any persuasion, threat, or
violence whatever, not even though they should kill their
children before their faces.

What hath puzzled our physicians, and prevented them
from setting this matter in the clearest light, is possibly
one simple mistake, arising from a very excusable ignorance;
that the passions of men are capable of swallowing food as
well as their appetites; that the former, in feeding, resemble
the state of those animals who chew the cud; and therefore,
such men, in some sense, may be said to prey on themselves,
and as it were to devour their own entrails. And hence
ensues a meagre aspect and thin habit of body, as surely
as from what is called a consumption.

Our farmer was one of these. He had no more passion

than an Ichthuofagus or Æthiopian fisher. He wished not
for anything, thought not of anything; indeed, he scarce
did anything or said anything. Here I cannot be understood strictly; for then I must describe a nonentity, whereas
I would rob him of nothing but that free agency which is
the cause of all the corruption and of all the misery of
human nature. No man, indeed, ever did more than the
farmer, for he was an absolute slave to labour all the week;
but in truth, as my sagacious reader must have at first
apprehended, when I said he resigned the care of the
house to his wife, I meant more than I then expressed,
even the house and all that belonged to it; for he was
really a farmer only under the direction of his wife. In
a word, so composed, so serene, so placid a countenance,
I never saw; and he satisfied himself by answering to every
question he was asked: "I don't know anything about it,
sir; I leaves all that to my wife."

Now, as a couple of this kind would, like two vessels of
oil, have made no composition in life, and for want of all
savour must have palled every taste; nature or fortune, or
both of them, took care to provide a proper quantity of
acid in the materials that formed the wife, and to render
her a perfect helpmate for so tranquil a husband. She
abounded in whatsoever he was defective; that is to say,
in almost everything. She was indeed as vinegar to oil,
or a brisk wind to a standing pool, and preserved all from
stagnation and corruption.

Quin the player, on taking a nice and severe survey of
a fellow-comedian, burst forth into this exclamation: "If
that fellow be not a rogue, God Almighty doth not write
a legible hand." Whether he guessed right or no is not
worth my while to examine; certain it is that the latter,
having wrought his features into a proper harmony to
become the characters of Iago, Shylock, and others of the
same cast, gave us a semblance of truth to the observation
that was sufficient to confirm the wit of it. Indeed, we
may remark, in favour of the physiognomist, though the
law has made him a rogue and vagabond, that Nature is
seldom curious in her works within, without employing
some little pains on the outside; and this more particularly
in mischievous characters, in forming which, as Mr. Derham
observes, in venomous insects, as the sting or saw of a
wasp, she is sometimes wonderfully industrious. Now,

when she hath thus completely armed our hero to carry on
a war with man, she never fails of furnishing that innocent
lambkin with some means of knowing his enemy, and fore-
seeing his designs. Thus she hath been observed to act
in the case of a rattlesnake, which never meditates a human
prey without giving warning of his approach.

This observation will, I am convinced, hold most true,
if applied to the most venomous individuals of human
insects. A tyrant, a trickster, and a bully, generally wear
the marks of their several dispositions in their countenances;
so do the vixen, the shrew, the scold, and all other females
of the like kind. But, perhaps, nature hath never afforded
a stronger example of all this than in the case of Mrs.
Francis. She was a short, squat woman; her head was
closely joined to her shoulders, where it was fixed somewhat
awry; every feature of her countenance was sharp and
pointed; her face was furrowed with the smallpox; and her
complexion, which seemed to be able to turn milk to
curds, not a little resembled in colour such milk as had
already undergone that operation. She appeared, indeed,
to have many symptoms of a deep jaundice in her look;
but the strength and firmness of her voice overbalanced
them all; the tone of this was a sharp treble at a distance,
for I seldom heard it on the same floor, but was usually
waked with it in the morning, and entertained with it
almost continually through the whole day.

Though vocal be usually put in opposition to instrumental
music, I question whether this might not be thought to
partake of the nature of both; for she played on two
instruments, which she seemed to keep for no other use
from morning till night; these were two maids, or rather
scolding-stocks, who, I suppose, by some means or other,
earned their board, and she gave them their lodging gratis,
or for no other service than to keep her lungs in constant
exercise.

She differed, as I have said, in every particular from
her husband; but very remarkably in this, that as it was
impossible to displease him, so it was as impossible to
please her; and as no art could remove a smile from his
countenance, so could no art carry it into hers. If her
bills were remonstrated against she was offended with the
tacit censure of her fair-dealing; if they were not, she seemed
to regard it as a tacit sarcasm on her folly, which might

have set down larger prices with the same success. On this latter hint she did indeed improve, for she daily raised some of her articles. A pennyworth of fire was to-day rated at a shilling, to-morrow at eighteenpence; and if she dressed us two dishes for two shillings on the Saturday, we paid half a crown for the cookery of one on the Sunday; and, whenever she was paid, she never left the room without lamenting the small amount of her bill, saying: "she knew not how it was that others got their money by gentlefolks, but for her part she had not the art of it." When she was asked why she complained, when she was paid all she demanded, she answered: "she could not deny that, nor did she know she had omitted anything; but that it was but a poor bill for gentlefolks to pay."

I accounted for all this by her having heard, that it is a maxim with the principal inn-holders on the Continent, to levy considerable sums on their guests, who travel with many horses and servants, though such guests should eat little or nothing in their houses; the method being, I believe, in such cases, to lay a capitation on the horses, and not on their masters. But she did not consider that in most of these inns a very great degree of hunger, without any degree of delicacy, may be satisfied; and that in all such inns there is some appearance, at least, of provision, as well as of a man-cook to dress it, one of the hostlers being always furnished with a cook's cap, waistcoat, and apron, ready to attend gentlemen and ladies on their summons; that the case, therefore, of such inns differed from hers, where there was nothing to eat or to drink, and in reality no house to inhabit, no chair to sit upon, nor any bed to lie in; that one third or fourth part, therefore, of the levy imposed at inns was, in truth, a higher tax than the whole was when laid on in the other, where, in order to raise a small sum, a man is obliged to submit to pay as many various ways for the same thing as he doth to the government for the light which enters through his own window into his own house, from his own estate; such are the articles of bread and beer, firing, eating, and dressing dinner.

The foregoing is a very imperfect sketch of this extraordinary couple; for everything is here lowered instead of being heightened. Those who would see them set forth in more lively colours, and with the proper ornaments, may read the descriptions of the Furies in some of the classical poets, or of the Stoic philosophers in the works of Lucian.

Monday, July 20 [15]. This day nothing remarkable passed; Mrs. Francis levied a tax of fourteen shillings for the Sunday. We regaled ourselves at dinner with venison and good claret of our own; and in the afternoon, the women, attended by the captain, walked to see a delightful scene two miles distant, with the beauties of which they declared themselves most highly charmed at their return, as well as with the goodness of the lady of the mansion, who had slipt out of the way, that my wife and their company might refresh themselves with the flowers and fruits with which her garden abounded.

Tuesday, July 21 [16]. This day, having paid our taxes of yesterday, we were permitted to regale ourselves with more venison. Some of this we would willingly have exchanged for mutton; but no such flesh was to be had nearer than Portsmouth, from whence it would have cost more to convey a joint for us than the freight of a Portugal ham from Lisbon to London amounts to; for though the water-carriage be somewhat cheaper here than at Deal, yet can you find no watermen who will go on board his boat, unless by two or three hours' rowing he can get drunk for the residue of the week.

And here I have an opportunity, which possibly may not offer again, of publishing some observations on that political economy of this nation, which, as it concerns only the regulation of the mob, is below the notice of our great men; though on the due regulation of this order depend many emoluments, which the great men themselves, or at least many who tread close on their heels, may enjoy, as well as some dangers which may some time or other arise from introducing a pure state of anarchy among them. I will represent the case, as it appears to me, very fairly and impartially between the mob and their betters.

The whole mischief which infects this part of our economy arises from the vague and uncertain use of a word called liberty, of which, as scarce any two men with whom I have ever conversed seem to have one and the same idea, I am inclined to doubt whether there be any simple universal notion represented by this word, or whether it conveys any clearer or more determinate idea than some of those old Punic compositions of syllables preserved in one of the comedies of Plautus, but at present, as I conceive, not supposed to be understood by any one.

By liberty, however, I apprehend, is commonly understood the power of doing what we please; not absolutely, for then it would be inconsistent with law, by whose control the liberty of the freest people, except only the Hottentots and wild Indians, must always be restrained.

But, indeed, however largely we extend, or however moderately we confine, the sense of the word, no politician will, I presume, contend that it is to pervade in an equal degree, and be, with the same extent, enjoyed by, every member of society; no such polity having been ever found, unless among those vile people just before commemorated. Among the Greeks and Romans the servile and free conditions were opposed to each other; and no man who had the misfortune to be enrolled under the former could lay any claim to liberty till the right was conveyed to him by that master whose slave he was, either by the means of conquest, of purchase, or of birth.

This was the state of all the free nations in the world; and this, till very lately, was understood to be the case of our own.

I will not indeed say this is the case at present, the lowest class of our people having shaken off all the shackles of their superiors, and become not only as free, but even freer, than most of their superiors. I believe it cannot be doubted, though perhaps we have no recent instance of it, that the personal attendance of every man who hath three hundred pounds per annum, in Parliament, is indispensably his duty; and that, if the citizens and burgesses of any city or borough shall choose such a one, however reluctant he appear, he may be obliged to attend, and be forcibly brought to his duty by the serjeant-at-arms.

Again, there are numbers of subordinate offices, some of which are of burthen, and others of expense, in the civil government—all of which persons who are qualified are liable to have imposed on them, may be obliged to undertake and properly execute, notwithstanding any bodily labour, or even danger, to which they may subject themselves, under the penalty of fines and imprisonment; nay, and what may appear somewhat hard, may be compelled to satisfy the losses which are eventually incident to that of sheriff in particular, out of their own private fortunes; and though this should prove the ruin of a family, yet the public, to whom the price is due, incurs no debt or obligation to preserve its officer harmless, let his innocence appear ever so clearly.

I purposely omit the mention of those military or militiary duties which our old constitution laid upon its greatest members. These might, indeed, supply their posts with some other able-bodied men; but if no such could have been found, the obligation nevertheless remained, and they were compellable to serve in their own proper persons.

The only one, therefore, who is possessed of absolute liberty is the lowest member of the society, who, if he prefers hunger, or the wild product of the fields, hedges, lanes, and rivers, with the indulgence of ease and laziness, to a food a little more delicate, but purchased at the expense of labour, may lay himself under a shade; nor can be forced to take the other alternative from that which he hath, I will not affirm whether wisely or foolishly, chosen.

Here I may, perhaps, be reminded of the last Vagrant Act, where all such persons are compellable to work for the usual and accustomed wages allowed in the place; but this is a clause little known to the justices of the peace, and least likely to be executed by those who do know it, as they know likewise that it is formed on the ancient power of the justices to fix and settle these wages every year, making proper allowances for the scarcity and plenty of the times, the cheapness and dearness of the place; and that *the usual and accustomed wages* are words without any force or meaning, when there are no such; but every man spunges and raps whatever he can get; and will haggle as long and struggle as hard to cheat his employer of twopence in a day's labour as an honest tradesman wil to cheat his customers of the same sum in a yard of cloth or silk.

It is a great pity then that this power, or rather this practice, was not revived; but, this having been so long omitted that it is become obsolete, will be best done by a new law, in which this power, as well as the consequent power of forcing the poor to labour at a moderate and reasonable rate, should be well considered and their execution facilitated; for gentlemen who give their time and labour gratis, and even voluntarily, to the public, have a right to expect that all their business be made as easy as possible; and to enact laws without doing this is to fill our statute-books, much too full already, still fuller with dead letter, of no use but to the printer of the Acts of Parliament.

That the evil which I have here pointed at is of itself worth redressing, is, I apprehend, no subject of dispute; for why should any persons in distress be deprived of the assistance of their fellow-subjects, when they are willing amply to reward them for their labour? or, why should the lowest of the people be permitted to exact ten times the value of their work? For those exactions increase with the degrees of necessity in their object, insomuch that on the former side many are horribly imposed upon, and that often in no trifling matters. I was very well assured that at Deal no less than ten guineas was required, and paid by the supercargo of an Indiaman, for carrying him on board two miles from the shore when she was just ready to sail; so that his necessity, as his pillager well understood, was absolute. Again, many others, whose indignation will not submit to such plunder, are forced to refuse the assistance, though they are often great sufferers by so doing. On the latter side, the lowest of the people are encouraged in laziness and idleness; while they live by a twentieth part of the labour that ought to maintain them, which is diametrically opposite to the interest of the public; for that requires a great deal to be done, not to be paid, for a little. And, moreover, they are confirmed in habits of exaction, and are taught to consider the distresses of their superiors as their own fair emolument.

But enough of this matter, of which I at first intended only to convey a hint to those who are alone capable of applying the remedy, though they are the last to whom the notice of those evils would occur, without some such monitor as myself, who am forced to travel about the world in the form of a passenger. I cannot but say I heartily wish our governors would attentively consider this method of fixing the price of labour, and by that means of compelling the poor to work, since the due execution of such powers will, I apprehend, be found the true and only means of making them useful, and of advancing trade from its present visibly declining state to the height to which

Sir William Petty, in his *Political Arithmetic*, thinks it capable of being carried.

In the afternoon the lady of the above-mentioned mansion called at our inn, and left her compliments to us with Mrs. Francis, with an assurance that while we continued wind-bound in that place, where she feared we could be but indifferently accommodated, we were extremely welcome to the use of anything which her garden or her house afforded. So polite a message convinced us, in spite of some arguments to the contrary, that we were not on the coast of Africa, or on some island where the few savage inhabitants have little of human in them besides their form.

And here I mean nothing less than to derogate from the merit of this lady, who is not only extremely polite in her behaviour to strangers of her own rank, but so extremely good and charitable to all her poor neighbours who stand in need of her assistance, that she hath the universal love and praises of all who live near her. But, in reality, how little doth the acquisition of so valuable a character, and the full indulgence of so worthy a disposition, cost those who possess it! Both are accomplished by the very offals which fall from a table moderately plentiful. That they are enjoyed therefore by so few arises truly from there being so few who have such disposition to gratify, or who aim at any such character.

Wednesday, July 22 [17]. This morning, after having been mulcted as usual, we dispatched a servant with proper acknowledgments of the lady's goodness; but confined our wants entirely to the productions of her garden. He soon returned, in company with the gardener, both richly laden with almost every particular which a garden at this most fruitful season of the year produces.

While we were regaling ourselves with these, towards the close of our dinner, we received orders from our commander, who had dined that day with some inferior officers on board a man-of-war, to return instantly to the ship; for that the wind was become favourable, and he should weigh that evening. These orders were soon followed by the captain himself, who was still in the utmost hurry, though the occasion of it had long since ceased; for the wind had, indeed, a little shifted that afternoon, but was before this very quietly set down in its old quarters.

This last was a lucky hit for me; for, as the captain, to whose orders we resolved to pay no obedience, unless delivered by himself, did not return till past six, so much time seemed requisite to put up the furniture of our bedchamber or dining-room, for almost every article, even to some of the chairs, were either our own or the captain's property; so much more in conveying it as well as myself, as dead a luggage as any, to the shore, and thence to the ship, that the night threatened first to overtake us. A terrible circumstance to me, in my decayed condition; especially as very heavy showers of rain, attended with a high wind, continued to fall incessantly; the being carried through which two miles in the dark, in a wet and open boat, seemed little less than certain death.

However, as my commander was absolute, his orders peremptory, and my obedience necessary, I resolved to avail myself of a philosophy which hath been of notable use to me in the latter part of my life, and which is contained in this hemistich of Virgil:

——*Superanda omnis fortuna ferendo est.*

The meaning of which, if Virgil had any, I think I rightly understood, and rightly applied.

As I was, therefore, to be entirely passive in my motion, I resolved to abandon myself to the conduct of those who were to carry me into a cart when it returned from unloading the goods.

But before this, the captain, perceiving what had happened in the clouds, and that the wind remained as much his enemy as ever, came upstairs to me with a reprieve till the morning. This was, I own, very agreeable news, and I little regretted the trouble of refurnishing my apartment, by sending back for the goods.

Mrs. Francis was not well pleased with this. As she understood the reprieve to be only till the morning, she saw nothing but lodging to be possibly added, out of which she was to deduct fire and candle, and the remainder, she thought, would scarce pay her for her trouble. She exerted, therefore, all the ill-humour of which she was mistress, and did all she could to thwart and perplex everything during the whole evening.

Thursday, July 23 [18]. Early in the morning the captain, who had remained on shore all night, came to visit us, and to press us to make haste on board. "I am resolved," says he, "not to lose a moment now the wind is coming about fair: for my own part, I never was surer of a wind in all my life." I use his very words; nor will I presume to interpret or comment upon them farther than by observing that they were spoke in the utmost hurry.

We promised to be ready as soon as breakfast was over, but this was not so soon as was expected; for, in removing our goods the evening before, the tea-chest was unhappily lost.

Every place was immediately searched, and many where it was impossible for it to be; for this was a loss of much greater consequence than it may at first seem to many of my readers. Ladies and valetudinarians do not easily dispense with the use of this sovereign cordial in a single instance; but to undertake a long voyage, without any probability of being supplied with it the whole way, was above the reach of patience. And yet, dreadful as this calamity was, it seemed unavoidable. The whole town of Ryde could not supply a single leaf; for, as to what Mrs. Francis and the shop called by that name, it was not of Chinese growth. It did not indeed in the least resemble tea, either in smell or taste, or in any particular, unless in being a leaf; for it was in truth no other than a tobacco of the mundungus species. And as for the hopes of relief in any other port, they were not to be depended upon, for the captain had positively declared he was sure of a wind, and would let go his anchor no more till he arrived in the Tajo.

When a good deal of time had been spent, most of it indeed wasted on this occasion, a thought occurred which every one wondered at its not having presented itself the first moment. This was to apply to the good lady, who could not fail of pitying and relieving such distress. A messenger was immediately dispatched with an account of our misfortune, till whose return we employed ourselves in preparatives for our departure, that we might have nothing to do but to swallow our breakfast when it arrived. The tea-chest, though of no less consequence to us than the military-chest to a general, was given up as lost, or rather as stolen; for though I would not, for the world, mention any particular name, it is certain we had suspicions, and all, I am afraid, fell on the same person.

The man returned from the worthy lady with much expedition, and brought with him a canister of tea, dispatched with so true a generosity, as well as politeness, that if our voyage had been as long again we should have incurred no danger of being brought to a short allowance in this most important article. At the very same instant likewise arrived William the footman with our own teachest. It had been, indeed, left in the hoy, when the other goods were re-landed, as William, when he first heard it was missing, had suspected; and whence, had not the owner of the hoy been unluckily out of the way, he had retrieved it soon enough to have prevented our giving the lady an opportunity of displaying some part of her goodness.

To search the hoy was, indeed, too natural a suggestion to have escaped any one, nor did it escape being mentioned by many of us; but we were dissuaded from it by my wife's maid, who perfectly well remembered she had left the chest in the bedchamber; for that she had never given it out of her hands in her way to or from the hoy; but William perhaps knew the maid better, and best understood how far she was to be believed; for otherwise he would hardly of his own accord, after hearing her declaration, have hunted out the hoy-man, with much pains and difficulty.

Thus ended this scene, which begun with such appearance of distress, and ended with becoming the subject of mirth and laughter.

Nothing now remained but to pay our taxes, which were indeed laid with inconceivable severity. Lodging was raised sixpence, fire in the same proportion, and even candles, which had hitherto escaped, were charged with a wantonness of imposition, from the beginning, and placed under the style of oversight. We were raised a whole pound, whereas we had only burned ten, in five nights, and the pound consisted of twenty-four.

Lastly, an attempt was made which almost as far exceeds human credulity to believe as it did human patience to submit to. This was to make us pay as much for existing an hour or two as for existing a whole day; and dressing dinner was introduced as an article, though we left the house before either pot or spit had approached the fire. Here I own my patience failed me, and I became an example of the truth of the observation: "That all tyranny and oppression may be carried too far, and that a yoke may be made too intolerable for the neck of the tamest slave." When I remonstrated, with some warmth, against this grievance, Mrs. Francis gave me a look, and left the room without making any answer. She returned in a minute, running to me with pen, ink, and paper in her hand, and desired me to make my own bill; "for she hoped," she said, "I did not expect that her house was to be dirtied, and her goods spoiled and consumed, for nothing. The whole is but thirteen shillings. Can gentlefolks lie a whole night at a public-house for less? If they can I am sure it is time to give off being a landlady: but pay me what you please; I would have people know that I value money as little as other folks. But I was always a fool, as I says to my husband, and never knows which side my bread is buttered of. And yet, to be sure, your honour shall be my warning not to be bit so again. Some folks knows better than other some how to make their bills. Candles! why, yes, to be sure; why should not travellers pay for candles? I am sure I pays for my candles, and the chandler pays the king's majesty for them; and if he did not I must, so as it comes to the same thing in the end. To be sure I am out of sixteens at present, but these burn as white and as clear, though not quite so large. I expects my chandler here soon, or I would send to Portsmouth, if your honour was to stay any time longer. But when folks stays only for a wind, you knows there can be no dependence on such!" Here she put on a little slyness of aspect, and seemed willing to submit to interruption. I interrupted her accordingly by throwing down half a guinea, and declared I had no more English money, which was indeed true; and, as she could not immediately change the thirty-six shilling pieces, it put a final end to the dispute. Mrs. Francis soon left the room, and we soon after left the house; nor would this good woman see us or wish us a good voyage.

I must not, however, quit this place, where we had been so ill-treated, without doing it impartial justice, and recording what may, with the strictest truth, be said in its favour.

First, then, as to its situation, it is, I think, most delightful, and in the most pleasant spot in the whole island. It is true it wants the advantage of that beautiful river which leads from Newport to Cowes; but the prospect here extending to the sea, and taking in Portsmouth, Spithead, and St. Helen's, would be more than a recompense for the loss of the Thames itself, even in the most delightful part of Berkshire or Buckinghamshire, though another Denham, or another Pope, should unite in celebrating it. For my own part, I confess myself so entirely fond of a sea prospect, that I think nothing on the land can equal it; and if it be set off with shipping, I desire to borrow no ornament from the terra firma. A fleet of ships is, in my opinion, the noblest object which the art of man hath ever produced; and far beyond the power of those architects who deal in brick, in stone, or in marble.

When the late Sir Robert Walpole, one of the best of men and of ministers, used to equip us a yearly fleet at Spithead, his enemies of taste must have allowed that he, at least, treated the nation with a fine sight for their money. A much finer, indeed, than the same expense in an encampment could have produced. For what indeed is the best idea which the prospect of a number of huts can furnish to the mind, but of a number of men forming themselves into a society before the art of building more substantial houses was known? This, perhaps, would be agreeable enough; but, in truth, there is a much worse idea ready to step in before it, and that is of a body of cut-throats, the supports of tyranny, the invaders of the just liberties and properties of mankind, the plunderers of the industrious, the ravishers of the chaste, the murderers of the innocent, and, in a word, the destroyers of the plenty, the peace, and the safety of their fellow-creatures.

And what, it may be said, are these men-of-war which seem so delightful an object to our eyes? Are they not alike the support of tyranny and oppression of innocence, carrying with them desolation and ruin wherever their masters please to send them? This is indeed too true; and however the ship of war may, in its bulk and equipment, exceed the honest merchantman, I heartily wish there was no necessity for it; for, though I must own the superior beauty of the object on one side, I am more pleased with the superior excellence of the idea which I can raise in my mind on the other, while I reflect on the art and industry of mankind engaged in the daily improvements of commerce to the mutual benefit of all countries, and to the establishment and happiness of social life.

This pleasant village is situated on a gentle ascent from the water, whence it affords that charming prospect I have above described. Its soil is a gravel, which, assisted with its declivity, preserves it always so dry that immediately after the most violent rain a fine lady may walk without wetting her silken shoes. The fertility of the place is apparent from its extraordinary verdure, and it is so shaded with large and flourishing elms, that its narrow lanes are a natural grove or walk, which, in the regularity of its plantation, vies with the power of art, and in its wanton exuberancy greatly exceeds it.

In a field in the ascent of this hill, about a quarter of a mile from the sea, stands a neat little chapel. It is very small, but adequate to the number of inhabitants; for the parish doth not seem to contain above thirty houses.

At about two miles distant from this parish lives that polite and good lady to whose kindness we were so much obliged. It is placed on a hill whose bottom is washed by the sea, and which, from its eminence at top, commands a view of a great part of the island as well as it does that of the opposite shore. This house was formerly built by one Boyce, who, from a blacksmith at Gosport, became possessed, by great success in smuggling, of forty thousand pounds. With part of this, he purchased an estate here, and, by chance probably, fixed on this spot for building a large house. Perhaps the convenience of carrying on his business, to which it is so well adapted, might dictate the situation to him. We can hardly, at least, attribute it to the same taste with which he furnished his house, or at least his library, by sending an order to a bookseller in London to pack him up five hundred pounds' worth of his handsomest books. They tell here several almost incredible stories of the ignorance, the folly, and the pride, which this poor man and his wife discovered during the short continuance of his prosperity; for he did not long escape the sharp eyes of the revenue solicitors, and was, by extents from the Court of Exchequer, soon reduced below his original state to that of confinement in the Fleet. All his effects were sold, and among the rest his books, by an auction at Portsmouth, for a very small price; for the bookseller was now discovered to have been perfectly a master of his trade, and, relying on Mr. Boyce's finding little time to read, had sent him not only the most lasting wares of his shop, but duplicates of the same, under different titles.

His estate and house were purchased by a gentleman of these parts, whose widow now enjoys them, and who hath improved them, particularly her gardens, with so elegant a taste, that the painter who would assist his imagination in the composition of a most exquisite landscape, or the poet who would describe an earthly paradise, could nowhere furnish themselves with a richer pattern.

We left this place about eleven in the morning, and were again conveyed, with more sunshine than wind, aboard our ship.

Whence our captain had acquired his power of prophecy, when he promised us and himself a prosperous wind, I will not determine; it is sufficient to observe that he was a false prophet, and that the weathercocks continued to point as before.

He would not, however, so easily give up his skill in prediction. He persevered in asserting that the wind was changed, and, having weighed his anchor, fell down that afternoon to St. Helen's, which was at about the distance of five miles; and whither his friend the tide, in defiance of the wind, which was most manifestly against him, softly wafted him in as many hours.

Here, about seven in the evening, before which time we could not procure it, we sat down to regale ourselves with some roasted venison, which was much better drest than we imagined it would be, and an excellent cold pasty which my wife had made at Ryde, and which we had reserved uncut to eat on board our ship, whither we all cheerfully exulted in being returned from the presence of Mrs. Francis, who, by the exact resemblance she bore to a fury, seemed to have been with no great propriety settled in paradise.

Friday, July 24 [19]. As we passed by Spithead on the preceding evening we saw the two regiments of soldiers who were just returned from Gibraltar and Minorca; and this day a lieutenant belonging to one of them, who was the captain's nephew, came to pay a visit to his uncle. He was what is called by some a very pretty fellow; indeed, much too pretty a fellow at his years; for he was turned of thirty-four, though his address and conversation would have become him more before he had reached twenty. In his conversation, it is true, there was something military enough, as it consisted chiefly of oaths, and of the great actions and wise sayings of Jack, and Will, and Tom of our regiment, a phrase eternally in his mouth; and he seemed to conclude that it conveyed to all the officers such a degree of public notoriety and importance that it entitled him, like the head of a profession, or a first minister, to be the subject of conversation among those who had not the least personal acquaintance with him. This did not much surprise me, as I have seen several examples of the same; but the defects in his address, especially to the women, were so great that they seemed absolutely inconsistent with the behaviour of a pretty fellow, much less of one in a red coat; and yet, besides having been eleven years in the army, he had had, as his uncle informed me, an education in France. This, I own, would have appeared to have been absolutely thrown away had not his animal spirits, which were likewise thrown away upon him in great abundance, borne the visible stamp of the growth of that country. The character to which he had an indisputable title was that of a merry fellow; so very merry was he that he laughed at everything he said, and always before he spoke. Possibly, indeed, he often laughed at what he did not utter, for every speech began with a laugh, though it did not always end with a jest. There was no great analogy between the characters of the uncle and the nephew, and yet they seemed entirely to agree in enjoying the honour which the red-coat did to his family. This the uncle expressed with great pleasure in his countenance, and seemed desirous of shewing all present the honour which he had for his nephew, who, on his side, was at some pains to convince us of his concurring in this opinion, and at the same time of displaying the contempt he had for the parts, as well as the occupation, of his uncle, which he seemed to think reflected some disgrace on himself, who was a member of that profession which makes every man a gentleman. Not that I would be understood to insinuate that the nephew endeavoured to shake off or disown his uncle, or indeed to keep him at any distance. On the contrary, he treated him with the utmost familiarity, often calling him Dick, and dear Dick, and old Dick, and frequently beginning an oration with "D—n me, Dick."

All this condescension on the part of the young man

was received with suitable marks of complaisance and obligation by the old one; especially when it was attended with evidences of the same familiarity with general officers and other persons of rank; one of whom, in particular, I know to have the pride and insolence of the devil himself, and who, without some strong bias of interest, is no more liable to converse familiarly with a lieutenant than of being mistaken in his judgment of a fool; which was not, perhaps, so certainly the case of the worthy lieutenant, who, in declaring to us the qualifications which recommended men to his countenance and conversation, as well as what effectually set a bar to all hopes of that honour, exclaimed: "No, sir, by the d— I hate all fools.—No, d—n me, excuse me for that. That's a little too much, old Dick. There are two or three officers of our regiment whom I know to be fools; but d—n me if I am ever seen in their company. If a man hath a fool of a relation, Dick, you know he can't help that, old boy."

Such jokes as these the old man not only took in good part, but glibly gulped down the whole narrative of his nephew; nor did he, I am convinced, in the least doubt of our as readily swallowing the same. This made him so charmed with the lieutenant, that it is probable we should have been pestered with him the whole evening, had not the north wind, dearer to our sea-captain even than this glory of his family, sprung suddenly up, and called aloud to him to weigh his anchor.

While this ceremony was performing, the sea-captain ordered out his boat to row the land-captain to shore; not indeed on an uninhabited island, but one which, in this part, looked but little better, not presenting us the view of a single house. Indeed, our old friend, when his boat returned from shore, perhaps being no longer able to stifle his envy of the superiority of his nephew, told us with a smile that the young man had a good five miles to walk before he could be accommodated with a passage to Portsmouth.

It appeared now that the captain had been only mistaken in the date of his prediction, by placing the event a day earlier than it happened; for the wind which now arose was not only favourable but brisk, and was no sooner in reach of our sails than it swept us away by the back of the Isle of Wight, and, having in the night carried us by

Christchurch and Peveral Point, brought us the next noon, *Saturday, July 25*, off the island of Portland, so famous for the smallness and sweetness of its mutton, of which a leg seldom weighs four pounds. We would have bought a sheep, but our captain would not permit it; though he needed not have been in such a hurry, for presently the wind, I will not positively assert in resentment of his surliness, shewed him a dog's trick, and slily slipt back again to his summer-house in the south-west.

The captain now grew outrageous, and, declaring open war with the wind, took a resolution, rather more bold than wise, of sailing in defiance of it, and in its teeth. He swore he would let go his anchor no more, but would beat the sea while he had either yard or sail left. He accordingly stood from the shore, and made so large a tack that before night, though he seemed to advance but little on his way, he was got out of sight of land.

Towards the evening the wind began, in the captain's own language, to freshen and indeed it freshened so much, that before ten it blew a perfect hurricane.

The captain having got, as he supposed, to a safe distance, tacked again towards the English shore; and now the wind veered a point only in his favour, and continued to blow with such violence, that the ship ran above eight knots or miles an hour during this whole day and tempestuous night till bed-time. I was obliged to betake myself once more to my solitude, for my women were again all down in their sea-sickness, and the captain was busy on deck; for he began to grow uneasy, chiefly, I believe, because he did not well know where he was, and would, I am convinced, have been very glad to have been in Portland Road, eating some sheep's-head broth.

Having contracted no great degree of good-humour by living a whole day alone, without a single soul to converse with, I took but ill physic to purge it off, by a bed conversation with the captain, who, amongst many bitter lamentations of his fate, and protesting he had more patience than a Job, frequently intermixed summons to the commanding officer on the deck, who now happened to be one Morrison, a carpenter, the only fellow that had either common sense or common civility in the ship. Of Morrison he inquired every quarter of an hour concerning the state of affairs: the wind, the care of the ship, and other matters of naviga-

tion. The frequency of these summons, as well as the
solicitude with which they were made, sufficiently testified
the state of the captain's mind; he endeavoured to conceal
it, and would have given no small alarm to a man who had
either not learnt what it is to die, or known what it is to
be miserable. And my dear wife and child must pardon
me, if what I did not conceive to be any great evil to
myself I was not much terrified with the thoughts of
happening to them; in truth, I have often thought they
are both too good and too gentle to be trusted to the power
of any man I know, to whom they could possibly be so
trusted.

Can I say then I had no fear? indeed I cannot. Reader,
I was afraid for thee, lest thou shouldst have been deprived
of that pleasure thou art now enjoying; and that I should
not live to draw out on paper that military character which
thou didst peruse in the journal of yesterday.

From all these fears we were relieved, at six in the
morning, by the arrival of Mr. Morrison, who acquainted
us that he was sure he beheld land very near; for he could
not see half a mile, by reason of the haziness of the weather.
This land he said was, he believed, the Berry Head, which
forms one side of Torbay: the captain declared that it
was impossible, and swore, on condition he was right, he
would give him his mother for a maid. A forfeit which
became afterwards strictly due and payable; for the
captain, whipping on his nightgown, ran up without his
breeches, and within half an hour returning into the cabin,
wished me joy of our lying safe at anchor in the bay.

Sunday, July 26 [21]. Things now began to put on an
aspect very different from what they had lately worn; the
news that the ship had almost lost its mizen, and that we
had procured very fine clouted cream and fresh bread and
butter from the shore, restored health and spirits to our
women, and we all sat down to a very cheerful breakfast.

But, however pleasant our stay promised to be here, we
were all desirous it should be short: I resolved immediately
to dispatch my man into the country to purchase a present
of cider, for my friends, of that which is called Southam, as
well as to take with me a hogshead of it to Lisbon; for it is,
in my opinion, much more delicious than that which is the
growth of Herefordshire. I purchased three hogsheads for
five pounds ten shillings, all which I should have scarce

thought worth mentioning, had I not believed it might be of equal service to the honest farmer who sold it me, and who is by the neighbouring gentleman reputed to deal in the very best; and to the reader, who, from ignorance of the means of providing better for himself, swallows at a dearer rate the juice of Middlesex turnip, instead of that Vinum Pomonæ which Mr. Giles Leverance of Cheeshurst, near Dartmouth in Devon, will, at the price of forty shillings per hogshead, send in double casks to any part of the world. Had the wind been very sudden in shifting, I had lost my cider by an attempt of a boatman to exact, according to custom. He required five shillings for conveying my man a mile and a half to the shore, and four more if he stayed to bring him back. This I thought to be such insufferable impudence that I ordered him to be immediately chased from the ship, without any answer. Indeed, there are few inconveniences that I would not rather encounter than encourage the insolent demands of these wretches, at the expense of my own indignation, of which I own they are not the only objects, but rather those who purchase a paltry convenience by encouraging them. But of this I have already spoken very largely. I shall conclude, therefore, with the leave which this fellow took of our ship; saying he should know it again, and would not put off from the shore to relieve it in any distress whatever.

It will, doubtless, surprise many of my readers to hear that, when we lay at anchor within a mile or two of a town several days together, and even in the most temperate weather, we should frequently want fresh provisions and herbage, and other emoluments of the shore, as much as if we had been a hundred leagues from land. And this, too, while numbers of boats were in our sight, whose owners get their livelihood by rowing people up and down, and could be at any time summoned by a signal to our assistance, and while the captain had a little boat of his own, with men always ready to row it at his command.

This, however, hath been partly accounted for already by the imposing disposition of the people, who asked so much more than the proper price of their labour. And as to the usefulness of the captain's boat, it requires to be a little expatiated upon, as it will tend to lay open some of the grievances which demand the utmost regard of our legislature, as they affect the most valuable part of the king's subjects—those by whom the commerce of the nation is carried into execution.

Our captain then, who was a very good and experienced seaman, having been above thirty years the master of a vessel, part of which he had served, so he phrased it, as commander of a privateer, and had discharged himself with great courage and conduct, and with as great success, discovered the utmost aversion to the sending his boat ashore whenever we lay wind-bound in any of our harbours. This aversion did not arise from any fear of wearing out his boat by using it, but was, in truth, the result of experience, that it was easier to send his men on shore than to recall them. They acknowledged him to be their master while they remained on shipboard, but did not allow his power to extend to the shores, where they had no sooner set their feet than every man became *sui juris*, and thought himself at full liberty to return when he pleased. Now it is not any delight that these fellows have in the fresh air or verdant fields on the land. Every one of them would prefer his ship and his hammock to all the sweets of Arabia the Happy; but, unluckily for them, there are in every seaport in England certain houses whose chief livelihood depends on providing entertainment for the gentlemen of the jacket. For this purpose they are always well furnished with those cordial liquors which do immediately inspire the heart with gladness, banishing all careful thoughts, and indeed all others, from the mind, and opening the mouth with songs of cheerfulness and thanksgiving for the many wonderful blessings with which a seafaring life overflows.

For my own part, however whimsical it may appear, I confess I have thought the strange story of Circe in the Odyssey no other than an ingenious allegory, in which Homer intended to convey to his countrymen the same kind of instruction which we intend to communicate to our own in this digression. As teaching the art of war to the Greeks was the plain design of the Iliad, so was teaching them the art of navigation the no less manifest intention of the Odyssey. For the improvement of this, their situation was most excellently adapted; and accordingly we find Thucydides, in the beginning of his history, considers the Greeks as a set of pirates or privateers, plundering each other by sea. This being probably the first institution of commerce before the Ars Cauponaria was invented, and merchants, instead of robbing, began to cheat and outwit each other, and by degrees changed the Metabletic, the only kind of traffic allowed by Aristotle in his *Politics*, into the Chrematistic.

By this allegory, then, I suppose Ulysses to have been the captain of a merchant-ship, and Circe some good ale-wife, who made his crew drunk with the spirituous liquors of those days. With this the transformation into swine, as well as all other incidents of the fable, will notably agree; and thus a key will be found out for unlocking the whole mystery, and forging at least some meaning to a story which, at present, appears very strange and absurd.

Hence, moreover, will appear the very near resemblance between the seafaring men of all ages and nations; and here perhaps may be established the truth and justice of that observation, which will occur oftener than once in this voyage, that all human flesh is not the same flesh, but that there is one kind of flesh of landmen, and another of seamen.

Philosophers, divines, and others, who have treated the gratification of human appetites with contempt, have, among other instances, insisted very strongly on that satiety which is so apt to overtake them even in the very act of enjoyment. And here they more particularly deserve our attention, as most of them may be supposed to speak from their own experience, and very probably gave us their lessons with a full stomach. Thus hunger and thirst, whatever delight they may afford while we are eating and drinking, pass both away from us with the plate and the cup; and though we should imitate the Romans, if, indeed, they were such dull beasts, which I can scarce believe, to unload the belly like a dung-pot, in order to fill it again with another load, yet would the pleasure so so considerably lessened that it would scarce repay us the trouble of purchasing it with swallowing a basin of camomile tea. A second haunch of venison, or a second dose of turtle, would hardly allure a city glutton with its smell. Even the celebrated Jew himself, when well filled with calipash and calipee, goes contentedly home to tell his money, and expects no more pleasure from his throat during the next twenty-four hours. Hence I suppose Dr. South took that elegant comparison of the joys of a speculative man to the solemn silence of an Archimedes over a problem, and those of a glutton to the stillness of a sow at her wash. A simile which, if it became the pulpit at all, could only become it in the afternoon.

Whereas in those potations which the mind seems to enjoy, rather than the bodily appetite, there is happily no such satiety; but the more a man drinks, the more he desires; as if, like Mark Anthony in Dryden, his appetite increased with feeding, and this to such an immoderate degree, *ut nullus sit desiderio aut pudor aut modus.* Hence, as with the gang of Captain Ulysses, ensues so total a transformation, that the man no more continues what he was. Perhaps he ceases for a time to be at all; or, though he may retain the same outward form and figure he had before, yet is his nobler part, as we are taught to call it, so changed, that, instead of being the same man, he scarce remembers what he was a few hours before. And this transformation, being once obtained, is so easily preserved by the same potations, which induce no satiety, that the captain in vain sends or goes in quest of his crew. They know him no longer; or, if they do, they acknowledge not his power, having, indeed, as entirely forgotten themselves as if they had taken a large draught of the river of Lethe.

Nor is the captain always sure of even finding out the place to which Circe hath conveyed them. There are many of those houses in every port-town. Nay, there are some where the sorceress doth not trust only to her drugs; but hath instruments of a different kind to execute her purposes, by whose means the tar is effectually secreted from the knowledge and pursuit of his captain. This would, indeed, be very fatal, was it not for one circumstance; that the sailor is seldom provided with the proper bait for these harpies. However, the contrary sometimes happens, as these harpies will bite at almost anything, and will snap at a pair of silver buttons, or buckles, as surely as at the specie itself. Nay, sometimes they are so voracious, that the very naked hook will go down, and the jolly young sailor is sacrificed for his own sake.

In vain, at such a season as this, would the vows of a pious heathen have prevailed over Neptune, Æolus, or any other marine deity. In vain would the prayers of a Christian captain be attended with the like success. The wind may change how it pleases while all hands are on shore; the anchor would remain firm in the ground, and the ship would continue in durance, unless, like other forcible prison-breakers, it forcibly got loose for no good purpose.

Now, as the favour of winds and courts, and such like, is always to be laid hold on at the very first motion, for within twenty-four hours all may be changed again; so, in the former case, the loss of a day may be the loss of a voyage: for, though it may appear to persons not well skilled in navigation, who see ships meet and sail by each other, that the wind blows sometimes east and west, north and south, backwards and forwards, at the same instant; yet, certain it is that the land is so contrived, that even the same wind will not, like the same horse, always bring a man to the end of his journey; but, that the gale which the mariner prayed heartily for yesterday, he may as heartily deprecate to-morrow; while all use and benefit which would have arisen to him from the westerly wind of to-morrow may be totally lost and thrown away by neglecting the offer of the easterly blast which blows to-day.

Hence ensues grief and disreputation to the innocent captain, loss and disappointment to the worthy merchant, and not seldom great prejudice to the trade of a nation whose manufactures are thus liable to lie unsold in a foreign warehouse, the market being forestalled by some rival whose sailors are under a better discipline. To guard against these inconveniences the prudent captain takes every precaution in his power; he makes the strongest contracts with his crew, and thereby binds them so firmly, that none but the greatest or least of men can break through them with impunity; but for one of these two reasons, which I will not determine, the sailor, like his brother fish the eel, is too slippery to be held, and plunges into his element with perfect impunity.

To speak a plain truth, there is no trusting to any contract with one whom the wise citizens of London call a bad man; for, with such a one, though your bond be ever so strong, it will prove in the end good for nothing.

What, then, is to be done in this case? What, indeed, but to call in the assistance of that tremendous magistrate, the justice of peace, who can, and often doth, lay good and bad men in equal durance, and, though he seldom cares to stretch his bonds to what is great, never finds anything too minute for their detention, but will hold the smallest reptile alive so fast in his noose, that he can never get out till he is let drop through it.

Why, therefore, upon the breach of those contracts, should not an immediate application be made to the nearest magistrate of this order, who should be empowered to convey the delinquent either to ship or to prison, at the election of the captain, to be fettered by the leg in either place?

But, as the case now stands, the condition of this poor captain without any commission, and of this absolute commander without any power, is much worse than we have hitherto shewn it to be; for, notwithstanding all the aforesaid contracts to sail in the good ship the *Elizabeth*, if the sailor should, for better wages, find it more his interest to go on board the better ship the *Mary*, either before their setting out or on their speedy meeting in some port, he may prefer the latter without any other danger than that of "doing what he ought not to have done," contrary to a rule which he is seldom Christian enough to have much at heart, while the captain is generally too good a Christian to punish a man out of revenge only, when he is to be at a considerable expense for so doing. There are many other deficiencies in our laws relating to maritime affairs, and which would probably have been long since corrected, had we any seamen in the House of Commons. Not that I would insinuate that the legislature wants a supply of many gentlemen in the sea-service; but, as these gentlemen are by their attendance in the House unfortunately prevented from ever going to sea, and there learning what they might communicate to their landed brethren, these latter remain as ignorant in that branch of knowledge as they would be if none but courtiers and fox-hunters had been elected into Parliament, without a single fish among them. The following seems to me to be an effect of this kind, and it strikes me the stronger as I remember the case to have happened, and remember it to have been dispunishable. A captain of a trading vessel, of which he was part owner, took in a large freight of oats at Liverpool, consigned to the market at Bearkey: this he carried to a port in Hampshire, and there sold it as his own, and, freighting his vessel with wheat for the port of Cadiz, in Spain, dropt it at Oporto in his way; and there, selling it for his own use, took in a lading of wine, with which he sailed again, and, having converted it in the same manner, together with a large sum of money with which he was entrusted, for the benefit of certain merchants, sold the ship and cargo in another port, and then wisely sat down contented with the fortune he had made, and returned to London to enjoy the remainder of his days, with the fruits of his former labours and a good conscience.

The sum he brought home with him consisted of near six thousand pounds, all in specie, and most of it in that coin which Portugal distributes so liberally over Europe.

He was not yet old enough to be past all sense of pleasure, nor so puffed up with the pride of his good fortune as to overlook his old acquaintance the journeymen tailors, from among whom he had been formerly pressed into the sea-service, and, having there laid the foundation of his future success by his shares in prizes, had afterwards become captain of a trading vessel, in which he purchased an interest, and had soon begun to trade in the honourable manner above mentioned.

The captain now took up his residence at an ale-house in Drury Lane, where, having all his money by him in a trunk, he spent about five pounds a day among his old friends the gentlemen and ladies of those parts.

The merchant of Liverpool, having luckily had notice from a friend during the blaze of his fortune, did, by the assistance of a justice of peace, without the assistance of the law, recover his whole loss. The captain, however, wisely chose to refund no more; but, perceiving with what hasty strides Envy was pursuing his fortune, he took speedy means to retire out of her reach, and to enjoy the rest of his wealth in an inglorious obscurity; nor could the same justice overtake him time enough to assist a second merchant as he had done the first.

This was a very extraordinary case, and the more so as the ingenious gentleman had steered entirely clear of all crimes in our law.

Now, how it comes about that a robbery so very easy to be committed, and to which there is such immediate temptation always before the eyes of these fellows, should receive the encouragement of impunity, is to be accounted for only from the oversight of the legislature, as that oversight can only be, I think, derived from the reasons I have assigned for it.

But I will dwell no longer on this subject. If what I have here said should seem of sufficient consequence to engage the attention of any man in power, and should thus be the means of applying any remedy to the most inveterate evils, at least, I have obtained my whole desire, and shall have lain so long wind-bound in the ports of this kingdom to some purpose. I would, indeed, have this work—which, if I should live to finish it, a matter of no great certainty, if indeed of any great hope to me, will be probably the last I shall ever undertake—to produce some better end than the mere diversion of the reader.

Monday [July 22]. This day our captain went ashore, to dine with a gentleman who lives in these parts, and who so exactly resembles the character given by Homer of Axylus, that the only difference I can trace between them is, the one, living by the highway, erected his hospitality chiefly in favour of land-travellers; and the other, living by the water-side, gratified his humanity by accommodating the wants of the mariner.

In the evening our commander received a visit from a brother bashaw, who lay wind-bound in the same harbour. This latter captain was a Swiss. He was then master of a vessel bound to Guinea, and had formerly been a-privateering, when our own hero was employed in the same laudable service. The honesty and freedom of the Switzer, his vivacity, in which he was in no respect inferior to his near neighbours the French, the awkward and affected politeness, which was likewise of French extraction, mixed with the brutal roughness of the English tar—for he had served under the colours of this nation and his crew had been of the same—made such an odd variety, such a hotch-potch of character, that I should have been much diverted with him, had not his voice, which was as loud as a speaking-trumpet, unfortunately made my head ache. The noise which he conveyed into the deaf ears of his brother captain, who sat on one side of him, the soft addresses with which, mixed with awkward bows, he saluted the ladies on the other, were so agreeably contrasted, that a man must not only have been void of all taste of humour, and insensible of mirth, but duller than Cibber is represented in the *Dunciad*, who could be unentertained with him a little while; for, I confess, such entertainments should always be very short, as they are very liable to pall. But he suffered not this to happen at present; for, having given us his company a quarter of an hour only, he retired, after many apologies for the shortness of his visit.

Tuesday [July 23]. The wind being less boisterous than it had hitherto been since our arrival here, several fishing-boats, which the tempestuous weather yesterday had prevented from working, came on board us with fish. This was so fresh, so good in kind, and so very cheap, that we supplied ourselves in great numbers, among which were very large soles at fourpence a pair, and whitings of almost a preposterous size at ninepence a score.

The only fish which bore any price was a John Dorée, as it is called. I bought one of at least four pounds weight for as many shillings. It resembles a turbot in shape, but exceeds it in firmness and flavour. The price had the appearance of being considerable when opposed to the extraordinary cheapness of others of value, but was, in truth, so very reasonable when estimated by its goodness, that it left me under no other surprise than how the gentlemen of this country, not greatly eminent for the delicacy of their taste, had discovered the preference of the dorée to all other fish: but I was informed that Mr. Quin, whose distinguishing tooth hath been so justly celebrated, had lately visited Plymouth, and had done those honours to the dorée which are so justly due to it from that sect of modern philosophers who, with Sir Epicure Mammon, or Sir Epicure Quin, their head, seem more to delight in a fishpond than in a garden, as the old Epicureans are said to have done.

Unfortunately for the fishmongers of London, the dorée resides only in those seas; for, could any of this company but convey one to the temple of luxury under the Piazza, where Macklin, the high-priest, daily serves up his rich offerings to that goddess, great as would be the reward of that fishmonger, in blessings poured down upon him from the goddess, as great would his merit be towards the high-priest, who could never be thought to overrate such valuable incense.

And here, having mentioned the extreme cheapness of fish in the Devonshire sea, and given some little hint of the extreme dearness with which this commodity is dispensed by those who deal in it in London, I cannot pass on without throwing forth an observation or two, with the

same view with which I have scattered my several remarks
through this voyage, sufficiently satisfied in having finished
my life, as I have probably lost it, in the service of my
country, from the best of motives, though it should be
attended with the worst of success. Means are always in
our power; ends are very seldom so.

Of all the animal foods with which man is furnished,
there are none so plenty as fish. A little rivulet, that
glides almost unperceived through a vast tract of rich
land, will support more hundreds with the flesh of its
inhabitants than the meadow will nourish individuals.
But if this be true of rivers, it is much truer of the sea-
shores, which abound with such immense variety of fish
that the curious fisherman, after he hath made his draught,
often culls only the daintiest part and leaves the rest of
his prey to perish on the shore.

If this be true it would appear, I think, that there is
nothing which might be had in such abundance, and
consequently so cheap, as fish, of which Nature seems to
have provided such inexhaustible stores with some peculiar
design. In the production of terrestrial animals she
proceeds with such slowness, that in the larger kind a
single female seldom produces more than one a year, and
this again requires three, four, or five years more to bring
it to perfection. And though the lesser quadrupeds, those
of the wild kind particularly, with the birds, do multiply
much faster, yet can none of these bear any proportion
with the aquatic animals, of whom every female matrix is
furnished with an annual offspring almost exceeding the
power of numbers, and which, in many instances at least,
a single year is capable of bringing to some degree of
maturity.

What then ought in general to be so plentiful, what so
cheap, as fish? What then so properly the food of the
poor? So in many places they are, and so might they
always be in great cities, which are always situated near
the sea, or on the conflux of large rivers. How comes it
then, to look no farther abroad for instances, that in our
city of London the case is so far otherwise that, except that
of sprats, there is not one poor palate in a hundred that
knows the taste of fish?

It is true indeed that this taste is generally of such
excellent flavour that it exceeds the power of French

cookery to treat the palates of the rich with anything more exquisitely delicate; so that was fish the common food of the poor it might put them too much upon an equality with their betters in the great article of eating, in which, at present, in the opinion of some, the great difference in happiness between man and man consists. But this argument I shall treat with the utmost disdain: for if ortolans were as big as bustards, and at the same time as plenty as sparrows, I should hold it yet reasonable to indulge the poor with the dainty, and that for this cause especially, that the rich would soon find a sparrow, if as scarce as an ortolan, to be much the greater, as it would certainly be the rarer, dainty of the two.

Vanity or scarcity will be always the favourite of luxury; but honest hunger will be satisfied with plenty. Not to search deeper into the cause of the evil, I should think it abundantly sufficient to propose the remedies of it. And, first, I humbly submit the absolute necessity of immediately hanging all the fishmongers within the bills of mortality; and, however it might have been some time ago the opinion of mild and temporizing men that the evil complained of might be removed by gentler methods, I suppose at this day there are none who do not see the impossibility of using such with any effect. *Cuncta prius tentanda* might have been formerly urged with some plausibility, but *cuncta prius tentata* may now be replied: for surely, if a few monopolizing fishmongers could defeat that excellent scheme of the Westminster market, to the erecting which so many justices of peace, as well as other wise and learned men, did so vehemently apply themselves, that they might be truly said not only to have laid the whole strength of their heads, but of their shoulders too, to the business, it would be a vain endeavour for any other body of men to attempt to remove so stubborn a nuisance.

If it should be doubted whether we can bring this case within the letter of any capital law now subsisting, I am ashamed to own it cannot; for surely no crime better deserves such punishment; but the remedy may, nevertheless, be immediate; and if a law was made at the beginning of next session, to take place immediately, by which the starving thousands of poor was declared to be felony, without benefit of clergy, the fishmongers would be hanged before the end of the session.

A second method of filling the mouths of the poor, if not with loaves at least with fishes, is to desire the magistrates to carry into execution one at least out of near a hundred Acts of Parliament, for preserving the small fry of the river of Thames, by which means as few fish would satisfy thousands as may now be devoured by a small number of individuals. But while a fisherman can break through the strongest meshes of an Act of Parliament, we may be assured he will learn so to contrive his own meshes that the smallest fry will not be able to swim through them.

Other methods may, we doubt not, be suggested by those who shall attentively consider the evil here hinted at; but we have dwelt too long on it already, and shall conclude with observing that it is difficult to affirm whether the atrocity of the evil itself, the facility of curing it, or the shameful neglect of the cure, be the more scandalous or more astonishing.

After having, however, gloriously regaled myself with this food, I was washing it down with some good claret with my wife and her friend, in the cabin, when the captain's valet de chambre, head cook, house and ship steward, footman in livery and out on't, secretary, and foremast man, all burst into the cabin at once, being, indeed, all but one person, and, without saying by your leave, began to pack half a hogshead of small beer in bottles, the necessary consequence of which must have been either a total stop to conversation at that cheerful season when it is most agreeable, or the admitting that polyonymous officer aforesaid to the participation of it. I desired him therefore to delay his purpose a little longer, but he refused to grant my request; nor was he prevailed on to quit the room till he was threatened with having one bottle to pack more than his number, which then happened to stand empty within my reach.

With these menaces he retired at last, but not without muttering some menaces on his side, and which, to our great terror, he failed not to put into immediate execution.

Our captain was gone to dinner this day with his Swiss brother; and, though he was a very sober man, was a little elevated with some champagne, which, as it cost the Swiss little or nothing, he dispensed at his table more liberally than our hospitable English noblemen put about those bottles, which the ingenious Peter Taylor teaches a led captain to avoid by distinguishing by the name of that generous liquor, which all humble companions are taught to postpone to the flavour of methuen, or honest port.

While our two captains were thus regaling themselves, and celebrating their own heroic exploits with all the inspiration which the liquor, at least, of wit could afford them, the polyonymous officer arrived, and, being saluted by the name of Honest Tom, was ordered to sit down and take his glass before he delivered his message; for every sailor is by turns his captain's mate over a can, except only that captain bashaw who presides in a man-of-war, and who upon earth has no other mate, unless it be another of the same bashaws.

Tom had no sooner swallowed his draught than he hastily began his narrative, and faithfully related what had happened on board our ship; we say faithfully, though from what happened it may be suspected that Tom chose to add perhaps only five or six immaterial circumstances, as is always I believe the case, and may possibly have been done by me in relating this very story, though it happened not many hours ago.

No sooner was the captain informed of the interruption which had been given to his officer, and indeed to his orders, for he thought no time so convenient as that of his absence for causing any confusion in the cabin, than he leapt with such haste from his chair that he had like to have broke his sword, with which he always begirt himself when he walked out of his ship, and sometimes when he walked about in it; at the same time grasping eagerly that other implement called a cockade, which modern soldiers wear on their helmets with the same view as the ancients did their crests—to terrify the enemy, he muttered something, but so inarticulately that the word *damn* was only intelligible; he then hastily took leave of the Swiss captain, who was too well bred to press his stay on such an occasion, and leapt first from the ship to his boat, and then from his boat to his own ship, with as much fierceness in his looks as he had ever expressed on boarding his defenceless prey in the honourable calling of a privateer.

Having regained the middle deck, he paused a moment while Tom and the others loaded themselves with bottles, and then descending into the cabin exclaimed with a thundering voice: "D—n me, why arn't the bottles stowed in, according to my orders?"

I answered him very mildly that I had prevented his man from doing it, as it was at an inconvenient time to me, and as in his absence, at least, I esteemed the cabin to be my own. "Your cabin!" repeated he many times; "no, d—n me! 'tis my cabin. Your cabin! d—n me! I have brought my hogs to a fair market. I suppose indeed you think it your cabin, and your ship, by your commanding in it; but I will command in it, d—n me! I will shew the world I am the commander, and nobody but I! Sir you think I sold you the command of my ship for that pitiful thirty pounds? I wish I had not seen you nor your thirty pounds aboard of her." He then repeated the words thirty pounds often, with great disdain, and with a contempt which I own the sum did not seem to deserve in my eye, either in itself or on the present occasion; being, indeed, paid for the freight of —— weight of human flesh, which is above fifty per cent dearer than the freight of any other luggage, whilst in reality it takes up less room; in fact, no room at all.

In truth, the sum was paid for nothing more than for a liberty to six persons (two of them servants) to stay on board a ship while she sails from one port to another, every shilling of which comes clear into the captain's pocket. Ignorant people may perhaps imagine, especially when they are told that the captain is obliged to sustain them, that their diet at least is worth something, which may probably be now and then so far the case as to deduct a tenth part from the neat profits on this account; but it was otherwise at present; for when I had contracted with the captain at a price which I by no means thought moderate, I had some content in thinking I should have no more to pay for my voyage; but I was whispered that it was expected the passengers should find themselves in several things; such as tea, wine, and such like; and particularly that gentlemen should stowe of the latter a much larger quantity than they could use, in order to leave the remainder as a present to the captain at the end of the voyage; and it was expected likewise that gentlemen should put aboard some fresh stores, and the more of such things were put aboard the welcomer they would be to the captain.

I was prevailed with by these hints to follow the advice

proposed; and accordingly, besides tea and a large hamper of wine, with several hams and tongues, I caused a number of live chickens and sheep to be conveyed aboard; in truth, treble the quantity of provisions which would have supported the persons I took with me, had the voyage continued three weeks, as it was supposed, with a bare possibility, it might.

Indeed it continued much longer; but as this was occasioned by our being wind-bound in our own ports, it was by no means of any ill consequence to the captain, as the additional stores of fish, fresh meat, butter, bread, etc., which I constantly laid in, greatly exceeded the consumption, and went some way in maintaining the ship's crew. It is true I was not obliged to do this; but it seemed to be expected; for the captain did not think himself obliged to do it, and I can truly say I soon ceased to expect it of him. He had, I confess, on board a number of fowls and ducks sufficient for a West India voyage; all of them, as he often said: "Very fine birds, and of the largest breed." This I believe was really the fact, and I can add that they were all arrived at the full perfection of their size. Nor was there, I am convinced, any want of provisions of a more substantial kind; such as dried beef, pork, and fish; so that the captain seemed ready to perform his contract, and amply to provide for his passengers. What I did then was not from necessity, but, perhaps, from a less excusable motive, and was by no means chargeable to the account of the captain.

But, let the motive have been what it would, the consequence was still the same; and this was such that I am firmly persuaded the whole pitiful thirty pounds came pure and neat into the captain's pocket, and not only so, but attended with the value of ten pounds more in sundries into the bargain. I must confess myself therefore at a loss how the epithet *pitiful* came to be annexed to the above sum; for, not being a pitiful price for what it was given, I cannot conceive it to be pitiful in itself; nor do I believe it is thought by the greatest men in the kingdom; none of whom would scruple to search for it in the dirtiest kennel, where they had only a reasonable hope of success.

How, therefore, such a sum should acquire the idea of pitiful in the eyes of the master of a ship seems not easy to be accounted for; since it appears more likely to produce in him ideas of a different kind. Some men, perhaps, are no more sincere in the contempt for it which they express than others in their contempt of money in general; and I am the rather inclined to this persuasion, as I have seldom heard of either who have refused or refunded this their despised object. Besides, it is sometimes impossible to believe these professions, as every action of the man's life is a contradiction to it. Who can believe a tradesman who says he would not tell his name for the profit he gets by the selling such a parcel of goods, when he hath told a thousand lies in order to get it?

Pitiful, indeed, is often applied to an object not absolutely, but comparatively with our expectations, or with a greater object: in which sense it is not easy to set any bounds to the use of the word. Thus, a handful of halfpence daily appear pitiful to a porter, and a handful of silver to a drawer. The latter, I am convinced, at a polite tavern, will not tell his name (for he will not give you any answer) under the price of gold. And in this sense thirty pounds may be accounted pitiful by the lowest mechanic.

One difficulty only seems to occur, and that is this: how comes it that, if the profits of the meanest arts are so considerable, the professors of them are not richer than we generally see them? One answer to this shall suffice. Men do not become rich by what they get, but by what they keep. He who is worth no more than his annual wages or salary, spends the whole; he will be always a beggar let his income be what it will, and so will be his family when he dies. This we see daily to be the case of ecclesiastics, who, during their lives, are extremely well provided for, only because they desire to maintain the honour of the cloth by living like gentlemen, which would, perhaps, be better maintained by living unlike them.

But, to return from so long a digression, to which the use of so improper an epithet gave occasion, and to which the novelty of the subject allured, I will make the reader amends by concisely telling him that the captain poured forth such a torrent of abuse that I very hastily and very foolishly resolved to quit the ship. I gave immediate orders to summon a hoy to carry me that evening to Dartmouth, without considering any consequence. Those orders I gave in no very low voice, so that those above stairs might possibly conceive there was more than one master in the cabin. In the same tone I likewise threatened the captain with that which, he afterwards said, he feared more than any rock or quicksand. Nor can we wonder at this when we are told he had been twice obliged to bring to and cast anchor there before, and had neither time escaped without the loss of almost his whole cargo.

The most distant sound of law thus frightened a man who had often, I am convinced, heard numbers of cannon roar round him with intrepidity. Nor did he sooner see the hoy approaching the vessel than he ran down again into the cabin, and, his rage being perfectly subsided, he tumbled on his knees, and a little too abjectly implored for mercy.

I did not suffer a brave man and an old man to remain a moment in this posture, but I immediately forgave him.

And here, that I may not be thought the sly trumpeter of my own praises, I do utterly disclaim all praise on the occasion. Neither did the greatness of my mind dictate, nor the force of my Christianity exact, this forgiveness. To speak truth, I forgave him from a motive which would make men much more forgiving if they were much wiser than they are, because it was convenient for me so to do.

Wednesday [July 24]. This morning the captain drest himself in scarlet in order to pay a visit to a Devonshire squire, to whom a captain of a ship is a guest of no ordinary consequence, as he is a stranger and a gentleman, who hath seen a great deal of the world in foreign parts, and knows all the news of the times.

The squire, therefore, was to send his boat for the captain, but a most unfortunate accident happened; for, as the wind was extremely rough and against the hoy, while this was endeavouring to avail itself of great seamanship in hauling up against the wind, a sudden squall carried off sail and yard, or at least so disabled them that they were no longer of any use and unable to reach the ship; but the captain, from the deck, saw his hopes of venison disappointed, and was forced either to stay on board his ship, or to hoist forth his own long-boat, which he could not prevail with himself to think of, though the smell of the venison had had twenty times its attraction. He did, indeed, love his ship as his wife, and his boats as children, and never willingly trusted the latter, poor things! to the dangers of the seas.

To say truth, notwithstanding the strict rigour with which he preserved the dignity of his station, and the hasty impatience with which he resented any affront to his person or orders, disobedience to which he could in no instance brook in any person on board, he was one of the best-natured fellows alive. He acted the part of a father to his sailors; he expressed great tenderness for any of them when ill, and never suffered any the least work of supererogation to go unrewarded by a glass of gin. He even extended his humanity, if I may so call it, to animals, and even his cats and kittens had large shares in his affections. An instance of which we saw this evening, when the cat, which had shewn it could not be drowned, was found suffocated under a feather-bed in the cabin. I will not endeavour to describe his lamentations with more prolixity than barely by saying they were grievous, and seemed to have some mixture of the Irish howl in them. Nay, he carried his fondness even to inanimate objects, of which we have above set down a pregnant example in his demonstration of love and tenderness towards his boats and ship. He spoke of a ship which he had commanded formerly, and which was long since no more, which he had called the *Princess of Brazil*, as a widower of a deceased wife. This ship, after having followed the honest business of carrying goods and passengers for hire many years, did at last take to evil courses and turn privateer, in which service, to use his own words, she received many dreadful wounds, which he himself had felt as if they had been his own.

Thursday [July 25]. As the wind did not yesterday discover any purpose of shifting, and the water in my belly grew troublesome and rendered me short-breathed, I began a second time to have apprehensions of wanting the assistance of a trochar when none was to be found; I therefore concluded to be tapped again by way of precaution, and accordingly I this morning summoned on board a surgeon from a neighbouring parish, one whom the captain greatly recommended, and who did indeed perform his office with much dexterity. He was, I believe, likewise a man of great judgment and knowledge in the profession; but of this I cannot speak with perfect certainty, for, when he was going to open on the dropsy at large and on the particular degree of the distemper under which I laboured, I was obliged to stop him short, for the wind was changed, and the captain in the utmost hurry to depart; and to desire him, instead of his opinion, to assist me with his execution.

I was now once more delivered from my burthen, which was not indeed so great as I had apprehended, wanting two quarts of what was let out at the last operation.

While the surgeon was drawing away my water the sailors were drawing up the anchor; both were finished at the same time; we unfurled our sails and soon passed the Berry Head, which forms the mouth of the bay.

We had not, however, sailed far when the wind, which had, though with a slow pace, kept us company about six miles, suddenly turned about, and offered to conduct us back again; a favour which, though sorely against the grain, we were obliged to accept.

Nothing remarkable happened this day; for as to the firm persuasion of the captain that he was under the spell of witchcraft, I would not repeat it too often, though indeed he repeated it an hundred times every day; in truth, he talked of nothing else, and seemed not only to be satisfied in general of his being bewitched, but actually to have fixed with good certainty on the person of the witch, whom, had he lived in the days of Sir Matthew Hale, he would have infallibly indicted, and very possibly have hanged, for the detestable sin of witchcraft; but that law, and the whole doctrine that supported it, are now out of fashion; and witches, as a learned divine once chose to express himself, are put down by Act of Parliament. This witch, in the captain's opinion, was no other than Mrs. Francis of Ryde, who, as he insinuated, out of anger to me for not spending more money in her house than she could produce anything to exchange for, or any pretence to charge for, had laid this spell on his ship.

Though we were again got near our harbour by three in the afternoon, yet it seemed to require a full hour or more before we could come to our former place of anchoring, or berth, as the captain called it. On this occasion we exemplified one of the few advantages which the travellers by water have over the travellers by land. What would the latter often give for the sight of one of those hospitable mansions where he is assured *that there is good entertainment for man and horse*; and where both may consequently promise themselves to assuage that hunger which exercise is so sure to raise in a healthy constitution.

At their arrival at this mansion, how much happier is the state of the horse than that of the master! The former is immediately led to his repast, such as it is, and, whatever it is, he falls to it with appetite. But the latter is in a much worse situation. His hunger, however violent, is always in some degree delicate, and his food must have some kind of ornament, or, as the more usual phrase is, of dressing, to recommend it. Now all dressing requires time, and therefore, though perhaps the sheep might be just killed before you came to the inn, yet in cutting him up, fetching the joint, which the landlord by mistake said he had in the house, from the butcher at two miles' distance, and afterwards warming it a little by the fire, two hours at least must be consumed, while hunger, for want of better food, preys all the time on the vitals of the man.

How different was the case with us! we carried our provision, our kitchen, and our cook with us, and we were at one and the same time travelling on our road, and sitting down to a repast of fish, with which the greatest table in London can scarce at any rate be supplied.

Friday [July 26]. As we were disappointed of our wind, and obliged to return back the preceding evening, we resolved to extract all the good we could out of our misfortune, and to add considerably to our fresh stores of meat and bread, with which we were very indifferently provided when we hurried away yesterday. By the captain's advice we likewise laid in some stores of butter, which we salted and potted ourselves, for our use at Lisbon, and we had great reason afterwards to thank him for his advice.

In the afternoon I persuaded my wife, whom it was no easy matter for me to force from my side, to take a walk on shore, whither the gallant captain declared he was ready to attend her. Accordingly the ladies set out, and left me to enjoy a sweet and comfortable nap after the operation of the preceding day.

Thus we enjoyed our separate pleasures full three hours, when we met again, and my wife gave the foregoing account of the gentleman whom I have before compared to Axylus, and of his habitation, to both which she had been introduced by the captain, in the style of an old friend and acquaintance, though this foundation of intimacy seemed to her to be no deeper laid than in an accidental dinner, eaten many years before, at this temple of hospitality, when the captain lay wind-bound in the same bay.

Saturday [July 27]. Early this morning the wind seemed inclined to change in our favour. Our alert captain snatched its very first motion, and got under sail with so very gentle a breeze that, as the tide was against him, he recommended to a fishing hoy to bring after him a vast salmon and some other fishing provisions which lay ready for him on shore.

Our anchor was up at six, and before nine in the morning we had doubled the Berry Head, and were arrived off Dartmouth, having gone full three miles in as many hours, in direct opposition to the tide, which only befriended us out of our harbour; and though the wind was perhaps our friend, it was so very silent, and exerted itself so little in our favour, that, like some cool partisans, it was difficult to say whether it was with us or against us. The captain, however, declared the former to be the case during the whole three hours; but at last he perceived his error, or rather, perhaps, this friend, which had hitherto wavered in choosing his side, became now more determined. The captain then suddenly tacked about, and, asserting that he was bewitched, submitted to return to the place from whence he came. Now, though I am as free from superstition as any man breathing, and never did believe in witches, notwithstanding all the excellent arguments of my Lord Chief Justice Hale in their favour, and long before they were put down by Act of Parliament, yet by what power a ship of burthen should sail three miles against both wind and tide, I cannot conceive, unless there was some supernatural interposition in the case; nay, could we admit that the wind stood neuter, the difficulty would still remain. So that we must of necessity conclude that the ship was either bewinded or bewitched.

The captain, perhaps, had another meaning. He imagined himself, I believe, bewitched, because the wind, instead of persevering in its change in his favour, for change it certainly did that morning, should suddenly return to its favourite station, and blow him back towards the bay. But, if this was his opinion, he soon saw cause to alter; for he had not measured half the way back when the wind again declared in his favour, and so loudly, that there was no possibility of being mistaken.

The orders for the second tack were given, and obeyed

with much more alacrity than those had been for the first. We were all of us indeed in high spirits on the occasion; though some of us a little regretted the good things we were likely to leave behind us by the fisherman's neglect; I might give it a worse name, for he faithfully promised to execute the commission, which he had had abundant opportunity to do; but *nautica fides* deserves as much to be proverbial as ever *Punica fides* could formerly have done. Nay, when we consider that the Carthaginians came from the Phœnicians, who are supposed to have produced the first mariners, we may probably see the true reason of the adage, and it may open a field of very curious discoveries to the antiquarian.

We were, however, too eager to pursue our voyage to suffer anything we left behind us to interrupt our happiness, which, indeed, many agreeable circumstances conspired to advance. The weather was inexpressibly pleasant, and we were all seated on the deck, when our canvas began to swell with the wind. We had likewise in our view above thirty other sail around us, all in the same situation. Here an observation occurred to me, which, perhaps, though extremely obvious, did not offer itself to every individual in our little fleet: when I perceived with what different success we proceeded under the influence of a superior power, which, while we lay almost idle ourselves, pushed us forward on our intended voyage, and compared this with the slow progress which we had made in the morning, of ourselves, and without any such assistance, I could not help reflecting how often the greatest abilities lie wind-bound as it were in life; or, if they venture out and attempt to beat the seas, they struggle in vain against wind and tide, and, if they have not sufficient prudence to put back, are most probably cast away on the rocks and quicksands which are every day ready to devour them.

It was now our fortune to set out *melioribus avibus*. The wind freshened so briskly in our poop that the shore appeared to move from us as fast as we did from the shore. The captain declared he was sure of a wind, meaning its continuance; but he had disappointed us so often that he had lost all credit. However, he kept his word a little better now, and we lost sight of our native land as joyfully, at least, as it is usual to regain it.

Sunday [July 28]. The next morning the captain told me

he thought himself thirty miles to the westward of Plymouth, and before evening declared that the Lizard Point, which is the extremity of Cornwall, bore several leagues to leeward. Nothing remarkable passed this day, except the captain's devotion, who, in his own phrase, summoned all hands to prayers, which were read by a common sailor upon deck, with more devout force and address than they are commonly read by a country curate, and received with more decency and attention by the sailors than are usually preserved in city congregations. I am indeed assured, that if any such affected disregard of the solemn office in which they were engaged, as I have seen practised by fine gentlemen and ladies, expressing a kind of apprehension lest they should be suspected of being really in earnest in their devotion, had been shewn here, they would have contracted the contempt of the whole audience. To say the truth, from what I observed in the behaviour of the sailors in this voyage, and on comparing it with what I have formerly seen of them at sea and on shore, I am convinced that on land there is nothing more idle and dissolute; in their own element there are no persons near the level of their degree who live in the constant practice of half so many good qualities. They are, for much the greater part, perfect masters of their business, and always extremely alert, and ready in executing it, without any regard to fatigue or hazard. The soldiers themselves are not better disciplined nor more obedient to orders than these whilst aboard; they submit to every difficulty which attends their calling with cheerfulness, and no less virtues and patience and fortitude are exercised by them every day of their lives.

All these good qualities, however, they always leave behind them on shipboard; the sailor out of water is, indeed, as wretched an animal as the fish out of water; for though the former hath, in common with amphibious animals, the bare power of existing on the land, yet if he be kept there any time he never fails to become a nuisance.

The ship having had a good deal of motion since she was last under sail, our women returned to their sickness, and I to my solitude; having, for twenty-four hours together, scarce opened my lips to a single person. This circumstance of being shut up within the circumference of a few yards, with a score of human creatures, with not one of whom it was possible to converse, was perhaps so rare as scarce ever to have happened before, nor could it ever happen to one who disliked it more than myself, or to myself at a season when I wanted more food for my social disposition, or could converse less wholesomely and happily with my own thoughts. To this accident, which fortune opened to me in the Downs, was owing the first serious thought which I ever entertained of enrolling myself among the voyage-writers; some of the most amusing pages, if, indeed, there be any which deserve that name, were possibly the production of the most disagreeable hours which ever haunted the author.

Monday [July 29]. At noon the captain took an observation, by which it appeared that Ushant bore some leagues northward of us, and that we were just entering the Bay of Biscay. We had advanced a very few miles in this bay before we were entirely becalmed: we furled our sails, as being of no use to us while we lay in this most disagreeable situation, more detested by the sailors than the most violent tempest: we were alarmed with the loss of a fine piece of salt beef, which had been hung in the sea to freshen it; this being, it seems, the strange property of salt water. The thief was immediately suspected, and presently afterwards taken by the sailors. He was, indeed, no other than a huge shark, who, not knowing when he was well off, swallowed another piece of beef, together with a great iron crook on which it was hung, and by which he was dragged into the ship.

I should scarce have mentioned the catching this shark, though so exactly conformable to the rules and practice of voyage-writing, had it not been for a strange circumstance that attended it. This was the recovery of the stolen beef out of the shark's maw, where it lay unchewed and undigested, and whence, being conveyed into the pot, the flesh, and the thief that had stolen it, joined together in furnishing variety to the ship's crew.

During this calm we likewise found the mast of a large vessel, which the captain thought had lain at least three years in the sea. It was stuck all over with a little shellfish or reptile, called a barnacle, and which probably are the prey of the rock-fish, as our captain calls it, asserting that it is the finest fish in the world; for which we are obliged to confide entirely to his taste; for, though he struck the fish with a kind of harping-iron, and wounded him, I am convinced, to death, yet he could not possess himself of his body; but the poor wretch escaped to linger out a few hours with probably great torments.

In the evening our wind returned, and so briskly, that we ran upwards of twenty leagues before the next day's [*Tuesday's*] observation, which brought us to lat. 47° 42'. The captain promised us a very speedy passage through the bay; but he deceived us, or the wind deceived him, for it so slackened at sunset, that it scarce carried us a mile in an hour during the whole succeeding night.

Wednesday. A gale struck up a little after sun-rising, which carried us between three and four knots or miles an hour. We were this day at noon about the middle of the Bay of Biscay, when the wind once more deserted us, and we were so entirely becalmed, that we did not advance a mile in many hours. My fresh-water reader will perhaps conceive no unpleasant idea from this calm; but it affected us much more than a storm could have done; for, as the irascible passions of men are apt to swell with indignation long after the injury which first raised them is over, so fared it with the sea. It rose mountains high, and lifted our poor ship up and down, backwards and forwards, with so violent an emotion, that there was scarce a man in the ship better able to stand than myself. Every utensil in our cabin rolled up and down, as we should have rolled ourselves, had not our chairs been fast lashed to the floor. In this situation, with our tables likewise fastened by ropes, the captain and myself took our meal with some difficulty, and swallowed a little of our broth, for we spilt much the greater part. The remainder of our dinner being an old, lean, tame duck roasted, I regretted but little the loss of, my teeth not being good enough to have chewed it.

Our women, who began to creep out of their holes in the morning, retired again within the cabin to their beds, and were no more heard of this day, in which my whole comfort was to find by the captain's relation that the swelling was sometimes much worse; he did, indeed, take this occasion to be more communicative than ever, and informed me of such misadventures that had befallen him within forty-six years at sea as might frighten a very bold spirit from undertaking even the shortest voyage. Were these, indeed, but universally known, our matrons of quality would possibly be deterred from venturing their tender offspring at sea; by which means our navy would lose the honour of many a young commodore, who at twenty-two is better versed in maritime affairs than real seamen are made by experience at sixty.

And this may, perhaps, appear the more extraordinary, as the education of both seems to be pretty much the same; neither of them having had their courage tried by Virgil's description of a storm, in which, inspired as he was, I doubt whether our captain doth not exceed him.

In the evening the wind, which continued in the N.W., again freshened, and that so briskly that Cape Finisterre appeared by this day's observation to bear a few miles to the southward. We now indeed sailed, or rather flew, near ten knots an hour; and the captain, in the redundancy of his good-humour, declared he would go to church at Lisbon on Sunday next, for that he was sure of a wind; and, indeed, we all firmly believed him. But the event again contradicted him; for we were again visited by a calm in the evening.

But here, though our voyage was retarded, we were entertained with a scene, which as no one can behold without going to sea, so no one can form an idea of anything equal to it on shore. We were seated on the deck, women and all, in the serenest evening that can be imagined. Not a single cloud presented itself to our view, and the sun himself was the only object which engrossed our whole attention. He did indeed set with a majesty which is incapable of description, with which, while the horizon was yet blazing with glory, our eyes were called off to the opposite part to survey the moon, which was then at full, and which in rising presented us with the second object that this world hath offered to our vision. Compared to these the pageantry of theatres, or splendour of courts, are sights almost below the regard of children.

We did not return from the deck till late in the evening; the weather being inexpressibly pleasant, and so warm that even my old distemper perceived the alteration of the climate. There was indeed a swell, but nothing comparable to what we had felt before, and it affected us on the deck much less than in the cabin.

Friday [Aug. 2]. The calm continued till sun-rising, when

the wind likewise arose, but unluckily for us it came from a wrong quarter; it was S.S.E., which is that very wind which Juno would have solicited of Æolus, had Æneas been in our latitude bound for Lisbon.

The captain now put on his most melancholy aspect, and resumed his former opinion that he was bewitched. He declared with great solemnity that this was worse and worse, for that a wind directly in his teeth was worse than no wind at all. Had we pursued the course which the wind persuaded us to take we had gone directly for Newfoundland, if we had not fallen in with Ireland in our way. Two ways remained to avoid this; one was to put into a port of Galicia; the other, to beat to the westward with as little sail as possible: and this was our captain's election.

As for us, poor passengers, any port would have been welcome to us; especially as not only our fresh provisions, except a great number of old ducks and fowls, but even our bread was come to an end, and nothing but sea-biscuit remained, which I could not chew. So that now for the first time in my life I saw what it was to want a bit of bread.

The wind, however, was not so unkind as we had apprehended; but, having declined with the sun, it changed at the approach of the moon, and became again favourable to us, though so gentle that the next day's observation carried us very little to the southward of Cape Finisterre. This evening at six the wind, which had been very quiet all day, rose very high, and continuing in our favour drove us seven knots an hour.

This day we saw a sail, the only one, as I heard of, we had seen in our whole passage through the bay. I mention this on account of what appeared to me somewhat extraordinary. Though she was at such a distance that I could only perceive she was a ship, the sailors discovered that she was a snow, bound to a port in Galicia.

Sunday [Aug. 4]. After prayers, which our good captain read on the deck with an audible voice, and with but one mistake, of a lion for Elias, in the second lesson for this day, we found ourselves far advanced in 42°, and the captain declared we should sup off Porte. We had not much wind this day; but, as this was directly in our favour, we made it up with sail, of which we crowded all we had. We went only at the rate of four miles an hour, but with so uneasy a motion, continually rolling from side to side, that I suffered more than I had done in our whole voyage; my bowels being almost twisted out of my belly. However, the day was very serene and bright, and the captain, who was in high spirits, affirmed he had never passed a pleasanter at sea.

The wind continued so brisk that we ran upward of six knots an hour the whole night.

Monday. In the morning our captain concluded that he was got into lat. 40°, and was very little short of the Burlings, as they are called in the charts. We came up with them at five in the afternoon, being the first land we had distinctly seen since we left Devonshire. They consist of abundance of little rocky islands, a little distant from the shore, three of them only shewing themselves above the water.

Here the Portuguese maintain a kind of garrison, if we may allow it that name. It consists of malefactors, who are banished hither for a term, for divers small offences—a policy which they may have copied from the Egyptians, as we may read in Diodorus Siculus. That wise people, to prevent the corruption of good manners by evil communication, built a town on the Red Sea, whither they transported a great number of their criminals, having first set an indelible mark on them, to prevent their returning and mixing with the sober part of their citizens.

These rocks lie about fifteen leagues north-west of Cape Roxent, or, as it is commonly called, the Rock of Lisbon, which we passed early the next morning. The wind, indeed, would have carried us thither sooner; but the captain was not in a hurry, as he was to lose nothing by his delay.

Tuesday. This is a very high mountain, situated on the northern side of the mouth of the River Tajo, which, rising about Madrid, in Spain, and soon becoming navigable for small craft, empties itself, after a long course, into the sea, about four leagues below Lisbon.

On the summit of the rock stands a hermitage, which is now in the possession of an Englishman, who was formerly master of a vessel trading to Lisbon; and, having changed his religion and his manners, the latter of which, at least, were none of the best, betook himself to this place, in order to do penance for his sins. He is now very old, and hath inhabited this hermitage for a great number of years, during which he hath received some countenance from the royal family, and particularly from the present queen dowager, whose piety refuses no trouble or expense by which she may make a proselyte, being used to say that the saving one soul would repay all the endeavours of her life.

Here we waited for the tide, and had the pleasure of surveying the face of the country, the soil of which, at this season, exactly resembles an old brick-kiln, or a field where the greensward is pared up and set a-burning, or rather a-smoking, in little heaps to manure the land. This sight will, perhaps, of all others, make an Englishman proud of, and pleased with, his own country. which in verdure excels, I believe, every other country. Another deficiency here is the want of large trees, nothing above a shrub being here to be discovered in the circumference of many miles.

At this place we took a pilot on board, who, being the first Portuguese we spoke to, gave us an instance of that religious observance which is paid by all nations to their laws; for, whereas it is here a capital offence to assist any person in going on shore from a foreign vessel before it hath been examined, and every person in it viewed by the magistrates of health, as they are called, this worthy pilot, for a very small reward, rowed the Portuguese priest to shore at this place, beyond which he did not dare to advance, and in venturing whither he had given sufficient testimony of love for his native country.

We did not enter the Tajo till noon, when, after passing several old castles and other buildings which had greatly the aspect of ruins, we came to the castle of Bellisle, where we had a full prospect of Lisbon, and were, indeed, within three miles of it.

Here we were saluted with a gun, which was a signal to pass no farther till we had complied with certain ceremonies which the laws of this country require to be observed by all ships which arrive in this port. We were obliged then to cast anchor, and expect the arrival of the officers of the customs, without whose passport no ship must proceed father than this place.

Here, likewise, we received a visit from one of those magistrates of health before mentioned. He refused to come on board the ship till every person in her had been drawn up on deck and personally viewed by him. This occasioned some delay on my part, as it was not the work of a minute to lift me from the cabin to the deck. The captain thought my particular case might have been excused from this ceremony, and that it would be abundantly sufficient if the magistrate, who was obliged afterwards to visit the cabin, surveyed me there. But this did not satisfy the magistrate's strict regard to his duty. When he was told of my lameness, he called out, with a voice of authority: "Let him be brought up," and his orders were presently complied with. He was, indeed, a person of great dignity, as well as of the most exact fidelity in the discharge of his trust. Both which are the more admirable as his salary is less than thirty pounds English per annum.

Before a ship hath been visited by one of those magistrates no person can lawfully go on board her, nor can any on board depart from her. This I saw exemplified in a remarkable instance. The young lad whom I have mentioned as one of our passengers was here met by his father, who, on the first news of the captain's arrival, came from Lisbon to Bellisle in a boat, being eager to embrace a son whom he had not seen for many years. But when he came alongside our ship neither did the father dare ascend nor the son descend, as the magistrate of health had not yet been on board.

Some of our readers will, perhaps, admire the great caution of this policy, so nicely calculated for the preservation of this country from all pestilential distempers. Others will as probably regard it as too exact and formal to be constantly persisted in, in seasons of the utmost safety, as well as in times of danger. I will not decide either way, but will content myself with observing that I never yet saw or heard of a place where a traveller had so much trouble given him at his landing as here. The only use of which, as all such matters begin and end in form only, is to put it into the power of low and mean fellows to be either rudely officious or grossly corrupt, as they shall see occasion to prefer the gratification of their pride or of their avarice.

Of this kind, likewise, is that power which is lodged with other officers here, of taking away every grain of snuff and every leaf of tobacco brought hither from other countries, though only for the temporary use of the person during his residence here. This is executed with great insolence, and, as it is in the hands of the dregs of the people, very scandalously; for, under pretence of searching for tobacco and snuff, they are sure to steal whatever they can find, insomuch that when they came on board our sailors addressed us in the Covent Garden language: "Pray, gentlemen and ladies, take care of your swords and watches." Indeed, I never yet saw anything equal to the contempt and hatred which our honest tars every moment expressed for these Portuguese officers.

At Bellisle lies buried Catharine of Arragon, widow of Prince Arthur, eldest son of our Henry VII, afterwards married to, and divorced from, Henry VIII. Close by the church where her remains are deposited is a large convent of Geronymites, one of the most beautiful piles of building in all Portugal.

In the evening, at twelve, our ship, having received previous visits from all the necessary parties, took the advantage of the tide, and having sailed up to Lisbon cast anchor there, in a calm and moonshiny night, which made the passage incredibly pleasant to the women, who remained three hours enjoying it, whilst I was left to the cooler transports of enjoying their pleasures at second-hand; and yet, cooler as they may be, whoever is totally ignorant of such sensation is, at the same time, void of all ideas of friendship.

Wednesday [Aug. 7]. Lisbon, before which we now lay at anchor, is said to be built on the same number of hills with old Rome; but these do not all appear to the water; on the contrary, one sees from thence one vast high hill and rock, with buildings arising above one another, and that in so steep and almost perpendicular a manner, that they all seem to have but one foundation.

As the houses, convents, churches, etc., are large, and all built with white stone, they look very beautiful at a distance; but as you approach nearer, and find them to want every kind of ornament, all idea of beauty vanishes at once. While I was surveying the prospect of this city, which bears so little resemblance to any other that I have ever seen, a reflection occurred to me that, if a man was suddenly to be removed from Palmyra hither, and should take a view of no other city, in how glorious a light would the ancient architecture appear to him! and what desolation and destruction of arts and sciences would he conclude had happened between the several eras of these cities!

I had now waited full three hours upon deck for the return of my man, whom I had sent to bespeak a good dinner (a thing which had been long unknown to me) on shore, and then to bring a Lisbon chaise with him to the seashore; but it seems the impertinence of the providore was not yet brought to a conclusion. At three o'clock, when I was, from emptiness, rather faint than hungry, my man returned, and told me there was a new law lately made that no passenger should set his foot on shore without a special order from the providore, and that he himself would have been sent to prison for disobeying it, had he not been protected as the servant of the captain. He informed me, likewise, that the captain had been very industrious to get this order, but that it was then the providore's hour of sleep, a time when no man, except the king himself, durst disturb him.

To avoid prolixity, though in a part of my narrative which may be more agreeable to my reader than it was to me, the providore, having at last finished his nap, dispatched this absurd matter of form, and gave me leave to come, or rather to be carried, on shore.

What it was that gave the first hint of this strange law is not easy to guess. Possibly, in the infancy of their defection, and before their government could be well established, they were willing to guard against the bare possibility of surprise, of the success of which bare possibility the Trojan horse will remain for ever on record, as a great and memorable example. Now the Portuguese have no walls to secure them, and a vessel of two or three hundred tons will contain a much larger body of troops than could be concealed in that famous machine, though Virgil tells us (somewhat hyperbolically, I believe) that it was as big as a mountain.

About seven in the evening I got into a chaise on shore, and was driven through the nastiest city in the world, though at the same time one of the most populous, to a kind of coffee-house, which is very pleasantly situated on the brow of a hill, about a mile from the city, and hath a very fine prospect of the River Tajo from Lisbon to the sea.

Here we regaled ourselves with a good supper, for which

we were as well charged as if the bill had been made on the Bath Road, between Newbury and London.

And now we could joyfully say:

Egressi optata Troes potiuntur arena.

Therefore, in the words of Horace:

——*hic Finis chartæque viæque.*

EXPLANATORY NOTES

For help in preparing the notes to *Jonathan Wild* I am grateful to Martin Durrell, Donald Fraser, H. R. A. Higgens, C. J. Rawson, W. H. Semple, and A. W. Shipps. In compiling the notes to *The Journal of a Voyage to Lisbon* I have profited from Austin Dobson's edition for the World's Classics (1907) and that by H. E. Pagliaro (New York, 1963), identified in the notes as Pagliaro.

OED identifies the *Oxford English Dictionary*, by permission of the Clarendon Press, Oxford.

JONATHAN WILD

p. 3. *l.* 18. *Plutarch, Nepos, Suetonius:* Plutarch (*c.* A.D. 46–after 119), author of the *Parallel Lives*; Cornelius Nepos (*c.* 99–*c.* 31 B.C.), author of *De Viris Illustribus* (*Concerning Famous Men*); and Suetonius (born A.D. 69?), author of *The Twelve Caesars*.

l. 25. *Aristides . . . Nero:* Aristides is cited by Plato in the *Gorgias* as an example of the virtue of justice, rare among statesmen; Marcus Junius Brutus was, particularly to the Augustans, another type of virtue (on both see, e.g., James Thomson, *Winter*, ll. 459 ff. and 524 ff.). The Spartan commander Lysander, known in part for his pride and fondness for praise, and Nero, are their antitypes. Brutus, incidentally, is named with Socrates as being an example of 'the great and good' in the Preface to Fielding's *Miscellanies*, vol. i (1743); see above, p. xx.

p. 4. *l.* 33. *the histories of Alexander and Caesar:* i.e., Plutarch's parallel lives of the two men. In *An Essay on Nothing* Fielding had asked rhetorically: 'What did *Alexander*, *Cæsar*, and all the rest of that heroic Band, who have plundered, and massacred so many Millions, obtain by all their Care, Labour, Pain, Fatigue, and Danger?— . . . Nothing' (*Miscellanies*, vol. i, ed. H. K. Miller, Oxford, 1972, p. 188).

p. 5. *l.* 26. *The Great:* the phrase would have been recognized at the time as an allusion to Sir Robert Walpole, prime minister from 1721 to 1742. See J. E. Wells, 'Fielding's Political Purpose in *Jonathan Wild*', *PMLA*, xxviii (1913), 14, and W. R. Irwin, *The Making of 'Jonathan Wild'* (New York, 1941), p. 44 ff. For important comments on 'greatness', see also Fielding's Preface to the *Miscellanies*, vol. i (in connection with *Jonathan Wild*), and the poem 'Of True Greatness' (*Miscellanies*, vol. i, ed. Miller, p. 19 ff.). In his 'Modern Glossary' in *The Covent-Garden Journal* for 14 January 1752 Fielding defined 'Great' as follows: 'Applied to a Thing, signifies Bigness; when to a Man, often Littleness, or

Meanness' (ed. G. E. Jensen, 2 vols., New Haven and London, 1915, i. 156).

p. 6. l. 6. Prince Prettyman: see George Villiers, Duke of Buckingham, and others, *The Rehearsal* (3rd edition, 1675), iii. 4, specifically the lines 'What Oracle this darkness can evince? / Sometimes a Fishers Son, sometimes a Prince', in which Prettyman burlesques Leonidas in Dryden's *Marriage à la Mode* (1672). (*The Rehearsal*, ed. Montague Summers, Stratford upon Avon, 1914, pp. 38, 113.)

p. 7. l. 23. This Edward: Sir Robert Walpole's grandfather was also called Edward: see Wells, 'Fielding's Political Purpose', pp. 19–20, for Fielding's possible parody in Wild's pedigree of Walpole in William Musgrave's *Brief and True History of Sir Robert Walpole and his Family* (1736). William J. Farrell, 'The Mock-heroic Form of *Jonathan Wild*', MP, lxiii (1965–66), 216–26, suggests a more general indebtedness to the *topoi* of traditional biography in this part of Book i, and in Book i as a whole notes affinities with Plutarch's *Life of Alexander*.

l. 33. Snap: 'a thief claiming a share in booty' (Eric Partridge, *A Dictionary of Slang and Unconventional English*, 5th edition, 1961, s.v.).

l. 37. abroad . . . American colonies: i.e., was transported; cf. i.7 (pp. 21–2).

p. 8. l. 1. Westminster Hall: the chief English law court.

l. 4. oranges: i.e., sexual favours (Partridge, *Dictionary of Slang*, s.v. orange). Compare Parson Oliver's letter to Parson Tickletext in *Shamela*: 'Her Mother sold Oranges in the Play-House'.

l. 7. Hockley-in-the-Hole: near Clerkenwell Green, famous for its Bear-Garden.

l. 17. Venienti occurrite morbo: 'remedy the disease at its first approach': Persius, *Satires*, iii. 64.

l. 18. Astyages . . . Asia: see Herodotus, *History*, i. 108.

l. 20. Hecuba . . . flames: see, e.g. Cicero, *De Divinatione*, i. 21.

l. 24. Mercury and Priapus: Mercury was, among other things, the planetary god of thieves (Ptolemy, *Tetrabiblos*, ii. 8). Priapus was a fertility god, usually represented (in his role of scarecrow) naked and with a very large phallus. See, e.g., Ovid, *Fasti*, i. 415 ff. For the joking pedantry about the quantity of the name, cf. *Joseph Andrews*, ii. 4, where Attalus is accorded similar treatment.

p. 9. l. 18. house . . . Covent Garden: Covent Garden was well-known for its brothels; a round-house was a prison. On the association of Wild with the plague, see Pat Rogers, *Grub Street: Studies in a Subculture* (1972), pp. 137–8.

l. 21. Mr. Titus Oates: born 1649, died 1705. Involved in the 'popish plot' of 1678. Tried for, and found guilty of, perjury in 1685.

p. 10. l. 20. Gradus ad Parnassum: a treasury of Latin synonyms, epithets, quotations, etc.

p. 11. l. 8. Alexander . . . King of Sweden: Alexander and Charles XII of Sweden (d. 1718) were commonly compared at the time as destructive tyrants: see Irwin, *The Making of 'Jonathan Wild'*, p. 48 ff. For Fielding's views on Alexander see *A Dialogue between Alexander the Great and Diogenes the Cynic* in *Miscellanies*, vol. i, ed. Miller, p. 226 ff.

l. 19. *Spanish Rogue . . . Cheats of Scapin:* Mateo Alemán's picaresque *Guzmán de Alfarache*, which had been translated into English by James Mabbe in 1622. C. J. Rawson, *Henry Fielding and the Augustan Ideal under Stress* (1972), p. 138n., suggests that Fielding refers either to the anonymous early eighteenth-century translation *The Spanish Rogue, Or, The Life of Guzman de Alfarache* (printed for Thomas Smith, n.d.), or the 1707 translation, *The Life of Guzman d'Alfarache, or the Spanish Rogue.* Thomas Otway's popular farce *The Cheats of Scapin* (1676) was an adaptation of Molière's *Les Fourberies de Scapin.*

p. 12. *l.* 42. *whisk and swabbers:* 'whisk' is the early name for whist; 'swabbers' are 'certain cards at the game of whist . . . , which entitled the holder to part of the stakes. *Whisk and swabbers:* a form of the game in which these cards were so used' (*OED*).

p. 13. *l.* 14. *freemasons:* for similar comments see *Tom Jones*, ii. 4 and v. 6.

l. 19. *play the whole game:* i.e., cheat (Partridge. op. cit., s.v.).

p. 15. *l.* 38. *Tower Hill . . . Tyburn:* state prisoners were executed at the former, common criminals at the latter.

p. 16. *l.* 10. *better to reign in Hell: Paradise Lost*, i. 263.

l. 37. *cog a die:* 'practise certain tricks in throwing dice' (*OED*).

p. 17. *fn.* 3. *Cant Dictionary:* there is no work with this exact title, but Hollis Rinehart, '*Jonathan Wild* and the Cant Dictionary', *PQ*, xlviii (1969), 220–25, suggests that Fielding used *A New Canting Dictionary* (London, 1725) since it contains these and other cant terms used in *Jonathan Wild.*

p. 18. *l.* 39. *night-cellar:* 'a cellar serving as a tavern or place of resort during the night for persons of the lowest class' (*OED*).

p. 20. *l.* 23. *plain Spanish:* ready money (Partridge. op. cit., s.v. Spanish).

p. 21. *l.* 14. *sneaking-budge:* defined as 'one that robs alone, and deals chiefly in petty Larcenies' in *A New Canting Dictionary* (Rinehart, art. cit., p. 221).

l. 33. *abroad for seven years:* the transportation period for petty criminals who were sent to America as plantation slaves (Irwin, p. 118, n. 160). In this chapter as a whole Fielding offers satire, common at the time, on the grand tour: see Pope's *Dunciad*, iv. 293 ff. and notes (Twickenham edition, vol. v, 1965, pp. 373–76), and Smollett, *Peregrine Pickle*, ed. J. L. Clifford, Oxford English Novels (1964), chap. xliii.

p. 23. *l.* 1. *hazard:* 'a game at dice in which the chances are complicated by a number of arbitrary rules' (*OED*).

l. 4. *Bob Bagshot:* there is a 'Robin of Bagshot' in John Gay's *The Beggar's Opera* (1728): both glance satirically at Sir Robert Walpole.

p. 24. *l.* 10. *the labourer worthy of his hire:* Luke 10: 7.

l. 23. *Aristotle . . . politics: Politics*, i. 1–2.

p. 25. *l.* 31. *hanger:* 'a kind of short sword, originally hung from the belt' (*OED*).

p. 26. *l.* 23. *toy-shop:* 'a shop for the sale of trinkets, knick-knacks, or small ornamental articles' (*OED*).

l. 28. *clout:* handkerchief.

p. 27. *l.* 3. *artificially:* with great art, skilfully.

l. 13. *Qui color . . . albo:* 'which once was white, and is now the opposite of white' (Ovid, *Metamorphoses*, ii. 541). Significantly, the line immediately precedes the story of the unchaste Coronis of Larissa.

p. 28. *l.* 31. *pinchbeck plate:* an alloy of copper and zinc, resembling gold (after the Fleet Street watch- and toy-maker Christopher Pinchbeck, who died in 1732). See *OED.*

l. 33. *plush:* 'a kind of cloth . . . having a nap longer and softer than that of velvet' (*OED*). Often used for the liveries of footmen.

l. 34. *dimity:* 'a stout cotton fabric, woven with raised stripes or fancy figures' (*OED*).

p. 30. *l.* 8. *Virgil:* the allusion is, of course, to the *Aeneid.*

p. 32. *l.* 33. *speaking with:* having to do with. A phrase from the *New Canting Dictionary*, where it is defined as meaning 'steal' (Partridge, s.v.).

p. 34. *l.* 20. *blown up:* betrayed, informed upon (*OED*, Blow, III. 27).

l. 27. *seedy:* defined in the *New Canting Dictionary* as 'poor, Moneyless, exhausted' (Rinehart, ' *Jonathan Wild* and the Cant Dictionary', p. 222).

p. 36. *l.* 30. *the Conv——n:* because of various disputes, the two convocations, of Canterbury and York, had been prorogued by the ministry in 1717 and 1741: Basil Williams, *The Whig Supremacy 1714–1760*, 2nd edition, rev. C. H. Stuart (Oxford, 1965), p. 82.

fn. l. 3. *the ordinary:* 'the Chaplain of Newgate prison, whose duty it was to prepare condemned prisoners for death' (*OED*).

p. 37. *l.* 20. *honour:* an important word in connection with Fielding's Augustan humanist preoccupation with linguistic corruption. See Glenn W. Hatfield, *Henry Fielding and the Language of Irony* (Chicago, 1968), passim, but esp. pp. 10–11, 19–20, and 103 ff. 'His Honour' was a phrase commonly applied to Walpole: see p. 172*n.* below, and C. B. Woods, 'Fielding and the Authorship of *Shamela*', *PQ*, xxv (1946), 255–56.

p. 39. *l.* 15. *rapping:* the *New Canting Dictionary* defines 'rapper' as 'a swinging great Lye' (Rinehart, art. cit., p. 222).

p. 40. *l.* 7. *whippers-in:* huntsman's assistants who manage the hounds: cf. *Joseph Andrews*, i. 2.

p. 41. *l.* 18. *Sic, sic juvat:* 'sic, sic iuvat ire sub umbras' ('Thus, thus it is pleasing to pass beneath the shades'): the words of the dying Dido, *Aeneid*, iv. 660.

l. 24. *whole nations . . . tears:* the reference is to Alexander, who wept because he had not conquered one of the infinite number of worlds (Plutarch, 'On Tranquillity of Mind', 466 D-E). Cf. iv. 4 (p. 136): 'I ought rather to weep with Alexander . . .'

p. 46. *l.* 23. *good-natured:* on Fielding and 'good-nature' as the sum of all virtues, see his poem 'Of Good-Nature' in *Miscellanies*, vol. i.

p. 53. *l.* 28. *Miss Molly Straddle:* J. E. Wells, 'Fielding's Political

Purpose in *Jonathan Wild'*, p. 29, notes that this encounter suggests Walpole's relationship with Maria Skerritt (or 'Molly Skerret'). The affair had begun before 1728, and Walpole married her after the death of his first wife in 1738.

l. 40. Rummer and Horseshoe: 'rummer' is a large drinking-glass (*OED*), but there is also a hint of 'thief' as in such contemporary canting compounds as 'rum diver', 'rum file', etc. (Partridge, s.v.); 'horseshoe' means 'the female pudend' (*ibid*, s.v.).

p. 54. l. 14. Penelope: Odyssey, xix.

p. 56. l. 22. the fair of Bartholomew: instituted in the middle ages and continuing until the mid-nineteenth century, the fair was held in Smithfield originally on 24 August (St Bartholomew's Day). In the mid-eighteenth century its duration was often limited to four days and many theatrical entertainments were offered there: see Sybil Rosenfield, *The Theatres of the London Fairs in the Eighteenth Century* (Cambridge, 1960).

l. 25. Derdæus Magnus: William Deard (d. 1761), well-known jeweller and toymaker. Referred to in *Joseph Andrews,* iii. 6, and *Covent-Garden Journal,* 4 January 1752 (ed. Jensen, i. 136).

p. 57. l. 29. sneaker: 'a small bowl (*of* punch)' (*OED*).

p. 63. l. 34. the Gate House: 'the apartment over the gate of a city or palace, often strongly built, and hence used as a prison; *spec.* that over the gate of the palace of Westminster' (*OED*).

l. 43. Mr. Ketch: from the early eighteenth century, the name was applied to any hangman (after Jack Ketch, public hangman from *c.* 1663 until 1686).

p. 64. l. 8. politics: cf. *An Essay on the Knowledge of the Characters of Men:* '. . . as it is impossible that any Man endowed with rational Faculties, and being in a State of Freedom, should willingly agree, without some Motive of Love or Friendship, absolutely to sacrifice his own Interest to that of another; it becomes necessary to impose upon him, to persuade him, that his own Good is designed, and that he will be a Gainer by coming into those Schemes, which are, in Reality, calculated for his Destruction. And this, if I mistake not, is the very Essence of that excellent Art, called *The Art of Politics*' (*Miscellanies,* vol. i, ed. Miller, p. 155).

l. 20. nab or trencher hat: the former is 'a very broad-brim'd Hat' (B.E., *A New Dictionary of the Terms . . . of the Canting Crew* (1699)), the latter is a hat with a flat top, of the academic type.

l. 24. shakebag: 'rogue, scoundrel' (*OED*).

oldnoll: seventeenth-century nickname for Oliver Cromwell. '*Nol(l),* abbr. *Oliver,* puns *noll,* the head, and *noll,* a simpleton' (Partridge, s.v. 'Old Nol(l)').

fn. l. 2. Aristotle: Wells, 'Fielding's Political Purpose', pp. 43–49, discusses the political significance of the hats passage, citing on p. 46 the 'Index to the Times' for *The Champion,* 24 April 1740, where, in an anti-Walpole context and after a reference to the adjournment of a parliamentary sitting, we find this paragraph: '*About the same Instant, a very learned Comment was exhibited at a public House in the Neighbourhood, on* Aristotle's *Chapter of Hats*'.

p. 65. fn. l. 3. Sophocles . . . Ajax: Sophocles, *Ajax,* 1285 ff., on the casting of lots, where the allusion is to Cresphontes who, after the conquest of the Peloponnesus, with Temenus and Aristodemus's two sons, agreed to cast lots for the cities. The first was for Argos, the second for Lacedaemon, the third for Messene. Cresphontes wanted Messene, and so put a lump of earth in the pitcher of water as his lot. It dissolved, so that only the other two lots (stones) came out (Apollodorus, *Library*, ii. 8. 4).

l. 6. *Achilles . . . dog's eyes*: *Iliad*, i. 159.

l. 15. *old hat*: 'the female pudend' (Partridge, s.v.).

p. 68. *l.* 21. *Peter Pounce*: the name of a character in *Joseph Andrews* who is modelled on the miserly and wealthy scrivener Peter Walter (1664?–1746) of Stalbridge Park, Dorset.

p. 69. *l.* 14. *prime minister*: the phrase could only have evoked Walpole: see *OED*.

p. 71. *l.* 8. *Drawcansir*: a reference to Buckingham's *Rehearsal* (see p. 6n.), iv. 1: 'I drink, I huff, I strut, look big and stare; / And all this I can do, because I dare'. As editor of *The Covent-Garden Journal* (1752) Fielding took the pseudonym Sir Alexander Drawcansir.

p. 75. *l.* 40. "*Kiss* ——": cf. *Shamela*, letter vi: '. . . I have a great Mind to kick your A——. You, kiss —— says I.'

p. 79. *l.* 13. *Nec Deus . . . nodus*: 'Let not a god intervene, unless the knot is worthy of such a deliverer' (Horace, *Ars Poetica*, l. 191). Also invoked in *Tom Jones*, viii. 1 and ix. 5.

l. 27. *Naturam . . . recurret*: 'You may drive out nature with a pitchfork, yet she will always hasten back' (Horace, *Epistles*, i. 10. 24; the original reads: 'Naturam expellas furca, tamen usque recurret').

p. 80. *l.* 22. *ab effectu*: from the performance.

p. 85. *l.* 8. *Herodotus*: *History*, iii. 14 (the story in fact concerns Psammenitus, and Crœsus weeps when he hears it). Fielding again thinks of Crœsus in connection with surprise in *Joseph Andrews*, i. 8.

p. 86. *l.* 27. *the following soliloquy*: a formal consolation, introducing the commonplaces of the tradition. Cf. *Joseph Andrews*, iii. 11; *Tom Jones*, v. 7; *Amelia*, vii. 2; and 'Of the Remedy of Affliction for the Loss of our Friends' in *Miscellanies*, vol. i.

p. 87. *l.* 34. *jointed baby*: doll or puppet.

p. 88. *l.* 34. *the excellent poet*: Edward Young, *The Complaint, or Night Thoughts on Life, Death, and Immortality* (1742–5), Night i. 376–8. Fielding quotes from memory; the original reads: 'Where is to-morrow? In another world. / For numbers this is certain; the reverse / Is sure to none.'

p. 89. *l.* 42. *Socrates . . . death*: see the opening of Plato's *Crito*.

p. 91. *l.* 25. *God's revenge against murder*: see p. 110n.

p. 92. *l.* 35. *Achates . . . Hephæstion*: Achates was Aeneas's armour-bearer and friend; Hephæstion was a close friend of Alexander and one of his generals.

p. 95. *l.* 7. *what was said . . . labour*: 'labor omnia vincit' (Virgil, *Georgics*, i. 145).

p. 97. *l.* 37. *Socrates . . . open*: see Plato's *Crito*, passim.

p. 98. *subtitle. Smithfield*: a 'Smithfield match' (cf. *Joseph*

Andrews, ii. 6) is a marriage for money, so named after the cattle market.

p. 99. *l.* 34. *the great Bubble-boy:* a 'bubble' is a trifle, and *OED* (s.v. Bubble-bow, -boy) defines 'Bubble-boy' as a 'lady's tweezer-case'. The reference is, presumably, to the toymaker William Deard, the 'Derdæus Magnus' of p. 56.

p. 100. *l.* 13. *academy of compliments: The Academy of Compliments: or, a new way of wooing. Wherein is a variety of love-letters* had appeared in 1685 and been reprinted in the mid-eighteenth century.

p. 101. *l.* 9. *Sallust:* Gaius Sallustius Crispus (86–34 B.C.).

l. 13. *Hurgo:* Fielding refers to the parliamentary reports in Edward Cave's *Gentleman's Magazine*. On 13 April 1738 the House of Commons resolved that accounts of debates should not be published. Cave's strategy was to offer his accounts (from June onwards) as 'Debates in the Senate of Lilliput'. These accounts were compiled by Cave's assistant William Guthrie, and later (from 1741) by Samuel Johnson. Although the gist of what they wrote was correct, the substance was the product of their own imaginations. The reports were signed 'Hurgo'. See James L. Clifford, *Young Samuel Johnson* (1955), pp. 188 ff. and 246 ff.

p. 102. *l.* 31. *caudle-cup:* caudle is 'a warm drink consisting of thin gruel, mixed with wine or ale, sweetened and spiced' (*OED*).

p. 107. *l.* 11. *why b——ch?:* cf. *Joseph Andrews*, i. 17. Francis Grose, *A Classical Dictionary of the Vulgar Tongue* (1785), s.v. Bitch, notes that this is 'the most offensive appellation that can be given to an English woman . . .'

p. 108. *l.* 14. *my Lady Betty Modish:* a character in Colley Cibber's *The Careless Husband* (1704). In Act iii she says of Lord Morelove: 'I want to cure him of that laugh now' (*Works*, 5 vols., 1777 edition, ii. 51).

l. 27. *Hymen . . . lighted torch:* a torch is the traditional emblem of Hymen, god of marriage (e.g., Ovid, *Fasti*, ii. 558).

l. 31. *liberties of the Fleet:* the Fleet was a debtors' prison; 'liberties' were minor privileges granted to prisoners therein.

p. 110. *l.* 22. *God's Revenge against Murder:* John Reynolds, *The Triumphes of Gods Revenge, against the crying, and execrable Sinne of Murther . . .* (London, 1621). Fielding possessed a copy of the 1635 edition, which is listed as item 450 in the sale catalogue of his library (reprinted in the appendix to Ethel M. Thornbury, *Henry Fielding's Theory of the Comic Prose Epic*, University of Wisconsin Studies in Language and Literature, xxx (Madison, Wis., 1931)).

p. 111. *l.* 21. *what a ravishing thought*, etc: Allan Wendt, 'The Moral Allegory of *Jonathan Wild*', *ELH*, xxiv (1957), 309, compares Fielding's *Champion*, 22 January 1739/40: 'What a glorious, what a rapturous consideration must it be to the heart of man to think the goodness of the great God of nature concerned in his happiness.'

p. 112. *l.* 8. *writ de homine replegiando:* the same as a writ of replevin, where replevin is 'the restoration to, or recovery by, a person of goods or chattels distrained or taken from him, upon his giving security to have the matter tried in a court of justice and to return the goods if the case is decided against him' (*OED*, s.v. Replevin).

l. 9. *capias in withernam:* 'In an action of replevin, the reprisal of other goods in lieu of those taken by a first distress and eloigned; also, the writ (called *capias in withernam*) commanding the sheriff to take the reprisal' (*OED*, s.v. Withernam).

p. 113. *l.* 31. *quomodo:* how (cf. *Tom Jones*, vii. 15).

p. 114. *l.* 6. *a puppet-show:* Wells, 'Fielding's Political Purpose', p. 34 ff., discusses Fielding's use of the metaphor, citing *Tom Jones*, xii. 6, and *The Champion*, 3 and 8 May 1740. Walpole was frequently satirized as player, puppet-master, etc.: see M. G. Largmann, 'Stage References as Satiric Weapon: Sir Robert Walpole as Victim', *Restoration and 18th Century Theatre Research*, ix (1970), 35–43.

p. 115. *l.* 7. *Nemo ... sapit:* 'No mortal is wise all the time' (Pliny, *Natural History*, vii. 40. 131): a favourite tag, used also in *Joseph Andrews*, iii. 5 and *Tom Jones*, xii. 13.

l. 8. *Ira furor brevis est:* 'anger is brief madness' (Horace, *Epistles*, i. 2. 62).

p. 116. *l.* 1. *dashed his head ... blow:* a familiar joke: cf. *Joseph Andrews*, ii. 9 and Butler's *Hudibras*, i. 2. 863: 'And dash'd his brains (if any) out.'

l. 19. *mittimus:* 'A warrant by which a justice commits an offender to prison' (Johnson's *Dictionary*).

p. 117. *l.* 1. *press-yard:* the yard in Newgate from which prisoners proceeded to execution. *OED* cites *The History of the Press-Yard* (1717): 'The Press-Yard being no part of the Prison, but taken in as a part of the Governor's House ... it is in the Keeper's Breast to refuse any Prisoner a Reception there without a Conditional Premium.'

p. 119. *l.* 20. *a place:* i.e., Bridewell, the house of correction for whores, etc.

p. 120. *l.* 1. *Blueskin:* an alias for Joseph Blake, at one time a member of the historical Jonathan Wild's gang. He left after disagreements with Wild over the sharing of booty, and was captured by him (in his role of thief-taker) on 2 October 1724. See Irwin, *The Making of 'Jonathan Wild'*, pp. 7–8.

p. 121. *l.* 5. *the chief magistrate ... public good:* an idea developed in iv. 6 (p. 140) and 11 (pp. 159–60). For a later example of Fielding's concern for the character of the magistrate, see *Covent-Garden Journal*, 7 January 1752, where Plato's *Republic* is quoted to the effect that 'a true Magistrate, is not so constituted that he may consult his own Good, but that he may provide for the Good of the Subject' (ed. Jensen, i. 144).

l. 24. *this bit of ribbon:* on the level of political allegory, which is to the fore here, an allusion to the Order of the Bath (Wells, 'Fielding's Political Purpose', pp. 31–2).

l. 30. *bubbled:* duped.

p. 124. *l.* 13. *a sincere Turk would be saved:* Parson Adams's identical belief (*Joseph Andrews*, i. 17) provokes a similarly hostile reaction. Fielding echoes a statement of Bishop Hoadly's in his sermon 'The Good Samaritan' that 'an honest *Heathen* is much more acceptable to [God], than a dishonest and deceitful *Christian*' (cit. M. C. Battestin, *Joseph Andrews*, Wesleyan edition, 1967, p. 83n.).

p. 126. *l.* 10. *Hicks's Hall:* 'a Sessions-House for the Justices of *Middlesex*' (John Stow, *A Survey of the Cities of London and Westminster*, augmented by John Strype, 2 vols., 1720, i. 288) founded by, and named after, Baptist Hicks, first Viscount Campden (1551–1629).

l. 30. *ut lapsu graviore ruant:* 'that they might tumble down with a severer fall' (Claudian, *In Rufinum*, i. 23). The context—in which Claudian begins by questioning then affirming Providential order —is relevant. Fielding quotes lines 14–19 in *Amelia*, i. 3.

p. 127. *l.* 1. *Blueskin . . . a knife:* after he had been captured by Wild in October 1724 (see p. 120n.) and sentenced, Wild visited Blueskin in Newgate and had his throat cut by him with a knife (Irwin, op. cit., p. 8).

l. 35. *a clause in an Act of Parliament:* the law of 1718 'which ma[de] it a Felony . . . to Receive and Return Stolen Goods, Knowing them to be so and not apprehending and prosecuting the Felon . . .' (Defoe's account in *Applebee's Journal*, 22 May 1725; cit. Irwin, p. 112, n. 33).

p. 128. *l.* 32. *garnish:* 'money extorted from a new prisoner, either as a jailer's fee, or as drink-money for the other prisoners' (*OED*).

p. 129. *l.* 23. *nubbed:* A *New Canting Dictionary* (1725) gives '*To be nubb'd*, to be hang'd' (Rinehart, '*Jonathan Wild* and the Cant Dictionary', p. 222).

l. 28. *cheat:* 'NUBBING-*Cheat*, the Gallows' (*Canting Dictionary*; cit. Rinehart, ibid.).

l. 40. *filing-lay:* '*The* FILE, . . . Pick-pockets'; 'LAY, an Enterprize, or Attempt' (*Canting Dictionary*; cit. ibid.).

p. 130. *l.* 28. *seedy:* see p. 34n. above.

p. 131. *l.* 2. *Roger Johnson:* the smuggler who oversaw the historical Wild's international dealings. Irwin (op. cit., p. 33) remarks that 'it is most unlikely that they were ever in Newgate together'.

p. 132. *l.* 42. *the liberties . . . plunder:* cf. p. 108n. above. Fielding's satirical point (whereby the language of politicians is seen as criminal cant) is discussed by Glenn W. Hatfield, *Henry Fielding and the Language of Irony* (1968), pp. 94–5.

p. 133. *l.* 18. *a very grave man:* identified by Irwin (p. 119, n. 191) as the staunch Tory and Jacobite William Shippen (1673–1743), who frequently opposed Walpole in parliament. But the 'grave man' appeasing tumult is familiar in Fielding: cf. *Tom Jones*, xii. 6, where the allusion is to *Aeneid*, i. 151. Bernard Shea, 'Machiavelli and Fielding's *Jonathan Wild*', *PMLA*, lxxii (1957), 59, compares *The Champion*, 15 January 1739/40 (as does Wells, 'Fielding's Political Purpose', pp. 25–6) and notes that Fielding draws here for his idea of 'the Authority of a Grave Man' on Machiavelli's *Discourse on the First Ten Books of Titus Livius*, i. 54. Cf. in addition *Covent-Garden Journal*, 28 January 1752 (ed. Jensen, i. 186).

p. 140. *l.* 8. *reprieve . . . Beggar's Opera:* the end of Act iii, where the Beggar yields to the Player's request that the opera should 'end happily'.

p. 156. *l.* 3. *the hedge of his teeth:* glancing at the Homeric phrase 'hedge (or barrier) of the teeth' (e.g., *Iliad*, ix. 409, *Odyssey*, x. 328).

l. 6. *amazon of Drury:* i.e., a whore.

l. 21. *My —— in a bandbox:* i.e., 'My arse in a bandbox', 'that won't do' (see Partridge, s.v. bandbox, though he dates it only from the late eighteenth century).

l. 40. *Doctor's Commons:* the courts to the south of St Paul's Cathedral which dealt particularly with marriage and divorce.

p. 162. *l.* 31. *Nec Judicis . . . vetustas:* 'Neither Jove's wrath, nor fire, nor sword, nor devouring age could destroy' (Ovid, *Metamorphoses*, xv. 871–2). Significantly, in view of the political and mock-heroic implications of *Jonathan Wild*, this is Ovid's cry at the end of the *Metamorphoses* for literary immortality, which he associates with the duration of the Roman empire. It immediately succeeds a reference to the reign of Augustus which looks forward to the time far off when the emperor will mount to heaven and there listen to the prayers of his people. Fielding also quotes the lines in 'On the Remedy of Affliction for the Loss of our Friends' (*Miscellanies*, vol. i, ed. Miller, p. 217).

p. 163. *l.* 4. *a GREAT dramatic poet:* the words are Gloucester's at the end of Colley Cibber's *Richard III*, iii. 1. Note the irony of 'GREAT': this passage is part of Fielding's continued satiric campaign against Cibber (see, e.g., *Shamela*, and *Joseph Andrews*, i. 1). See below, p. 261n.

p. 164. *l.* 2. *Those who do evil . . . angels:* Matthew 25 : 41.

l. 16. *Cicero, or . . . Tully:* the same man (Marcus Tullius Cicero).

l. 19. *ear hath not heard . . . conceive:* paraphrasing I Corinthians 2 : 9

p. 165. *l.* 12. *death . . . poet says:* Wild looks back in a very general way to his schoolboy acquaintance with the ancients.

p. 166. *l.* 31. *the gravel:* 'a term applied to aggregation of urinary crystals . . . also, the disease of which these are characteristic' (*OED*). Commonly applied to any difficulty in passing urine. Irwin, pp. 117–18, n. 156, notes that 'the drunkenness and irreligion of the ordinaries of Newgate was traditional' at the time.

p. 167. *l.* 17. *To the Greeks FOOLISHNESS:* I Corinthians 1 : 23.

p. 171. *l.* 24. *Suave mari magno . . . laborem:* 'Sweet it is, when on the great sea the winds are buffeting the waters, to gaze from the land on another's great struggles' (Lucretius, *DE rerum natura*, ii. 1–2; ed. and trans. Cyril Bailey, 3 vols., Oxford, 1947, i. 237).

p. 172. *l.* 22. *Jonathan Wild had every qualification*, etc.: Bernard Shea, 'Machiavelli and Fielding's *Jonathan Wild*', p. 72, compares Machiavelli's *Life of Castruccio Castracani of Lucca* (in *Works*, trans. H. Nevile, 1695 edition, p. 250): 'He had all the Qualities that make a Man great: Grateful to his Friends, Terrible to his Enemies, just with his Subjects, crafty with Strangers; and where Fraud would do the Business, he never troubled himself to conquer by Force. No Man was more forward to encounter with danger . . .'

l. 34. *Honosty:* more anti-Walpole satire. Specific illumination comes from Fielding's *The Vernoniad* (1741), p. 10, n. 24, where Fielding refers to Walpole as 'a certain Magician called [Osonos] or [Usonos], or according to the *Laconians* [Usonor], in Latin *Hishonour*—This Magician is said to have invented a certain *Aurum potabile*, by which he could turn men into Swine or Asses, whence some think he had his Name; [Us] signifying a Swine, and [Onos], *Laconicè* [Onor], an Ass' (cit. M. C. Battestin, 'Pope's *Magus* in Fielding's *Vernoniad*: The Satire of Walpole', *PQ*, xlvi (1967), 139).

p. 173. *l.* 33. *He laid down several maxims:* Shea, art. cit., p. 71n., offers parallels with Machiavelli's *Prince* and *Discourses*.

p. 174. *l.* 32. *the twelve excellent and celebrated rules:* the rules were supposed to have been found in Charles I's study after his death. They were known throughout the eighteenth century from their appearance on a woodcut of Charles's execution, and could be found in cottages and public houses. Cf. Goldsmith, 'Description of an Author's Bedchamber', l. 12, and *The Deserted Village*, l. 232.

p. 175. *l.* 8. *the tragic poet:* unidentified.

l. 13. *Lætius est . . . honestum:* 'virtue rejoices when it pays dear for its existence' (Lucan, *The Civil War*, ix. 404; Loeb edition, trans. J. D. Duff, 1928, p. 535). Ironically, this is from Cato's patriotic speech of encouragement to his soldiers as he proposes to cross the African desert.

p. 177. *l.* 31. *we may say with the divine:* unidentified.

THE JOURNAL OF A VOYAGE TO LISBON

p. 181. *Dedication to the Public:* this accompanied both 1755 editions of the work, but was written either by Fielding's publisher, Andrew Millar, or Arthur Murphy, Fielding's first editor. The *Voyage* was published together with Fielding's *A Fragment of a Comment on L. Bolingbroke's Essays*.

p. 183. *l.* 12. *peregrinations to a proper use,* etc.: Fielding's view of travel is the traditional Augustan one. Compare (among many other possible parallels) Johnson's *Idler* 97, 23 February 1760.

p. 184. *l.* 3. *Doctor Zachary Gray:* Zachary Gray's elaborately annotated edition of Samuel Butler's *Hudibras* was published in 1744.

l. 7. *collection of the late Doctor Mead:* Dr Richard Mead (1673–1754), well-known physician and collector, possessed a collection of 30,000 volumes. Pope's *Epistle to Burlington*, l. 10, refers to 'Books for Mead'.

p. 185. *l.* 17. *Burnet and Addison:* Gilbert Burnet, *Some Letters containing an account of what seemed most remarkable in Switzerland, Italy, some parts of Germany* (1686), and Joseph Addison, *Remarks on Several Parts of Italy . . .* (1705).

l. 32. *Longinus:* Dionysius Longinus, *On the Sublime*, sec. ix.

l. 33. *the Telemachus: Les Avantures de Télémaque fils d'Ulysse* (1699), by François de Salignac de la Mothe Fénelon (1651–1715).

l. 37. *Hesiod:* the reference is to Hesiod's *Theogony* (an account of the origin of the world and the birth of the gods).

p. 186. *l.* 12. *Ut speciosa dehinc miracula promant:* 'that they then might relate striking and marvellous things' (Horace, *Ars Poetica*, l. 144; in the original the verb is singular: 'promat').

l. 21. *Pliny:* Fielding refers to parts of Pliny's *Natural History*.

p. 187. *l.* 16. *what no man . . . himself:* in the original (1743) *Jonathan Wild*, iv. 9 (not reprinted in the present edition) Fielding had offered 'a burlesque on the extravagant accounts of travellers' (see the Preface to the *Miscellanies*, vol. i, excerpted above, p. xix).

l. 25. *facts of so common a kind:* a common criticism: cf. Johnson's *Idler* 97.

l. 35. *a play:* Aphra Behn's (1640–89) *The Feign'd Courtezans* (1679), esp. i. 2 and iii. 1. Susanna Centlivre (1667?–1723) was a prolific comic dramatist.

p. 188. *l.* 19. *my Lord Anson's:* George Anson (1697–1762); *A Voyage Round the World by George Anson* (1748) was compiled by Richard Walter (chaplain on Anson's flagship *Centurion*) from Anson's notes.

l. 22. *the speeches . . . Thucydides:* compare the passage on 'ancient historians' in *Jonathan Wild*, iii. 6 (p. 101); and cf. Thucydides, *History*, i. 22.

p. 189. *l.* 17 *Mr. Richardson:* Author's Preface to *Clarissa* (1747–1748): '. . . considerate readers will not enter upon the perusal of the piece before them, as if it were designed only to divert and amuse. It will probably be thought tedious to all such as dip into it, expecting a light novel, or transitory romance . . .' (Everyman edition, 4 vols., 1962, i, p. xv). Fielding makes a similar allusion in *Covent-Garden Journal*, 4 February 1752 (ed. Jensen, i. 193).

l. 19. *Mr. Addison: Spectator* 85, 7 June 1711: 'I once met with a Page of Mr. *Baxter* under a *Christmas* Pye. Whether or no the Pastry-Cook had made use of it through Chance, or Waggery, for the defence of that Superstitious *Viande*, I know not' (ed. D. F. Bond, 5 vols., Oxford, 1915, i. 361).

l. 32. *the Rehearsal:* see p. 6n. above. Fielding here alludes to *The Rehearsal* (3rd edition, 1675), ii. 4, where Gentlemen-Usher and Physician achieve 'a very silent change of a Government' by drawing their swords and sitting on 'two great Chairs'.

p. 191. *l.* 2. *Duke of Portland's medicine:* a powder consisting of birthwort, gentian, germander tops and leaves, ground pine and lesser centaury, prescribed as a remedy for gout (see *OED*, s.v. Portland).

l. 4. *Mr. Ranby:* John Ranby (1703–73): cf. *Tom Jones*, viii. 13.

l. 15. *His Grace the Duke of Newcastle:* Thomas Pelham-Holles, first Duke of Newcastle (1693–1768). Lincoln's Inn Fields was the site of his home, Newcastle House.

p. 194. *l.* 4. *my clerk:* Joshua Brogden.

fn. l. 1. *A predecessor of mine:* Sir Thomas de Veil (1684?–1746).

l. 11. *my great patron:* John, 4th Duke of Bedford (1710–71).

l. 20. *my brother:* John Fielding (1721–80), who succeeded his half-brother as J.P. for the City and Liberties of Westminster. He was knighted in 1761.

p. 195. *l.* 22. *Judge Burnet:* Sir Thomas Burnet (1694–1753), third son of Gilbert Burnet, Bishop of Salisbury. He was made a judge in the court of common pleas in 1741.

l. 26. *the late Duke of Marlborough,* etc.: Fielding refers to Blenheim Palace, built for John Churchill, first Duke of Marlborough (1650–1722) by the government after his victory at the battle of Blenheim (1704). Fielding praised Marlborough in, e.g., 'Of True Greatness' (1741), ll. 99–100, and 'Liberty', l. 122.

p. 196. *l.* 20. *Dr. Ward:* Dr Joshua Ward (1685–1751), known as 'Spot' Ward, attended George II. Cf. the end of *Tom Jones,* viii. 9.

l. 28. *Mr. Pelham:* Henry Pelham, born in 1696 and prime minister since 1743, had died on 6 March 1754. Fielding had dedicated his *Proposal for Making an Effectual Provision for the Poor* (1753) to him.

l. 34. *diaphoretic:* perspiration-inducing.

p. 197. *l.* 4. *a little house of mine:* at Fordhook (see p. 200), on the Uxbridge Road, between Acton and Ealing.

l. 7. *Kensington Gravel Pits:* Kensington is on gravel soil. It became famous when William III established his palace there shortly after his accession in 1688. Defoe remarks that 'the Air agreed with and was necessary to the Health of the King' (*Tour thro' the whole Island of Great Britain,* Letter vi, ed. G. D. H. Cole, 2 vols., 1968, i. 390).

l. 39. *the late Bishop of Cloyne:* George Berkeley (1685–1753), *Siris: a Chain of Philosophical Reflexions and Inquiries concerning the Virtues of Tar Water* (1744). A copy is listed as item 221 in the library sale catalogue.

l. 42. *author of the Female Quixote:* Charlotte Lennox (1720–1804), whose *Female Quixote* (1752) was praised by Fielding in *Covent-Garden Journal,* 24 March 1752 as 'a most extraordinary and most excellent Performance' (ed. Jensen, i. 282).

p. 198. *l.* 4. *Sydenham:* Thomas Sydenham (1624–89), well-known physician.

l. 10. *anasarca:* 'a dropsical affection of the subcutaneous cellular tissue of a limb or other large surface of the body, producing a very puffed appearance of the flesh' (*OED*).

l. 24. *trochar:* 'a surgical instrument consisting of a perforator or stylet enclosed in a metal tube or cannula, used for withdrawing fluid from a cavity, as in dropsy' (*OED*).

p. 199. *l.* 16. *Michaelmas quarter:* one of the four divisions of the legal year, it began on 29 September (the feast of St Michael).

p. 200, *l.* 3. *the captain:* Captain Veal, master of *The Queen of Portugal.*

p. 201. *l.* 18. *My wife . . . my eldest daughter:* Fielding's second wife, Mary Daniel, whom he married in 1747 (his first wife, Charlotte Cradock, had died in 1744); the daughter's name was Eleanor Harriot.

l. 27. *Redriffe:* a flourishing township known for its docks, etc.

Defoe, *Tour*, Letter v (ed. Cole, i. 317), comments that although it is written 'Rotherhith' it is pronounced 'Redriff'.

l. 29. *king's Proclamation Day:* a day on which the sovereign issued a decree which empowered him to legislate; such decrees to carry the authority of Acts of Parliament.

l. 34. *contra bonum publicum:* against the public good.

p. 202. *l.* 8. *Mr. Welch:* Saunders Welch, Fielding's high constable: see, e.g., W. L. Cross, *The History of Henry Fielding*, 3 vols. (New Haven, Conn., 1918), ii. 226, 229, 235–6, 251, 262, etc.

l. 27. *gauntlope:* an original form of gauntlet (see *OED*). C. J. Rawson, *Henry Fielding* (1968), p. 128n., comments on the ironic appropriateness of the word here.

p. 203, *l.* 12. *King's Arms:* Pagliaro (p. 140) suggests that Fielding refers to the King's Arms tavern in Exchange Alley.

l. 41. *Hogarth . . . look at:* William Hogarth's 'The Enraged Musician' of November 1741.

p. 204. *l.* 24. *it seems . . . my pen alone:* an allusion to *Don Quixote*, Part ii, chap. 74 (identified by Austin Dobson, *Voyage*, p. 161n.).

p. 205. *l.* 8. *Society of Antiquarians:* the Society of Antiquaries was originally founded in Elizabeth's reign but had been suppressed by James I in 1604. It was revived in 1718 and given a charter by George II in November 1751.

l. 15. *The King of Prussia . . . science:* Austin Dobson, *Voyage*, p. 161n., suggests an allusion to Hogarth's 'March to Finchley' print (December 1750), which Hogarth had originally dedicated to George II. But the king's ignorant reaction to the print had so upset Hogarth that he rededicated it, this time to Frederick II, King of Prussia. The dedication reads: 'To His Majesty the King of Prussia, an Encourager of Arts and Sciences!' (see Ronald Paulson, *Hogarth's Graphic Works*, 2 vols., New Haven and London, 1965, i. 279). The story may be apocryphal.

p. 206. *l.* 4. *virtuosi:* triflers in collecting curios, antiquities, etc. A common Augustan satirical target.

l. 40. *Aristotle: Politics*, i. 1. 5–6. Cf. *Jonathan Wild*, i. 8 (p. 24).

l. 43. *Mr. Montesquieu:* the reference is to Montesquieu's *De l'Esprit des Lois*, xxi. 2–3.

p. 208. *l.* 1. *the liturgy:* Fielding refers to the Litany in the *Book of Common Prayer*: 'That it may please thee to preserve all that travel by land or by water . . .'.

l. 35. *Sir Courtly Nice . . . Surly:* see *Sir Courtly Nice* (1685) by John Crowne (1640?–1703?).

p. 209. *l.* 6. *as many offices as Scrub in the play:* George Farquhar, *The Beaux' Stratagem* (1707), iii. 2.

l. 14. *Mr. Hunter:* William Hunter (1718–83), the Glasgow-trained physician who came to London in 1741. He spent some time as lecturer on surgery to navy surgeons.

p. 210. *l.* 33. *the Royal Anne:* built at Woolwich in 1704, of 1,721 tons burden, and carrying 100 guns and 780 men. But as Dobson, *Voyage*, p. 163n., observes, the *Royal Sovereign* of 1701 was larger, displacing 1,882 tons and carrying 110 guns and 850 men.

p. 211. *l.* 23. *Marshal Saxe:* Maurice de Saxe (1696–1750), who defeated the English army under William, Duke of Cumberland

(1721–65), at Laffeldt (La Val) in July 1747 in one of the battles in the War of the Austrian Succession.

p. 212. *l.* 18. *the Royal Hospital at Greenwich:* designed by Sir Christopher Wren and Nicholas Hawksmoor. Begun in 1696 and substantially completed by the 1730s.

l. 23. *romantic:* i.e., having no foundation in fact.

p. 213. *l.* 30. *Nocet empta dolore voluptas:* 'pleasure bought with pain is harmful' (Horace, *Epistles,* i. 2. 55).

p. 214. *l.* 2. *late separation . . . companies:* in 1745 the Company of Barber Surgeons was dissolved and the surgeons given their own company. (Cf. *Tom Jones,* viii. 6.)

l. 22. *Sir Courtly Nice declares:* Crowne, *Sir Courtly Nice,* Act iv: 'Oh! there's nothing so charming as admirable teeth. If a lady fastens upon my heart it must be with her teeth' (*The Dramatic Works of John Crowne,* 4 vols., 1873–4, iii, 1874, 318–19).

p. 215. *l.* 17. *Robin Hood Society:* a debating society which met at the Robinhood inn in Butcher-Row, London, and ridiculed by Fielding in *Covent-Garden Journal,* 28 January and 1 February 1752. For a full account, see Jensen, ii. 167–9.

l. 18. *Woman's Almanac:* no such title appears to be listed in the relevant volume of *The New Cambridge Bibliography of English Literature.* Doubtless Fielding is just making a general satirical point.

l. 21. *a young lady of her sister:* Jane and Margaret Collier, daughters of the metaphysician Arthur Collier (d. 1732). After they were orphaned they were brought up with the Fielding children at Salisbury. Margaret accompanied Fielding to Lisbon.

l. 27. *knight-marshal:* 'an officer of the English royal household, who had judicial cognizance of transgressions . . . within a radius of twelve miles from the king's palace' (*OED*).

p. 217. *l.* 7. *Plato: Laws,* iv. 713–14. The Serrani edition of Plato's *Works* is item 481 in the sale catalogue of Fielding's library.

l. 28. *There is . . . trade:* cf. the discussion on trade among other things between Adams and the innkeeper in *Joseph Andrews,* ii. 17.

p. 220. *l.* 13. *Æolus:* god of the winds.

p. 221. *l.* 34. *a great lady's name:* Elizabeth Yorke, who had married Lord Anson (first lord of the admiralty) in 1748.

p. 223. *l.* 28. *Mr. Addison's observation: Tatler* 117, 7 January 1709/ 1710: '. . . whoever can read it without growing giddy, must have a good head, or a very bad one' (*The Tatler,* ed. G. A. Aitken, 4 vols., 1898–9, iii, 1899, 20).

p. 226. *l.* 7. *hoy:* 'a small vessel, usually rigged as a sloop, and employed in carrying passengers and goods, particularly in short distances on the sea-coast' (*OED*).

l. 14. *Omnia . . . ponto:* 'all was sea, and the shores were absent from the sea' (Ovid, *Metamorphoses,* i. 292).

l. 38. *bubble:* dupe.

p. 230. *l.* 4. *White's:* the well-known chocolate house in St James's Street.

l. 19. *charde, perigord-pie, ortolan:* respectively the central leaf-stalk of artichoke, blanched for use at table (or stalks of white beet); meat pie flavoured with truffles or highly seasoned; small bird of delicate flavour.

l. 25. *an Act of Parliament:* 17 Geo. II, cap. 5. See Sir William Blackstone, *Commentaries on the Laws of England*, iv. 13: among 'idle and disorderly persons are . . . [those] who wander abroad, and lodge in ale-houses, out-houses, or in the open air, without giving a good account of themselves' (1809 edition, 4 vols., iv. 169).

p. 231. *l.* 1. *Hearn:* John Herne the lawyer (*fl.* 1660), who published collections of precedents: *The Pleader* (1657); *The Law of Conveyances* (1658), etc.

l. 9. *Sunday, July 19:* for a comment on Fielding's misdating, see F. S. Dickson, 'The Early Editions of Fielding's "Voyage to Lisbon"', *The Library*, 3rd Series, viii (1917), 26–7.

l. 20. *wind:* not in *OED*, etc. Fielding is being facetious at the expense of rough English wine and punning on the French for port (vin de Porto). In nautical slang 'wind' meant 'intoxicated' (*OED*, Wind, sb., 20g). Cf. Fielding's references to 'Port Wind' in his letter to John Fielding of 22 July 1754 (Cross, *Henry Fielding*, iii. 41).

p. 233. *l.* 6: *grand climacteric:* i.e., 63. A climacteric is a period 'containing a certain number of years, at the end of which some great change is supposed to befal the body' (Johnson's *Dictionary*); climacteric years were the 7th and its multiples (7 was the number of the body) and the 9th and its multiples (9 was the number of the soul). The most important was that produced by multiplying 7 by 9.

l. 41. *Cornaro:* Luigi Cornaro (1467–1566), *Trattato della vita sobria* (1558) had appeared in an English translation (by W. Jones) in 1702 under the title: *Sure and certain Methods of attaining a long and healthful Life. . . . Written by Lewis Cornaro . . . when he was near an hundred Year of Age'.

p. 234. *l.* 6. *Cheney, Arbuthnot:* Dr George Cheyne (1671–1743), physician friend of Richardson and Fielding, wrote a large number of works on diet; Dr John Arbuthnot (1667–1735), friend of Pope, produced *An Essay concerning the Nature of Aliments* in 1731.

l. 8. *Dr. James's Dictionary:* Robert James (1705–76), *A Medical Dictionary* (1743–5).

l. 9. *very common food*, etc: Fielding refers to John Ranby's (see p. 191n.) charge that the physicians who had attended the dying Walpole were incompetent. See R. C. Jarvis, 'The Death of Walpole: Henry Fielding and a Forgotten "Cause Célèbre"', *MLR*, xli (1946), 113–30.

l. 27. *Diodorus Siculus:* Diodorus Siculus (1st cent. B.C.), *History*, iii. 15 ff., talks about the 'fish-eaters' (Ichthyophagi). The 'self-eaters' are a joke of Fielding's.

p. 235. *l.* 28. *Quin:* James Quin (1693–1766), the celebrated actor: see *Joseph Andrews*, iii. 10, and *Covent-Garden Journal*, 31 March 1752, for other references. On Fielding's attitude to physiognomy (the subject of this and the following paragraph), see *An Essay on the Knowledge of the Characters of Men*, in *Miscellanies*, vol. i, ed. Miller, p. 157, and *Joseph Andrews*, ii. 17.

l. 41. *Mr. Derham:* the physico-theologian William Derham, D.D*
(1657–1735). Dobson (*Voyage*, p. 171n.) suggests a reference to his
Physico-Theology (1713), iv. 14.

p. 237. *l.* 34. *pay . . . for the light:* the window tax of 1696 had been
increased in 1747. The landlady in *Tom Jones*, vii. 13 complains:
'Why now there is above forty shillings for window-lights, and yet
we have stopt up all we could . . .'.

p. 238. *l.* 2. *Lucian:* the Greek satirist (*c.* A.D. 120–), one of Fielding's favourite authors whom he praises in *Covent-Garden Journal*,
30 June 1752.

p. 239. *l.* 1. *one of the comedies of Plautus:* Plautus (*c.* 254–184 B.C.)
flourished as a writer during the second Punic War. Fielding
refers to the play *Poenulus* (*The Little Carthaginian*).

p. 240. *l.* 22. *the last Vagrant Act:* the Act of 1752. Cf. p. 230n.

l. 33. *spunges:* 'obtain[s] by pressure or extortion' (*OED*).
raps: snatches.

p. 242. *l.* 1. *Sir William Petty:* Sir William Petty (1623–87), the
political economist who wrote several essays on 'political arithmetic'. Fielding refers to the volume *Political Arithmetick, or a
Discourse concerning the extent and value of Lands . . .* (published
posthumously by his son in 1690). Item 546 in the sale catalogue
of Fielding's library.

l. 3. *the lady:* probably a Mrs Roberts, who had an estate at
Appley, a mile east of Ryde (Cross, *Henry Fielding*, iii. 38–9).

p. 243. *l.* 19. *hemistich:* section of a line of verse.

l. 20. *Superanda omnis fortuna ferendo est:* 'all fortune is to be
overcome by enduring' (*Aeneid*, v. 710).

p. 244. *l.* 25. *mundungus:* bad tobacco.

l. 29. *Tajo:* the river Tagus. Lisbon harbour, where Fielding lands,
is on the Tagus estuary (see p. 282).

p. 247. *l.* 4. *Denham . . . Pope:* Sir John Denham's important topo-
graphical poem *Cooper's Hill* (1642) and Pope's *Windsor Forest*
(1713) are implied here.

l. 13. *the late Sir Robert Walpole:* Walpole had died in 1745.
The reference to him as 'one of the best of men' is doubtless
ironic.

p. 254. *l.* 7. *Vinum Pomonæ:* wine of Pomona (goddess of fruit).
Cross, iii. 40 suggests that 'Cheesehurst' is 'probably Churston
Ferrers'.

p. 255. *l.* 16. *sui juris:* his own master.

l. 32. *the strange story of Circe: Odyssey*, x. The episode was
traditionally given a moral interpretation: '*Homer* intended to
teach, as *Eustathius* remarks, that pleasure and sensuality debase
men into beasts' (Pope's translation of *The Odyssey of Homer*,
5 vols., 1725–6, iii. 55; note to Book x. 242). For warnings against
'the inchantmentes of *Circes*, the vanitie of licencious pleasure,
the inticements of all sinne', see also Roger Ascham, *The Schole-
master*, Book i (1863 edition, ed. J. E. B. Mayor, p. 76 ff.).

l. 41. *Thucydides: History*, i. 5.

p. 256. *l.* 1. *Ars Cauponaria:* the art of trading (literally, of shop-
keeping).

l. 3. *Metabletic . . . Chrematistic:* that pertaining to barter; that pertaining to money-making (for the latter *OED* cites *Amelia*, ix. 5).

l. 35. camomile: 'an aromatic creeping herb. . . . The flowers are employed in medicine for their bitter and tonic properties' (*OED*).

l. 39. calipash and calipee: respectively 'that part of the turtle next to the upper shell, containing a dull green gelatinous substance' and 'that part next the lower shell, containing a light yellowish gelatinous substance' (*OED*). Cf. *Tom Jones*, i. 1. Fielding's Jew has broken dietary law and is undergoing a 24-hour fast in atonement, as Pagliaro (p. 146) suggests.

l. 42. Dr. South: Robert South (1634–1716), sermon on Proverbs 3 : 17 ('Her ways are the ways of pleasantness': 'How vastly disproportionate are the pleasures of the eating and of the thinking man! Indeed as different as the silence of an Archimedes in the study of a problem, and the stillness of a sow at her wash' (*Sermons*, 5 vols., Oxford, 1842, i. 11).

p. 257. l. 7. like Mark Anthony in Dryden: Dryden, *All for Love* (1678), iii: 'There's no satiety of Love in thee;/Enjoy'd, thou still art new . . .'; though the phrase 'appetite increased with feeding' clearly echoes *Hamlet*, i. 2.

l. 9. ut nullus . . . modus: 'that there is no sense of shame about, or restraint on, longing'. Cf. Horace, *Odes*, i. 24. 1–2: 'Quis desiderio sit pudor aut modus/tam cari capitis?'

p. 259. l. 18. doing what he ought not to have done: echoing the general confession in the morning and evening service in the *Book of Common Prayer* ('we have done those things which we ought not to have done').

p. 261. l. 14. Axylus: Iliad, vi. 12–19. To Pope, in his note on this passage, he is a type of 'that ancient Hospitality which we now only read of' (*Translations of Homer*, Twickenham edition, ed. Maynard Mack, vii. 323). Fielding uses the name in *The Covent-Garden Journals* for 25 February, 10 March, and 11 April 1752.

l. 40. Cibber . . . in the Dunciad: Colley Cibber (1671–1757) was created poet laureate in 1730. As a satiric target of Pope's, he was enthroned as the laureate of Dulness in place of Lewis Theobald (1688–1744) in the 4-book *Dunciad* of 1743. See above, p. 163n.

p. 262. l. 12. John Dorée: popular name for the dory, 'a fish . . . found in European seas, and much esteemed as food' (*OED*).

l. 22. Mr. Quin: see p. 235n.

l. 26. Sir Epicure Mammon: see Jonson's *The Alchemist* (1610).

l. 33. Macklin: Charles Macklin (1697?–1797), the actor, who opened a tavern under the North Piazza, Covent Garden in March 1754. See William Appleton, *Charles Macklin: An Actor's Life* (Cambridge, Mass., 1961), p. 98 ff.

p. 264. l. 19. bills of mortality: published weekly by the Company of Parish Clerks, they listed the deaths in the London parishes; the phrase became applied to the district itself.

l. 24. cuncta prius tentanda: 'all things must first be tried'; *cuncta prius tentata:* 'all means have been previously tried' (Ovid, *Metamorphoses*, i. 190).

l. 27. that excellent scheme of the Westminster market: in 1749 an act was passed 'for making a free market for the sale of fish in the city of Westminster; and for the preventing the forestalling and monopolizing of fish' (22 Geo. II, cap. 49).

p. 266. l. 1. Peter Taylor: a friend of Fielding's, he died in 1757. *led captain:* hanger-on or parasite.

l. 4. methuen: name for Portuguese wines imported under a treaty of 1703 concluded by Sir Paul Methuen, English envoy to the Portuguese court.

p. 272. l. 22. Sir Matthew Hale: the judge, who lived from 1609 to 1676. He believed in witchcraft, and it was in his court on 10 March 1661/2 that Rose Cullender and Amy Drury were convicted of witchcraft. They were subsequently executed. Witchcraft was abolished as a crime in 1736. I have been unable to identify the 'learned divine'.

p. 275. l. 7. nautica fides . . . Punica fides: sailor's faith (faithlessness); Punic 'faith' (treachery).

l. 35. melioribus avibus: 'with better omens' (literally 'birds', from which the Romans took their omens).

p. 279. l. 9. Virgil's description of a storm: Aeneid, i. 50–150.

p. 280. l. 3. Juno: for Juno's enmity towards Aeneas, see especially the opening of the *Aeneid.*

l. 34. snow: small sailing-ship similar to a brig.

l. 37. a lion for Elias: Elijah, or Elias, is introduced in I Kings 17 and there is a lion in I Kings 13: 24–5. Sunday, 4 August, was the 8th after Trinity, the two lessons for which day were I Kings 13 (Matins) and 17 (Evensong). The captain misreads the second under the influence of the first.

p. 281. l. 20. Diodorus Siculus: History, i. 60.

l. 37. an Englishman, etc.: Cross, iii. 48 remarks: 'This is an Englishman's way of saying that the old mariner had turned Roman Catholic and been received there into the beautiful monastery of the Hieronymites hewn out of the rock.' The 'present queen dowager' was Maria Anna of Austria, widow of King John V of Portugal.

p. 282. l. 30. Bellisle: 'Rather strangely, Fielding, whose ear must have been slow to catch foreign sounds, persisted to the last in writing "Bellisle" for Belem, pronounced Belain, the final syllable being a nasal' (Cross, iii. 49).

p. 284. l. 6. the Covent Garden language: cf. John Gay, *Trivia* (1716), iii. 255–7: 'I need not strict enjoin the pocket's care, / When from the crowded play thou lead'st the fair; / Who has not here or watch or snuff-box lost?'

l. 11. Catharine of Arragon: Catherine of Braganza is buried at the convent of Belem; Catherine of Aragon at Peterborough.

p. 285. l. 33. Virgil tells us: Aeneid, ii. 15.

p. 286. l. 4. Egressi . . . arena: 'egressi, optata potiuntur Troes harena': 'disembarking, the Trojans gain the longed-for shore' (*Aeneid,* i. 172). *l. 6. hic Finis chartæque viæque:* 'this is the end of the story and the journey'; echoing the end of Horace's *Satires,* i. 5. 104 ('Brundisium longae finis chartaeque viaeque est'), the account of a journey to Brundisium.

1973.   DOUGLAS BROOKS.